PRAISE FOR

FIREBORN

'Brilliant, epic, exhilarating! A sequel that is even better than
its predecessor – I absolutely loved it'
Hannah Gold, author of *The Last Bear*

'Frightening new monsters and mighty challenges aplenty
await Twelve, as the glorious, big-hearted Fireborn-saga
from the former Waterstones Children's Book of the Month
author continues'
Waterstones, Books You Need to Read in 2023

'Breathtakingly imaginative – I felt like I was right there,
fighting fearsome monsters!'
Natasha Hastings, author of *The Miraculous Sweetmakers*

'The best kind of children's fantasy story: thrilling
and imaginative'
B. B. Alston, author of *Amari and the Night Brothers*

'A monster-filled adventure set in a wildly imaginative frozen
world, with axe-wielding action scenes that'll make your
heart race! I couldn't put it down'
A. F. Steadman, author of *Skandar and the Unicorn Thief*

'This remarkable debut pulsates with energy and drama'
Daily Mail, Best Children's Books of the Year

'I loved this whirlwind adventure! A brilliant novel weaving fantasy, friendship, heartbreak and hope together really superbly. I have pledged my heart to FIREBORN'
Cerrie Burnell, author of *Harper and the Sea of Secrets*

'Atmospheric, fast-paced'
Guardian

'A richly imagined story, bursting with thrilling magic, terrifying monsters and an epic adventure that leaves you wanting more'
Catherine Doyle, author of *The Storm Keeper's Island*

'A high-energy, fast-paced action story with some truly terrifying monsters'
The Week Junior

'FIREBORN is an exciting adventure that will make you want to set off on your own epic journey to battle mythical monsters'
Katie Tsang, co-author of *Dragon Mountain*

'This is monster-hunting at its finest, from a superb new voice in children's fiction'
Aisha Bushby, author of *A Pocketful of Stars*

'An action-packed roller-coaster of a ride, with tons of twists and surprises . . . Nail-bitingly tense and vivid'
Tolá Okogwu, author of *Onyeka and the Academy of the Sun*

Books by Aisling Fowler

FIREBORN:
Twelve and the Frozen Forest
Phoenix and the Frost Palace
Starling and the Cavern of Light

Aisling Fowler wishes that she had grown up in a magical, mountainous kingdom, but was actually raised in Surrey on a diet of books and *Buffy the Vampire Slayer*. After earning a BSc in Biology and working as a support worker and then a nurse, the idea for Fireborn came to her as she moved back and forth between London and the US.

Now based in Los Angeles, when she is not reading or writing, Aisling loves cooking and plotting adventures (for herself as well as her fictional characters).

Phoenix and the Frost Palace is the second Fireborn book.

FiREBORN

PHOENIX AND THE FROST PALACE

AISLING FOWLER

Illustrated by Sophie Medvedeva

HarperCollins *Children's Books*

First published in the United Kingdom by
HarperCollins *Children's Books* in 2023
Published in this paperback edition in 2023
HarperCollins *Children's Books* is a division of HarperCollins*Publishers* Ltd
1 London Bridge Street
London SE1 9GF

www.harpercollins.co.uk

HarperCollins*Publishers*
Macken House, 39/40 Mayor Street Upper
Dublin 1, DO1 C9W8, Ireland

2

ISBN 978-0-00-839422-6

Aisling Fowler and Sophie Medvedeva assert the moral right to be identified
as the author and illustrator of the work respectively.

A CIP catalogue record for this title is available from the British Library.

Typeset in Sabon by Palimpsest Book Production Ltd, Falkirk, Stirlingshire

Printed and bound in the UK using 100% renewable electricity
at CPI Group (UK) Ltd

For my brilliant agent, Claire, whose faith and support made this series possible.

EMBER

ICEGAARD

THE FROZEN WASTES

N

THE FROZEN FOREST

The Heart Grove

THE FANGS

MOUNTAIN CLAN

THE
ENDLESS
OCEAN

The Hunting Lodge

Netherfoss

Ledge

Safe Path

GRASS CLAN

RIVER CLAN

The Ilara

The Embrace

THE RIVERLANDS

FOREST CLAN

Safe Path

The Clasp

THE GREAT WOODS

POA

Lake Ilara

The Floating Market

NEWT

Safe Path

THE SCOUR

Safe Path

BOG CLAN

DESERT CLAN

CHAPTER 1

Phoenix's legs ached as she climbed higher and higher, up steep steps roughly hewn into the cliff face. In spite of the exertion, her heart was light. For the first time in days, the clouds had dropped below Ledge, revealing a bold blue sky above the mountain-clan village where the Hunters were staying. Finally, the rain had stopped and it was the perfect weather for a hunt.

'We're never going to reach the top!' Five groaned, trailing behind her with Seven and Six.

'L-let's take another break,' Seven gasped.

'Yes,' Six panted, just as out of breath as his sister.

Five heaved a sigh of relief. 'Genius idea, Seven.'

Phoenix glanced back and saw the three of them had already staggered to a stop. They slumped against one another, hair damp with sweat in spite of the cold bite to the air. She swallowed her complaint – they'd just had a break and really wouldn't reach the top at this rate – and nodded instead.

'Maybe just a quick stop then,' Phoenix said. It *was* quite nice to catch her breath.

On her shoulder, Widge, her squirrel, flicked his tail cheerfully, his chestnut fur gleaming in the sunlight. His bright eyes were fixed on something high above their heads and Phoenix puffed out a breath, craning her neck to look too. The cliff soared up and away from them, steps winding back and forth across it. Their destination was at the very top, where a red-painted platform poked out over the precipice. It was the place mountain-clan gliders launched and landed, and an edgeworm had apparently taken up residence there.

Phoenix groaned softly; it still looked miles above them. 'You've got the best deal,' she muttered to Widge. 'Wish someone would carry me!' He chirped merrily, unmistakably pleased with himself.

She glanced down and quickly regretted it. Clouds shifted beneath them, blocking the ground from view. Even Ledge, the colourful mountain-clan settlement, was completely obscured. Her stomach dropped and she averted her eyes quickly, focusing back on the red speck instead.

'Looks much closer,' she said to the others.

Five snorted. 'You are *such* a liar, Twelve!' Dark hair obscured his flushed face.

'I'm Phoenix now,' she reminded him with a grin. 'And we must be closer! Come on!'

With a sigh, her three friends fell in behind her, pressing themselves against the cliff as they climbed. The mountain clan did not believe in safety ropes and the vast drop clawed at them, making them all nervous.

'Have you two had any more ideas for your Hunter names?' asked Seven, glancing back at Five and Six.

Five brightened immediately. 'Funny you should ask. I've come up with a shortlist.' He paused and aimed a pointed look at Six. 'Yes, *another* shortlist.'

'Me too,' grinned Six. 'I thought "Popinjay" would suit you perfectly.'

Phoenix laughed. 'What? Those rowdy, colourful birds?'

Six nodded, unable to hide his amusement at Five's outrage.

'Or m-maybe "Peacock"?' Seven suggested innocently.

'You two are both awful,' Five sniffed. 'No, I was thinking something more like –' he paused for dramatic effect – 'Nighthawk.'

Seven caught Phoenix's eye and they both looked away quickly, trying not to laugh.

Six shook his head, struggling to quell the telltale twitching at the corner of his lips. 'Terrible.'

'Really?' Five shrugged as everyone nodded vigorously. 'All right, how about Bladewielder?'

'No!'

'Grim-stalker?'

'Definitely not!' Six rolled his eyes. 'And when have you ever stalked a Grim anyway?'

Phoenix couldn't help but shiver at the mention of that particular dark creature. It had only been three months since one of them had taken her mentor Silver's life at the Hunting Lodge.

A shadow passed over Seven's face too, and Phoenix wondered if she was remembering her kidnap on that same day. Or the resulting battle, where Phoenix had accidentally destroyed the lodge with her newly discovered elemental power . . .

She shook the thought away and forced herself to concentrate on the conversation around her. 'I think it's your turn, Six,' she said, forcing a grin on to her face. 'I keep coming back to "Goat" for you.'

'What?' Six's horror was comical.

'You're really sure-footed.' Phoenix strove to keep a straight face.

'That's true!' Seven grinned. 'He always has been!'

Five nodded seriously. 'Nice one, Phoenix. "Goat" is *definitely* a contender.'

'You take it if you like it so much,' Six snorted.

Together, the four friends bickered their way upward until an hour later, quite unexpectedly, the steps flattened out and suddenly they were at the top. The air was thin, the view so beautiful it silenced them. Far below, a milky ocean of cloud stretched to the horizon and from its rolling depths sprang mountain beyond mountain, each peak dipped in glittering snow.

'Thank the frost,' Five groaned, sinking to his haunches.

'Right,' Six said, suddenly looking purposeful. 'Shall we run over what we know about the edgeworm?' He offered Five a hand and hauled him back to his feet.

'Elder Hoarfrost said that three days ago it nearly got one of the gliders,' Phoenix said.

The gliders were the most respected people in the mountain clan after the chief himself. They used handmade wings to ride the thermals, often warning of dangers long before they arrived.

'He thinks it's probably still waiting there at the end of the platform,' Five said, wincing. 'But I'm hoping it might have got sick of all the rain and moved on.'

'Five!' Six exclaimed. 'That is not a Hunter attitude, especially not on our first proper hunt!'

'Even I'm h-hoping it'll be there,' Seven said brightly.

'You don't have to face it,' muttered Five.

'I'll learn so m-much though.' She smiled sweetly. 'From your mistakes.'

'Oi!'

'There won't be any mistakes,' Phoenix said firmly, leading the group towards the red boards that jutted out over the hair-raising drop.

A little back from it stood an A-frame building: the wing shed. The roof was carved into a pair of downbeating wings, their brilliant white blinding against the blue sky.

Steps down from the entrance led straight on to the gliding platform. Just looking at the red planks gave Phoenix goosebumps. The thought of stepping on to them, walking to the edge, strapping on some bits of wood covered in feathers, then jumping and hoping for the best . . . She shook herself, pushed away the jolt of fear.

'No mistakes,' she muttered again to calm herself. Widge squealed his agreement, tail swishing cheerfully.

'According to *A Magical Bestiary*, edgeworms are only a problem for the mountain clan, aren't they?' Six said.

Phoenix nodded.

Five sighed. 'Go on then. We all know you know it off by heart.'

Phoenix grinned and mentally flipped to the *Magical Bestiary* entry on edgeworms.

'*Edgeworms are unpleasant pests of the mountains*,' she recited. '*They lurk at the top of steep drops, taking on the appearance of their surroundings. By flattening themselves to the ground and extending themselves beyond a cliff's true edge, they can make the precipice appear up to six feet further away than it truly is. Anyone unfortunate enough to step on one will plummet to their death, whereupon the edgeworm descends to devour its victim's remains.*'

'*So* disgusting,' said Five.

Phoenix ignored him. '*If attacked, these unpleasant creatures assume their true many-legged form. Their jaws are bone-crushingly strong and their whip-like tail is covered in poisonous barbs. Avoid the tail at all costs: its poison is paralytic.*'

'And the stats?' Six prompted her, checking his quiver of arrows.

Phoenix grinned. '*Aggression: four out of ten. Danger posed: six out of ten. Difficulty to disable: four out of ten.*'

'Pfft,' Five snorted. 'Four out of ten difficulty? We've faced *way* worse. We'll be fine.' He shot a sidelong glance at Seven. 'Won't we . . .?'

Phoenix frowned at him. Ever since they'd discovered that Seven was a Seer, they'd all struggled with the temptation to quiz her about what she saw in their futures. They knew how uncomfortable it made her.

Seven shook her head slowly. 'I haven't Seen anything, Five. I'm s-sorry.'

He shrugged, trying to look unconcerned. 'Come on then,' he said, drawing his sword. 'Time to give Seven a faultless lesson in how to dispatch an edgeworm.'

Beside him, Six strung his bow and Phoenix pulled the axes off her back.

Phoenix glanced at Widge. 'Why don't you stay with Seven?' The little squirrel's claws tightened on her shoulder and his eyes narrowed. He was staying exactly where he was. 'Suit yourself,' she said with a sigh. Then, to the others: 'Come on.'

'Good luck!' Seven called after them. 'N-not that you need it,' she added quickly.

Phoenix took a deep breath and stepped up on to the platform.

CHAPTER 2

'I wish they hadn't painted it red,' Six muttered.

'Yeah, bit gaudy, isn't it?' said Five, grimacing.

'Easier for the gliders to spot from the sky,' Phoenix murmured.

Blood-red wood, planed as smooth as slate, stretched before them into an infinite ocean of blue.

Phoenix's stomach jerked unpleasantly as the wood creaked beneath her. She focused instead on her axes, their familiar weight reassuring in her hands.

Next to her, Five whistled softly. 'Not that comforting to think there's just these planks between us and the ground,' he said. 'How high did Chief Soar say we were up here?'

'Let's not think about that,' Six said from Phoenix's other side, taking a cautious step forward.

The end of the platform was about ten feet away.

Phoenix scanned the boards for any alteration in colour or texture. Five was using his sword to prod the wood every few inches ahead of him. Six was doing the same with an arrow.

'Nothing yet,' Five whispered, pressing the tip of his sword into another board. There was no hint of humour about him now. Every line of his face was tense and watchful.

Eight feet from the edge.

Phoenix advanced cautiously, her vision filled with a seamless red. On her shoulder, Widge was stiff and still, his eyes fixed on the painted wood too.

Seven feet.

Six's arrow dug into the grain with barely a sound.

Six feet.

Phoenix tried to stop her eyes from flicking forward to the drop, to the endless blue that awaited them if they made a mistake.

Five feet.

A prickle of sweat stood out on Five's forehead. 'We must be *very* close,' he whispered, stretching out his blade again.

'There!' With sudden certainty, Phoenix saw a tiny change in the pattern of the wood, an alteration so slight you'd never notice it unless you were looking hard. Her hand shot out and grabbed Five's wrist just before the tip of his blade touched down.

'Here?' Six whispered. 'Yes, I see it!'

As one, they took a step back. The edge of the platform had appeared to be about five feet away. Really, it was no more than an inch ahead of them.

One more step and they would have plummeted to their deaths.

The silence around them was absolute; even the wind seemed to hold its breath. Then, in an explosion of movement, Five sprang forward. His sword sank deeply into the creature at their feet and he leaped away again as a furious shriek rent the silence.

Side by side, Five, Six and Phoenix moved further back as a mind-bending flood of change spread from the wound Five had inflicted. The red planks rippled, bucking and twisting as their colour and texture morphed. A moment later, a rough, scaly creature was visible in front of them. Its yellow eyes regarded them balefully as its low, leggy shape tensed, ready to attack.

'Look out!' Five cried as the whip-like tail cracked towards them. Phoenix ducked, feeling the air ripple over her head. Widge, sensibly, chose this moment to dive into her furs.

The edgeworm advanced, its mouth gaping, teeth slick with mould, breath so foetid Five retched beside her.

'Ugh,' he gasped.

The momentary lapse in attention was all the creature needed. Its tail whipped forward again, lightning-fast, and would have impaled Five if Phoenix hadn't leaped in front of him, her axe relieving the tail of several poison barbs. Screaming, the creature whirled away from her, dark green blood oozing from its wound.

Her leap carried her further than she'd intended and suddenly Phoenix was right at the end of the platform, the creature between her, Five and Six.

'Don't step back!' Six yelped, his face draining of colour.

Phoenix clenched her teeth against a snapped reply, forcing herself to focus on the creature in front of her. The spark of annoyance seemed to catch inside her though, and, with dawning horror, she felt the heat of her power stir.

No, no, no.

She adjusted her grip on her axes and took a deep breath, trying to calm herself, but it was too late. Threads of warmth were already creeping through her, coiling and spreading. She could feel the fire beginning to build, pulsing with every heartbeat, demanding to be let out.

The timing really couldn't have been worse.

The creature's gaze flickered between the three Hunters, sizing up the easiest target.

Phoenix tried to take the deep, steady breaths that helped dissipate the fire. Usually when this happened, she would close her eyes and sit in a quiet place for a few minutes. That wasn't an option now, and the fire seemed to know it. Stronger and stronger it surged within her until her hands began to tingle unpleasantly and sweat beaded on her brow.

'Come on, Wormy,' Five said through gritted teeth,

stepping back with Six, trying to lead the creature away from Phoenix, give her a bit more space. 'It's us you want.'

For a moment, it looked like it would work. The creature took a step towards the boys, but then suddenly whirled back to Phoenix, its many legs a blur as its maimed tail lashed forward, trying to hook her ankles out from under her.

She reacted slowly, her attention split between the creature and the fire trying to explode out of her. With a vicious downward slice, she just managed to hack the rest of its tail off. She kicked out at the scuttling creature as it launched itself at her, but her angle was all wrong and it crashed heavily into her knees.

'NO!' Seven's scream sounded very distant.

Almost in slow motion, Phoenix felt herself lose her balance and begin to topple back, arms windmilling. The sky filled her vision as she and the edgeworm tumbled over the end of the platform.

CHAPTER 3

'PHOENIX!' Six yelled.

With all her might, Phoenix twisted in mid-air and drove her axe down, through the tail end of the creature and into the wood at the very edge of the platform. Then she was half falling, her feet scrabbling for purchase while her body hung over a seemingly infinite drop, clouds swirling beneath her.

The fire inside her vanished as a flood of ice-cold terror swept it aside. Only her axe anchored her. Her heart was racing, sweat stinging her eyes as she gripped the haft with everything she had. Beside her, the edgeworm thrashed furiously, and, with a horrifying splintering sound, Phoenix felt the axe blade begin to work its way out of the planks holding her.

Bright white panic emptied her mind. At the corner of her vision, the edgeworm's teeth flashed as it twisted to snap at her. Acting on pure instinct, she hacked at it with the axe in her other hand. It screamed again and writhed harder, desperately trying to pull itself away from the blade pinning it. Phoenix felt the axe give way a little more under their combined weight. With a yell, she pulled herself higher, every muscle in her arm screaming as she fought the deadly pull of gravity. Something grabbed her other arm and pulled her viciously upward. Then she was face down on sun-warmed red planks, the sound of Five and Six dispatching the edgeworm loud in her ears.

She took a slow, deep breath, trying to steady the thunderous pounding of her heart, the tremor in her hands.

'Phoenix, are y-you all right?' Hands were pulling her up and Phoenix found herself staring into Seven's frightened face, her red hair whipping wildly in a sudden breeze.

'I think so,' she lied. She couldn't believe what had just happened. Her powers had risen up at the worst possible moment, distracted her, almost got her killed.

Relief made Seven laugh with delight. 'Five pulled you up j-just in time. If he hadn't . . .' She didn't need to finish the sentence.

'By the frost,' Five gasped, his knees looming in her vision as he threw himself on to the boards. 'That was close.'

Six collapsed beside them. 'I thought you'd gone over for a second, Phoenix. I . . .' His voice trembled.

'I thought so too,' Phoenix admitted, her voice betraying how shaken she was. She sat herself up. Widge popped his head out of her bearskin, his eyes wide as he stared between them.

'Oh, Widge,' Phoenix sighed, scratching his cheek. 'I really wish you'd stayed with Seven.' The look he gave her seemed to agree.

'A Magical Bestiary was obviously wrong,' Five scowled, wiping blood off his sword. 'That was way harder than a four out of ten!'

'I wondered about that too,' said Six, frowning. He snuck a glance at Phoenix. 'Are you sure you remembered the right rankings?'

'This is the thanks I get for memorising a whole book?' Phoenix sputtered.

'Yup,' said Five with a smirk. 'And, when we get back down to Ledge, I'm reading that entry myself.'

'Why wait?' Phoenix scowled. She nodded at her bag, lying near the wing shed. 'It's in there.'

Six and Seven stared at her.

'You brought it with you, but . . . didn't check it?' Six asked.

'I told you, I know it off by heart!' said Phoenix as Five dragged the heavy book out of her bag. He dropped it with a thud on to the wooden boards, then flopped down beside the others, flipping the pages to the entry on edgeworms, ignoring the dark look Phoenix was giving him.

'Aggression: four out of ten,' he read. 'Danger posed:

six out of ten. Difficulty to disable –' Five's eyes widened – '*SIX* out of ten!'

'Huh?' Six leaned over his shoulder to look.

'You said it was FOUR out of ten!' Five howled.

'No way!' said Phoenix, snatching the book from him and poring over the page. 'There's no way I'd misremember something so—' She broke off as her eyes found the relevant line. 'Oh.'

Widge stared up at her, his expression full of recrimination.

Phoenix winced and closed the book quickly. 'Oh well. No harm done really.' She'd been aiming for a breezy tone, but her voice sounded strained, even to her.

'No harm . . .' Five stared at her, agog. 'Did you *see* what just happened? If I hadn't been there to save you—'

'NOLLYWADDLING NINCOMPOOPS!'

The angry roar made all four leap to their feet as Elder Hoarfrost stamped across the boards towards them, eyes black and furious. 'Could ye have made that tiddly edgeworm look any ruddy harder?'

CHAPTER 4

By the time Phoenix and her friends were halfway back to Ledge, they were in no doubt over how shoddy Elder Hoarfrost thought their work was – no detail of their hunt had gone uncriticised; everything from their strategy to the way they held their weapons had been judged and found wanting.

'I've never seen a sadder performance,' Hoarfrost growled in conclusion.

Phoenix was right behind him, her jaw aching with the effort of biting back her retorts. No one had ever implied her axemanship was anything less than superb and she wasn't enjoying his critique at all. Added to that, Five was still muttering, '*Four* out of ten,' under his breath and they'd descended into the layer of cloud that seemed to exist permanently round Ledge. A light, persistent rain was steadily drenching them. As water trickled down Phoenix's neck, she felt thoroughly miserable. She missed the clean, cold frost of the higher mountains where the Hunting Lodge was. Or rather where it had been – before she'd accidentally destroyed it.

Through the mist, the colourful roofs of the village slipped in and out of view beneath them. The people of Ledge lived their lives vertically. Higgledy-piggledy stone buildings rested precariously on supports sticking straight out of the cliff. Narrow steps cut back and forth between them if you were lucky. If not, there were hair-raising rope bridges and ladders instead.

As the group drew level with Ledge's highest buildings, the broad steps they were on split into a multitude of smaller, narrower ones cobwebbing across the cliff to give access to all areas of the village. Hoarfrost peeled away from them with a final glare, heading down to the building that had been given over for his use. His face was like thunder and Phoenix suddenly had the feeling it wasn't just the edgeworm causing his bad mood.

'Any n-news from those Hunters you sent out to the clans?' Seven called after him, clearly thinking the same thing.

Hoarfrost stopped and turned round to scowl at her. 'Nothing useful,' he said, balling his fists. 'None of 'em have found hide nor hair of that wriggling wretch, Victory, or that goblin mage . . .' Hoarfrost frowned, grasping for the right name.

'Morgren,' Phoenix said with a grimace.

The last time she'd seen him, her elemental fire had blasted him across the lodge's training ground. She wasn't even sure he'd survived. Her feelings about Victory were even darker. The Hunting Lodge's ex-weaponsmaster had betrayed them all. She'd helped goblins gain access to the lodge and would've happily killed everyone there if Phoenix's previously undiscovered powers hadn't prevented it. The depths of Victory's treachery went even deeper though: she had led the attack on Phoenix's home two years before, an attack that resulted in the slaughter of her whole village.

'Aye,' Hoarfrost nodded, oblivious to Phoenix's racing thoughts. 'Morgren. No word of him nor that Croke creature neither.' His scowl deepened.

Phoenix couldn't suppress a shudder at the mention of the Croke: the faceless, cloaked monster who'd invaded her mind and memories three months earlier. Even more than Morgren or Victory, the Croke haunted her dreams, seemed to lurk in every shadowy place.

'Total blimmin' silence from the witches, an' none of the clans have a clue about this so-called "Master",' Hoarfrost went on, oblivious to Phoenix's discomfort. 'Ruddy *useless*, the lot of 'em! A whole army of goblins, just upped an' vanished into Ember!' He threw his arms in the air, but beneath his bluster Phoenix could tell he was worried. 'And,' Hoarfrost continued, warming to his subject, 'not only can the chiefs not help us, but now they're coming 'ere, demanding I split my Hunters equally between all the tribes! Ridiculous!'

'The Hunting Lodge is supposed to be impartial,'

said Five. '*Clearly*, it doesn't look that way with us lot living here in Ledge.'

Hoarfrost's face turned puce. 'Ye reckon I don't know that? What was I supposed to blimmin' well do? Have my Hunters live in tents through the winter? The mountain clan is the closest to us . . .'

Five raised his eyebrows.

'. . . geographically!' Hoarfrost roared, seeing his look. 'It's far from ruddy ideal.' The Elder puffed out his cheeks and shook his head, turning from them to head down into the village. 'Have to meet Chief Sundew from the bog clan now. Right old battle-axe she is too.'

Phoenix winced. 'Good luck,' she said, trying to sound encouraging.

'Luck?' Hoarfrost grunted. 'No need for it. Born diplomat, me.'

Happily, he didn't hear her snort of laughter as he hurried away, rain closing behind him like a curtain.

'Shall we visit Dog after dinner?' Six asked.

Phoenix grinned. 'Good idea,' she said, brightening at the prospect of seeing the Hunting Lodge's Guardian again.

The only way into Ledge was to be hauled up in a basket. Neither the basket nor the people manning the ropes were strong enough to lift Dog, so he was forced to stay at the base of the great cliff, guarding the snagglefeet – the Hunters' sturdy, shaggy mounts. It was not a situation anyone was pleased with, but the only option was to go down to see him, which they did every day.

Later on, as the sun dipped in the sky, Six, Seven and Five followed Phoenix through the village, down steps that weaved over, round and under the buildings. It still felt odd to Phoenix to look up and see the bottom of a house suspended above her head, especially ones that were so beautiful: indigo dye covered the struts and base while the constellations favoured by the family inside were painted in gold. The sky was revered above all else by the mountain clan. Nowhere was that more visible than in the decoration of their buildings.

Beneath Ledge, the cliff continued down, sheer rock and tapering steps dropping towards the basket that would carry them to the gloom at the bottom.

'I *hate* this bit,' Five hissed as the light faded. 'Is something to hold on to too much to ask?'

The path had narrowed to barely three feet, empty space sucking at them from beyond the edge.

'You can grab on to me if you like,' Six whispered.

'Oh . . . um . . . er . . . thanks,' Five said. Phoenix could practically hear him blushing.

In the Frozen Forest, Five had been forced to reveal he had feelings for Six by Oakhammer, one of the forest's malevolent Heart Trees. The two boys remained the firmest of friends, but Phoenix felt sure there were moments when Five wished they were something more. She'd tried to broach the topic with him, but had been gently rebuffed.

Up ahead, a speck of orange light bled into the gathering darkness.

'Thank the frost, they're lighting the torches,' Five said.

One man and one woman manned the basket platform, impressively broad shoulders straining through their furs.

'Welcome to the almost-bottom, little Hunters!' The woman grinned, her teeth gleaming in the light of the torches. Eagle feathers and shining quartz were braided through her hair.

'Not many outside the clan like those steps this close to dark,' the man chuckled, taking in Five's pallor and Phoenix's careful aversion of her eyes from the edge.

In the middle of the platform was a large round hole. Two ropes attached to a pulley ran through it into the blackness beneath. Somewhere under them, a huge basket hung and the two mountain folk began cranking a great wheel to pull it up.

'Hop in,' the man said, steadying the basket for them a moment later. 'Ring the bell down there when you want us to bring you back up.'

Five was the last one in and straight away the basket

began to lower in fits and starts, dropping a few feet, then stopping and inching down more slowly. Everyone's knuckles were white on the sides, their faces drawn.

'This is the b-bit I don't like,' Seven groaned, squeezing her eyes closed as the basket lurched again.

Six gulped. 'Agreed . . .'

Widge was the only one who looked cheerful. As if to make a point, he bounded lightly round each of their shoulders before returning to Phoenix.

'No one likes a show-off,' she muttered. Widge's trilled response sounded a lot like squirrel laughter.

The lights of the village were so far above them now that Phoenix could have been looking at a settlement in the sky. Which she supposed, in a way, it almost was.

A few heart-stopping minutes later and they were scrambling gratefully out of the basket on to uneven, rock-strewn ground.

Six grinned. 'Right, let's find that Guardian of ours!'

CHAPTER 5

'D-Dog?' Seven called.

The group stood in the pool of light by the basket, peering hopefully into the shadows around them. The moon was barely a sliver, just peeping through clouds that had thinned and risen above Ledge to veil the starlight.

The darkness shifted and swirled ahead of them. Then came the crunch of steps.

On Phoenix's shoulder, Widge bounced in excitement as a shape shifted in the gloom, moving steadily closer until it resolved into the Guardian. In the dim light, his reddish stone fur looked almost black and he appeared more enormous than ever.

'Phoenix,' said Dog, his voice deep and gravelly. He nudged her shoulder with a surprising gentleness before turning to the others. 'Six, Five and Seven,' he said, his voice a smile. 'I am glad to see you all.'

On Phoenix's shoulder, Widge gave an indignant squeal and Dog laughed. 'And little Widge,' he added. 'I had not forgotten you.'

Mollified, Widge touched noses with Dog, his tail flicking a happy pattern in the air.

'Thought we might bump into each other down 'ere,' came a familiar voice from the darkness. A moment later, Hoarfrost appeared, feet crunching across the scree.

'Hoarfrost has been telling me of your battle with the edgeworm,' Dog said, his tail beginning to wag. 'It seems you acquitted yourselves very well. No less than I expected, of course.'

'Acquitted ourselves . . . well?' Five said, shooting a surprised look at Hoarfrost. He recovered quickly to nod enthusiastically. 'More than well,' he exclaimed. 'Dog, you should have seen us! We were all superb, but *especially* me. I saved Phoenix's life! Did Elder Hoarfrost mention that?'

Phoenix jabbed him hard with her elbow. 'You did not.'

'Enough of that,' Hoarfrost snapped. 'Ye killed the edgeworm an' survived the experience. 'Twas an *adequate* performance.'

'That's not—' Five stopped talking abruptly at the thunderous look Hoarfrost gave him.

'Did you come down here just to tell Dog about us?' Six asked.

'I'll speak to the Guardian whenever I like,' said Hoarfrost sharply. 'An' without feeling the need to run it past ye.'

Six winced. 'Of course, but . . .?'

Hoarfrost sighed and passed a hand over his face, looking suddenly tired. 'I'm still waiting for a hawk from young Pine's team. Sent his lot to speak to the river clan, keep an eye out for the goblins in those parts. He's late checking in.' The Elder sniffed. 'Ain't like him to be late.'

Five hesitated. 'You haven't . . .' He broke off and shook his head. 'Never mind.'

'Spit it out, boy,' Hoarfrost said impatiently.

'The witches . . .' Five shrugged. 'We still haven't heard anything from them. Do you—'

'The witches!' Hoarfrost boomed, suddenly furious. Five flinched. 'There's another blimmin' thorn in my side. Ye'd think when I write to tell 'em of what happened to the Hunting Lodge, of Phoenix an' Seven both having some sorta magic, they'd respond with —' he threw up his hands – 'interest at least.'

'Or advice,' Six suggested.

'Or horror,' said Phoenix. 'Apparently, I'm the bad kind of witch.'

'A harbinger of doom!' Five grinned, perking up. 'I knew it from the first day I met you!'

The punch she landed on his arm was not gentle.

'You'd think they'd respond with ruddy SOMETHING!'

'An elemental witch, a Seer and the return of goblin magic.' Five sighed. 'If that's not enough to get a reaction from them, then *clearly* nothing is.'

Hoarfrost nodded unwillingly. 'You have the right of it, Five.'

Somewhere high above them, there was a burst of fire. A moment later, the crackle of sound reached them.

Hoarfrost threw back his head to track the falling sparks. 'What the . . .?'

'A flare,' Dog said, his voice humming with sudden urgency. 'Ledge's alarm signal. Back in the basket. Quickly. Before they pull it up.'

Phoenix saw immediately that he was right. The basket was already lifting off the ground. Widge gave a sharp shriek of alarm.

Above them, another flare went off as they rushed forward. Phoenix froze as something appeared in the sky above Ledge, the blaze of light throwing an immense birdlike shadow on to the high clouds.

'What in Ember . . .?' Five gasped, his mouth hanging open.

Another burst of brilliance and this time Phoenix saw the shape more clearly. It *was* a bird: enormous and as pale as pearl in the dark.

Hoarfrost's knuckles were white as he stared up.

Above them, the great bird pulled back its wings to enter a near-vertical dive, streaming down the side of the cliff straight for them.

'I don't ruddy believe it,' Hoarfrost whispered.

'What?' Five asked, his eyes wide as he reached for his sword. 'What is that?'

It was Dog who answered. 'That is an ice eagle,' he said, his voice filled with wonder. 'A witch has come.'

CHAPTER 6

Hoarfrost seemed frozen to the spot, the first time Phoenix had ever seen him so uncertain.

The enormous bird, an unearthly gleaming white in the moonlight, pulled out of the dive at the last possible moment to land lightly nearby. From its back, a woman slipped to the ground, walking towards them with her chin held high. She was tall, her hair twisted on top of her head making her appear even more so. Her face was all angles, sharp cheekbones prominent beneath warm brown skin. From her shoulders flowed a long cloak made of the same snow-white feathers as her bird.

'Greetings, Hoarfrost,' she said, her voice soft. Close up, her hair was streaked with silver, her eyes edged with fine lines.

'Nara?' Hoarfrost frowned, his eyes searching her face. 'That you?' His surprise was obvious.

The woman's smile was relieved. 'I wasn't sure you'd remember me.'

Five nudged Phoenix. *They know each other?* he mouthed.

Phoenix shrugged. On her shoulder, Widge's eyes were huge, darting from face to face, trying to take everything in.

'Course I remember ye,' Hoarfrost said gruffly, some of his bluster returning. 'It's been more than forty years an' I might be getting on, but this is still working just fine.' He tapped his forehead with a scowl.

She nodded, amused, and her eyes swept over the group, lingering on Dog with interest. 'We received your letter,' she said, turning back to Hoarfrost, her face becoming more serious.

His wild eyebrows shot up. 'The one I sent three months ago? An' you decided to reply. How *very* kind of ye.'

The witch drew her beautiful feathered cloak round herself. 'We should talk,' she said quietly. 'Much has happened. Icegaard's silence hasn't been without reason.'

'Silence?' Hoarfrost snorted. 'More like total flipping disapp—' He pulled himself up sharply.

'I am here now,' Nara said with quiet dignity, 'to explain. And to discuss the contents of your letter. You said you have a fire elemental in the ranks of your Hunters?'

Phoenix stiffened.

Above their heads, torches were flaring to life in Ledge, feet hurrying on the narrow paths. The basket winch-woman hollered down to Hoarfrost and he roared back that all was well.

'Might be best we stay down here for now,' he said to Nara. 'Bit more privacy.' He hesitated, then seemed to come to a decision. 'This is Phoenix,' he said, jerking his head in her direction. 'And yes, I'd say she's a fire elemental for sure, though we're keeping it under wraps, for obvious reasons.'

'Of course,' Nara said softly. 'The old superstitions around them live on.' Her gaze on Phoenix was so intense that Widge scurried back into her furs. On either side of her, she felt her friends move protectively close.

'You lot better stay if this concerns Phoenix,' Hoarfrost grunted, leading the group to a circle of rocks they could sit on.

'Yes, that would be helpful,' Nara said, following him.

Phoenix exchanged a look with Six. The witch seemed nervous. Hoarfrost could see it too.

Nara took a deep breath, finally peeling her eyes away from Phoenix to offer them all a shaky smile. 'You wrote asking for our help,' she began. 'But I am here to ask for yours instead.'

Whatever Hoarfrost expected, it hadn't been that. Phoenix could practically see the questions and expostulations itching to burst out of him, but he just nodded and said, 'Go on.'

'Morgren,' Nara said. 'The goblin mage you wrote of.'

A stillness came over the assembled group and a growl broke free from Dog. Five caught Phoenix's eye, his confusion obvious.

'What of 'im?' Hoarfrost asked, his hands clenching into fists.

'He has paid Icegaard a visit,' Nara said.

Phoenix hugged herself, shock coursing through her. So Morgren *had* survived their battle at the Hunting Lodge. Widge emerged to make a low growling sound, pressing himself protectively against her throat.

'Grottering gimlets!' Hoarfrost sprang to his feet. 'Is he still there? Is that army of his with 'im?'

Nara shook her head, apparently unfazed by the Elder's outburst. 'Three weeks ago, he appeared from nowhere on the ice outside the frost palace. Some sort of portal magic, I expect. He was there only a few minutes before vanishing again, but unless there's more than one goblin mage it was definitely him.' She took a deep breath. 'He . . . did something. Icegaard is in grave danger as a result.' She winced. 'All of Ember may be in danger.'

'What do you mean, "he did something"?' Five frowned.

'Ember is in danger?' Dog asked at the same time.

Nara nodded quickly. 'For this to make sense, I must

explain what happened forty years ago.' Her eyes met Hoarfrost's. 'Why it was that we disappeared.'

In spite of her shock, Phoenix was intrigued. It was hard not to be. Throughout Ember, the witches were a half-forgotten story. There were times when she'd wondered if they were even real. But now there was one sitting right in front of her, her cloak of ice-eagle feathers glimmering in the moonlight, as real as Widge on Phoenix's shoulder. She looked at her friends and saw the same combination of wonder and disbelief on their faces.

'Go on,' Hoarfrost said.

Nara took a deep breath, her expression pained.

CHAPTER 7

'You know that Icegaard bound goblin magic at the end of the Dark War,' Nara said carefully. 'That we held it, secret and safe, for hundreds of years.'

Hoarfrost nodded.

'Well, forty years ago, one of our witches asked the Headwitch for permission to study it, to try to . . . work with it.'

'Why do I suddenly have a bad feeling about this?' Hoarfrost growled.

'We will never know exactly what happened . . .' Nara went on as though he hadn't spoken. 'She was studying goblin portal magic. But, when she attempted her first spell, the Shadowseam appeared in Icegaard.'

'Shadowseam?' said Five. 'What's that?'

Nara gave a sad laugh. 'The truth is that, even after all these years, I cannot answer that question. It's some kind of dark substance. It caused a magical illness the likes of which we'd never seen before: we called it seam-sickness. None of our healing spells worked. There were almost a thousand of us. Within weeks, only fifty of the young ones were left. I was among the oldest to survive.'

There was a long silence before Hoarfrost spoke, as shaken as Phoenix had ever seen him. 'You were the oldest left?' he asked. 'But you'd barely have been . . . what? Sixteen?'

The silence grew deeper and darker as the meaning of Nara's words sank in. On Phoenix's shoulder, Widge shivered, made himself small.

'By the frost . . .' Hoarfrost's whisper trailed into silence.

The four friends stared at one another, their eyes wide.

Hoarfrost's fist thudded against his knee. 'Why didn't ye tell us? Call for assistance! We woulda helped. The banemages woulda helped!'

'We lived in terror that we would pass the illness across the Frozen Wastes into Ember,' Nara said. 'Before she died, our Headwitch decreed no contact with the outside world until we destroyed the Shadowseam and knew how to treat the disease. She feared even a letter could be catastrophic.'

The air around Phoenix felt heavy, the horror of Nara's words a physical weight.

'It ended eventually,' Nara said quietly. 'But it had already taken too many of us. There was no one left to teach the Unfledged; so much of our knowledge was almost lost.' She drew a shuddering breath. 'We have been relearning our own magic for the last forty years, trying to recover. We never found a way to destroy the Shadowseam though. That is why you have not heard from us.'

'What does this have to do with Morgren though?' Five asked, earning a mortified look from Six. '*What?*' he muttered. 'She told us it was connected.'

Nara gave a shaky laugh. 'It is,' she said. 'For forty years, we have held the Shadowseam inside an oculus.'

Six looked puzzled. 'Inside a . . . what?'

'A sort of magical trap,' she explained.

Behind her, the great white eagle clicked her beak softly, dipping her head to rest on Nara's shoulder. The witch reached up to stroke the feathers beneath the bird's fierce amber eyes, seemed to draw strength from her. 'Since Morgren visited us, the Shadowseam has been growing.' When Nara met Phoenix's gaze, there was a wild fear in the witch's eyes. 'It hasn't grown in forty years.'

'You're worried about the illness returning?' Hoarfrost said.

Nara's laugh was slightly hysterical. 'Of course. But we're even more worried that it will destroy the entire frost palace.'

Phoenix stared.

'We've already renewed the oculus spell four times,'

Nara said unsteadily, 'which is unheard of. Each time, the Shadowseam becomes harder to contain. And it's . . .' She shook her head. 'Somehow it's draining the magic out of Icegaard, even from within its trap. *That* should be impossible too. The whole point of an oculus is to . . .' She trailed off at their blank expressions and shrugged tiredly. 'It shouldn't be happening. If it continues like this, Icegaard doesn't have long left. It is magic that holds the frost palace's structure together. Without it . . .'

'What?' Five snorted. 'It'll fall down?'

Hoarfrost was staring hard at Nara. 'You can't mean what I think you do?'

The witch nodded. 'You saw Icegaard once, Hoarfrost. You know what it is. If its magic fails, it's not just the witches who will suffer. All of Ember would be in danger.'

Phoenix caught Seven's eye. The other girl looked as confused as she felt.

Hoarfrost shook his head slowly. 'What is it ye think Hunters can do, Nara? We fight dark critters. This ain't that though. This is pure magic, an' that's witch knowledge, not ours.'

Nara's voice was quiet but fiercely urgent. 'The Shadowseam must be destroyed to prevent more damage to the frost palace, before it grows large enough to break out of the oculus holding it.' Her hands clenched convulsively. 'If it escapes our containment, it would be free to move beyond Icegaard, perhaps even across the Fangs into the clan lands. And, if seam-sickness returns, then all we have done over the last forty years, the sacrifices we've made . . .' She closed her eyes. 'They would all have been for nothing.'

Hoarfrost stood suddenly, began to pace.

Nara's eyes tracked the Elder. 'You must see that everything is at stake: not just the future of Icegaard, but of the clans too – all of Ember.'

'Course I see that,' Hoarfrost muttered, still pacing.

Phoenix shivered as the witch carried on speaking. 'We have tried everything to get rid of it.' She raised her gaze to Phoenix. 'Or rather almost everything.'

A sudden understanding flared bright in Phoenix. 'Everything except elemental fire,' she said.

'Exactly.' Nara's face was full of desperate hope. 'Will you come with me to Icegaard, Phoenix? Will you help me destroy the Shadowseam?'

'Hang on,' Hoarfrost cut in, his face suddenly sharp and wary. 'You want her to do what now?'

Phoenix was grateful for his interruption. Her heart was skipping a strange rhythm in her chest and she was suddenly slick with sweat. Nara wanted her to *use* her powers? She'd spent the last three months desperately trying to suppress them.

'Morgren and his allies attacked the Hunting Lodge,' Nara said steadily to Hoarfrost. 'Now they're moving against Icegaard. They hope to seize my home and use the magic contained inside it to threaten all of Ember. They will turn Icegaard into a weapon.' She paused. Phoenix bit her lip as all eyes turned to her. 'If she is what you say, Phoenix is our only hope of destroying the Shadowseam and thwarting their plan.'

CHAPTER 8

Shortly after making her request, Nara left the group to consider it. 'I'll be back at first light for your decision.'

Phoenix watched the enormous bird climb, then vanish over the top of the cliff, feathers gleaming in the moonlight.

'What do you wanna do, Phoenix?' Hoarfrost asked, shifting to face her. The surprise on everyone's faces made him shrug. 'Ye're Hunters now,' he said. 'Means ye know yer own strengths an' weaknesses, means ye make yer own decisions. I never force my Hunters to accept a hunt . . .' He broke off and frowned. 'Not that this *is* a hunt, strictly speaking, far as I can see.'

Phoenix felt the group's eyes on her, but couldn't organise her thoughts into words. Fear, sharp and sour, rose in her. Widge sensed it, licked her earlobe and pressed himself closer. She'd spent the last three months pretending her powers didn't exist, quietly hoping they might fade away if she didn't use them, but the opposite seemed to be true. More and more regularly, the fire rose in her, stronger every time, demanding to be used.

And every time she pushed it down her fear of it grew. If she went with Nara, she would *have* to use it. The thought filled Phoenix with horror.

She looked up and saw Seven watching her with worried eyes.

Five sat forward on his rock, his elbows on his knees as he spoke. 'I think there are two options,' he said finally. 'One: we go. Or two: we don't.'

Phoenix's snort of laughter took her by surprise, even as hope sparked in her: he'd said 'we'.

Six rolled his eyes. 'Is that really the best you can do?'

Five grinned and shrugged.

'This is serious, Five,' Seven said, her brow furrowed as she thought. 'Nara's news changes everything.'

'It does, doesn't it?' Six said. The humour had vanished from his face.

'Seven is right,' Dog growled. 'We have been looking for Morgren and Victory—'

'Wondering what their next move will be,' Phoenix cut in, raising a hand to stroke Widge, whose tail was twitching with agitation. Her heart was beating faster, her hands clammy on the squirrel's fur.

'Exactly.' Dog nodded. 'And now we know.'

Hoarfrost stayed quiet, watching them all.

Five's face was scrunched into a frown. 'Let me get this straight. Morgren's done who-knows-what to this Shadowseam thingy to get it to destroy Icegaard,' he said slowly. 'And if he manages that then the seam will be free to attack Ember too.'

'And, if the s-seam spreads that illness through the clans, they'll be s-so diminished they won't stand a chance against a goblin army anyway,' said Seven.

'Two snarrows with one stone,' Six said grimly. 'Get rid of the witches *and* weaken the clans.' He shook his head. 'It makes sense when you think about it. Nara said it was a goblin spell that first created the Shadowseam. If anyone knows what it actually is, how to manipulate it, it'd be Morgren.'

Phoenix nodded, her heart in her mouth.

Hoarfrost shook his head slowly. 'The threat to Ember is twofold. If Icegaard's structure fails, the frost palace itself will be a threat to us, even without the Shadowseam inside it.' He noticed their baffled expressions. 'Ye'll have to take my word for it. If ye see the frost palace for yerselves, ye'll understand.'

As Phoenix listened to her friends, her fear began to slide towards anger, slowly at first, then in a hot rush. Morgren. Victory. The Croke. The three monsters responsible for the deaths of her parents and her sister. Responsible, in fact, for the deaths of everyone she'd once known. The three of them haunted her dreams at night, and not a day had gone by when she hadn't wondered where they were, what horrors they were planning next. Now, finally, she knew.

The fire inside her sensed her anger and, hopeful, began to build. She pushed it down viciously.

'I'll go,' she said, her voice unsteady. 'I want to help the witches destroy the Shadowseam. I want to stop whatever it is Morgren's trying to do.' Dread washed through her at her own words. What if she hurt someone with her powers? *Killed* someone? Killed . . . everyone?

Five and Six glanced at each other and nodded. 'We're coming with you,' they said together.

Phoenix didn't quite trust herself to speak, gratitude tying a tight knot in her throat. She nodded back at them instead, hoping her smile was enough to convey everything she was feeling.

A hawk swooped out of the darkness to land on Hoarfrost's shoulder, a curl of paper tied round its leg. ''Bout ruddy time,' the Elder muttered to it, turning away to tilt the note into the moonlight.

'I w-want to go with you too,' Seven said, the determination in her voice startling Phoenix. 'I know I'm not a H-Hunter yet, but this isn't a hunt, not in the normal sense anyway. It's about magic and . . . and Phoenix isn't the only one w-with that.' Seven's eyes were wide on each of them, urgent. 'I might be able to learn more about my Sight at Icegaard, maybe even improve it.'

Five and Six exchanged a glance and Seven hurried on, speaking faster, trying to convince them. 'I'll keep up my t-training of course – weapons practice with you every day—'

'Of course you're coming with us, Seven,' Phoenix said. 'You're one of us. We can't just leave you behind!'

The delight on Seven's face almost made her laugh and Widge trilled merrily, his tail waving a cheery pattern behind him.

'WHINGERING WHEEVERS!' Hoarfrost's roar cut through the night's peace, sending a flock of feathercoos exploding into the sky from a nearby bush. In their enclosure, the snagglefeet snorted, tossing their heads and rolling their eyes. Phoenix nearly jumped out of her skin.

'What is it?' Dog yelped, springing to Hoarfrost's side.

When the Elder turned back to face the group, Phoenix was shocked at the change that had come over him. The hand holding the note was trembling, his face as pale and dangerous as lightning.

'That . . . that *abomination*!' he spat. 'That wriggling *wretch*!' The venom in his voice was startling.

Five caught Phoenix's eye, bemused. Then, to the group's horror, Hoarfrost sat down suddenly and buried his face in his hands.

'I don't ruddy believe it,' he whispered, his voice shaking. 'I never really thought . . . How *could* she?'

A sharp and powerful fear filled Phoenix and she saw the same disquiet on the others' faces.

'What has happened?' Dog asked again.

In the silence before the Elder spoke, Phoenix noticed a dark smear on the paper in his hand. She tried to tell herself it was mud, but the lie wouldn't stick. Widge chittered nervously and began nibbling a hank of her hair.

'Pine's team found Victory in the riverlands.' Hoarfrost stopped to take a juddering breath.

'Sh-she killed them, didn't she?' Seven said softly. 'All of them but Pine.'

Hoarfrost looked up sharply, then nodded. Every line of him tightened, hardened. 'Aye,' he whispered. 'All of 'em but Pine.' His voice grew ragged. 'Victory trained those boys an' girls herself. She . . .' He stopped talking and stood abruptly, turning his back to them again.

Dog's hackles had risen, his lips quivering round a snarl. 'Victory?' he growled. 'Victory attacked a team of Hunters?'

Hoarfrost nodded, his back still to them. 'Aye. They saw her, tried to track her. Didn't work, of course. She knew all their tricks, taught 'em everything they know.' He grimaced, corrected himself. 'Everything they knew.'

Phoenix saw Six close his eyes, Five shake his head in disgust, and a roaring fury coursed through her. Victory had killed her family, killed her mentor, Silver, and now she was slaughtering her own pupils.

'Is there a chance this is c-connected to what Morgren did at Icegaard?' Seven asked.

Everyone stared at her and Seven flushed. 'They're

b-both working for the same . . . c-creature,' she said. 'The Master.' She shivered 'M-maybe this is the next phase of their plan . . . whatever that is.'

Phoenix forced herself to think. Seven was right, of course. Both Victory and Morgren had revealed themselves within days of each other, but on opposite sides of Ember. 'Perhaps they're hoping the Hunters will split into two groups,' she murmured, thinking hard. 'Try to go after both of them at once.'

Hoarfrost began to pace, his hands clenching and unclenching by his sides. 'You might be right, Phoenix,' he muttered. 'We'd be weaker divided. She's a decent strategist is Victory. Always was.' He stared into the darkness, then spun back to them, his eyes fixed on Dog. 'Guardian, I want you in the riverlands. I wanna know what that varmint, Victory, is up to, an' I wanna know where she's hiding so I can bring her in myself.'

Phoenix stiffened. 'I thought Dog would come to Icegaard,' she said, her heart missing a beat at the thought of being separated from him. 'With me – us, I mean.'

Hoarfrost shook his head. 'He's under my command an' I'm sending 'im after Victory. No one else'll get there so fast. No one else can track her back to her rat hole without being in mortal danger.' Hoarfrost turned to Dog, his expression steely. 'Don't be seen, Guardian. Scent-tracking only. Don't let her know ye're on to her or we don't stand a chance of catching her unawares.'

Dog's distress matched Phoenix's. 'Surely I should stay with—'

'You're the Guardian of the lodge, not of Phoenix,' Hoarfrost said sharply, glancing between them. Phoenix saw that the others looked as stricken as she felt. 'Ye're not part of their team. Never will be.' His gaze softened slightly at Dog's startled anguish. 'I'll let ye say yer goodbyes. Then I want ye off.'

'Tonight?' Phoenix gasped, the unfairness of it making her want to scream. This was too much, too quickly.

'Aye,' Hoarfrost nodded, merciless. 'You lot'll be gone tomorrow anyway an' ye don't want that ex-weaponsmaster of ours to get away any more'n I do,' he said. His eyes were sharp on her, daring her to disagree.

The Elder's mind was made up, Phoenix saw, and nothing was going to alter his decision. She and Dog would be taking separate paths.

CHAPTER 9

When Hoarfrost left them, Phoenix and her three friends flung themselves at Dog, arms wrapping round his neck.

'It will be all right,' Dog said gruffly, nudging each of them with his nose. 'You will be fine. I will be fine. We will be reunited soon and with many tales to tell.'

'I just assumed you'd be coming with us,' Five said, his voice husky.

'I thought the same,' Dog admitted. 'But it is not to be. And that ice eagle would struggle to carry me anyway.'

Phoenix snorted a laugh, furiously blinking away the tears stinging her eyes. Widge had leaped on to Dog's back and was lovingly grooming a patch of his stony fur.

The Guardian turned to her, dropping his head to look her in the eye. 'What you have agreed to do is very noble,' he said gently. 'The witches often helped the Hunters in the past. It is rarer for us to assist them in such a meaningful way. You will be re-establishing a relationship that is centuries old.'

Phoenix winced. 'I'm not doing it because of that,'

she admitted. 'I need to be *doing* something.' She shrugged at their confused looks. 'We've all spent months wondering if Morgren's alive, worrying about him and Victory and . . . and what they're planning.'

To her horror, she realised she couldn't speak the Croke's name out loud, her fear of that creature too visceral. She found herself glancing over her shoulder, wondering if the patch of deepest darkness at the base of the cliff held a cloaked, faceless figure. She caught herself doing things like that more often than she would have liked.

Phoenix shook her head, forced herself to concentrate on what she was saying. 'Now we finally have something on them.' She tried to sound pleased, decisive. 'And maybe we can do something to stop them instead of just . . .'

'Waiting,' Seven filled in.

'Exactly.' Phoenix nodded, pushing down another wave of fear. 'This is a good thing. To have the chance to stop Morgren. It's excellent.'

Five, Six, Seven and Dog stared at her.

'You're worried about using your powers, aren't you?' Six asked, his ability to know what she was thinking uncanny. 'You won't be alone though. We'll be with you all the way.'

'*Obviously!*' Five exclaimed. He paused, a small frown on his face. 'Well, maybe you'll be alone for some of it since, you know, we aren't elementals, but—'

Six elbowed him hard, drawing a yelp from the other boy.

Phoenix swallowed a smile. 'I haven't used my powers since the battle at the Hunting Lodge,' she said, trying not to sound as worried as she felt. 'And I have no idea what a Shadowseam is. I just . . .'

'Nara will help you,' Seven said with perfect confidence.

Hope flared in Phoenix's chest. 'Did you See that? You know it for sure?'

Seven hesitated, then nodded. 'She wants to teach you, help you control your fire. You won't have to face the Shadowseam until you're ready.'

Phoenix's relief was sword-sharp. She'd half imagined Nara leading her straight to this seam thing on arrival at Icegaard, expecting her to destroy it immediately. Perhaps it wouldn't be quite like that though. On her shoulder, Widge chirped softly, his tail tickling the back of her neck.

A comfortable silence fell between them. Dog glanced up at the moon; there was something tense in him that wasn't lost on Phoenix.

'Do you really have to go tonight?' she asked.

'You heard Hoarfrost,' the Guardian replied. 'Time is of the essence. Victory must be caught before she harms anyone else.'

'Will you be all right?' Five asked. He went on quickly,

'After what Oakhammer did to you . . . it seemed like you felt pain more easily.'

Phoenix winced, remembering how the Heart Tree in the Frozen Forest had tortured Dog, laughed at his first experience of pain. Somehow, perhaps unintentionally, Oakhammer had permanently changed Dog that day. He said he *felt* everything more now, not just pain.

'I did and still do,' Dog said gently. 'Perhaps I am less impervious than I once was. Less stone. But I am still more than a match for Victory.'

Phoenix couldn't help but notice that the Guardian looked troubled. 'What is it?' she asked. 'There's definitely something you're not telling us.'

Dog's laugh rattled like pebbles shaken together. 'I cannot get anything past you.'

'Of course not,' Phoenix scowled. 'We're your friends – you're not supposed to get anything past us.'

For a moment, Dog looked stunned. 'Friends,' he murmured. 'No one has ever said that to me before.'

'Stop trying to change the subject,' Five said. 'What is it you're worried about?'

Dog sighed and shook his head. 'Hoarfrost wishes me to travel unseen.'

'You think that'll be difficult?' Phoenix asked.

'In places,' Dog admitted. 'But there is one I am thinking of in particular. The fastest route to the riverlands passes through the Great Woods. The forest clan are more vigilant than ever. I think I must travel beneath the River Clasp – underwater – to avoid being seen by them.'

'*Under* the Clasp?' Five spluttered.

The four friends stared at one another, their eyes wide and fearful. The Clasp was notorious throughout Ember, its waters imbued with strange powers. It was said that a sip of it could strip away a person's memories, that bathing in it would send you mad.

'That's r-really dangerous, Dog,' Seven said.

'Especially if you're more vulnerable after Oakhammer,' Phoenix said, fear for him leaping in her chest, making breathing suddenly difficult.

'Can't you go round the woods instead?' Six asked, grimacing as he spoke. That route would add another three days to Dog's trip.

'I must get there as fast as possible to give myself the best chance of catching Victory,' Dog said. He shook himself. 'Do not worry about me. I will be fine.'

He stood, glancing up at Ledge.

A wild panic flared in Phoenix. 'You're going *now*?'

'I must,' Dog said gently. 'I shall miss you all so much.' He shook himself again quickly. 'This is the right thing to do though.'

Phoenix leaned against him, a sick sadness rolling inside her. It didn't feel like the right thing. But saying that out loud wouldn't change the situation. Instead, she said, 'We should say goodbye then.'

'Yes,' Dog said quietly. 'I will think of you every day and look forward to when we are reunited. I have no doubt you will excel at Icegaard, that each of you will do everything you can to thwart Morgren.'

Phoenix was glad it was so dark when the Guardian left them, the tears on her cheeks all but invisible as he disappeared into the night.

CHAPTER 10

Dog padded into the darkness, away from Phoenix and the others, his heart as heavy as it had ever been.

The night air smelled of rain and stone and possibility, but he couldn't revel in the scents as he usually did. Everything was tainted with the cloying odour of sadness.

He'd promised himself that he wouldn't look back, but the temptation was too strong. The four of them were still just visible by the snagglefeet, huddled together, consoling one another as friends should.

Friends.

His eyes found Phoenix and it was hard to tear them away again. She'd called him her friend. No one had ever done that, and he hadn't dared to hope anyone ever would.

He forced himself to turn away.

Now he was alone again as he'd been so often before.

Now he had a mission and he'd succeed in it as he always did.

Dog only managed to take two paces before his paws

stopped, seemingly of their own accord, so he could sneak another look back at them.

His friends.

The urge to howl was almost too strong to resist. Instead, Dog forced himself to turn and break into a long, ground-eating lope towards the distant green silence of the Great Woods. Towards the unknown danger of the River Clasp. And, somewhere beyond that, his enemy – Victory.

CHAPTER 11

Phoenix had lain awake for what felt like hours, eyes peering into the gloom of her room, worrying about Dog, wondering what Icegaard would be like.

Icegaard.

In spite of Victory and Morgren, in spite of the Shadowseam, there was a part of her that fizzed with excitement at the thought of actually getting to see the frost palace. What would Poppy have said if she'd known her big sister would one day visit it? Phoenix didn't have to think hard about that at all: Poppy would have exploded with glee. Her little sister had been fascinated by the world beyond Poa. It was she who'd been most excited when, three years before, their da told them he'd take them to the floating market – the first time Phoenix and her little sister had ever travelled beyond the grasslands.

She closed her eyes, allowed herself to drift into a memory of their first day there.

'There you are,' Starling gasped, relief flooding her as Poppy appeared suddenly beside where she was sitting in their da's cart. 'Where've you been?'

'Looking around, of course.' Poppy blinked. Behind her, the floating market seethed with activity and noise, brightly coloured stalls jostling for space alongside one another. Beyond them, the shining water of Lake Ilara spread in every direction, gleaming in the warm afternoon light.

Starling shivered, averted her eyes. The shore looked much too far away. Earlier, when the clan bridges had unrolled like bobbins from the island to the shore, when she'd crossed with her da and Poppy, she'd been excited. That feeling was gone now. The bridges had been reeled back in, wouldn't unfurl again until the next day, and she felt trapped. Trapped with the other clans on all sides. Trapped in all their strangeness.

She shuddered as she felt the cart beneath her bob up and down in time with the island. She hadn't realised before they arrived that the floating market wasn't a real island, but an artificial one. Bundles of reeds laid over old reeds laid over even older ones. The ground was soft and springy, the island free to twirl across the lake with the breeze. Everything about it felt fragile and unnatural. Starling hated it.

'Have you seen the river-clan stalls?' Poppy asked, not noticing her sister's expression. 'Kingfisher feathers in colours I've never seen before! And fish scales that shimmer like silver. It's beautiful.' The last word came out as a sigh.

'You should've stayed with me,' Starling said, reaching for her. 'You know Da asked me to look out for you.'

Poppy leaped lightly out of reach. 'But I want to explore and you won't.'

'That's not true.'

'It is,' Poppy snorted. 'If you wanted to see things, you wouldn't be sitting on the back of our cart. You can see that any old day. Everything else though . . .' She turned, sweeping her arms wide to take in the bustle of the market, a sharp contrast to the perfect stillness of the lake. 'We're only here for four days. Then we go home.' She sighed, her arm dropping as a cloud passed in front of the sun. 'Reed says we have to make the most of it.'

Starling stiffened. 'Reed? Who's Reed?'

Poppy beamed. 'My new friend!'

'We've only been here a couple of hours,' Starling snapped. 'You can't have made a new friend already.'

'Can.'

'Can't!'

'All right then –' Poppy shrugged – 'then I'm going to play with nobody.' She danced off, her expression mischievous as she shouted over her shoulder, 'Nobody is going to teach me to swim!'

'What?' Starling leaped to her feet, the cart shifting beneath her. 'No! You can't, Poppy. That's dangerous. I . . . I forbid it.'

Poppy didn't dignify that with a response, her mouth

quivering with suppressed laughter as she glanced back at Starling.

'I'll tell Da!' Starling shouted, hating herself a bit. Bringing their father into it was a low blow.

But it worked.

A slight pause in her little sister's step. 'Come with me then,' Poppy said, turning round, her eyes bright. 'Reed'll teach you too. I know he will!'

Warring feelings raged back and forth in Starling. If she went with Poppy, at least she'd know her sister was safe. But she didn't want to learn to swim. She was grass clan, not river. What if this river-clan boy was dangerous or . . . or . . .

'Come on!' Poppy called. Tired of waiting, she turned on her heel and scampered towards the hubbub of the main market.

'Wait!' Starling cried. Her little sister was too quick though, already weaving away between the colourful stalls and press of bodies. Not wanting to lose her, Starling jumped down from the cart and gave chase, her eyes drinking in the sights she'd been watching with an uncomfortable mix of suspicion and fascination.

A desert-clan stall blazed with the jewel colours of dyed wools, glinted with polished discs of desert glass larger than she'd ever seen. Next to it sat a forest-clan stall, its frontage blocked by a jostling crowd, the haggling for ymbre heated.

Further on, a bog-clan stall groaned under the weight of hundreds of harvested plants, some dried, some still dripping moisture from their roots, but each neatly labelled with its medicinal property and price. Starling's jaw dropped at one tiny plant, its roots meticulously wrapped, which cost as much as a month's corn.

The stallholder grinned at her, clearly amused by her reaction. 'Never seen woundwort before?'

Starling blinked, shaking her head mutely.

'Stops bleeding,' the stallholder explained. 'Mash up these leaves and smear it on to any wound, even a lost limb, and it'll stem the blood immediately.' Starling's eyes widened and the man nodded. 'Saved countless lives it has, 'specially up at the Hunting Lodge.'

'Starling! Are you coming?' Poppy's voice summoned her back to the moment, somehow cutting through the shifting crowd and excited haggling.

With a quick nod, Starling followed, trying her best to catch Poppy but failing – her little sister was fast. Eventually, just as she thought her heart would burst out of her chest, she sprinted round the final stall and almost crashed into her sister's back.

Poppy had stopped abruptly and was chattering away happily with a boy around Starling's age, dressed in a fish-skin jerkin of the river clan.

'Reed,' Starling guessed, immediately wary.

The river clan had no argument with the grass clan

for now, but the history between them stretched back centuries and had rarely been easy.

Reed grinned and nodded, oblivious to her rushing thoughts. 'Are you here to learn to swim too?'

'No,' she said. 'And neither is Poppy. It's not a grass—'

A splash cut her off and she spun, horrified to see that Poppy had stripped to her underclothes and jumped straight into the lake.

'Poppy!'

Reed stared, his jaw slack with surprise.

Coughing and spluttering, Poppy's head broke the surface, gasping in a breath before sinking out of sight again.

'Poppy!'

Panic threatened to choke Starling as she flung herself down at the edge of the lake, plunging her arms into the water, feeling frantically for her little sister. Nothing – it was too deep. She stood, about to jump in after her, but a small hand pulled her back.

'If you can't swim, you can't help her,' Reed said.

Before Starling could respond, he'd dived into the spot where Poppy had vanished, the water seeming to part for him with barely a ripple.

Starling stood in the sudden quiet, a horror of uncertainty breaking over her. An instant later, she stepped to the edge, about to hurl herself in, when the surface broke and two heads appeared, Reed hauling Poppy up behind him.

'Idiot!' he laughed at Poppy, blinking water from his eyes. 'You're supposed to have the lesson first!'

Starling stared at her little sister, her heart hammering, unable to understand the amusement on Poppy's face. Why wasn't she terrified?

'I saw fishes, Starling!' Poppy exclaimed, reaching for her hand so she could be dragged on to the soft bank. 'Swimming!'

'By tomorrow, you'll be swimming just like them,' Reed promised.

Poppy's beaming smile matched Reed's, even when another fit of coughing shook her and Starling had to slap her on the back.

'Poppy,' she hissed. 'You'll drown.'

Reed stared at her, his small face confused. 'If you can swim, you'll never drown.' He hesitated, then added, 'Unless you meet a ripplewrack.'

Poppy waved this away airily. 'I'm not scared.' Her face was as excited as Starling had ever seen it. 'Teach me.'

Later, as they walked back to their da's stall, Poppy was very quiet, glassy-eyed.

'You all right?' Starling asked.

'Do you feel it?' Poppy whispered.

'Feel what?'

'How incredible it is,' Poppy said softly, her face alight. Then, in response to Starling's confused expression, 'The world, Starling! It's so big and so full of wonder.' She sighed happily. 'When I'm older, I'm going to be an explorer and see every bit of it.'

Phoenix smiled a small, painful smile in the dark, tried to keep the memory light and whole in her mind.

It's so big and so full of wonder.

She'd almost forgotten how delighted her little sister had been with the floating market: the sounds and smells, the different clans, the new foods, the water. She'd wanted to be an explorer so she could discover even more.

Phoenix closed her eyes with a sigh, trying to hold on to some of Poppy's happiness in her mind. Yes, she would have loved the chance to visit Icegaard.

But when Phoenix finally drifted off, it was the Croke, as always, that slipped into her dreams, reminding her that her sister was gone, that her whole family was gone. It twisted her memories and warped them into nightmares.

CHAPTER 12

The next morning, it was a pale and sombre group that made their way down through Ledge. Although she was awake and surrounded by her friends, fragments of Phoenix's nightmares still echoed within her. She'd considered taking dream milk again to hold them at bay, but quickly rejected the idea. She remembered her family much more clearly without it and wouldn't sacrifice that for anything. The Croke felt close though, seemed to watch her from every shadow. Widge nibbled nervously on a strand of her hair as the basket was lowered from Ledge, his weight and warmth a comfort to her.

'They're already down there,' Five said, nodding at Hoarfrost and Nara, just visible beneath them. A muscle was working in his jaw and he was unusually quiet.

Phoenix stared down as the basket descended, her heart twisting. Dog should be there too. It felt so wrong that this was happening without him.

'There ye are,' Hoarfrost said. He scanned each of them quickly as they clambered out of the basket. 'Good, ye've got yer weapons, I see.' He pinned Five, Six and

Phoenix with a sharp look. 'Ye three are Hunters now.' He nodded at Seven. 'She's still a huntling. Which means ye're responsible for her safety, her training an' speaking the Pledge. Got it?'

They nodded.

'An' by the frost, Five an' Six, ye've got to choose yer Hunter names soon.'

The two boys nodded again quickly.

'We're narrowing it down all the time,' Five said.

Phoenix suppressed a snort. That definitely wasn't true.

'Hmph,' Hoarfrost said. Not much got past him. He turned to Nara. 'Well, here they are.'

The witch's snow-white feathered cloak seemed to glow in the pre-dawn light as she stepped forward, her eyes bright and fixed on Phoenix. 'Thank you,' she said, the strength of her emotion making her voice shake. 'My thanks to *all* of you. I know it must feel strange to be whisked away by me before we get to know one another,' she said. 'But time is truly of the essence and I'd like to leave as soon as possible.'

Phoenix winced at a sharp stab of fear. *Time is truly of the essence.* Nara was depending on her ability to control her fire, her ability to destroy this Shadowseam. All of Icegaard would be depending on her, perhaps all of Ember. Phoenix wished with every fibre of her being that the Shadowseam was something she could just fight with her axes: she would have had more confidence then.

Instead, she just felt a cold, rising dread. What if she couldn't do it? What if she ended up damaging Icegaard the way she'd damaged the Hunting Lodge? What if that somehow harmed Ember?

'We've got everything we need with us,' Six said, his voice betraying his eagerness. For once, he appeared oblivious to what Phoenix was thinking.

'W-we're ready,' Seven agreed.

'Are we flying to Icegaard? On your eagle?' Five asked, his eyes wide.

Behind Nara, the great bird landed on silent wings.

'In a manner of speaking.' Nara smiled, moving to stroke the bird's cheek feathers. 'I left a portal near Icegaard. If I create another one here, we'll be able to fly through, straight to the frost palace.'

'What's a p-portal?' Seven asked.

'It's very safe,' Nara reassured them quickly. 'Where two portals exist, you can join them, travel between them, as easily as stepping across a threshold. But there must be two and they must be connected. It took me a week to fly here on Chiara, but it will only take us moments to return once I open the second portal and connect it to the one at Icegaard.'

She smiled at the eagle beside her, who inclined her head gently. With a start, Phoenix noticed the intelligence in the bird's gaze. From her shoulder, Widge stared too, as fascinated as she was.

'I do *not* like the sound of that,' Five muttered, drawing a surprised look from Six.

Nara smothered a smile. 'I think that our magic has been forgotten in Ember,' she said. 'But, starting now, we would like that to change. Will you trust me?' The question was so open and direct that it took Five by surprise.

'I think I have to,' he murmured, looking awkward. 'So, how will it work?'

Nara turned to her ice eagle with a smile. 'I'll let Chiara answer that.'

To Phoenix's amazement, the bird began to speak. Her shock was reflected on everyone's faces except for Hoarfrost and Widge, who began to groom himself. Chiara's voice was soft like Nara's, so quiet they strained to hear her.

'It is simple,' the bird said. 'You will climb on to my back with Nara, and I will take off. When we are airborne, Nara will create the portal and we will fly through. From the other side, it is only a short flight to Icegaard. I ask only that you try not to pull my feathers.'

'All right then,' Nara said, her smile a little nervous. 'It's time.' She waved them forward as Chiara ducked her head, spreading her wings so it was easier for them all to climb on. Nara boosted them up, directing them to the bird's long glossy back. Phoenix was last, and she marvelled at the river-silk smoothness of the feathers, their icy brightness. She tried not to tug any of them as she made her way to where the others were sitting, all looking amazed and terrified in equal parts.

'There's nothing to hold on to,' Five muttered wildly. '*Nothing!*'

He was right, Phoenix saw with a ripple of unease. But then Nara leaped up lightly, settling herself just behind the eagle's great head.

'Phoenix, hold on to me,' she said. 'You others hold on to Phoenix. We'll fly nice and straight and smooth, but just in case . . .' She passed back a length of rope and waited patiently as they all tied themselves to one another. Five tested and retied all their knots four times before he was happy.

'Excellent,' the witch said when he was finally done. 'Then we will take our leave.' She raised her hand to Hoarfrost in a farewell salute.

'Look after my Hunters,' Hoarfrost growled, raising his hand in return.

Then they were all calling goodbye as Chiara spread her wings and, with a powerful leap, took flight.

CHAPTER 13

Five made a strangled, high-pitched sound that might have been a smothered scream. Phoenix couldn't contain a whoop as the ground fell away; the feeling of freedom was too immense. Widge poked his head curiously out of her collar and closed his eyes, enjoying the fresh breeze in his cheek fur and round his ears. A gentle purr vibrated through him and Phoenix laughed in delight.

'Ember's only flying squirrel,' she said with a grin. Widge looked rather pleased with that.

'This is a-amazing!' Seven cried, her voice bubbling with delight.

Nara turned back, her eyes bright. 'No one ever forgets their first ice-eagle flight,' she called, the air whirling her words away.

'I don't doubt it,' Five groaned. 'I'm not feeling so good.'

Phoenix glanced back at him. His eyes were squeezed tightly shut. 'Five, if you're sick on me . . .'

'I thought this was a dream of yours?' Six laughed from behind him. 'To fly on an ice eagle.'

'I didn't think it through,' Five said, squeezing his eyes even tighter. 'Why can't we fly closer to the ground?'

Six tried and failed to smother more laughter. 'You are ridiculous,' he gasped. 'Open your eyes, Five. You can't miss this – it's too incredible!'

At Six's urging, Five opened one eye. His arms tightened round Phoenix so much that she could barely breathe. But when he spoke again it was with awe. 'This is . . . this is . . .'

Behind him, Six beamed.

Phoenix stared in amazement as they climbed. Ledge was tiny, a bright spot quickly gone as the detail beneath them blurred. Then there was only the dawning, cloud-brushed sky with the promise of a rising sun on the horizon, and the mountains, silvery and mysterious, caught on a knife edge between night and day.

Behind her, everyone was silent, and, when she turned to look at them, she saw her own wonder reflected. They smiled at one another; there were no words.

A while later, Nara looked back again. 'It is beautiful here,' she called, 'but it's time to return to Icegaard. When I open the portal, you'll see a disturbance in the air. Once we've flown through, I'll close the portal there, but I'll leave this side open to make your return trip easier.'

Before anyone had time to respond, she faced forward, raised her arm and whispered something that Phoenix couldn't catch.

Chiara banked to the left, turning towards a patch of brightening air. The sky there rippled and swirled before calming, except . . . Phoenix blinked, barely able to understand what she was seeing.

The sky around Ledge had lightened to a silvery-blue as the sun peeped above the mountains. But ahead of them was a perfect circle of star-filled darkness: the sky of a place where dawn was still hours away.

Phoenix's heart began to race. Widge became very still and Five's grip tightened even more.

'Icegaard is much further north than Ledge,' Nara called over her shoulder. 'At this time of year, the sun only rises for a few hours each day.'

Phoenix found herself holding on to the witch more tightly as they approached the portal. For an instant, there was the roar of a storm, a confusing brightness and darkness, then an icy, brutal cold that hit Phoenix like a bare-knuckled punch. Behind her, she heard her friends' teeth chattering alongside her own.

Nara craned to look behind them, and with a look of intense concentration whispered something else. Once again, the word escaped Phoenix, slipping through her senses like an eel until it disappeared. She twisted round just in time to see the circle of blue sky shrink and vanish behind them.

'I've left the portal at Ledge open,' Nara called to Phoenix, seeing her surprise. 'But it's not safe to leave two connected and open, even in the sky. We have too many glintwings here to risk it.'

'What in Ember . . .?' Six whispered, staring around.

Phoenix felt words fail, surprise muting her as she followed Six's gaze: the mountains were gone, the breaking day was gone. It seemed as if *everything* was gone. The land they'd emerged into was empty, locked in night. Ghostly, moon-silvered ice spread as far as the eye could see and a throttling cold blanketed everything, already seeping into her bones. A less hospitable place Phoenix couldn't have imagined if she'd tried.

Nara raised her hand and murmured something. Suddenly the bitter cold eased. 'A warmth spell,' she said. 'One of our most important pieces of magic out here, as you can imagine.'

Five grimaced. 'Thanks . . . I think.' Then, more quietly: 'Shouldn't she ask before doing magic on us?'

'I d-don't mind if it keeps the cold away,' Seven whispered back. 'A few minutes of that and I'd be frozen solid.'

They only flew for a short while before Phoenix became aware of a low, repetitive, booming sound.

'What's that noise?' she called to Nara.

'The Endless Ocean,' the witch replied, pointing to something ahead of them in the darkness.

The ocean! Phoenix's heart fluttered. Her ma's ma had seen it once as a girl, the story of it passed down like an heirloom through the generations. She strained her eyes towards it, to the rolling, gleaming sheet of restless movement. Its surface shone sword-steel dark: dangerous, beguiling, hungry. Just as her ma had heard it described, and later described it to her.

Nara noticed her expression. 'It's beautiful on a clear day in summer,' she said. 'But it's more powerful than we can fathom and contains more dark creatures than all of Ember. It always pays to remember that.'

Phoenix nodded slowly, unable to tear her eyes from it as Chiara turned to follow a series of sharp cliffs just north. That was how she missed the first glimpse of Icegaard.

'What's that?' Seven called from behind her, jolting Phoenix out of her ocean reverie. She was pointing along the coastline. In the darkness, something glinted, rising vastly out of the ocean to curl over the cliff like a shining claw.

'That,' Nara said with a smile, 'is the frost palace.'

Phoenix could only stare, her astonishment increasing the closer they got.

'But it's a w-wave!' Seven exclaimed at last, putting Phoenix's thoughts into words. 'I think?'

'It is,' Nara smiled. 'Part of a wave that would have wiped away all of Ember had it not been frozen in time since long before our records began. We don't know what happened to stop it in its tracks like that, but it's been our home for over a thousand years.'

Phoenix stared. 'A wave that would have wiped away Ember . . .' It sounded outlandish, yet there it was, frozen at the moment it had begun to surge over the cliffs, its crest trailing back into the pounding black waters of the ocean. The closer they got, the more the scale of it staggered her. It was like a mountain: the walls of the Hunting Lodge could have been stacked up fifty times and still not come close to the lofty heights of the wave's spray-whipped peak.

It is magic that holds the frost palace's structure together. Phoenix remembered Nara's words to them with a terrible lurch. Magic that the Shadowseam was devouring. Suddenly the danger to Ember was abundantly clear.

'That. Is. Terrifying.' Five's eyes were huge.

With a swoop that made Phoenix's stomach heave, Chiara dived under the magnificent curling lip of the frost palace to land on the clifftop beneath it. A barrelled wall of ice surged up and over them at an impossible angle, blocking out the stars. It looked like it was about to crash to the ground at any moment, yet it didn't.

In a sudden rush, all Phoenix's fears crowded in on her, leaving her feeling sick and breathless. She was here, at Icegaard, and it was more enormous than she'd ever imagined. If the Shadowseam truly threatened this place, what in Ember could *she* do about it? She was only one person: one girl who felt particularly small standing before the frost palace.

The goosebumps prickling up her arms had nothing to do with the cold.

'Do you f-feel that?' Seven whispered.

'Feel what?' Six asked.

But Phoenix knew what she meant. There was something in the air here, something that made her chest tight. She'd felt it in the Frozen Forest too, months earlier.

'Magic,' she murmured, not realising she'd spoken aloud. Widge trilled his agreement, only his ears and eyes visible above her furs.

'If magic is freezing and smells like fish,' Five muttered. His fingers were still digging into Phoenix even though Chiara was on the ground now. She gently prised them off. 'I don't understand,' he said to Nara, gazing around. 'Where *actually* is Icegaard?'

Nara smiled. 'It's here,' she said, gesturing at the huge wave as she helped them down from the great bird's back. 'This is the frost palace.'

Five stared at the wall of frozen water, looking as worried as Phoenix had ever seen him. 'You can't live in a lump of ice,' he said, speaking very slowly, as though explaining something difficult. 'Even one as obscenely large as this.'

Nara laughed. 'It will make sense once you're inside, I promise.' Then: 'Thank you, Chiara.'

The affection between Nara and her ice eagle was

obvious. Chiara ducked her head to the witch. 'Our first true adventure,' she said in her soft voice.

'Worth the very long wait, I think,' Nara replied, resting her forehead momentarily against the bird's beak.

The ice eagle inclined her beautiful head, then took off again, flying out from beneath the curving crest of the wave to vanish, the sound of her powerful wingbeats disappearing a moment later.

Five watched her go, his eyes huge.

'Look,' Seven whispered, pointing.

At the base of the frost palace, right in front of them, lines of light were appearing in the ice, tracing intricate patterns across the gleaming surface.

'Doors,' Phoenix breathed as two shapes were completed. She swallowed hard, wonder displacing her fears. She'd just flown on an ice eagle. She was about to enter the frost palace. How she *wished* she could show Poppy.

Nara smiled, her feathered cloak billowing behind her as she set her weight against the doors' icy surface, then turned to wave the others forward.

'Welcome to Icegaard.'

CHAPTER 14

Phoenix could feel Widge's heart racing and she raised a hand to touch him, drawing comfort from his soft fur as they both stared into the frost palace.

A vast cavern had been hollowed out of the solid wave. And inside it was a lake, perfectly still and as clear as the finest desert glass. Phoenix hadn't expected that. Fish swam beneath its surface, trails of coloured light streaming behind them as they moved.'

Two lines of enormous ice statues rose from the depths of the water, leading away from the entrance. Each figure on its plinth depicted a different woman, incredibly realistic, but many times the size of a normal person. And all of them appeared to be alive. Their eyes were fixed on Phoenix and her friends, blinking as they leaned over to whisper to one another.

The group had followed Nara forward without even realising it, their eyes drinking in every impossible detail.

The two columns of statues swept back to a frozen island where a group of women stood silently, most of them wearing feathered cloaks like Nara's. Phoenix barely noticed them – it was the tree behind them that demanded her attention. It dominated the small area of land, the whole of the cavern in fact. It sprang straight from the ice, its green, leafy branches reaching vastly across the water. This tree made even Oakhammer seem barely a sapling.

Phoenix could see steps winding round the trunk. She traced them up, and discovered that the tree was even taller than the cavern it stood in. The upper reaches of its trunk and branches vanished into the curved ice high above them.

'It's . . . it's . . .' Seven broke off, unable to continue.

'Beautiful,' breathed Six, his eyes huge.

Phoenix had never agreed with him more. The ice glowed with a mysterious light of its own, the darting fish drew rainbows of colour in the water and a multitude of warm orange orblights hovered over everything. Several of them floated lazily across the lake towards where Phoenix was standing. She stared, fascinated, her eyes moving ceaselessly, trying to take in everything at once.

'This is a thousand times worse than I imagined,' Five whispered. 'There's magic *literally* everywhere.'

Phoenix glanced at him, about to laugh, and did a double take. Five's face was pale and clammy, his hands clenched into fists. 'Are you all right?' she whispered.

Five gave a tight nod, then flinched as the nearest ice statue waved merrily at them. His hand touched the pommel of his sword convulsively and every line of him hummed with tension. Six moved to stand beside him and Five managed a grateful grin.

'Are those the other witches?' Phoenix asked Nara, nodding to the group of women across the water.

Nara smiled. 'They are.'

'Is there a boat?' Six asked, gazing uncertainly at the shining gulf of water between them and the island.

'No need for that,' Nara laughed. 'We can walk.' She stepped across the threshold and each ice statue raised an arm to the figure opposite it, forming a tunnel of sorts. When their fingertips touched, the water beneath them froze rapidly until a frozen bridge of ice spread from Nara's feet, between the statues and towards the island.

Five made a choking sound as Six tugged him forward after Nara, who was now making her way slowly across the bridge, greeting and being greeted by each of the statues she passed.

'Icemother Sanna, Icemother Linnet,' she said, inclining her head and smiling.

'Greetings, Sister Nara,' they murmured, before turning their attention to Phoenix, Seven, Five and Six.

'Hunters,' the giant statues whispered to one another. 'Just like before . . .'

'I don't know – not like before. They look rather young to me.'

'The icemothers defend the frost palace,' Nara explained over her shoulder. 'If anyone or anything tried to force entry, they'd receive quite a different sort of welcome.'

'Does that . . . er . . . happen often?' Five asked, grimacing at the statues' curious stares.

'Never,' Nara said. 'But it's reassuring to have such excellent defences nonetheless.'

'That's what we said about the lodge walls too . . .' Five said darkly, drawing a furious look from Six.

'This is incredible,' Seven whispered, moving closer to Phoenix.

Widge chirped, his eyes wide, but Phoenix could only nod, suddenly feeling overwhelmed. She was quietly grateful when Seven slipped an arm through hers.

The closer they got to the island, the clearer the faces of the waiting witches became. The first thing Phoenix noticed was how few of them there were, barely fifty, their number made even smaller by the enormity of Icegaard around them. For the first time, Phoenix truly understood how devastating the sickness had been all those years ago.

Scattered through the group she saw a few children. Everyone's eyes were wide with excitement and curiosity.

One of the women broke free of the crowd to welcome

them as they stepped off the bridge, her feathered cloak brushing the frozen ground behind her. A smile lit her face as she swept up to greet them.

'Welcome to Icegaard,' she said, her gaze warm.

She was very tall and fair, her russet hair plaited in a complicated braid. Fine lines around her eyes suggested laughter and her whole presence radiated calm.

'My name is Yelara, and I am the Headwitch,' she smiled.

Phoenix tensed as the woman placed both her hands on her shoulders and kissed her cheek. For an instant, she was enveloped in warmth before Yelara moved on, greeting Seven, Five and Six in turn.

It was a very different welcome to a Hunter's gruff thump. Six flushed bright red and Five surreptitiously rubbed the kiss from his cheek as Yelara embraced Nara.

'Welcome home,' Yelara murmured. 'It's good to see you safe. What an adventure you must have had. I can't wait to hear of it.' There was something like longing in her voice.

Nara nodded, her face bright as the Headwitch led them to the cluster of waiting witches where whispers gusted back and forth like a breeze. Phoenix fidgeted as their eyes swept over her.

'*Clearly*, no one's told them staring is rude,' Five murmured, shifting closer to Six and the others. His voice was tense and his gaze jumped nervously from face to face. 'Guess manners get rusty when you cut yourself off from civilisation.'

'Five!' Six looked slightly panicked in case anyone had heard him. 'Can we wait a bit longer before offending everyone here?'

'First impressions count,' Five whispered.

'Exactly!'

If Yelara heard, she gave no sign, turning instead to her witches and raising her hands for quiet. The murmur of voices hushed, the ice statues stilled, and Icegaard seemed to hold its breath. And then she spoke.

CHAPTER 15

The Headwitch's voice carried effortlessly.

'For the first time in over forty years, we welcome Hunters to Icegaard,' Yelara said. 'And within their ranks stands an elemental.' A ripple of excited whispers spread through the witches as the Headwitch gestured to Phoenix.

Phoenix squirmed, not enjoying the sensation of so many eyes on her at once. On her shoulder, Widge nudged her chin encouragingly.

'She comes to assist us in a time of great peril,' Yelara went on, her words growing in volume, 'and our gratitude should know no bounds.' She took a deep breath. 'I promised you all when I took the Headwitch cloak that witches would once again venture out into the world, and that we would welcome the world to Icegaard.'

She looked around slowly, meeting the eyes of many. 'These are not the circumstances that I imagined when I made that promise. I know we are all living in fear of the Shadowseam, that it is hard – very hard – to think of anything else. But I urge you to see our guests' arrival for what it is: momentous, a turning point in our history, and one full of hope for our future.'

In the Hunting Lodge, such a proclamation by the Elders would have been met with grunts of approval at most, but the witches' reactions were far less reserved. Joy lit up every face as the witches whooped their pleasure, some even flinging balls of light up into the air in bright crackling displays of delight.

Five yelped in shock and grabbed Six's arm.

Phoenix managed a sickly smile, a sudden wave of nausea rolling through her. This was a hundred times worse than she'd imagined. She was being introduced as some sort of saviour without even having seen the Shadowseam, this thing she was supposed to deliver them all from.

'No pressure then,' Five muttered, recovering his composure. He sounded sympathetic. 'You must be even more nervous than me right now.'

Phoenix managed a weak smile. 'I've felt better.' She shot a glance at Five. He still looked clammy, his eyes darting around ceaselessly. 'Are you all right?'

Five shrugged, looking awkward. 'I guess all this magic is putting me on edge.' He touched the pommel of his sword again without seeming to notice he was doing it. 'I'm sure I'll get used to it though. Eventually.'

Yelara turned to face the little group. 'Come,' she said, waving them closer. 'I want you to meet our Unfledged.'

Seven and Phoenix exchanged a baffled look as, from between the ranks of the witches, three younger faces appeared, working their way through the press of bodies to the front. The young witches stared at the Hunters unashamedly, and Phoenix stared back. Widge flicked his tail excitedly, his nose twitching as he examined them in turn.

Unlike the older witches, each of them wore a cloak of a rich blue wool rather than ice-eagle feathers.

'This is Libbet,' Yelara said, gesturing to the smallest girl, olive-skinned and tawny-haired, no more than eight years old. Libbet beamed, her excitement palpable in the way she was bouncing on the balls of her feet.

'Then we have Thea,' Yelara continued, smiling at the girl next to Libbet. Thea was a couple of years older than Libbet, her features so pale and delicate that it looked like she might break, her eyes a startling turquoise. The smile she gave Phoenix was dazzling.

'And this is Zenith,' Yelara finished, her eyes warm on the oldest girl.

Around fifteen years old, Zenith stood behind Thea and Libbet, protectively close. Her skin was dark brown, her hair braided and her expression intensely curious. Her gaze swept over Phoenix and her friends in a frank assessment. Phoenix suddenly wished she'd straightened her furs before meeting everyone; Widge began frantically cleaning his whiskers.

'Girls,' Yelara said to the young witches, 'meet Seven, Five, Phoenix and Six. I'd like you to show them round Icegaard, help them settle in.' She paused to look at Phoenix and her friends. 'That is, if you feel ready for a tour?'

The friends nodded and Yelara smiled, turning back to the young witches. 'Why don't you start with the feasting tree?'

Before Phoenix could say anything, Libbet, the youngest of the Unfledged, was pulling her forward through the ranks of witches and suddenly the new arrivals were surrounded by a sea of faces old and young, but all eager, each wanting to shake a hand or pat a shoulder.

'Did she say *feasting* tree?' Six asked, linking his arm through Phoenix's so they weren't separated by the crowd carrying them forward.

Phoenix frowned. 'I think so,' she said, squeezing his arm with relief. On her shoulder, Widge squealed hopefully at the mention of possible food. She rolled her eyes at him.

'You don't think the food here will be magic, do you?' Five asked, leaning closer, looking worried. 'I mean, *can* you eat magic? Is it safe?'

Before they could answer, the little group broke free of the witches, and the tree they had seen from the other side of the lake stood before them, unobstructed.

'It's huge!' Phoenix gasped.

At the same moment, Seven said, 'It's magnificent!'

The oldest girl, Zenith, grinned at them, seeming almost relieved. 'You're the first people I've ever seen see it for the first time.' She frowned for a moment. 'Did that make sense?'

Phoenix nodded silently, still overawed by the tree's size. The trunk's girth was so vast that even if every witch and Hunter present joined hands they'd still be unable to encircle it. Its bark was a rich chestnut brown, deeply ridged with age and giving off a comforting resinous scent. The leaves were unusual: small pleated ovals that rustled overhead in spite of there being no breeze.

Zenith led them to a wide wooden staircase spiralling up round the trunk into the branches above. Together, the group climbed past enormous boughs. Seven nudged Phoenix, nodding at tables and benches that seemed to be growing from the branches themselves. Her expression was as awestruck as Phoenix's. Beneath them, the lake slowly receded until it was just flashes of light-streaked water caught between glossy greenery. Zenith kept glancing at the friends, clearly fascinated by their reactions. Further back, witches peeled off the steps to sit round the tables, chatter and laughter following the group as they continued their ascent.

'Are you really a Hunter?' squeaked a little voice

next to Phoenix. She looked down to see Libbet staring up at her with huge brown eyes, still bouncing on the balls of her feet. 'Are you the elemental? Are those axes yours? Why do you have a handprint on your face?'

Phoenix swallowed a smile at the barrage of questions delivered without breath.

'I'm Phoenix,' she said, introducing herself. She turned and saw that Thea and Zenith were listening too. 'And yes, I'm a Hunter.'

'You seem so young,' Thea said. Her voice was surprisingly strong given how fragile she looked.

'We're the youngest in five generations!' Five exclaimed, brightening suddenly. 'But don't be fooled by our youth. We're *very* fearsome.'

Zenith gave a snort of amusement. She glanced back at them again, but didn't stop climbing.

Libbet was still staring at Phoenix expectantly, waiting for answers to the rest of her questions.

'This is from a firesprite,' Phoenix explained, pointing to the scar on her cheek – she remembered Sharpspark with a conflicted mix of affection and dread as Libbet's eyes widened – 'and, like Five said, we *are* Hunters, even though we're young. And yes, I'm the elemental.'

Elemental. The word tasted strange, sent a cold shiver through her. It felt odd to say it out loud after so many weeks of keeping it a secret.

'You're a fire elemental, aren't you?' Zenith said,

slowing down, her expression curious. 'Nara told us about you before she left.' She studied Phoenix. 'I know fire elementals are the most destructive, but . . . No offence, but it's hard to imagine that you'll be able to achieve what fifty witches couldn't. I hope I'm wrong obviously—' She shook herself and shot a reassuring smile at Phoenix, oblivious to the churning she'd just set off in the other girl's stomach. 'Anyway, Nara's going to teach you herself.'

'She's giving me lessons?' Phoenix asked. A flare of hope and fear leaped inside her when Zenith nodded.

Lessons. *Magic* lessons. She found, to her surprise, that part of her was excited by the idea. The fear of her power was strong, but it stemmed from the fire's unpredictability: the way it rose up in her at the slightest provocation, fighting to get out. How it seemed to be getting stronger. But, if she could control it, perhaps all that would change. Maybe it could even be useful. Either way, Phoenix was pleased that it would be Nara teaching her; the witch had seemed trustworthy and level-headed.

A dreamy look came into Zenith's eyes. 'Hopefully, this is just the beginning – the first step towards Icegaard being welcomed back into Ember again.'

Five shivered. 'Just what Ember needs. More unknown magic.'

Zenith blinked. 'Icegaard's magic would help the clans, like it always has.' She stared at their uncertain expressions. 'The clans . . . do remember everything we've done for them, don't they?'

'Everything you've done?' Five frowned, momentarily distracted from his wide-eyed fearfulness. 'Like what? No one's heard from a witch in decades.'

Phoenix saw shock sweep across the other girl's features. '*Like what?*' she echoed faintly. She drew herself up to her full height. 'Who was it who brokered the peace treaty between the ice giants and the mountain clan? Who managed to confine darkwater to the Clasp, preventing it from contaminating the other rivers?'

Phoenix and her friends exchanged an uneasy look.

Zenith stared at them, aghast. 'Are you serious?'

'I think we learned about the ice-giant treaty at the lodge,' Six said, scrunching his eyes up as he tried to remember. 'It happened a really long time ago though.'

'So what?' Zenith gasped. 'Without it, the mountain clan would've been pounded into rock dust! Are you really telling me no one remembers that we saved them?'

'I'm sure the mountain clan would,' Phoenix said quickly, her tone conciliatory. 'But it's true that the clans are focused on more recent developments. Er . . . within their lifetime.'

'Just because our contributions happened a few years—'

'Centuries,' Five whispered.

'—ago, doesn't make them any less meaningful!' Zenith exclaimed.

Phoenix bit her lip. This wasn't going how she'd hoped.

Five shrugged. 'That's wishful thinking. Icegaard's pretty much been forgotten.'

'Five!' Six exclaimed.

Zenith looked horrified. For a moment, Phoenix thought she was going to say something else, but instead she turned from them and swept up the curving steps, her blue cloak billowing behind her as she vanished from view.

'Wonderful,' Six groaned. 'We've made friends already.'

Five winced. 'I'm sorry, all right? I'm probably not . . . thinking as clearly as I usually do. This place . . .' He glanced around and shivered again.

'Is it true?' Libbet asked hesitantly. She'd stopped bouncing on the balls of her feet, looked smaller, much younger. 'Has Ember really forgotten us?'

'Well . . .' Five trailed off, grimacing as Six shot him another furious glare.

He was saved by Zenith's reappearance, a scroll of paper in her hand. She was scribbling on it frantically as she made her way back down to them.

'Right,' she said, businesslike. 'Thea, Libbet and I already have a whole tour planned: everything from the sluice rooms to the eyrie.'

'We've been talking about it since we found out Nara was going to ask you to come back with her,' Thea said.

Zenith nodded to the paper she'd been writing on. 'I've made a quick list of the most important bits of Icegaard's history too, in case, you know . . . anyone needs their memory jogged.' Her smile became forced as she glanced Five's way.

'Great!' Six said brightly, nudging Five until he nodded too.

The young witch seemed to relax. 'Great,' she echoed. 'Then follow me!'

CHAPTER 16

Dog had run all night and made good progress, the softer, greener scent of the grasslands already hinted at in the warmer air. Now, as the sky began to lighten, he paused and allowed himself to look back again. The lights of Ledge were long gone and probably, by now, so was Phoenix. If anything though, the ache in Dog's heart was heavier, the pain amplified by the distance from his friend.

He shook his head and continued on, forcing himself to focus on his mission. He thought of Victory, of her betrayal and the terrible things she'd done. He would need to be at his sharpest to track her successfully, to do it without her knowledge. But, no matter how hard he tried to concentrate, his thoughts kept drifting back to Phoenix. Would she be at Icegaard by now?

Somewhere beneath the earth, a small creature was snoring and up ahead was the scritch of unknown claws on rock. Dog sniffed, picked up a hint of foulness in the air and adjusted his course to circle past whatever was lurking there. Usually, he would have taken pride in hunting down whatever it was, but not today.

Alone. Alone. Alone.

The word yawned round him like a chasm, cold and deadening.

'Ridiculous,' he growled to himself. The sound of a voice, even just his own, was a sharp relief. 'You have worked alone for centuries. This is no different.'

Except that it was. He found himself reliving again his journey with the huntlings to rescue Seven; how irritating he'd found them all to start with; how their incessant squabbling had mellowed to something sweeter; how he'd started to enjoy carrying Phoenix on his back. When he'd watched over them at night, he had felt, for the first time in a very, very long time, that he was doing something important.

'Enough,' he snarled, breaking into his long, ground-eating lope again.

'Do you always talk to yourself?' The voice was painfully high-pitched and somewhere just above his head.

The sound Dog made was somewhere between a yelp and a yowl, his stony fur standing on end as he skidded to a halt, twisting to see who'd spoken.

A tiny, burning-bright figure hovered behind him, wings ablur, hands on hips and head tilted to one side.

'Sharpspark!' Dog exclaimed, too surprised to say more. The air was suddenly full of his scent: fire and glee and wildness.

'You're extremely easy to creep up on,' Sharpspark said, his flames a deep liquid gold. 'Of course, I am the very stealthiest of my kind.'

'What are you doing here?' Dog sputtered. 'And where have you been?'

Sharpspark shrugged and fluttered higher so Dog had to crane his neck to gaze up at him. 'Hoarfrost sent me away.'

Dog frowned. The last time he'd seen Sharpspark, the sprite had been helping the Hunting Lodge kitchens to burn down. 'You did destroy his home.'

'Only a little bit.' Sharpspark rolled his eyes. 'People are too attached to their *things*. You didn't mind.'

Dog squirmed. The guilt-riddled truth was that he hadn't minded at all. Usually when a battle was finished, he was required to return to the walls of the Hunting Lodge, their stone absorbing his body and his whole sense of self until the Hunters needed protecting once again. Sometimes the wait was a hundred years or more. The lodge's destruction had given him a freedom he'd never expected. Where once there'd been walls, now there were possibilities: new duties, new experiences, *friends*. So no, he was definitely not sorry his former home had fallen, nor for the part Sharpspark had played in it.

'You have not said where you went,' Dog said, changing the subject adroitly.

To his surprise, Sharpspark's fire dimmed. 'The firepits.'

'They . . . were not to your liking?' Dog asked, surprised by the sprite's reaction. The firepits were lava-filled crevasses deep inside the Scour: a place of raging flames, choking smoke and sulphurous gases. He couldn't think of anywhere more likely to please a firesprite.

'The pits were excellent. My task was not,' Sharpspark said. His wings slowed and his fire dimmed further. 'I bade farewell to Brightfire and Burnfoot.'

Dog winced. The two other firesprites had died fighting Morgren, during the final battle for the Hunting Lodge. 'I am sorry.'

'Sorrow is pointless,' Sharpspark said, his colour returning. He looked around. 'Where are the others? Where is the fiery girl?'

Dog sighed. 'Gone to Icegaard,' he said.

'Oh.' Sharpspark's fire dimmed again for a moment. 'You are sad because of it.'

'Yes,' Dog said quietly.

'Sorrow is pointless,' Sharpspark reminded him. 'You should burn something instead.' He rolled his eyes at Dog's blank look and fluttered down to settle on the end of the Guardian's nose. 'I think I will come with you,' he said, an uncomfortable warmth spreading from his tiny feet.

'Why?' Dog frowned. 'You do not even know where I am going.'

'*Why?*' Sharpspark laughed, orange sparks flying from his wings as he stretched lazily. 'You'll need my protection. Like I said, you're *very* easy to creep up on!'

An outraged snarl quivered on Dog's lips, but the firesprite didn't notice.

'Also,' he added, yawning, '*why not?*'

Dog paused, a strange feeling uncurling in him. It took a moment for him to identify it as relief. Relief so unexpected and so strong that he wasn't sure he could speak.

He wouldn't be alone after all.

He nodded once, briskly, still not trusting his voice, then picked up his pace again, the firesprite flying alongside him, heading south-west, towards the distant green silence of the Great Woods.

CHAPTER 17

The tour of Icegaard had barely begun and already Phoenix was fascinated. The more Zenith talked about the frost palace, the more animated she became. She marched them swiftly up the stairs, trailing facts behind her like a comet.

'The feasting tree was grown from a nut by Allania the First over nine hundred and fifty years ago and totally changed our existence up here.' She glanced back at them. 'Before that, the witches mainly survived on gifts from the villages we'd helped, like the Hunting Lodge does. Now we've moved beyond that and the tree feeds us.'

'What do you mean?' Six asked.

It was Thea who answered, her turquoise eyes bright as she spoke. 'You sit at a table and ask the tree for whatever you'd like to eat, a bud grows down to you—'

'Then you pick it and it's full of custard tart!' Libbet beamed.

'If you've asked for custard tart,' Thea said pointedly. 'Which you only do *after* dinner.'

Libbet nodded quickly, her face a picture of innocence.

'You'll see for yourself at lunch,' Zenith said, grinning at everyone's disbelief. 'We're lucky to have this tree; what it produces is always delicious. Before it was mature enough to bud, witches and their ice eagles were constantly flying back and forth between Icegaard and the clan lands, ferrying magic across the Fangs and bringing food back from the grateful . . .' Her voice faded as she rounded the stairs above them and disappeared from sight.

'*Really* lucky they have this tree then,' Five muttered. 'None of the clans will be volunteering to provide them with food any time soon.'

'Five!' Phoenix hissed. Widge gave him a disapproving look.

'Sorry, sorry,' he grumbled. He flinched as an orblight floated past, looking for a moment as though he might actually draw his sword. 'I'm on edge.'

'We can see that,' Phoenix muttered through gritted teeth.

Thea and Libbet trotted up the stairs ahead of them. 'You're going to love this!' Thea called back. 'We're about to leave the main cavern.'

A moment later, Phoenix understood what she meant. She'd already seen that the feasting tree was taller than the cavern they'd entered. As they climbed, the steps funnelled her through the roof and into a large, round ice tunnel, wide enough for several people to walk abreast. It spiralled upward round the tree, encased in ice, the bark of its trunk still just visible through the thick rime covering it. Phoenix felt she was somewhere else entirely, the lake, the fish, the statues all suddenly gone.

Their way was lit by the soft glow emanating from the ice itself, and the floating orblights that seemed to be everywhere, some drifting aimlessly, some – to Five's chagrin – following the group.

Zenith was waiting patiently, her gaze drinking in their amazed expressions with hungry delight. She gestured around them. 'These tunnels, and the rooms they lead to, were carved out over generations,' she explained. 'The crypts below the lake too. Creating these tunnels was always the priority though, so Fledged and Unfledged witches could reach the eyrie without going outside.'

She shrugged at their confused expressions. 'Partly because of the cold, partly because of fathomghasts. Most winters, they gather at the base of the cliffs here. Come on – it's not much further to the witcheries.'

Fathomghasts. Phoenix shuddered as Zenith led them on and Widge began to nibble her hair nervously.

'Fledged? Unfledged? What do those actually mean?' Six asked Thea.

She stared at him in amazement, her turquoise eyes huge. 'You really don't know?' She glanced round at the others for confirmation, and they all shook their heads.

'Fledging is how we become proper witches,' Libbet

said cheerfully, bouncing on the balls of her feet again. The hundreds of steps weren't bothering her at all.

'It's a spell,' Thea clarified, seeing Phoenix's confusion. 'A very difficult one. If you can perform it, you've proven yourself a fully competent witch and can wear a cloak of ice-eagle feathers.'

'It can take years to make one of those cloaks,' Libbet said, stroking her blue cape dreamily.

'We collect the ice-eagles' feathers only when they moult,' Thea said. 'Which doesn't happen that often.'

'I see,' said Phoenix slowly, not seeing at all. 'And this Fledging spell . . . does what exactly?'

'Makes an ice eagle, of course!' Libbet said, laughing.

Phoenix stopped walking, stared at the girl. '*Makes* an ice eagle?' she said, disbelief threaded through every syllable. She thought of the enormous bird she'd flown on to get to Icegaard, of her size, beauty and obvious intelligence. 'Makes it from what? How?'

'From ice.' Thea shrugged. 'And magic.' She smiled at Phoenix's startled expression. 'There's a reason the spell is so difficult.'

A sudden yowl from Five made them all jump. 'What is *that*?' he cried, grabbing Phoenix's arm and pointing towards the wall of ice. At first, Phoenix could only see a shadow, but, as she moved closer, it resolved into something that made her flinch too.

A face, orange-eyed and lifeless, leered out at her.

CHAPTER 18

'What in Ember . . .?' Phoenix leaped back, the frozen face staring past her with dead eyes. Widge dived into her furs.

Zenith hurried back down to them, drawn by the commotion. Her gaze raked the group and landed on the dark shape inside the wall. 'But you're Hunters!' she said, confused. 'Surely you aren't scared of our glimmers?'

'*Scared?*' Two bright spots of colour appeared on Five's cheeks, but Zenith didn't seem to notice.

Phoenix stepped forward again, axes now in her hands as she peered at the face in the ice. In a moment of inspiration, she reached into her pocket and pulled out her moonstone, wondering if it would let her see more clearly.

'Ooh, is that a runestone?' Zenith asked eagerly as it flared to brightness in Phoenix's hand.

'A – what?'

'A runestone,' Zenith said again, stepping closer, eyes fixed on it. 'The cave clan mines them, don't they? Nara said some of them can even break through illusions.'

'I think you might have misheard her,' Six said, stifling a smile. 'They're called moonstones, not runestones.'

'Oh.' Zenith's expression slipped into a frown. 'Are you sure?'

'Very sure,' Six said.

'Moonstone,' Zenith said ruminatively as though tasting the word. She hadn't taken her eyes off the stone in Phoenix's hand. 'I like that. And I suppose that makes more sense. Its light *is* like moonlight.'

Phoenix nodded, her attention still caught by the creature trapped in the ice. In the silvered light, it was terrifyingly clear. Even in death, its eyes were vivid orange, its deadly triangular teeth bared. Widge poked his head up from her collar to peek at the creature, and gave a low croon of horror. Zenith was right, Phoenix saw immediately: it was a glimmer. What was it doing there though?

'Why are you using axes?' Zenith asked, breaking into her thoughts.

Phoenix reshouldered them. The creature was thoroughly encased in ice, long dead and clearly no threat. 'What do you mean?' she asked, turning to Zenith.

'If you're an elemental, then why are you using ordinary weapons instead of your fire?' Zenith frowned. She eyed Phoenix curiously, her gaze flicking from the moonstone to the axes and back again. A horrified realisation flashed over her features. 'You can't summon safely, can you?' she said. 'That's the most basic— *Please* tell me I'm wrong?'

'I—'

'We live in a palace made of *ice*,' Zenith said a little wildly.

'So . . . er . . . *why* is there a monster in the wall?' Six asked.

Phoenix sighed in relief as the others' attention slid away, but Zenith's eyes remained on her, fearful.

'We don't know,' Thea admitted. 'They've always been there. We think they must've been on the cliff when the palace was created and got swept up in all the water.'

'They?' Seven asked, eyeing the glimmer with concern. 'There are m-more?'

'They're all over the place,' Zenith said. 'They aren't anything to worry about though.' Her gaze flicked back to Phoenix. *Unlike you.* 'So, Nara didn't tell you when you'd be starting your lessons?'

Phoenix frowned. 'No.'

'Hopefully, soon,' Libbet said solemnly. 'I'd want as many classes as possible before even looking at the Shadowseam.'

'You've seen it then?' Phoenix asked, her stomach lurching. 'What's it like?'

Thea shook her head. 'Only Fledged witches work with it.' She drew her blue cloak more tightly round herself.

'You're going to destroy it, aren't you?' Libbet spoke cheerfully and with perfect confidence.

'I . . .'

'Stop it, Libbet,' Thea said, frowning. 'She hasn't even seen it yet.'

Phoenix shot Thea a grateful look. Widge chirped softly, clambering out of her furs to return to her shoulder.

Libbet watched him, wide-eyed, then gave a gasp of delight as he leaped lightly from Phoenix's shoulder on to her head, sniffing her tangled tawny hair.

Phoenix grinned. 'He likes you – he doesn't do that for everyone.'

'Come on,' Zenith said, gesturing for them to follow again. 'Lots more to see.'

Libbet beamed when it became clear Widge had no intention of leaving his new spot. She walked slowly up the curving stairs, careful not to jiggle the squirrel balancing proudly on top of her head.

'This is the witchery level,' Zenith called back to them, rounding a corner.

Phoenix saw there was an arch leading away from the tree's trunk into another wide, bright passage. A multitude of smaller archways fed off the corridor into interconnected rooms. Phoenix peered into each of them hungrily as they walked, her excitement quickly turning to confusion. Most of the rooms were totally empty. In a few of them, the ice appeared to have stopped glowing. Some of the doorways were pitch-black, as cold as the ice they were made of. Chill air swirled round Phoenix's ankles as she passed.

Zenith was waiting for them. 'These are the old witcheries,' she explained, seeing the group staring into the dark spaces. 'Our workrooms. After a witch Fledges, she's given her own witchery to carry out whatever studies she likes.' She hesitated. 'All these rooms were in use once. Before the seam-sickness came. Now there aren't enough of us to occupy them.'

Phoenix saw the young witch's hands curl into fists by her side. 'It's the Shadowseam that's draining the magic from them though; that's why some of them have gone dark. Apart from the crypts, there were no lightless places in Icegaard before that goblin came. Now they're appearing everywhere, spreading.'

Goosebumps rose along Phoenix's arms. Beside her, Seven shivered. The blackness at the back of the witchery seemed to reach for them.

'Come on, Phoenix, Seven. There are much nicer things to see. We're about to enter the ingredients store,' Zenith called back, jolting Phoenix out of her reverie.

The rest of the group had followed Zenith further down the passage. She and Seven hurried to catch up.

'Don't touch anything unless you fancy growing an extra arm or turning into a snarrow,' Zenith grinned as they ducked under an arch and into a space dazzlingly lit by a multitude of floating orblights.

'An extra arm might be useful,' Six whispered. Phoenix forced herself to smile.

'By the f-frost,' Seven whispered. 'This is amazing.'

Once Phoenix's eyes adjusted, she had to agree. The room was long and wide. Straight down its centre sat a workbench large enough for half the lodge to sit comfortably round. Higgledy-piggledy shelves crammed every inch of the walls with long ladders on runners positioned round the room to allow access to the higher sections. Phoenix threw back her head and felt her jaw slacken: the shelves didn't stop at the top of the walls, but arched across the ceiling, directly over her head and down the other wall. Desertglass bottles of every hue winked at her, showing no inclination to obey gravity and fall.

She looked down quickly, her head swimming.

The wonder she felt was reflected in the others' faces as they turned on the spot, taking it all in. Zenith watched them eagerly, pleased with their reactions.

'These are the ingredients,' she explained, gesturing at the bottles. Her face was bright and she looked more relaxed than Phoenix had seen her so far. 'Some of them can be gathered here in the Frozen Wastes, but many of them can't. They haven't been replaced for forty years. Maybe now that—'

'What's that noise?' Five interrupted. The air in the room hummed softly and his shoulders had hunched up round his ears. He looked incredibly worried. 'And ingredients for what?' he added, reading a couple of the labels and wrinkling his nose.

'They're magical ingredients, of course,' Zenith said. 'For potions.'

Curious, Phoenix moved closer to the shelves, twisting her head to read some of the labels herself.

A clear bottle containing a pinch of silver fur was marked PELT OF VEILED FOX. The bottle next to it was larger and oily black, the stopper an elaborate twist of wickedly jagged glass. DARKWATER FROM THE RIVER CLASP read the label.

Phoenix thought immediately of Dog, her stomach lurching. Where was he now? Was he safe? She hoped with every fibre of her being that he would find a way to avoid that dangerous water; even contained in a bottle, something about it made her skin prickle warningly.

She forced her gaze on to the next jars:

FANG OF YGREX

SAP OF BABWINKLE

MARSHMADDER MIASMA

MILK OF DEATH'S-HEART FROG

HAIR OF GRIM

YMBRE

On and on the bottles stretched, each ingredient more intriguing than the last. Phoenix followed the shelves until she was distracted by Widge arriving abruptly back on her shoulder with a warning squeal.

Phoenix turned to see Zenith talking to a pale-faced Five.

'You're so lucky,' the witch was saying, 'to be able to go wherever you like, see whatever you want.'

'Lucky?' Five's voice held a sharp edge. 'Do you even know why most of the huntlings end up at the lodge? It's not by choice, you know.'

'I didn't mean . . .' Zenith trailed off. 'I just meant you're lucky to be here.' She winced as the words left her mouth. 'No, that came out—'

'Oh yes,' Five snorted, cutting her off, 'I'm delighted to be here, helping you witches with Ember-knows-what after decades of silence. Such an *honour*.'

'Helping us?' Zenith went from awkward to angry in an instant. 'It's not *you* helping us – it's her!' Zenith gestured at Phoenix. 'If she doesn't completely destroy our home first, that is.'

Phoenix winced. Widge growled. 'I—'

'As if we'd need help from *you*!' Zenith continued. 'Some jumped-up little Hunter who's afraid of magic. You're pathetic!'

'Little? Pathetic?' Five made a sound like a pan boiling over. 'What would you know about anything? What's pathetic is you singing the witches' praises for things they did *centuries* ago. You've never left the Frozen Wastes. You have no idea what life in Ember is like, but you're *obviously* clinging on to a fantasy where the witches are heroes to the clans. Let me be *very* clear: they're not. No one cares about you or this place.'

Zenith swayed as though Five had slapped her, but he didn't stop speaking. 'Most of Ember thinks the witches are dead and gone. Those that don't won't have anything good to say about magic though. You're deluded if you imagine otherwise. Why do you suppose this place makes me so nervous? The only magic out there now belongs to *monsters*.'

Phoenix reeled. On the other side of the room, she saw Seven flinch too. Surely he hadn't meant that? Two of his closest friends had magical powers; how could he possibly equate magic with monstrousness? She caught Seven's eye, saw she looked as hurt as Phoenix felt.

'Zenith, don't—'

Thea's cry came too late. With an arm movement like a shove and a word that didn't want to be heard, Zenith sent a vortex of air spinning across the room towards Five. He dodged the first one, but her second one caught him full in the chest. With a furious yell, he was flung up and pinned against the shelves several feet above their heads. Brightly coloured bottles tumbled to the ground, smashing beneath him to scatter their contents across the floor. A curl of snake-like vine reared up to snap at his ankles before crumbling into dust, two columns of smoke entwined to catch fire and lightning crackled in a pillow-sized thundercloud.

'What in Ember is going on?' Headwitch Yelara appeared in the doorway, horrified as she took in Five suspended against the shelves, the broken bottles beneath him. Her eyes found Zenith's and her expression became dangerous. 'I hope you have a *very* good explanation, Zenith.'

CHAPTER 19

'He insulted Icegaard,' Zenith said, trembling with fury. 'He belittled our history, the witches' contributions to Ember.'

The air around her was still quivering with magic, tiny tornadoes lifting the braids from her shoulders, fluttering the edges of her cloak. No part of her looked repentant and her eyes flashed defiantly at the Headwitch.

Five brushed the last of the broken glass from his furs and eyed a singed patch on them. He was worryingly quiet, a muscle flickering in his neck. Six looked like he wanted to launch himself at the young witch. Seven was staring at her with mingled curiosity and dislike.

Phoenix drew a calming breath, unable to tear her eyes from the witchling in front of her. The air in the room felt electric, tension sparking between them all, and in the centre of it stood Yelara, visibly trying not to lose her temper with Zenith.

'How could you?' Yelara said, her voice shaking. 'How could you be so . . .' She shook her head, shook the words away. 'Olva has just caught a reel of stinkworms. She's in the sluice rooms. You will take her place and spend the rest of the day preparing them. I'll find you later.'

Zenith's lip curled in disgust, but something in the Headwitch's face must have convinced her that arguing was futile. She shot Five a venomous look, then marched out of the room, her head held high. Seven and Six watched her go with narrowed eyes, matching expressions of satisfaction on their faces.

Phoenix was close enough to hear the air whistle through Yelara's nostrils as she watched the young witch leave.

'Thea, Libbet,' the Headwitch said, turning to the girls, 'I think your part in the tour is finished. I will take over from here.' She softened slightly at the disappointment on their faces. 'You'll have plenty of time with our guests later.' Without waiting for a response, she turned to Phoenix and her friends. 'Is everyone all right? I'm so sorry.'

'We're fine,' Five muttered, a dull flush spreading over his cheeks.

Phoenix realised with discomfort that Yelara was watching her more than anyone else.

'We're not going to leave, if that's what you're worried about,' Phoenix said, her voice sharper than she'd intended. She wasn't used to Elders apologising to her and she wasn't sure she liked it. She especially didn't appreciate that it was only happening because Yelara needed something so desperately from her.

She pushed away her discomfort and took a deep breath, glad her voice came out businesslike. 'But I would like to see the Shadowseam now.' She glanced at her friends and they nodded encouragingly.

'Of course,' Yelara said quickly.

Phoenix shrugged. 'No use putting it off.'

She hoped she sounded calm, but anticipation was building in her unpleasantly. She wanted to see what she was there to face. There was no way it could be worse than what she was imagining.

A short while later, Yelara was leading the four friends along passage after passage. All of them were carved into the ice and glowing softly, each confusingly similar to the last. Seven walked beside Phoenix, her expression thoughtful. Behind them, Six was chastising Five for his part in what had just happened with Zenith.

'You provoked her!' Phoenix heard him hiss.

'Do you think Five meant what he said, about thinking magic is monstrous?' Seven asked suddenly.

Phoenix blinked, her stomach dropping. 'I . . . hope not.'

'Same,' Seven murmured, unsettled. 'I mean . . . t-two of his best friends have magic. He can't think *we're* monstrous? Can he?'

Seven's thoughts chimed uncomfortably with Phoenix's own, but she shook them away. 'No, of course not,' she said with more confidence than she felt. 'He's just rattled by Icegaard.'

'Right,' Seven said. She looked unconvinced. 'It was extreme though, even f-for him.'

Phoenix bit her lip. There was nothing she could say in Five's defence – Seven was right.

Yelara spoke over her shoulder, dragging them back to the moment. 'The Shadowseam is trapped where it first appeared, in quite a remote part of the frost palace. We're hoping that will buy us some more time . . .' The Headwitch trailed off, her hands clenching involuntarily.

Six and Five hurried to catch them up, the shock of what had happened with Zenith still simmering between them.

'The ice is dimming,' Seven said, stepping closer to Phoenix. 'Just like in the witcheries.'

'Makes sense,' Six murmured. 'We're getting closer to the Shadowseam.'

Five nodded his agreement. It was definitely getting darker in the corridor, the luminous glow from within the ice fading as they walked. Flaming torches appeared in makeshift brackets on the wall and a thin layer of water beneath their feet cast rippling reflections through the hall. The effect was eerie: it was suddenly as though they were somewhere else entirely.

'It's more serious than it appears,' Yelara said. 'As the seam drains away Icegaard's magic, the ice loses its light first, then it begins to weaken.'

'Weaken?' Five asked, staring around with fresh concern.

Yelara hesitated. 'Touch it,' she said a moment later, nodding at Phoenix. 'It will help you understand, I think.'

With her friends watching, Phoenix stepped forward, stretching out her fingertips to the wall. She flinched immediately, surprised. It didn't feel like ice at all, not even completely solid. With a frown, she tried again, pressing slightly harder, and gasped as her hand suddenly sank *through* the wall, a thin membrane seeming to burst beneath her fingers so her hand was plunged into freezing water up to the wrist.

'What the . . .?' She leaped back, half expecting the liquid wall to fall on her. It held its shape, but rippled strangely in the flickering torchlight, its watery nature undeniable.

'We're close to the Shadowseam here and too much of the magic has already been drained away,' Yelara said by way of explanation. She glanced at the others, her face deadly serious. 'From here, try to walk softly. The closer to the seam we get, the more fragile the magic – and the ice – becomes.'

Phoenix didn't move, still staring at the shimmering water. Suddenly she understood what the film of water under her boots was, saw what it meant: Icegaard's destruction had already begun.

She looked up, saw Yelara watching, torchlight dancing on her grief-stricken face.

'What will happen if I can't stop it?' she asked, her voice unsteady.

Yelara took a shaky breath. 'As the magic weakens, Icegaard will return to its original form: water. When it fails completely, the wave will sweep across the Wastes into Ember, as it would have done eons ago if magic hadn't stopped it.'

She looked each of them in the eye, saving Phoenix for last. 'You saw the size of the frost palace when you arrived. "Wave" doesn't really do it justice: it's more of a mountain. The devastation it would wreak is unimaginable. And of course, once we can no longer reach the Shadowseam to renew the containment spell, that will break free too, to follow the wave into Ember. If the illness affects the clans the way it did us witches . . .' She broke off, unable to continue.

Hoarfrost's words came back to Phoenix: *The threat to Ember is twofold.* How horribly right he'd been.

'All that . . . but only if the Shadowseam isn't destroyed,' Phoenix whispered, a sick squirming sensation in her stomach.

Yelara nodded. Widge shuddered beneath Phoenix's furs and Seven squeezed her hand. It wasn't enough to halt the avalanche of fear that threatened to sweep her away though. Suddenly this all felt far too real, the pressure enormous, smothering. No wonder the witches had all stared at her so fiercely, so hungrily, when she'd arrived earlier.

When the group began to walk again, it was in deep silence, everyone lost in their own thoughts.

'Here we are,' Yelara announced all too soon.

Phoenix's skin prickled all over and goosebumps dotted her arms. It felt like something very dark was very close.

Yelara had led them to an elaborately carved archway, its patterns sinking and resurfacing as it battled to hold its shape. 'The Shadowseam is in here,' she said softly, waving them forward.

A cold wind swept out from the room beyond, lifting Phoenix's hair, sending more goosebumps racing down her collar. It ruffled the water beneath her feet into dark, murmuring wavelets that raced out from the archway, from what lay beyond. An instant later, a terrible creeping, scratching sensation erupted all over her, and, from her bearskin, Widge gave a high, sharp alarm call. The feeling was enough to freeze Phoenix to the spot. Dark creatures made her flesh creep – a useful warning if one was nearby – but this was something else entirely. The last time she'd felt such intense horror, such pure dread, had been when the Croke was standing right in front of her. Her heart quailed and she remained frozen to the spot as the others moved forward.

'By the frost . . .' Six whispered, his voice strangled as he stepped through the arch.

Phoenix took a shuddering breath, then forced herself to follow.

CHAPTER 20

'If you went faster, we'd get there sooner!'

Dog gritted his teeth. 'This would be much easier if you stopped saying that. I am going as fast as I can.'

High above him, Sharpspark flared white with annoyance before swooping down to hover in front of Dog. 'You are a terrible travel companion,' he hissed, his features contorting in rage. 'Never again will I accompany one who can't fly!'

'You knew I would be walking when you joined me,' Dog growled, trying not to let his temper get the better of him. He'd learned the hard way that it took surprisingly few cross words for Sharpspark to fly into a fireball-slinging fury. Instead, he focused on the line of green growing ever thicker on the horizon: the Great Woods. 'We will be there soon.'

'Not until dusk,' Sharpspark complained, flopping between Dog's ears, his fire dimming again.

'That is good,' Dog reasoned. 'We need to stay hidden.'

Sharpspark made a noncommittal sound.

'Sharpspark,' Dog said warningly. 'You know we must remain out of sight.'

'Skulking is not in a firesprite's nature,' the sprite replied airily. 'I expect it comes easily to you, but for me it is very hard. Eyes are naturally drawn to me.' He paused, and then said very quietly, very longingly, 'And there's so much good burning in the woods.'

'I heard that,' Dog snapped. 'You are sitting next to my ears. You will not set fire to a single tree!'

Sharpspark thought for a moment. 'I'll decide later.'

'The forest folk will defend their home-trees with everything they have,' Dog growled, worry gnawing at him suddenly. 'Many of your kind have met their end in the Great Woods.'

He wished he could see the sprite, who'd fallen silent. 'Sharpspark?' he prompted. 'I do not want anything to happen to you. We will not be able to travel together through the woods. I cannot help you if you are in trouble.'

'I know,' Sharpspark sighed. 'No wings and no fire; you're no help at all.' He paused, then patted Dog's head. 'You try hard though.'

Dog swallowed a growl. The sprite's ego was as enormous as it was tiresome.

As the trees grew closer and the sun dipped, Sharpspark listed the innumerable ways he felt he was vital to Dog's journey. By the time they reached the banks of the River Embrace, Dog's dignity was singed and his temper frayed.

Beyond the wide expanse of water, the Great Woods loomed. A barrage of smells, familiar from long ago, washed over him. First among them was the rich scent of ymbre, the home-trees' deep gold sap that flowed through the trunk and walls of the forest-clan homes, keeping them warm even in the depths of winter.

'Quiet,' he whispered to Sharpspark.

The grass on the riverbank was long enough to hide in, but the forest clan were vigilant and protected their borders vigorously. To his relief, the firesprite dimmed his fire and fell silent.

Across the water, high up in the branches of the home-trees, Dog could hear the hum of voices, see a couple of the strange abodes. The forest clan did not build their own houses: they asked their family's tree to grow them one. As a result, huge swellings like beehives protruded from the enormous trunks. Windows and doorways glowed with warm orange light while networks of rope bridges and ladders connected them all.

Dog knew that there was only one way he could pass through these woods unseen: underwater. He eyed the burbling river with concern. He would have to travel along the Embrace's riverbed, find where the smaller river, the Clasp, joined it, then follow that waterway through the Great Woods.

The thought of the Clasp filled him with a shifting unease. Darkwater was found there, said to drive people mad, to steal memories, and sometimes to put others in their place.

Once through the woods, Dog hoped tracking Victory would be simple in comparison.

'What about one tree?' Sharpspark asked hopefully, pulling Dog out of his reverie. 'Just a small one. Look, there's a tiny one over there. They wouldn't miss that.'

Dog snorted. 'They certainly would. Do you not know anything of the forest clan?'

Sharpspark shrugged, which Dog took as a no.

'They bury their Elders with a home-tree nut in their mouths,' he explained. 'That "small" tree over there is a grave. The sapling may already have the memories of an Elder flowing in its ymbre. You cannot desecrate it.'

Sharpspark wrinkled his nose. 'Disappointing *and* disgusting.'

Dog sighed and stepped towards the river, his foreboding growing. 'I will see you on the other side,' he said, glancing back at the hovering sprite. 'Try to stay out of trouble.'

Sharpspark made a rude noise, whirling up and away. Dog watched him go ruefully. He would miss him.

With a sigh, he walked into the river and allowed the water to close silently over his head.

CHAPTER 21

The room containing the Shadowseam was enormous and perfectly round. The curved walls and domed ceiling were covered with flaming torches, their light reflected in streaks through the rippling film of black water on the ground.

Phoenix barely saw any of it though. For her, there was only the Shadowseam.

Before her raged something that seemed like a hole in the fabric of the world, seething with darkness and fury, frantically trying to escape its prison, to devour everything around it. She had to tilt her head back to take in the full monstrous scale of it. It spread across her vision, blocking out everything else, a great clot of living night. She felt its hunger, saw a tentacle reach for her and be repelled, then reach again. The fire inside her leaped to the surface as though summoned, and a hot liquid terror surged through Phoenix as she fought to push it down. Breathing suddenly seemed very difficult.

She felt rather than saw Yelara come to stand beside her, place a warm hand on Phoenix's arm.

'You see the layer of movement around it?' Yelara asked, pointing to the very edge of the seam's darkness.

Phoenix shook herself, feeling like she was surfacing from underwater, and looked where the Headwitch pointed. There was indeed a layer of swirling motion round the seam, a whirling, vivid vortex of air that sent a chill breeze coiling down her neck. She understood immediately that this was the only thing containing it. It seemed far too thin, too insubstantial to be effective.

'I see it,' she said unsteadily.

'That's the oculus,' Yelara said. 'One of our most powerful spells. It creates a cage of sorts, to trap magical substances.' She shook her head. 'It's only partly working though. The Shadowseam shouldn't be able to exert any influence whatsoever from inside one of these. It should be harmless, like we hoped it was before Morgren came here.' Phoenix stiffened at the name. 'Instead, its power is spreading through the frost palace, draining magic even as far away as the witcheries.'

She glanced at Phoenix. 'You saw them, I assume? The dark rooms before the ingredients store? They're still solid for now, but we expect within a couple of weeks that they'll become more like the passages that brought us here: unstable.'

Phoenix nodded weakly, barely able to take in anything except the enormity of her task. The enormity and the impossibility. The Shadowseam leered at her, its power undeniable, filling her vision with darkness.

Behind her, Seven, Five and Six all stood in a line, their heads thrown back, their jaws slack.

'What in Ember is it?' Six murmured.

Yelara shook her head slowly. 'The truth is that we still don't really know.' She gestured around them. 'This space was given to a witch called Jira to allow her to study goblin magic—'

'Why?' Five said, his horror obvious. 'That sounds like a terrible idea!'

Yelara's smile was the saddest Phoenix had ever seen. 'So easy to say that now,' she said. 'Her reason was simple: portals. You've already seen that our portal spell requires two doorways to be in place: one where the witch currently is and one where she wishes to go. The goblin mages of old required only one portal, a single doorway to go wherever they desired. It was a huge benefit to them in battle, but we wanted it for –' Yelara choked out a ragged laugh – 'for convenience.'

'Oh.' Seven's voice was tiny, her eyes fixed on the Headwitch rather than the Shadowseam.

Yelara's gaze was far away now, fixed somewhere in the past. 'Jira studied the goblin spells for years. She was sure she'd learned enough to attempt one of their portals.' The Headwitch jerked her head at the Shadowseam.

'Instead of a doorway to the floating market, she got this.'

'Must've been a shock,' Five muttered.

'I imagine so,' Yelara said tightly, 'though we'll never know for sure. Jira was already dying when she was found. She'd clearly battled the seam, had managed to trap it in an oculus. But the illness that arrived with it – seam-sickness – had almost finished her. From her, it tore through the whole frost palace.' Yelara sighed. 'When Jira died, we lost our expert on goblin magic. She'd kept most of the original texts and her notes on them in here, but those were lost too, destroyed in her battle to contain the seam. We've tried everything we know to get rid of it, but . . .' She trailed off.

There was a long silence. Phoenix found her gaze pulled magnetically back to the Shadowseam, her flesh crawling. 'But it *was* contained,' she said softly, remembering what Nara had said at Ledge. 'Until . . .'

'Until M-Morgren came,' Seven finished.

'Yes.' Yelara's shoulders slumped. 'I wish we knew what he did, but, like I said, our expert on goblin magic was Jira. All her work was lost. There just wasn't enough left for us to teach ourselves too.'

The Shadowseam massed against the oculus before them, strands of darkness reaching out, only to be knocked back by the whirling magic containing it.

Phoenix's heart stuttered.

'Yelara,' she said, turning to the Headwitch, deciding it was better to be honest from the start, 'I don't think I can—'

'I don't expect you to do anything now,' Yelara said quickly. 'In fact, I wouldn't want you to, even if you were willing. Nara has already told me that your power is very new to you, that you haven't used it in months.' She paused and passed a hand over her face. 'I realise how dangerous what we're asking of you is. And I would never want you to attempt it unless you thought you could succeed.'

Phoenix pushed down a wild urge to laugh. She would never – *never* – be able to destroy this thing. She was a Hunter, used to weighing her strengths against an opponent. She already knew this was a battle she couldn't win. It was like asking her to fight an ice giant alone with one arm tied behind her back and only snowballs for weapons.

'Yelara,' she tried again, shaking her head, 'I—'

'Let Nara help you,' the Headwitch said hastily, the pleading note in her voice unmistakable. 'Please. She's always had an interest in elemental magic. She's the closest thing to an expert in all of Ember. If anyone can help you learn to control your fire, it's her. And, if anything can destroy the Shadowseam, it's you. You're our only hope.'

Phoenix took a deep breath through her nose, trying

to calm the nausea she was feeling. What she wanted to do was turn round and walk away. She wanted to demand to be returned to Ledge, where fighting monsters was simple and her axes were all she needed. But she was a Hunter. And the witches were asking for her help.

She forced herself to take one last, long look at the Shadowseam before turning her back on it. She'd seen more than enough.

Around her, the torches burned on, oblivious to the horror they were illuminating.

'I'll try,' Phoenix said quietly to Yelara, dread almost choking her. 'That's all I can do.'

CHAPTER 22

The Embrace was a murky brown and the current stronger than Dog had expected. He had to dig his paws deep into the soft mud on the bottom before he took a step to stop himself being rolled along like a pebble. Long skeins of tangled riverweed soon streamed off his legs and silt clogged his nose. Fish goggled at him in amazement: a curious crowd of them circled, fins flashing in the dim light, before vanishing again. A ripplewrack snarled at him from its scraped-out hole in the bank, sharp teeth glinting, long, strangling fingers curled into fists.

One foot in front of the other, Dog forced his way through the water, straining for a hint of where the Clasp joined the Embrace. Finally, just as he began to feel an awful certainty that he'd passed the conflux, a flume of colder water swept past him, unmistakably ymbre-scented.

With a sigh that was part relief, part dread, Dog fought the current to get to the other side of the river, tracking back along the colder water until, with an abruptness that was startling, he realised he must now be in the smaller river. The light was dimmer and greener, the current gentle. It was quieter too. Where the Embrace had raced and burbled, the Clasp crept along, gathering the whispered secrets of the home-trees.

Dog longed to climb out of the water and look around him. It had been centuries since he'd set foot in the Great Woods. He knew better than to try though; he must not be seen and this would be the very worst place to surface. There were bound to be more guards so close to the river border, and the Hunting Lodge's Guardian suddenly appearing unannounced would raise some very awkward questions.

Instead, he made his way to the deepest part of the channel and began to walk, surprised and grateful that the softer current allowed him to move with relative ease.

On and on he went. He walked until he lost all track of time, until he felt dizzy and confused and so very, very tired. He sank into a memory without even noticing.

The wall spat him out and his senses returned in a crashing, whirling rush. Dog blinked and shook his head, ready for anything, his teeth already bared in a snarl. But, as his vision returned, he saw there was no need for immediate action; a woman stood before him – probably an Elder – her iron-streaked hair pulled back severely from her face. A gleaming scimitar hung at her waist and her hand was stained with the blood of whichever creature she'd used to summon him.

'Guardian,' she said, her eyes running over him, appraising. 'My name is Elder Grit-in-the-Eye. Welcome back.'

It was a moment before the overwhelming feeling of his senses returning had subsided enough to speak, but then he lowered his head and replied, 'Greetings, Elder Grit-in-the-Eye.'

She nodded, satisfied, and beckoned him to follow her, a torrent of words falling from her lips as he gazed round the training ground, curious. Everything looked exactly the same, even down to the position of the woodpile. A sudden wild hope flared in him: perhaps he hadn't been gone long.

'Is Fox still here?' he asked.

'What?' Elder Grit-in-the-Eye frowned at the interruption, then her expression cleared. 'Ah, Fox. Of course, you knew him, didn't you?'

She said 'knew', not 'know'. Dog's heart sank as he nodded.

'A fine Hunter,' she said brusquely. 'Lost a hand to a spineghast, but insisted on still taking part in hunts.' She sniffed. 'Died young, of course.'

He took a moment to crush the grief rising in him. Fox had thrown snowballs at him, taught him to play hide-and-seek even though Dog was terrible at it. He'd enjoyed Fox's company immeasurably. Now he was gone. It was a moment before Dog could speak again.

'Of course,' he said. Then, with a spark of dangerous hope, 'What of Flick? And Ranger?'

Surprise and irritation chased themselves across the Elder's face. 'Both dead,' she snapped. 'You've been gone sixty years, Guardian. You can't possibly think there'd still be anyone here that you know?'

Dog dragged himself free of the memory and snarled, horrified to find he'd stopped walking, had stood statue-still for who knew how long. Around him the water was black and weighty.

Dread filled him; this was darkwater. And he was definitely not immune to it.

CHAPTER 23

Phoenix sat with her friends at one of the tables in the feasting tree, Widge nervously nibbling a hank of her hair. Beneath them, the lake gleamed bright, the fish trailing complicated multicoloured patterns through the water. The enormous statues – the icemothers – had left their plinths and were milling about in groups on the lake, the water freezing where their feet touched it, the murmur of their voices just audible.

Whenever Phoenix closed her eyes, the Shadowseam raged behind her eyelids. One thought dominated: if Ember's survival depended on her destroying that thing, then it was already doomed. She shook the conviction away, but it kept sliding back to her.

'You haven't said much,' Six said gently, his worried eyes on her. 'You know we'll help you any way we can, don't you? That's why we came with you.'

'E-exactly. You're not alone,' Seven said, her pale face serious.

Phoenix managed a weak smile.

'Who else wishes this Jira character had left goblin magic alone?' Five sighed, shaking his head.

'She thought she was just opening a portal,' Six reminded him.

'She did,' said Five with a groan, slumping back in his chair. 'One straight to our doom.'

Phoenix looked up, amused in spite of herself.

Six rolled his eyes. 'So dramatic.'

'Hard not to be,' Five said gloomily. 'A tidal wave of saltwater and an illness that's already wiped out most of the witches. Morgren and Victory won't even need a goblin army to take Ember: they'll be able to just stroll right in.'

'You don't think I can destroy it, do you?' Phoenix said, watching him closely.

'Well . . .' He hesitated. 'Do *you* think you can?'

His gaze met hers and she saw fear as wild as her own there.

'Five, you're unbelievable!' Six exclaimed.

'I'm being honest,' Five said, frowning, 'which is more than you're doing. We're not going to be able to help Phoenix in any way that really matters. You saw that thing. You know that.'

Six shook his head. 'You were out of line with Zenith and you're out of line now.'

Two bright spots of colour appeared on Five's cheeks as he opened his mouth to reply.

'That's enough.' Seven cut them off, uncharacteristically sharp. 'Don't you t-two usually spar around this t-time?'

The boys stared at her in surprise. Six recovered first. 'Uh, we do, yes. But—'

'Well, m-maybe you should do that,' Seven said. 'Now.' A silent look passed between her and her brother. An instant later, Six nodded.

'What?' Five said, an eyebrow raised. 'Have we just been *dismissed*?'

Six already had him by the elbow and was leading him away. 'Come on – she's right. You do need to practise. Yesterday you were awful.'

'That's *so* untrue!' Five's outraged voice faded as Six marched him away.

Phoenix stared at the girl next to her.

Seven shrugged. 'I c-can be firm when I need to be,' she said, looking awkward. 'I might not be able to save you from an edgeworm, but I c-can get rid of my brother easily enough. And Five goes wherever he goes.'

'Thank you,' Phoenix said with sincerity. 'I'm not sure I could've dealt with an argument between them right now.'

'W-we all believe in you,' Seven said softly. 'I don't think Five meant what he said.'

Phoenix shook her head. 'He's right, you know. This task . . . it will be a test of strength: my magic against the Shadowseam's. None of you can help me with that. Not really.'

'Y-you and Five have both forgotten something important,' Seven admonished. 'Having friends who support you counts for a lot. That *c-can* make a difference. I'm h-here if you want to talk.'

In spite of the Shadowseam, Phoenix's heart swelled. Seven was the quietest of her friends, the one who demanded the least attention, was happy – perhaps even *preferred* – walking in the shadow of the others. But it was moments like these that reminded Phoenix that Seven was also the most thoughtful, the kindest of them all. It had been Seven who had given her Widge, something she was grateful for every single day.

As though hearing her thoughts, Widge nestled closer to her cheek, his bright eyes warm on Seven.

'It's—' Phoenix broke off, shook her head. Why was it so hard to talk about how she felt? She took a breath, tried again. 'It's a lot of pressure.'

To her surprise, Seven laughed.

'That's . . . funny?'

Seven smiled. 'No, just r-really obvious.' She grew thoughtful. 'You have to concentrate on the things within your control though. It's the only way to get through this.'

'Nothing feels within my control,' Phoenix sighed.

'Your lessons with Nara will be,' Seven said firmly. 'Those are what you need to focus on. Think of your axes. It took you time to learn to use them so well, didn't it? Maybe controlling your fire will be the same: a skill to be mastered like any other.'

Phoenix nodded, trying to take heart from her friend's words.

'I believe in you, Phoenix,' Seven said, her gaze warm. 'If there's anyone who can do this, it's you. The world is so big and so full of wonder—' She broke off at Phoenix's stricken expression. 'What? Did I say something wrong?'

Phoenix felt hot and cold at the same time.

So big and so full of wonder . . . Poppy's words from Seven's mouth. The hairs stood up along her arms.

Seven was staring at her, her face crinkled with concern.

'My sister.' Phoenix swallowed hard. 'Poppy. She said almost exactly the same thing to me once.' She laughed, a ragged sound. 'I was just thinking about it last night.'

Seven grew very still. 'You've never said her name before,' she murmured. 'But she was right, of course. There's so much out there and all of it needs saving now. It sounds like Poppy was wise.'

'Wise?' Phoenix smiled in spite of her aching heart. 'I think she probably was, although I never saw it that way at the time.'

Seven hesitated. 'What was she like?'

Phoenix shivered. 'It still feels . . . hard to talk about her. I used to block her out, block everyone out really.

But I don't want to do that any more. I don't want to forget her.'

Seven nodded, remained silent. How to describe Poppy with all of her wonderful contradictions?

'She was so many things,' Phoenix said slowly. 'She was kind and curious. Much friendlier than me. I think she might have been braver than me too, although I only saw that side of her now and then.'

'If she were here now, what do you think she'd say to you?' Seven said.

'"Don't you dare let Ember be destroyed before I've seen any of it!"' Phoenix spoke without thinking, but her little sister's voice rang true in the words. She almost laughed out loud; Poppy suddenly felt very close.

'She was definitely wise,' Seven smiled. 'And what would you say back?'

The smile slipped from Phoenix's face. For a moment, she could almost see Poppy in front of her, head tilted to one side as she awaited Phoenix's response. 'I'd promise her to stop it, of course,' she said slowly. 'I'd owe it to her. In . . . in a really twisted way, I'm living her dream. She would've loved to visit the Hunting Lodge, to see Ledge. She would've exploded with excitement if she'd come to Icegaard. It should be her here, but . . .' Phoenix broke off, swallowed the lump in her throat. 'I'd promise her anything to make up for that.'

The words had weight, felt like a bond. Determination

slipped in to replace some of Phoenix's fear: she would keep this promise to her little sister.

Seven looked away, blinking hard. It was a moment before she spoke again. 'I wish there were some way I could really help you . . . beyond just being here for you, I mean.'

Phoenix shook her head. 'Don't—'

'Yelara said there's a library just beneath the eyrie,' Seven said suddenly, sitting up straighter. 'I can't help you t-train your power, but I *can* go there and find everything there is about goblin magic and the Shadowseam. M-maybe the witches missed something!'

The air around Seven seemed to crackle with energy and Phoenix felt herself buoyed by her friend's sudden excitement, some of her fear of the Shadowseam melting away. What a glorious thing it was to have a friend like her.

'I hope I'm not interrupting?' came a voice from behind them.

The two girls turned to see Nara watching them.

'Phoenix,' the witch said, 'I was hoping you'd be willing to start your lessons with me straight away. We should try to maximise the time we have before . . .' She winced.

Phoenix's stomach dropped, and the happy feeling she'd had just a moment ago faded away. 'How long do we have until the Shadowseam . . . breaks free?' she asked, finding her voice.

Nara hesitated. 'At the rate its influence is spreading, the frost palace probably only has a few weeks.' She shook her head. 'And that's an optimistic guess. As the seam grows, the oculus becomes harder to maintain. If that fails and the Shadowseam can spread unchecked . . .' Her eyes filled with sudden determination. 'We have a lot of work to do. Are you ready?'

Seven caught Phoenix's eye and nodded encouragingly.

Phoenix took a deep breath and turned to Nara. 'I'm ready.'

CHAPTER 24

There was no time for Dog to prepare. The darkwater pressed closer to him, whispering its secrets. Before he knew what was happening, he was wrenched into another memory – only this time it wasn't his.

He stood in the training ground of the Hunting Lodge, his arm shaking under the weight of a sword as a taller boy rained blow after blow on him. He tried so hard, but could barely deflect them. Sweat trickled down his face in spite of the frigid air and a raging desperation grew in him. Why wasn't he stronger? Why wasn't he better after so, so many hours of practice?

The other boy smirked as he walked away. 'Think I've made my point, Titch,' he laughed. 'You'll never be a Hunter. Give up. Go back to grubbing for snails or frogs or whatever it is you lot eat out in the bogs.'

'My name's not Titch!' he shouted, hating how raw and small his voice sounded.

More laughter sounded behind him, and he turned, full of fury, his grip tight on the blade. His brow crinkled in confusion: there was no one there. Then, suddenly, a girl rippled into view, seemingly out of thin air. A blue cloak lifted from her shoulders in the breeze and she tugged it back round herself.

'You again,' he sighed, sheathing his sword. 'You're always creeping up on me. How are you doing that?'

'It's called the Veil,' the young witch said, beaming. 'It's a difficult spell, but I'm very good at it, aren't I?'

He glared at her. 'You laughed,' he said. 'It gave you away.'

'Cheer up.' The girl flashed him a gap-toothed grin. 'I wasn't laughing at you. You were much better today.'

'Really?' he asked, suddenly hopeful.

'Definitely.' She nodded firmly. 'And a witch never lies.'

'I thought you weren't a proper witch yet,' he said. But he could feel the beginnings of a smile forming.

'I'm Unfledged,' she corrected him. 'But I was born a witch.'

Dog fought the memory off even as surprise flooded him. The huntlings he'd just seen had known one another's clans, spoken openly of them. That hadn't been the case at the Huntling Lodge for over a thousand years – and meant the darkwater had preserved a memory even older than him.

His momentary distraction was enough for the darkwater to strike again. It pressed another stranger's memory on to him, overwhelming his senses until their past was all he could see and feel.

The wailing was unbearable; she wanted to put her fingers in her ears. She wanted to run back to the home-tree and climb, climb, climb to the very highest branches. She wanted to press her lips against the bark and let the sweet ymbre flow down her throat until she could lose herself in her tree's memories, see her grandmother again, watch her grow up, see her as a young woman discovering that she was a tree whisperer.

Instead, she was here in the grove of rebirth, her grandmother's shroud stitched from leaves while the tribe beat their chests and howled their grief. Only she had to hold herself tight. Only she had a job to do.

It wasn't fair.

She stepped forward and took a breath, calmed her shaking hands and reached for the cup of fresh ymbre. The wails died as she slipped the shroud from the beloved face.

The flow of the liquid was steady and true, pouring straight into her grandmother's mouth.

'Return to the earth,' she whispered, 'and live again.'

Next, the nut, a solid weight in her pocket. She pulled it out now, glossy and dark.

That something so small could contain such multitudes.

She raised it to her lips and kissed it, then stood quietly as it was passed reverently from hand to hand, every tribe member kissing it, until it finally returned to her. She placed it in her grandmother's mouth and covered her face again.

'Return to the earth,' hundreds of voices whispered, 'and live again.'

Dog realised he'd once more stopped moving. The power of the darkwater, of the memories, was growing. He shook himself, silt flying from his fur and mouth. He drew his lips back in a warning snarl, but the water flowed carelessly past him, the ripples round his ears sounding eerily like laughter. The weight of the memories pressed down on him like fear and he suppressed the urge to howl. Where was Phoenix? Where was Sharpspark? Were they safe? Was he?

He squeezed his eyes shut and ducked down, trying to make himself as small and unnoticeable as possible, creeping forward step by step, trying to focus only on what was beneath his paws. Memories scratched at him, but he found that if he concentrated very hard, blotted out everything, he could just about hold them off.

He pressed forward with more confidence until something else brought him up short. There was a faint glow in the river: light unspooled from something upstream to be pulled past him like wool unravelled from a ball. It formed a bright, wavering, thread-like trail.

Curiosity won over caution and Dog fought his way towards it, noticing as he did how the darkwater grew calmer, the battering assault of its memories reduced. He followed the quiet path created by the filament of light, his curiosity growing greater all the time.

On and on it led him, through water dark and dangerous, all the time keeping the shadows at bay. It could have been hours or days that he followed it, until abruptly he realised he was no longer in the Clasp at all. The water was fresher, and the thick, cloying scent of ymbre was gone.

The source of the shadow-banishing light was on the bank, half in, half out of the water at the edge of the Great Woods. It wasn't until he was very close that Dog realised what he was looking at: a lutra, the sacred creature of the river clan, the reason they protected their waters so carefully. Six feet long with a strong tail and webbed paws, it was otter-like in appearance. Its silver fur gleamed despite the light-filled blood seeping from the knife in its side.

With growing horror, Dog moved closer.

It was lithe and sleek although curled up in pain, and a bright intelligence shone in its pain-filled eyes as it tracked Dog's progress, whiskers twitching. It was one of the most beautiful things Dog had ever seen. And it was unmistakably dying. The urge to howl was almost too strong to bear as he dragged himself out of the water towards it.

The wind whispered through the nearby trees, but everything else was very quiet. Even the river flowed silently, as though shocked by what lay before it.

Dog didn't know what to do. He was standing on the

bank, in full view of anyone who happened towards the river. But he knew he couldn't leave the lutra to die alone.

'I am sorry,' he murmured, coming to sit sphinx-like in the mud next to the creature. 'I have found you too late. But I will stay with you until the end. That is all I can do.'

The lutra's gentle eyes were fixed on him, and Dog thought he saw acquiescence there, so he shuffled a little closer, making sure he kept a respectful distance between them, laid his head on his paws and thought. After a moment, he began to speak, telling the creature of what he remembered of its home. He spoke of the vast beauty of a sunset he'd once seen over the tranquil waterscape of the riverlands, and of the peace he'd found in the sun-dappled waters of the Ilara.

The lutra listened, he thought. Its eyes half closed, its breath ever slower. Dog closed his eyes too, racking his brain for another memory, something luminous that might bring the creature comfort.

When he opened his eyes again, the lutra had pulled itself closer to him, its breathing laboured as it touched its whiskered nose to Dog's cheek.

Dog had heard stories of the power in a lutra's touch – people said they could cure any illness, bestow unusually long life – but it was like nothing he could have imagined. He felt as though he'd heaved an enormous breath where before he'd been smothered. An immense feeling of opening swept through him, spreading brightness and warmth from his ears to his tail, filling him with new, richer sensations: the mud of the riverbank was pleasingly squelchy beneath his belly and the pads of his paws. Scents sharpened in the air and the silt in his mouth tasted earthy, faintly sour.

A taste! He would have leaped to his feet and barked with delight if at that moment a memory from the lutra hadn't washed through him, drawn perhaps by some lingering presence of the darkwater.

The trout was fat and fast and clever, darting and flicking in the current, light flashing iridescent on its scales. Chasing it was joyous: the bubbles dancing in the water, the power in her own body as she raced after it, the water almost seeming to part for her. Shafts of light pierced the river from above and the river grasses below stretched up, tickling her belly, billowing in the gentle currents.

She dived down, hoping to get beneath the trout, then surged up towards it, the fish's outline frantic against the watery sky above. With a great flick of its tail, it was up and out of the water, leaping desperately away from her grasping paws.

Delight blossomed in her: what a noble opponent this trout was! She paddled faster, lashing her tail for extra propulsion, and powered out of the water behind it, droplets flying from her whiskers. Every fibre in her strained forward, teeth snapping shut a hair's breadth short of the trout's tail.

A movement on the bank caught her eye as she began to arc back down towards the water. Two figures stood staring at her: a tall human woman and a goblin in a decadent cloak. They reeked of magic and ill-intent, more so even than the banemages who sometimes came to hunt her kind. It was enough to make her forget the trout. Every instinct developed through her long, long life told her to flee.

So she did. Or rather she tried to. She twisted back down towards the safety of the water and heard a shout go up from the bank. She caught a flash of violet light and realised to her horror that she was no longer moving. Instead of slipping neatly back into the rippling water, she was suspended unnaturally above it.

For a moment, the surprise was so great that she couldn't move. Then she began to fight with all her might. But no matter how she struggled, wrenching herself left and right, she could not twist free of the magic holding her.

'Wriggly, isn't it, Victory?' laughed the goblin. 'Like that fish it was chasing.'

'Let's get this done, Morgren,' the woman, Victory, said, her voice tight. She glanced over her shoulder as she spoke. 'If we're seen, everything is ruined. This isn't how I would have chosen to do it.'

'There's no one around,' Morgren shrugged. 'I'd know.'

She realised now that she was being pulled over the surface of the water towards the two figures. The more she scented of them, the more fearful she became: power, ruthless ambition and cruelty. Their smell spoke of painful deaths and something even darker, something old and malevolent, something that had no place in Ember. She fought harder.

'Set it down there,' Victory said, pointing at the bank.

She dropped, hitting the sodden earth hard, but before she could move a great weight pressed down on her. She looked up and saw the goblin standing over her, his hands outstretched, pinning her without even touching her.

The woman reached to the belt at her waist and drew out a leaf-shaped blade that shone copper in the winter sun.

As Victory crouched over her, she struggled harder than ever. Then the blade flashed – and suddenly she felt very cold, her limbs taking on a new, leaden weight.

'Efficient as always,' Morgren grinned. 'You're sure this is the best place for it though?'

'Definitely,' Victory said, standing and turning away.

Morgren sniggered. 'Then let the battle begin.'

'We should get back,' Victory said, rolling her shoulders. 'It must be nearly time.'

'Not yet,' said Morgren. 'She's arrived at Icegaard,

but only just. The Croke says she's changed her name to Phoenix.'

A strange, bitter smile twisted the woman's face. 'Phoenix.' Her laughter was forced. 'She thinks a lot of herself, that one.'

Morgren shrugged. 'Seems appropriate 'after what we did to Poa.' His face darkened. 'After what she did to me.'

'You'll get your chance with her again. Soon.'

An ugly look played across the goblin's features. 'I can't wait until she meets our master.' He glanced around, unmoved by the beauty of the landscape, suddenly restless. 'I've had enough of this place. Let's go.'

He waved a hand and they were gone.

The sun was still shining, but some of the light seemed to have gone from it, the sky bleached to grey. The river sounded very far away.

The memory ended so abruptly that Dog lurched, thrown off balance. Panic latched on to him as he came back to himself. *Phoenix.* She was in danger.

The light of the lutra suddenly dimmed, then vanished entirely as she died.

A terrible weight pressed down on Dog, his heart leaden. He'd just witnessed something unspeakably wrong. Goodness had radiated from the creature like warmth, but Victory had attacked her, left her to bleed to death.

The river clan's sacred creature, dead at the edge of the Great Woods. And killed with an unmistakably forest-clan blade.

Wars had started over much, much less. And war was what Victory wanted.

Dog realised he'd spent so much time planning how he would find Victory that he'd never paused to wonder what she was actually doing in the riverlands. Now all was horribly clear, and an impossible decision lay before him. Should he go to Icegaard to protect Phoenix, or stay in the riverlands and try to prevent some of the terrible harm Victory intended? For the first time ever, his heart and his head were telling him different things.

Dog stood in the weak winter light as though frozen, a furious battle raging inside him.

CHAPTER 25

'This is the sparring room,' Nara said to Phoenix, throwing a pair of doors open. 'We use it for practising battle magic.' She paused. 'Or rather we used to. Before the seam-sickness.' She waved Phoenix inside. 'This is where we'll have our lessons.'

'Are we going to spar?' Phoenix asked doubtfully.

The room was an enormous cuboid, each wall of ice polished to a mirror shine, remarkable only in its lack of ornamentation. A big table with two stools sat right in the middle, but other than that it was just a gleaming white box, empty and clean. A few orblights floated around, but most of the light came from the walls themselves.

'No,' Nara smiled. 'We're here because this room has more magical defences round it than any other part of the palace. Well . . . apart from where the Shadowseam is, of course. Given that elemental fire is notoriously destructive, I thought coming here would be sensible.'

Phoenix gulped, feeling herself grow clammy as Nara led her to the large table. On her shoulder, Widge's tail flicked, his eyes bright with curiosity as he looked around.

'It's a very efficient use of space,' Nara said.

Then, noting Phoenix's blank look, she pointed to the centre of the table where a small keyhole lay flush with the surface. From her pocket, she pulled a key and inserted it, turning it with a soft click. To Phoenix's amazement, the tabletop flipped slowly open to reveal a storage compartment, much larger than should have been possible.

Nara pulled out various books, bottles, a cauldron and a long cloak made of a strange scaly material before closing the tabletop and setting the objects down on it.

'Sandmadder skin,' Nara explained. She shrugged off her beautiful feathered cloak and pulled the scaly one on instead. 'It's fireproof,' she added, seeing Phoenix's confusion.

'Right,' Phoenix muttered, trying to ignore the way her heart was jumping about in her chest. Widge trilled soothingly.

'Sit,' Nara said, gesturing at one of the stools, then settling herself opposite. Phoenix couldn't help but notice that Nara looked excited while she still only felt a nauseating dread.

'I've been thinking about how best to start,' the witch said. 'But it occurred to me that you might have an idea yourself?'

Phoenix shook her head quickly. 'I've just been trying to stop the fire, not use it.'

'What do you mean?' Nara asked.

Phoenix shifted uncomfortably. 'Sometimes I feel like it's bubbling up inside me, that it could just burst out.' She hesitated. 'It's been getting worse recently.' She kept her eyes on Nara's face, watching for her reaction.

'It just means its strength is growing,' Nara said calmly, 'which is good. You will need every ounce of power to destroy the seam.' She paused and frowned slightly, didn't notice how Phoenix paled at mention of the Shadowseam. 'It does also mean that mastering it is becoming more important. How often do you experience this "bubbling"?'

Phoenix shrugged. 'Every day.'

Nara went quiet at that, narrowing her eyes as she thought. Eventually, she shook herself and stood up.

'I think a demonstration would be best,' she said, gesturing for Phoenix to stand too. 'So we know what we're dealing with.'

'What?' Phoenix yelped. 'No!'

Nara's expression switched to one of curiosity. 'I know Hoarfrost told you not to use your magic in Ledge, but you're in Icegaard now.'

'You don't understand,' Phoenix said, panic rising in her. 'Last time I used my powers, I destroyed the Hunting Lodge, and it was pure luck I didn't kill anyone.

Everyone. Do you know how much danger you're putting Icegaard in?'

Nara sat back down again, placing her palms flat on the table. 'Phoenix,' she said carefully, 'to train your magic, to understand it, you'll have to use it. Think of it as a bubbling pot over a flame. If you don't take the lid off now and then, it *will* boil over.'

A horrible shiver racked Phoenix and she suddenly felt icy cold, her breath tight in her chest. Widge wriggled free of her furs to butt his head gently against her chin, shooting Nara a dirty look.

'I want to teach you control so absolute that it becomes like breathing,' Nara said gently. 'So that even when you're asleep it never slips.'

Phoenix looked up sharply at that. She hadn't told anyone about how sometimes she woke up from her nightmares to find her sheets smoking. She thought she'd hidden the evidence well.

The witch paused and took a deep breath. 'You have to trust me.'

Phoenix looked into Nara's clear, determined eyes, and nodded weakly. What choice did she have?

'How will it work?'

'We'll have to feel our way,' Nara said. 'I don't think this has ever been done before. Elementals of old were not welcome at Icegaard.'

Phoenix absorbed that in silence.

'You already have a significant ability with it—'

'I do?' Phoenix sputtered. 'Where did you get that from?'

'You used your fire the night the Hunting Lodge was attacked to defeat a goblin mage,' Nara said patiently. 'And you said you're suppressing it every day. Both of those things suggest a level of command.'

Phoenix nodded slowly. She hadn't thought of it like that before.

'Is the fire connected to your emotions?' Nara asked. 'Anger?'

Phoenix nodded again, surprised. How did the witch know that?

'We'll start there then,' Nara said briskly. 'I want you to think about something that makes you angry, then send a single, short-lived burst of flames down the room.' She pointed to the far end, away from the door. 'There.'

Phoenix's limbs felt heavy, cold with dread. 'What if I can't stop it?' she whispered.

'I've thought of that,' Nara said, picking up a small bottle from the table, 'and come up with a rather blunt solution.' She held up the vial. 'I brewed this earlier; it will knock you out if things start getting out of control.'

'How?' Phoenix asked, staring at the bottle doubtfully.

'If I unstopper it beneath your nose, the fumes will render you unconscious.' Nara looked pleased, then added quickly, 'Only temporarily, of course.'

Phoenix nodded slowly. 'That should work,' she said, feeling a flicker of hope.

'In your own time then,' Nara said, taking her gently by the shoulders and turning her away from the big table.

Phoenix took a deep breath, tried to allow herself to believe she could do this. Something about Nara reminded her of Dog, inspired confidence. The thought of the Guardian tugged at her, worry for him rising through her all over again. She knew that wishing he was here with her was pointless, but couldn't seem to stop herself.

'Get off, Widge,' Phoenix whispered, forcing herself to concentrate on the blank wall of ice in front of her. But the stubborn little squirrel dug his claws in, tension vibrating through him. She took a deep, calming breath, then shook herself. She wasn't supposed to be calming down: she needed to get angry.

She thought of the Shadowseam, its seething darkness, the crawling feeling it gave her, as though every dark creature in Ember was creeping towards her. She waited for the threads of fire to build, to respond, but nothing happened. If anything, her flames died down rather than springing to the surface.

Phoenix swallowed hard, the sound loud and wet in the emptiness of the sparring room. The Shadowseam didn't make her angry: it terrified her. She turned her thoughts away from what that meant.

Without even meaning to, her brain leaped to Five instead, the words he'd said to Zenith. *The only magic out there now belongs to monsters.* Surely he hadn't meant that, had spoken rashly in a moment of anger? If anyone could understand that impulse, then Phoenix could. Still, she felt the threads of fire sink even lower inside her, further from the surface.

'Phoenix?' Nara prompted gently.

Phoenix nodded quickly, forced herself to concentrate. She settled on Victory, on her many, many betrayals, on how Phoenix's family was dead because of her. For a moment, the weaponsmaster's face was clear before her, and immediately her power leaped inside her, skeins of heat building and spreading through her chest. She clamped down on it automatically, shocked by the suddenness of it.

Beads of sweat formed on her brow and she wiped them away, cursing quietly.

'Try to think of it as just another training session,' said Nara. 'You must've had plenty of them at the Hunting Lodge.'

Phoenix nodded – that was true enough. 'Just another training session,' she muttered to herself. Again, she thought of Victory and the heat began to flicker through her, building until her fingertips began to throb. Fear screamed at her not to do it, but she pushed it aside and raised her right hand.

Then there was only the fire.

It tore out of her in a twisting, vengeful torrent, slamming into the ice wall with unimaginable force. Where the golden flames hit, the wall rippled with heat, and, for a wondrous instant, Phoenix could actually see Icegaard's magic embedded in the ice, glowing brilliantly white, tested by the fire rolling over it.

Behind her, Nara gave a small cry. 'Enough, Phoenix,' she said, her voice raw. 'That's more than enough.'

Phoenix tried to pull back, tried to close the floodgates, but the magic was too strong for her. On and on it raged, tearing through her until she felt her limbs grow shaky and her breath begin to labour.

'Phoenix!'

Her knees cried out in pain as they hit the ground. A moment later, everything was black.

She blinked desperately, trying to get her eyes to adjust, but it was as though all the light had been sucked out of the world. And, in the closing darkness, she felt something shift, something watchful, its attention suddenly latched on to her with a cold, unalterable malevolence.

'I see you, Phoenix.' The voice was flat and empty and lifeless. The voice of the Croke.

Her breath hitched, the sound impossibly loud. Her heart fluttered as though it could fly free and her dread grew and grew until she was paralysed by it.

She sensed the Croke move closer, the sound soft and deadly and somehow all around her at—

'Phoenix? Phoenix! Can you hear me?'

Someone was shaking her. Peeling open her eyelids felt like hefting rocks. Nara was crouched over her, her face a worried blur. Phoenix blinked several times until the witch's features swam into focus.

She was lying on the ground. Widge was on her chest, paws on her chin, peering at her fearfully. Her limbs felt leaden, exhaustion permeating every inch of her.

'What happened?' she murmured, pushing the dream-fragment as far away as she could.

'You couldn't stop it,' Nara said. Phoenix could see she was trying to stay calm, but struggling. 'I had to knock you out.'

Phoenix nodded weakly as Widge licked her chin.

The witch helped her up and set her on a stool.

'How do you feel?' she asked.

'Awful,' Phoenix muttered. Even stroking Widge required a monumental effort.

'You rest there,' Nara said, her eyes searching Phoenix's face. 'I'm going to brew you a strengthening potion, one that's nice and strong.'

Swaying with exhaustion, Phoenix watched as Nara built a small fire on the tabletop. When the flames flared, she set a tripod suspending a small cauldron over them, and began to add ingredients from the various bottles.

Every now and then, Nara whispered something Phoenix couldn't quite catch, and the contents of the cauldron sent up a shower of sparks.

'Why can't I hear what you're saying?' Phoenix asked after it had happened for a third time. Each time, it made her more uncomfortable: she relied on her senses, often her life depended on them, but something about the witch's magic seemed to evade her hearing altogether.

'It is called quietspeech,' Nara said, looking up from stirring. 'It's the language of our magic. Only a witch able to wield its power can read, hear or speak it. You are a witch, but not of my type of magic, so you cannot hear it.' She kept stirring and smiled. 'It used to be how we found new witches, you know. Those born in the clans rather than here.'

She saw Phoenix's surprise and nodded. 'It happens. The quickest way to identify them is simply to say a word of quietspeech and have them say it back. If they can hear it and repeat it, they have the ability to use it.'

The witch frowned and when she next spoke she sounded sad. 'There must be many out there now, their magical abilities undiscovered.' She spooned some of the liquid from her cauldron into a cup, offering it to Phoenix.

Widge sniffed the potion curiously, but didn't object, which Phoenix took as a good sign. Her first sip was so sour it felt like her eyelids were turning inside out, but almost immediately she felt a flush of strength race through her.

'Thanks,' she said, sitting up straighter and taking another tentative sip. 'You're not going to make me do that again, are you?'

'No, I don't think it would be helpful for either of us,' Nara said gently. 'Can you tell me what happened though?'

Phoenix shrugged. 'I couldn't stop it,' she said. She tried to sound casual, but the tremble in her voice gave her away. 'It was like trying to close a door on a herd of stampeding snagglefeet.' She bit her lip. 'It was too strong for me.'

Nara sat across the table from her, her face thoughtful. 'You think of using your magic as opening a door,' she said a minute later, 'which is interesting. Is it possible you could only open that door a crack instead of fully?'

Phoenix thought, then nodded slowly. 'Maybe.' She clamped down on the magic so tightly most of the time, but, when she used it, she let the fire have total freedom. But perhaps she didn't have to. 'I don't see how that will help with the Shadowseam though. I'll need more power, not less.'

'One thing at a time,' said Nara. 'Control is crucial, whether you're facing the seam or not. If you can't stop it when it floods out of you like that, then we need to start with something smaller. That is what we'll concentrate on tomorrow,' she said cheerfully. 'Yes, tomorrow,' she laughed, seeing Phoenix's face. 'Time is—' She broke off suddenly, her eyes fixed on something behind Phoenix's shoulder.

'What?' Phoenix frowned, turning to look.

At first, she didn't see it, didn't know what she was looking for, until Nara's finger directed her gaze.

'The magic. It's . . . beginning to fail,' Nara said, her voice flat with dread.

Phoenix followed the witch's gesture and saw a small patch of ice that was darker than the rest, the light within it flickering oddly.

Nara walked over to it, eyes fixed on the fist-sized space, her face clouded with dismay. 'But this is one of the most protected rooms,' she whispered, seeming to have forgotten Phoenix was there.

'The Shadowseam is doing that?' Phoenix asked, her heart sinking.

She stared round the spare beauty of the sparring room and bit her lip. If Nara was right – and Phoenix had no doubt that she was – then soon this place would be as dark and forbidding as the abandoned witcheries, as fragile as the tunnel leading to the Shadowseam's cell.

'If it's trapped, then how is it doing this?' she asked.

Nara shook her head slowly. 'We don't know,' she said quietly. Then, more angrily, 'There's so much we don't know about it.' She grimaced, struggling to calm herself. 'The only thing we can do is destroy it. That's why our lessons together are so important.' She offered a weak smile as Phoenix's heart plummeted, her doubt pressing round her.

The glow in the darkened patch of ice flickered once more, then died.

CHAPTER 26

Dog didn't know how long he'd stood on the riverbank, indecision raging in him, the murdered lutra at his feet.

'I found you!' Sharpspark whirled round the Guardian's head until Dog could taste smoke and cordite in the air. The sprite's voice was hot and gleeful. 'You're almost as bad at skulking as I am. I thought—' Sharpspark broke off abruptly when he saw the lutra lying on the ground. His fire dimmed.

'I found her here,' Dog said, his voice rough. 'I could do nothing to save her.'

Sharpspark hovered, silent. 'Lutras are pure spirits,' he said finally. 'Even firesprites have no quarrel with them. Who did this?' His burning eyes lingered on the creature's wound, the knife still in its side. His flames pitched to a dangerous blue-white.

'It was Victory,' Dog said. 'Victory and Morgren. I do not know if the creature showed me willingly or if there was still darkwater clinging to me, but I saw it through her own eyes.' He couldn't stop himself from snarling, his hackles rising.

Sharpspark stared at him, his expression suddenly changing to one of surprise. 'She touched you,' he said. It wasn't a question.

'Yes,' Dog said warily. 'How did you know?'

The sprite tilted his head to one side, thinking. 'I'm not sure,' he said finally. 'But there's something different about you.'

Hesitantly, Dog moved towards the water, peering down at his reflection. His fur was still made of stone, still the same reddish colour as before, his ear still torn. But he didn't doubt the sprite was right. He felt different, as though everything in him had been slightly shifted, subtly rearranged.

Sharpspark fluttered over his head, examining him critically before landing in his usual spot between Dog's ears.

Dog had never felt pain like it. Twin bolts of pure energy seemed to explode from the sprite's feet. He leaped back and twisted away, shaking Sharpspark off him with a yowl.

The surprise on Sharpspark's face would have been comical if Dog hadn't been so shocked.

'Definitely different,' the sprite said eventually. He paused, wrinkled his nose. 'Does this mean I have to fly all the time now?'

'I thought that was what you wanted anyway,' Dog said, recovering enough to speak. The spot between his ears felt unpleasantly tight and hot. He peered at his reflection again, almost expecting to see a burn, but there was nothing there.

Sharpspark made a sound of annoyance. 'It was quite comfortable sitting there.'

'I can taste now,' Dog admitted quietly, gazing up at him. 'I have never been able to taste anything before.'

Sharpspark shrugged. 'An overrated sense; firesprites have no need for it.'

Dog stared at him for a moment, then smiled. There was something grounding in Sharpspark's disinterest. 'And there was me thinking it was something to be excited about.'

The firesprite shook his head. 'Wings would be exciting. Fire would be magnificent. Taste is just . . . taste.'

Dog would have laughed if it wasn't for the lutra. Instead, he said, 'I am very pleased to see you. And relieved your trip went smoothly through the woods.'

To his surprise, the sprite folded his arms, every angle of him suddenly defiant. 'It wasn't me,' he said, scowling, his features sharpening with displeasure. 'And how did you know anyway?'

'Know what?' Dog asked, his heart sinking.

'The small tree,' Sharpspark said. 'The dying one. It was already broken when I found it.'

'I think I need more explanation,' Dog said, careful

to sound calm in spite of the sudden panic racing through him.

'Besides, I would burn it, not chop it,' Sharpspark went on, as though Dog hadn't spoken, glaring into the river. 'Not that they believed me.' The sprite wrinkled his nose. 'Until they found that feather anyway.'

'Feather?' Dog frowned. 'What are you talking about?'

'Kingfisher,' the sprite said finally, pleased with himself. 'They found a kingfisher feather there and forgot all about me.'

'You're saying a home-tree was destroyed?' Dog said slowly. 'And the forest clan found a kingfisher feather nearby?'

'Yes.' Sharpspark nodded. 'And I had nothing to do with it whatsoever . . . well, until later.'

It was too much for Dog to take in. Victory and Morgren were even cleverer than he'd thought. The lutra had been killed with a forest-clan knife. A forest-clan home-tree had been desecrated and the river clan's symbol found nearby.

'How long ago did they find the home-tree?' Dog asked, the question humming with urgency. How long did he have to defuse this situation?

'Hours ago,' Sharpspark said with a shrug. 'They are on their way here. I had to fly fast to stay ahead of them.'

Dog wanted to throw back his head and howl.

'If Victory did this, why are we still here?' Sharpspark

frowned. 'Tracking her was why you brought us here. She's gone.'

It took all of Dog's self-control not to snap at him. 'A war is about to start,' he growled. 'And we might be the only ones who can stop it. But –' he shook his head hard, a whine tearing from him – 'Phoenix . . .'

'What's the fiery one got to do with this?' Sharpspark was starting to look very annoyed.

'That's where Victory and Morgren are headed,' Dog said. 'They know she is at Icegaard.'

'Then we must go there,' Sharpspark said simply.

Dog looked up at his small, fierce form, suddenly more grateful than he could express for the sprite's presence. 'Yes,' he said, his tail beginning to wag, 'we—'

A cry from the water interrupted him. A small canoe floated in the river, its prow carved into the likeness of a mallard's head. The face of the boy paddling it was slack with shock as he took in the lutra lying at Dog's feet.

'Wait!' Dog cried.

But it was too late. With a scream that must have carried for miles, the boy expertly spun the canoe round and paddled downstream as fast as he could.

Dog had no doubt that, within minutes, he would have company. He squeezed his eyes shut, throwing his head back in a howl of frustration.

When the first forest-clan arrow struck him a moment later, it turned into a yelp of pain.

CHAPTER 27

Two days later, Phoenix saw that the black mark in the sparring room had grown. A lot. Half of the wall now throbbed with the ever-spreading blot of darkness, its magic draining away.

She stood in front of it, jangling with nerves. She'd already prodded it several times to make sure the ice was still solid and she resisted the urge to do it again. Widge's tail twitched, agitated, and he retreated into her furs.

Nara shook her head at it. 'It's safe for today,' she said. 'But I'll have to find somewhere else for us to train tomorrow.'

Phoenix tried not to look too relieved. The growing patch of un-magic was almost as unsettling as the Shadowseam itself.

A couple of hours into their lesson, just after Nara had knocked her out for the third infuriating time, a chiming sound filled the air.

'What's that?' Phoenix asked blearily, taking Nara's proffered hand and allowing herself to be pulled to her feet. The witch's face was drawn tight and she hurried away as soon as Phoenix was standing.

'It's a signal from the icemothers,' she called over her shoulder. 'It's probably nothing, but I'll just check. Wait here for me and I'll be back in a few minutes.' With that, she slipped out of the door and was gone.

Phoenix blinked and shook her head, still shaky from failing to control the fire. She took a sip of the strengthening potion Nara had left for her.

'A signal from the icemothers?' she said, glancing at Widge. 'What does that mean?' His bright-eyed gaze mirrored her own curiosity, which she took as a sign of encouragement. A moment later, she was making her way down the trunk stairs towards the lake.

'Hey, Phoenix!' Five was puffing behind her, hurrying to catch up.

'Weapons training with Seven?' she guessed.

'As if,' he snorted. 'It's like she doesn't respect our authority as Hunters at all. When Six and I went to collect her from the library, she just said no, that she was too busy! Again!' He shook his head sadly. 'This would *definitely* not be happening if Dog were here. Can you believe her?'

Phoenix's heart lurched at the mention of Dog, the constant weight of missing him growing heavier. Would he have reached the Great Woods by now? Was Hoarfrost right that Victory wouldn't be able to harm him?

'You all right?' Five asked, shooting her a sideways glance.

Phoenix bit her lip.

The only magic out there now belongs to monsters.

Five's words had been replaying in her mind a lot. She was being ridiculous. She knew he didn't really think that she or Seven were monsters. And yet his words kept popping into her head at unexpected moments and . . . he was clearly bothered by all the magic in Icegaard. He couldn't look at an icemother without frowning, even gazing at the glowing walls with suspicion.

Phoenix took a deep breath, making up her mind. She had to know. 'In the ingredients store, what did you—'

'What *is* that noise?' Five interrupted.

As they descended the steps, the sound of chimes grew louder, beautiful but chilling.

'Some sort of signal,' Phoenix replied, half disappointed, half relieved to change the subject. 'Nara left as soon as she heard it so—'

'You're following her,' Five finished cheerfully. 'Excellent.'

Beneath them, the lake came into view, and it was immediately obvious that something was happening. None of the icemothers were on their plinths.

Footsteps clattered on the stairs behind them and Six sprinted into view.

'What's going on?' he panted, then his eyes scanned the lake beneath. 'Where are all the icemothers?'

'There,' Five said, pointing straight down.

Phoenix followed his gaze and saw he was right. The huge statues were clustered along the edge of the island, the water frozen beneath their feet as they leaned down to speak to Yelara. It seemed most of the witches were already there, Zenith among them. The three friends sped towards her.

'We'll worry about that later,' Yelara was saying, raising her voice so everyone could hear. 'The most important thing is to find it and stop it as soon as possible.'

'What's happened?' Phoenix asked Zenith when they left the feasting tree's steps. For a moment, she thought the witch wasn't going to say anything, the glower she shot Five speaking volumes.

'There's a dark creature inside Icegaard,' she said eventually. 'The icemothers say it crawled out of the lake.'

'What?' Phoenix felt her jaw slacken, turning to look at Zenith properly. The young witch's eyes were wide. She looked frightened. 'How—'

'"How" doesn't matter,' Zenith interrupted. '"Where" is what's important. Didn't you hear what Yelara just said? It needs to be found.' Her eyes darted to the feasting tree and back as she spoke.

'Bet you're glad there are some – what was it? – "jumped-up little Hunters" here now.' Five looked positively cheery.

Zenith stared at him, and Phoenix fought down the urge to step between them.

Instead of lashing out, the young witch made a jerky motion with her head, half nod, half toss. 'Nothing like this has ever happened before,' she said, a brittle tension visible in her. 'If you can find this thing, stop it from hurting anyone . . . yes, I'll be glad of it, of course.'

Phoenix could see how much it cost her to say that. Even Five didn't push her any further, his smile fading as he nodded.

'It's what Hunters do,' he shrugged. 'It doesn't matter if we're in a tiny bog-clan village or Icegaard, our job is to track dark creatures and stop them. We'll help any way we can.'

Zenith stared at him for a moment, then heaved a sigh. 'I'm sorry about the other day,' she muttered, so quiet and muffled and grudging that Phoenix thought she'd misheard.

Five's grin returned, even bigger than before. 'Sorry, Zenith, I didn't quite catch that. What did you say?'

'Five!' Six elbowed him hard and turned to Zenith. 'You're probably wondering if he's always this annoying – it's yes, I'm afraid. I'm trying to convince him his Hunter name should be Mosquito.'

Five gave a snort of amused laughter and the corner of Zenith's mouth twitched.

'I . . .' Five squared his shoulders, facing Zenith properly. 'I'm sorry,' he said, talking quickly. 'I was out of line and . . . you were just trying to—'

'I shouldn't have lashed out,' Zenith said at the same time.

'But I antagonised you.' Five winced. 'I'm good at that.'

'You are.' Six and Phoenix spoke together and everyone snorted with laughter.

Phoenix was surprised by the sudden relief she felt – she liked Zenith. Maybe they could start again.

'What kind of dark creature is it?' she asked.

Her question carried into a sudden silence that had fallen. The icemothers and the witches all turned at the same time, and she tried not to shrink under the focus of so many eyes.

It was one of the icemothers who spoke, crouching down so she was only slightly taller than Phoenix. The ice she was made of squeaked and popped gently as she moved, her eyes as colourless as the rest of her. Phoenix tried not to shiver at the cold that flowed from the living statue, even as her eyes drank in her impossibility. 'It was a wheever that we saw.'

Behind her, the other icemothers nodded their agreement. Phoenix felt Six sway with surprise beside her. Widge squealed his confusion.

'What's a wheever?' Zenith whispered, drawing an amazed look from Five.

'It's a creature of the grasslands,' he said. 'How can you know all about ice-giant treaties, but never have heard of a wheever?'

'I know the dark creatures around Icegaard,' Zenith said, a little defensively. 'And I've read loads about the clans, but . . . just not the dark creatures beyond the Fangs.' She shrugged. 'The clans are more interesting than the dark creatures.'

Five stared at her for a moment. 'You can never properly understand the clans without understanding the creatures they live alongside,' he said, uncharacteristically serious.

Zenith opened her mouth, then closed it again.

Six glanced between them. 'So how about a swap?' he said. Then, in response to everyone's confused looks, 'Zenith knows about Icegaard and the creatures of the Wastes. We know about the clans and creatures south of the Fangs.' He shrugged as though it was obvious. 'So, I propose a trade. A fact for a fact. Simple.' He grinned at them.

Zenith's smile was slow. 'I like that.'

'So do I!' Five said enthusiastically. 'And I know LOADS about the clans. Way more than you'd read in any book. My father was—' He stopped talking abruptly, paled as he realised how close he'd come to revealing something about his life before the Hunting Lodge. 'Sorry,' he said, glancing nervously at Phoenix and Six.

'Don't worry,' Phoenix said quickly. 'You didn't tell us anything.'

She was sure she'd known what he was going to say though: when they'd faced Oakhammer in the Frozen Forest, he'd forced Five to reveal that his father had been a chief. She realised that Five probably wasn't exaggerating; if he'd grown up in a chief's household, he *would* know a lot about the clans.

'It's a good idea,' she said instead. 'We can learn from one another.'

For a moment, the four of them smiled at each other.

'But how can there be a wheever *here*?' A witch's voice rose above the others, jerking Phoenix back to the moment.

She turned to the icemothers, her thoughts racing. 'It's impossible,' she said, speaking up. 'Wheevers never venture north of the Fangs.'

'This we know to be true,' the icemother said, her frozen face grave. 'And yet a wheever is what we all saw.' Behind her, the other icemothers nodded again. 'It dragged itself out of the lake here –' she pointed to the spot where Yelara was standing – 'and headed straight for the feasting tree. It was quick. So fast that we failed to catch it before it was beyond our reach.'

'It seemed to know where it was going,' said another icemother, frowning.

'We should split up,' Phoenix said, turning to Yelara, plans and strategies wheeling through her mind. 'Search the palace in groups of no less than three. Can your witches defend themselves against a dark creature?'

Yelara nodded, although she didn't appear quite as confident as Phoenix would have liked.

'Where are Thea and Libbet?' Phoenix asked, looking around.

'On the eyrie,' said Zenith quickly. 'I sent them there. The ice eagles will protect them.'

The relief on Yelara's face was telling. 'Well done. And you should join them; you're Unfledged too.' Before Zenith could object, Yelara pointed to two witches: an older woman with tight grey curls, and a small mousy-haired one who looked like she wouldn't say boo to a snarrow. 'Fliss and Britt, can you two make sure she gets there safely?'

'Could you go via the library?' Six asked quickly. 'Seven is in there.'

'Of course, dearie,' said Fliss, her grey curls bobbing as she nodded. 'She'll be safe with us.'

'We're battle-magic trained,' Britt added cheerfully, seeing Six's concern.

He nodded, his relief obvious.

Muttering furiously and looking thoroughly put out, Zenith followed the witches back to the feasting tree.

Five watched her go. 'You know, she might not be so bad after all,' he said thoughtfully.

Yelara was organising everyone into groups. She turned to Phoenix, Five and Six. 'Can you three search the sleeping quarters?'

A minute later, the three of them were running back up the trunk stairs, witches' feet pattering all round them as they peeled off into various passages to search different parts of the palace.

'A wheever?' Six panted as they ran. 'The icemothers must've made a mistake.'

'Yes, they must have,' Phoenix gasped. 'We should be ready for anything.'

'Strange luck, isn't it?' he replied, putting on a burst of speed to overtake Phoenix. 'A dark creature breaking in just after Hunters arrive here for the first time in decades.'

His words snagged in Phoenix's mind. 'Strange luck' didn't even begin to cover it. This was a coincidence of monumental proportions.

Five seemed to be thinking the same thing, his feet slowing in time with hers. Ahead of them, Six slowed too, until all three of them were standing stock-still, frowning into space.

'Whatever it is, why *is* it here?' Five said aloud. 'And why now?'

A suspicion formed in Phoenix's mind, so strong that

she was certain she was right. She turned to Five at the same time as Six spun back to them. When they spoke, it was with one voice.

'The Shadowseam.'

CHAPTER 28

'Are you sure you remember the way?' Six gasped as they pelted higher up the stairs. 'All these passages look the same to me.'

'I'm sure,' Phoenix panted, wishing her axes didn't weigh quite so much. 'It's this way.'

'Are we certain we're right about this?' Six asked, his face clouding.

'Why else would it be here now?' Phoenix said breathlessly. 'You heard Zenith: Icegaard has never been broken into.'

'Just like the lodge until three months ago,' Five added, between heaving breaths. 'Then Morgren turns up, does something to the Shadowseam, and now we have a dark creature inside the walls here too. Does that sound like a coincidence to you?'

Six shook his head, too breathless to speak.

'Me neither,' Phoenix said, her heart racing. 'This is connected to Morgren, Victory and the Croke. It has to be.'

Her saliva seemed to vanish when she mentioned the

Croke. She resisted the urge to look over her shoulder as they dashed into the dark part of the tunnel. She couldn't help but notice that the water beneath her feet seemed deeper than before. And all around her was a trickling sound.

They splashed round the final corner, the arch to the Shadowseam's cell appearing before them. The three friends slowed, approaching as quietly as they could, silent ripples spreading from their feet. Widge poked his head out of Phoenix's collar, giving a tiny squeal of concern as he looked around.

'Don't worry, Widge,' Phoenix whispered. The look he gave her was far from convinced.

'What's that?' Five murmured, throwing an arm out to stop them and pointing at something floating nearby.

It looked like a sun-bronzed stem of grass, but when Phoenix picked it up she could see immediately that it wasn't: the edges were too sharp, the tip deadly. It was unmistakably a wheever quill.

'The icemothers were right,' Six said, unable to mask his surprise. 'It *is* a wheever. But how—' He stopped, confused.

Phoenix's mind immediately turned to *A Magical Bestiary*, even as she pushed down a wave of fear. A wheever was a dark creature of the grasslands, where she'd grown up. She remembered vividly her ma drawing its outline in the dirt outside their home in Poa, the point of her stick freshly sharpened.

'*What's this?*' *she asked, her tone warning the two small girls in front of her that this was no laughing matter.*

'*A wheever,*' *they chorused, smothering their giggles.*

'*And what do you do if you see it?*' *she said, her eyes heavy on them.*

'*Run!*' *they both shouted.*

Their ma swallowed a smile, frowned to compensate. '*And if it gives chase?*'

Here, Poppy hesitated, and Starling quickly filled the silence. '*Split up, but don't lose sight of each other. Run faster. Get help.*'

Poppy jumped when Starling nudged her, then caught on and nodded fervently.

Phoenix shook the memory away, tried to ignore the sudden ache in her chest.

'Do you remember the wheever entry from *A Magical Bestiary*?' Six whispered.

'Is that a good idea?' Five asked. 'After the edgeworm, I mean . . .'

'Oi!' Phoenix whacked him none too lightly on the arm. 'I made *one* mistake.'

'One absolutely *ginormous*, life-or-death mistake,' Five said.

'An unfortunate incident,' Phoenix said, her irritation

growing. 'Which mainly affected *me*, not you! And, by the way, feel free to learn the whole book off by heart yourself, Five.'

'Shh,' Six muttered. 'Can you both focus? There's a wheever in there! What do you remember, Phoenix?'

Ignoring Five, Phoenix thought back to the entry in her book and recited: '*These strange creatures thrive in the temperate grasslands and enjoy an omnivorous diet. Their dense, grass-like hair is both their distinguishing feature and effective camouflage. When grazing, wheevers stick to their folded form: four-legged, large and rather bumbling in appearance. These should be treated with caution and avoided where possible. However, if the creature unfolds into its bipedal hunting form – signalling an appetite for meat – it is to be greatly feared. These predators are lithe and fast, incredibly strong and patient. Beware the—*' Phoenix broke off with a frown.

Five's eyebrows shot up. 'Er . . . beware the what? Don't stop now – it was just getting good!'

'Something about its quills,' Phoenix muttered, scouring her memory and finding it infuriatingly blank.

'What about the rankings?' Six asked nervously.

With a grimace, Phoenix shook her head again.

'Not even one? Anything would help.'

'Let's just guess *four* out of ten,' Five muttered darkly under his breath.

'I'm sorry,' Phoenix groaned, ignoring Five. 'It's gone.

I haven't had enough time to study the *Bestiary* recently.' She thought quickly. 'I know we'll be all right if it's in its four-legged form though. Grass-clan villages take care of those themselves, don't even call for Hunters.'

'Great,' Five muttered. 'Let's all hope it's not feeling carnivorous then.'

'All right,' Six whispered. 'Weapons ready?'

Phoenix nodded quickly. All eyes were now on the open doorway. Shadows danced and flickered in the rippling water and already she could feel the chill breeze from the oculus. Her heart beat faster.

On either side of her, Five and Six readied themselves.

Then, in a burst of motion, the three of them leaped through the doorway together.

CHAPTER 29

The Shadowseam was the first thing they saw. It filled the oculus completely, pressing against it and writhing furiously, drawing their attention like a disaster unfolding.

'Phoenix! Six! Concentrate!' Phoenix heard Five hiss. 'Where's the wheever?'

Phoenix tore her eyes away only with difficulty, shuddering. They were lucky the wheever hadn't been lurking by the door: it would have made an easy meal of them.

'Must be behind the oculus,' Six whispered, voicing Phoenix's thoughts. 'We can't see through the seam.'

Together, the three of them edged past the Shadowseam, black water lapping round their ankles, sticking close to the wall where the torches flickered. A few of them guttered in the oculus breeze, their smoke staining the ice with oily black smears.

'Listen,' Five breathed.

Beneath the crackle of the flames, the whirling of air and the distant, reverberating boom of the ocean, there was another noise: a sinister popping, cracking sound. An instant later, they saw what was making it.

'Oh great,' Five muttered.

Phoenix's jaw dropped as the wheever in front of them shifted into its hunting form, the pops and cracks coming from its joints realigning themselves. She stared, aghast, as limbs lengthened, stubby paws stretched into dangerously sharp talons, and its flat, rodent-like jaw lengthened into a wolfish snout filled with gleaming teeth.

'Don't suppose you've remembered those rankings yet?' Six gasped, backing away, scrabbling to string his bow.

'No,' Phoenix said, trying not to panic. 'But they're just numbers, aren't they?'

'Er,' Six said. 'Well—'

'*Incredibly* useful numbers that it'd be *really* helpful to have!' Five cried, his knuckles white round his sword.

'We'll be fine if we stick together,' Phoenix said quickly, hoping she sounded reassuring.

The two boys nodded.

'What's wrong with its eyes?' Six asked a moment later.

Phoenix looked, and immediately saw what he meant. It seemed as though the Shadowseam was reflected in the creature's eyes, but then it turned and she saw it was something much stranger: the darkness was *inside* them, the whites and irises obliterated in a swirling black void.

'That's not normal,' she whispered, backing away and clutching her axes tighter.

'What about this is?' Five snorted, never taking his eyes from the creature.

The dancing torchlight cast shifting shadows, everything confusingly doubled by its reflection in the water on the ground. Phoenix tried to force herself to refocus as the wheever finished unfolding, its stout body lengthening into a tall, streamlined figure ten feet tall. The wet crunches that accompanied this, along with the creature's own agonised yowl, were enough to make her feel nauseous. Widge vanished into her furs and she could feel him curled into a tight, quivering ball against her.

She desperately tried to organise her thoughts, but the sight of the creature morphing was so horrible, so outlandish, that she couldn't concentrate.

'We'd better not get too close to the seam,' Five whispered, sounding almost as shaken as Phoenix felt.

'Agreed,' Six muttered. 'Doesn't leave us a lot of room though.'

Phoenix bit her lip, staring around. Six was right; the Shadowseam filled most of the width of the cell, leaving just enough space at the sides to edge round it. Behind and in front of it, there was a clear space of about thirty feet, but that wasn't enough, especially given that she wasn't sure whether the oculus would prevent them from falling into the Shadowseam, a thought that made her cringe with horror.

Six fired his first arrow just as the creature reached its full height, grassy quills trailing from its back. The wheever's head whipped towards them as the arrow embedded itself in its arm. Its roar was deafening and the friends leaped back, engulfed in the scent of dried grass undercut with something metallic and sour. Six fired two more arrows in quick succession. Both found their mark, and the creature sprang forward. With a spine-tingling hiss, its arm shot out – its reach easily twice what any of them would have expected – and swiped the bow from Six's hands. The weapon snapped with a horrible crack and, to everyone's horror, passed straight through the oculus and into the Shadowseam, vanishing immediately.

Six gave a cry of dismay and Phoenix's heart sank; if a bow could fall into the seam, then a person could too.

The wheever leaped towards them once more, its black eyes unreadable, but its intention clear as it lunged again for Six. Five wrenched him back just in time, cursing how the water slowed him down as he hacked at the creature's arm, nicking it to draw another terrifying howl.

The Shadowseam swelled, massing behind the oculus closest to where the fight was, as though inflamed by it.

'Careful!' Phoenix shouted as Five bundled Six round the seam to the safer side of the oculus. She slashed furiously at the wheever, driving it back a pace.

'I've still got my dagger!' she heard Six cry.

'Yeah, very useful, I'm sure,' Five muttered, reappearing, only to duck as the wheever lashed out again.

A moment later, to their shock, Six emerged from the other side of the seam, right behind the wheever.

'What are you doing?' Phoenix yelled.

'If we're on both sides of it, we can distract it from each other!' Six called back.

Along the creature's spine, its quills quivered. Phoenix stared, frantically trying to remember what *A Magical Bestiary* had said about them. It came to her in a sudden, horrifying rush.

'The quills are projectile!' she yelled just as several of them fired at Six with deadly accuracy. He managed to avoid them only by hurling himself to the wet ground, the spines piercing the softening ice only a few inches above him.

'Yep,' he gasped. 'So I see!'

An instant later, the wheever had turned from Five and Phoenix, sensing Six's weakness. Now its back faced them and they were the ones in danger from the quills.

'Are you thinking what I'm thinking?' Five called.

'I have no idea,' Phoenix replied, diving aside to avoid more of the creature's spines. Widge squeaked his annoyance as cold water seeped through her furs.

'Six's bow vanished into the seam!' Five said. 'Do you think a wheever would vanish too?'

'You want to drive it into the oculus?' she asked, half horrified, half impressed.

'Worth a try!' Six yelled, diving under the wheever's arms and circling towards them. He was dripping wet. 'It might make our job a whole lot easier. It's too tall to easily kill, especially now I've lost my bow.'

The wheever whipped round to face the three of them, side by side again. The creature was now directly between them and the Shadowseam, its reflection making it seem twice as tall as it was. Phoenix nodded, Six's words sparking an idea in her. She backed away from her two friends, her axes in her hands. Her eyes never left the wheever as it crept closer, surrounded by its own flickering shadows and the gathering darkness of the seam behind it.

'I think I know how to do it,' she called. 'Six, get down on your hands and knees.'

'What?'

'Just do it!'

As he knelt down, grumbling at the coldness of the water, Phoenix was already running towards him at full tilt. In three strides, she splashed across the space between them, then leaped forward, planting her foot firmly between his shoulder blades, using him as a springboard to hurl herself up at the wheever.

It gave her the extra height she needed, and she slammed hard into its chest, driving her axe into its shoulder. She felt the wheever hiss and totter backwards, her momentum catching it off guard. Its jaws snapped dangerously close to her face, then they were both falling, the creature's arms windmilling on either side of her, Five and Six's shouts ringing in her ears.

'Jump, Phoenix!' both boys screamed, voices laced with panic. Phoenix saw with horror that the creature had staggered back far enough that its top half would fall straight into the oculus, taking her with it.

The Shadowseam loomed larger and larger in front of her, its mass writhing even faster, as though excited. With a twist and a furious wrench, she managed to pull her axe free and throw herself away from the wheever, just as its head passed through the containment spell. She hit the ground hard, water exploding from beneath her, and rolled away. Her heart beat frantically as Five and Six hauled her up, dragging her further back.

For the first time, she became aware of other voices, raised and drawing closer every second, but her eyes were latched on to the oculus. The wheever's head and shoulders had vanished into the Shadowseam while its legs scrabbled desperately for purchase in the film of shadowy water outside the oculus.

Suddenly there were witches all around them, pulling them further back, calling instructions to one another to renew the oculus.

But Phoenix couldn't take her eyes off the wheever's legs. The scrabbling faded to a horrible twitching, then they were still. Abruptly, with a speed that made her cry out in surprise, the wheever was tugged into the Shadowseam and disappeared completely.

Phoenix felt the air leave her lungs, her knees suddenly shaky. That could so easily have been her. Or Five. Or Six. Her fear of the Shadowseam grew even more powerful. The witches might claim not to know what it was, but she did: a monster so strong that it devoured other monsters. She couldn't shake the uncomfortable feeling that she'd just fed it.

Five and Six pulled her out of her reverie.

'I can't believe it broke my bow,' Six said, outraged, squeezing water from his sopping furs. 'And Phoenix *jumped* on me.'

Phoenix opened her mouth to reply, but Five got there first. 'You let her,' he snorted.

'I had no idea that's what she was planning to do!' Six exclaimed.

'The wheever was too tall for me!' Phoenix spluttered,

defensive. 'It was the only way! And I jumped *off* you, not on to you! There's a difference!'

Five grinned. 'If you say so. But let's face it, that wasn't exactly Six's most dignified moment.'

To Phoenix's intense relief, Nara joined them, gently pulling them away from the circle of witches forming round the Shadowseam. 'Are you all right?'

She relaxed only when they'd each assured her several times that they were fine.

'It's certainly impressive what you can do with those axes, Phoenix,' Nara said. Then, to all of them: 'Was it some Hunter instinct that made you realise the creature was in here?'

'Not really,' Six said. 'We wondered if it might have been attracted to the Shadowseam.' He gestured around them. 'It obviously was.'

Nara nodded slowly, her face troubled. 'How in Ember did it get this far north though, let alone *inside* Icegaard?'

Yelara broke from the circle of witches and came to join them, her face grave. 'That,' she said, 'is something we must discover as quickly as possible.'

'It's got to be the seam,' Phoenix said quietly. 'It's devouring Icegaard from the inside, and now it's drawing other creatures to it too, maybe to help it, maybe just to eat them.' She realised with a jolt of shock that she almost felt sorry for the wheever.

Yelara crossed her arms tightly, a muscle flickering in her cheek. Phoenix could feel the force of will it took for the Headwitch not to look at her, not to ask how her lessons were going, when she'd be ready to destroy the seam.

The pressure was smothering and, as Phoenix turned to leave the watery, torch-lit chamber with Five and Six, it took all of her willpower not to run.

CHAPTER 30

Phoenix's feet were carrying her to find Seven before she'd even realised where she was going. After the chaos and danger of the wheever attack, more than anything she wanted her friend's reassuring presence, her quiet calm.

On the eyrie, she discovered Seven had returned to the library the moment she'd found out it was safe. And, now that Phoenix was outside it, the place itself piqued her curiosity. The doors in front of her were three times her height, carved with scenes from Ember that constantly shifted and changed. A frost-deer wandered across a snow-strewn meadow, ears swivelling as it dipped its graceful head to graze. A moment later, the scene vanished to be replaced by an enormous river-clan village floating along the Ilara, alarmed trillpeeps bursting from the dense reeds it brushed past.

Phoenix shook herself: the doors were mesmerising, but Seven was on the other side of them. Suddenly buzzing with anticipation, she stepped forward and pushed them open.

Ice. Light. Paper.

Her breath left her in a sigh; the library was wildly beautiful.

The oval space was huge and gleamed with the ethereal light of the frost palace's ice. The Shadowseam's influence hadn't reached this far at least. Phoenix tilted her head back to better take it all in. Books and scrolls lined every inch of the soaring, curved walls. A score of balconies wound themselves round the room, glittering, ice-carven staircases spiralling up between them.

Phoenix's senses reeled, stretched in every direction. Seven had said the library was enormous, but that felt like a ridiculous understatement: a person could spend years in here and still not have studied everything it held.

Where was Seven though?

Phoenix turned on the spot, examining each balcony level until she spotted a flash of bright red hair high above her. Widge gave a cheery trill, his whiskers twitching happily when he saw her too.

'Seven?' Phoenix called.

The other girl was so intent on her reading that she didn't hear. Phoenix climbed up the nearest stairs spiralling up to Seven's level.

Phoenix's first thought was that she was lucky to have spotted Seven at all: her friend was sitting on the floor with so many books and scrolls piled up around her, she was in danger of being buried by them. They rustled madly as Seven glanced at one, then shoved it aside in favour of another.

'Careful!' Phoenix gasped as a haphazard pile of books wobbled, dangerously close to toppling on her friend's head.

Seven's yelp was almost a shriek and two of the books she'd been looking at flew over the balcony edge, pages flapping wildly before they landed with dual resounding slaps on the floor far below.

'Phoenix!' Seven squeaked, spinning to face her and sending more scrolls flying. The pile of books teetered and Phoenix leaped forward to stop them falling on the other girl.

'What are you doing here?' Seven asked. To Phoenix's surprise, she saw her hurriedly pull a scroll over one of the books she'd been examining.

'I just came to tell you about the wheever—' Phoenix broke off, her curiosity too strong. 'What's that you're looking at?'

'This lot?' Seven laughed uneasily. 'A b-bit of everything.' She picked up a ragged scroll and waved it at Phoenix. 'Some goblin magic mentioned in here.' Another scroll. 'This one t-talks about something called a "rift". I thought it might be related to our Shadowseam, but –' Seven shook her head and tossed it aside –'I don't think it is.' She picked up a book bound in red silk.

'This has some exercises for clarifying visions that I'm going to t-try this evening—'

'And what about—'

Phoenix pointed at the book Seven had covered up. But, before she could finish, Seven interrupted. 'Wait! D-did you just say you wanted to tell me about a *wheever*?'

'You haven't heard?' Phoenix asked. 'Didn't Zenith tell you on the eyrie?'

Seven scowled at the mention of the young witch.

'She's all right, you know,' Phoenix said cheerfully. 'She and Five made up. Five even apologised!'

To Phoenix's surprise, Seven didn't meet her eye, just shrugged and began shuffling some loose pages. Phoenix stared at her for a moment, confused. 'Seven?'

'What?' Seven asked, looking up. The challenge was as surprising as it was unmistakable. What reason did Seven have to dislike Zenith any more than the others?

'So . . . she didn't tell you about the wheever?' Phoenix said awkwardly when it became clear Seven wasn't going to break the silence.

Seven shook her head, looking relieved. 'Two witches came with her: Fliss and Britt. They were very insistent I go with them, so I took some books up with me.' She shrugged, awkward. 'They were all talking, but I didn't really listen. I was reading.'

A few minutes later, Phoenix had filled Seven in, and

the other girl was staring at her with frank amazement. 'It was *inside* the frost palace? But how? They're never normally—'

'Found outside the grasslands,' Phoenix finished for her. 'I know.' She shook her head. 'I suppose the Shadowseam lured it here, but . . .' She trailed off, bit her lip. 'It just doesn't make sense.'

Seven frowned. 'No, it doesn't.' She pointed to the untidy stack of books teetering nearby. 'Those are the witches' records of the seam – an entry every day for the last forty years. It's never attracted dark creatures before.'

'So . . . Morgren might've . . . changed it into something else?' Phoenix asked hesitantly.

'I don't know.' Seven scrubbed a hand over her face. Only then did Phoenix notice how pale she looked. 'I've scoured the shelves for g-goblin texts, but there's very little left. Jira must have taken everything to where she was working – which means it was all lost.' Her shoulders slumped. 'I'm so sorry, Phoenix.'

'Don't apologise,' Phoenix said quickly, even as her heart sank. 'We knew it'd be a long shot.'

'I thought I could help you,' Seven murmured, her head bowed.

'You have,' Phoenix said firmly. 'Not by solving unsolvable problems though, just by being you.'

Seven gave her a rather watery smile as the library

doors burst open to admit Five and Six, both talking loudly.

'There!' Five crowed, pointing up. '*Told* you Phoenix would be here too!' He lowered his voice, but not enough to prevent Phoenix hearing him add, 'Hopefully, she's studying *A Magical Bestiary*. She *really* needs to brush up on it.'

'Seven,' Six called hurriedly, seeing Phoenix's annoyance, 'you haven't trained for days now. If there are dark creatures roaming around the frost palace, you need to be able to defend yourself.'

'Yeah,' Five said. 'Also, Hoarfrost will kill us if he ever finds out we didn't train with you every day.'

Seven gestured at all the thousands of shelves. 'Do you think I've finished reading all these yet?'

'Hopefully,' Five said. 'You've been up there long enough.'

'Have you ever actually r-read a book?' Seven snorted. 'You have no concept of the time it takes!'

Five shrugged, unrepentant. 'Are you coming down or not? Personally, I'd rather you weren't gobbled up by the next nasty thing that wanders through here.'

'Same,' Six said quickly, his eyes fixed on his sister, silently pleading with her.

'It might be a good idea to take a break anyway,' Phoenix said gently. 'Do something different for a bit, then come back fresh.'

Below them, Six nodded eagerly. 'That sounds sensible to me!'

'Fine.' Seven sighed, rising to her feet and heading for the stairs. 'Can we do it in here though? I want to get back to work as soon as possible.'

Phoenix turned to follow her, then hesitated, remembering the book Seven had hidden from her. She knew it was a sneaky thing to do, but, before she could think about it too hard, she'd reached out to brush the scroll off the open book, twisting her head to read the words. Except there weren't any – both pages were perfectly blank. And, when Phoenix flicked a few pages back and forth, they were blank too.

Strange.

Six's outraged voice distracted her. 'Seven, *where* is your dagger?'

Phoenix hurried down the gleaming spiral staircase to join them.

'Oh.' Seven glanced down at her belt, conspicuously empty of her knife. 'I must've forgotten to pick it up this morning.'

'So you have no weapons,' Five said flatly. 'Honestly, it's like you *want* to be eaten by a monster!' Shaking his head, he unbuckled his own dagger. 'Here, take mine. But don't forget yours tomorrow, all right?'

Seven nodded miserably. Phoenix could practically see the focus she'd had moments before vanishing. Her shoulders hunched as Six handed her a wooden sword. Really, there was no one less suited to becoming a Hunter. Phoenix pushed the thought away as soon as it came.

'Just relax,' she advised. 'You fight so much better when you're not worrying about it.'

'It's h-hard not to worry when you have so many weapons pointed at you,' Seven said darkly, eyeing the axes Phoenix had swung off her back without really noticing. Beside her, Five had drawn his sword and Six his dagger.

Widge gave a sharp squeak of agreement, then leaped to Seven's shoulder to offer his support.

'Traitor,' Phoenix muttered, but Seven brightened the moment the squirrel landed on her.

'Why don't we work on your attack today?' Six suggested, planting himself in front of his sister. 'See if you can land a blow on me.' Then, seeing her concern, 'Don't worry – I won't hurt you.'

Seven smiled weakly. 'M-maybe I'm worried about hurting you.'

'That's the spirit,' Five grinned. 'Fighting talk!'

'Yes, go for it, Seven,' said Phoenix. 'You can do it.'

'Hey!' Six exclaimed, glancing back at them both. 'It's like you want her to win! Wasn't being jumped on by Phoenix— OUCH!'

While Six was looking away, Seven had crept closer and bopped him firmly on the head with her wooden sword.

'What was that for?' he gasped, rubbing his skull.

'We're practising, aren't w-we?' Seven said, her mouth twitching. 'You w-were distracted. It seemed like a good opportunity. Isn't d-distraction one of the things I'm supposed to take advantage of during an attack?'

Five sniggered. 'She makes a good point.'

A few minutes later, Phoenix was having to hold her breath and avoid Five's eye to stop herself from laughing out loud. Seven had managed to land blows on Six multiple times through various unconventional means, including pointing out his laces were undone and pretending she'd sprained her ankle.

Unfortunately, Six's patience was clearly running out. 'You're not taking this seriously,' he said, rubbing his arm where she'd just whacked him again. 'What dark creature is going to stop because you may or may not have hurt your ankle?'

Seven grinned, clearly surprised to be enjoying herself. 'I d-don't know, but you're the one attacking me now and these t-tactics seem to be working just fine.'

Six sighed. 'You're missing the point on purpose.'

Seven shrugged. 'Well, I'm never going to beat you if I play by your rules, am I? So I'm doing it my way.'

'There is a logic there,' Five said thoughtfully. 'But I think Six's right. I'm not sure what you're doing would work against a Grim.'

'My turn,' Phoenix said, stepping forward to replace Six before an argument could break out.

'Checked your laces?' Seven grinned. On her shoulder, Widge trilled merrily.

'You're really staying on her side?' Phoenix asked him, her eyebrows raised.

Then she yelped in surprise. Seven was suddenly pelting towards her, yowling at the top of her lungs and whirling her sword round her head at speed. Phoenix gawped, so disconcerted she almost forgot to hurl herself aside; Seven's wooden sword caught in her hair, pulling out a few strands.

'What was that?' she choked, half amused, half cross.

'A surprise attack,' Seven said, smiling beatifically. '*Another* one.'

'You have to admit, she *is* quite good at finding ways to catch us off guard,' Five said, stepping forward. 'My turn. I have to warn you though, Seven, you'll find me *much* harder to take by surprise than— Hey! Where are you going?'

Instead of running towards Five, Seven had darted away, up the nearest spiral staircase.

'You're s-supposed to be a dark creature, aren't you?' Seven called over her shoulder. 'Shouldn't you be chasing m-me?'

She grinned as Five followed, a scowl on his face. 'A dark creature would probably be making some sort of noise too,' she called down. 'Maybe grunting or oinking or— What? Don't you want this to be realistic?'

'This is demeaning,' Five said flatly, ignoring Six's howl of mirth. He glanced at Seven as he trudged up the stairs after her. 'What are you going to do with that?' he asked, nodding at a huge book in her hands.

Seven shrugged. 'Make you read it?'

Then, while Five was rolling his eyes extravagantly, she threw the heavy tome, catching him hard in the chest. Three more followed in quick succession, knocking him back a few steps.

'Oi! That's not fair!' Five yelped as Phoenix and Six collapsed with laughter.

'I think it is,' Seven beamed, Widge bouncing cheerfully in agreement. 'And, since I've now beaten all three of you, I'm going to return to my reading.' With that, she headed back to her pile of books. 'You were right, Phoenix. I do feel better for having done something else for a bit,' she called over her shoulder. 'Thanks!'

With a happy trill and a complex wave of his tail, Widge sprang from Seven's shoulder and streamed back to Phoenix's where he stared at her fixedly until she reached up to scratch his cheek the way he liked it.

Five stomped back to Phoenix and Six. 'You're right, Six,' he muttered, shaking his head. 'She didn't take that seriously at all.'

'I don't know,' Phoenix said, grinning, inexplicably

buoyed. 'I think we underestimated her and she took advantage of it.'

'Quite clever really,' Six said grudgingly, still rubbing his head.

Five made a sound of disgust.

High above them, the top of Seven's vibrant hair vanished behind an enormous pile of scrolls.

CHAPTER 31

'Stop shooting at me!' Dog barked, his hackles rising as yet another woodpecker-fletched arrow bounced off him.

Several groups of forest-clan warriors were pouring out of the Great Woods, each of them heavily armed.

A man pushed to the front of the crowd, his breastplate made of dense black wood hardened with ymbre. 'What are you doing here, Guardian?' he called. His eyes were narrowed, suspicious. Then he caught sight of the lutra by Dog's feet and staggered with the shock of it.

Dog knew he had only moments to act. 'Listen to me!' he cried. 'One of your home-trees was attacked and you are certain the river clan are responsible. Correct?' The man glowered, then gave a grudging nod. Dog lowered his nose to the lutra. 'Here lies a murdered lutra. The knife that killed her is of forest-clan design. The river folk will be convinced that you were responsible.'

Roars of furious dissent spread through the angry group before him.

'Silence!' Dog barked, standing as tall as he possibly could.

The people before him were furious and perhaps the only thing they would respond to was a strength they perceived greater than their own. His tactic seemed to work and they quietened.

'We had nothing to do with that,' the lead warrior said, nodding at the lutra.

'I know it,' Dog growled.

The time for secrecy was over; Victory was long gone. He had perhaps only a few minutes to avert disaster.

'The lodge's own weaponsmaster was responsible for both these crimes.'

He saw the hesitation on the warriors' faces and spoke faster to convince them.

'You have heard of the misfortune of the Hunting Lodge,' he called, raising his voice so they could all hear. 'That our weaponsmaster betrayed us. She was seen in this area three days ago. She killed three Hunters here.'

The warriors nodded; they'd heard this.

'Bad business,' one woman muttered, her hand still tight round her spear.

'Victory's treachery goes further still,' Dog barked. 'She seeks to sow hatred. It was she who harmed your home-tree and murdered this lutra, in the hope of starting a war between your clans. She thinks all she needs to be successful is a feather and a knife. But I know you will prove her wrong.'

'What evidence do you have?' challenged the man in the black breastplate.

'Honestly,' scowled Sharpspark, his wings a hot blur beside Dog's ear, 'how can you stand to be quizzed by them? Shall I teach them a lesson for you?'

'Quiet, Sharpspark,' Dog said, but it was too late. The eyes of the forest clan were on the firesprite, and their horror was obvious.

'That's him!' shouted someone. 'That's the sprite who set fire to the broken tree!'

Dog gazed at Sharpspark in dismay, and the sprite shrugged, unapologetic.

'It was already dying,' he said. 'I saw no harm. It was a glorious blaze, a fitting end.' An arrow shot past him as he spoke, close enough to make him wobble in mid-air. His flames brightened until he was painful to look at. 'How *dare* you!' he shrieked.

Dog could feel his control of the situation slipping away.

And that was the moment the river clan arrived.

Behind him came the rhythmic slice and sweep of many oars in the water. When he turned, his heart in his mouth, he saw the boy's canoe had been joined by many, many others. Each full of river folk, all armed to the teeth.

'Greetings,' he called, all too aware of the tension

humming through the group behind him, the arrows nocked and drawn tight. 'I am—'

'It's true!' The howl came from the lead boat, raw with fury and pain. A woman stood in the prow, pointing at the lutra, her fish-skin jerkin gleaming.

Roars of horror and rage rose behind her and the paddling doubled in speed.

'Hear me!' barked Dog. 'Listen!'

'Warriors, ready yourselves!' He heard the cry go up from the forest clan behind him, saw the light glint off the leaf-shaped spear tips as the first canoe touched the bank.

In one smooth movement, the woman in the prow leaped out, landed next to the lutra and pulled the knife from its side. The blood on the knife no longer shone, but the shape of the blade itself was unmistakable. She held it over her head so those still on the water could see it and their howls of fury cut to a silence far more ominous.

'It's too late to stop this,' Sharpspark whispered to Dog, careful not to touch him as he fluttered uncomfortably close to his maimed ear. Dog could feel the sprite's heat searing him as never before. 'You tried, but they won't be turned from one another now. We should leave, warn the fiery girl of what you saw.'

Dog growled. He wanted nothing more than to leave this place. But he couldn't let these two groups slaughter one another.

When the first forest-clan spear was hurled, he did the only thing he could, and sprang to meet it, snapping it in two with a quick crunch of his jaws.

Immediately, cries of outrage rose.

'He works with the river clan!'

'He protects *them*!'

Dog wished he was bigger, wished he was louder. 'Listen to me!' he barked. 'I represent the Hunting Lodge as I have done for a thousand years!'

He hoped the mention of his great age would lend him authority, but it was not to be. The forest clan pressed forward and the river clan followed suit, baring their teeth, the air between them alive with violence. Dog could feel the electricity of it fizzing between them, knew a single spark would tip everything beyond the point of no return.

Another arrow was fired, this time from the river clan, and Dog leaped to block it with his shoulder, only just managing to swallow his yelp of pain.

'The person responsible for this is Victory!' he barked, turning on the spot with Sharpspark above him, trying to meet every eye. '*She* is the one who must be caught. *She* is the one who must be punished. Why do you think I am here?'

'River clan, hold your fire!'

The voice came from the water, from one of the boats yet to reach the bank. Dog recognised it immediately though and turned to it, a hopeful whine building in his throat.

'Chief Torrent?' he called.

Behind him, the forest folk murmured their shock. The river-clan chief was as elusive as an eel, the rumours about her as strange as her authority was unquestioned. Even Sharpspark looked interested. If Dog could just convince *her* that Victory had done this . . .

She was exactly as he remembered. Sturdy and river-beaten, she stepped out of the canoe with a lightness that belied her age. Her fish-skin jerkin shone like polished silver over a riversilk shirt while gold-brushed fishbones and green mallard feathers decorated her coiled black hair. She looked every inch the chief that she was.

Sharpspark fluttered closer to Dog's ear. 'There's something strange about her,' he whispered, none too quietly.

'Shh,' Dog growled.

'Well met, Guardian,' Torrent said, her gaze warm on Dog, curious on Sharpspark. 'How long has it been?'

'Eighty-four years,' Dog replied, sensing the ripple of unease from the forest warriors. Sharpspark made a rather undignified sound of surprise.

Even Dog could barely believe it. He stared at Torrent, almost against his will, hunting for differences in her, even tiny ones, and finding none. At least some of the rumours about her must be true: she looked exactly the same as when he'd last set eyes on her all those years ago. Even her scent was unaltered: intelligence, waterlilies, discipline.

The river clan clustered round their chief, their protective instincts warring with the need to keep a respectful distance from her.

Torrent knelt by the lutra, and bowed her head over the creature.

Dog knew he should wait, but too many thoughts were leaping round his head. He stepped closer, trying to ignore the fishing spears and daggers suddenly levelled at him.

'Torrent,' he said, hoping his desperation wasn't obvious, 'the forest clan did not do this. I promise you.'

When she looked up at him, her expression was lost. 'This is the lutra that saved me as a child,' she whispered. 'I was drowned by a ripplewrack and this creature brought me back. Did you know that, Guardian?'

Dog nodded. It was one of many stories told about her. 'I have heard that, yes.' He dipped his head to where she crouched, hoping to offer some measure of solace. 'I am sorry.'

Torrent stood slowly, and Dog saw the moment her grief slipped into rage, the sudden fire that blazed up in her. Her fists were clenched, but her voice stayed steady when she spoke. 'If not them –' her eyes raked the forest-clan warriors, and Dog saw one actually step back – 'then who?'

Her gaze was a fishhook, impossible to escape.

'She is fierce!' Sharpspark whispered in his ear, clearly impressed. Dog ignored him with difficulty: this was too important to allow himself to be distracted by the sprite.

'Victory,' he said simply. 'It was her.'

'How can you be so sure?'

Dog's eyes slipped to the lutra. 'She showed me.'

Suddenly Torrent's hands were on either side of Dog's face, her grip fierce. Her eyes searched his, his nose almost touching hers, until she pulled back suddenly.

'She touched you too,' Torrent whispered, her shock obvious. 'I see it in you.'

Dog nodded.

The chief turned to her warriors. 'Take the lutra,' she said. 'Prepare her for a river burial as lovingly as you would a member of your own family.' She raised her eyebrows when they didn't immediately respond. 'Go!'

The crowd around her shifted uncertainly.

'We cannot leave you here alone,' someone whispered. 'Unprotected.'

'Not with *them*,' spat another, all eyes turning to the forest clan.

'I am not alone. I am with the Guardian of the Hunting Lodge,' Torrent replied. She levelled her gaze at the forest-clan warriors, their dark and mutinous stances. 'But I see the Guardian's explanation has not satisfied you on the subject of your home-tree. This must be addressed. I call a moot, on this spot, one week from now.'

The warrior who'd spoken before stepped forward, nodded to Torrent. 'A moot. Here. One week from now. I will tell Chief Broadleaf.' With that, the forest folk seemed to melt into the shadows, vanishing back into the trees.

'Uncanny,' Torrent said softly to Dog, 'how they do that.' Then they both watched in silence as the lutra was placed gently in a canoe and paddled away by an ageing warrior, his face salted with tears.

'Do you think this moot will resolve the destruction of the home-tree?' Dog asked Torrent, the woods drawing his gaze. 'I can offer no absolute proof, but I know it was Victory.'

Torrent's lips pressed together. 'Broadleaf is a reasonable man. But his tribe are restless and there have been too many incidents between our clans recently.' She shook her head slowly. 'I have delayed the bloodshed. That is all.'

Dog nodded, tension itching through him. He needed to leave this place; he needed to get to Icegaard, to Phoenix. Sharpspark seemed to feel the same, flying higher, his flames brightening.

'There is somewhere else you need to be,' Torrent said, her eyes flicking between Dog and the firesprite.

Dog nodded. 'Your lutra showed me Victory attacking her. In the moments afterwards, the weaponsmaster threatened someone I know. I believe I know where she is going.'

'This "someone" is very dear to you,' Torrent surmised.

Dog nodded again, ignoring sounds of impatience from Sharpspark above him.

'Then you must go,' Torrent said softly. Her eyes narrowed. 'But, when you catch Victory, I expect her to be brought to me to answer for her crimes. Will you promise that, Guardian?'

'I promise,' Dog said, turning to leave. 'Although there are others who share the right to judge her.' He felt tightly coiled, the need to run shivering through him. He had to get to Icegaard, and as quickly as possible.

Torrent rested her hand on his shoulder, hesitated before she spoke. 'A lutra's touch is a strange gift, Guardian.'

Dog looked back at her, an inexplicable fear suddenly in him. 'Do you know what it will do to me?'

Torrent shook her head slowly. 'It bestows health, heals all disease, cures all ills. I myself am one hundred and fifty years old, yet I feel the same as I did at thirty.' Her eyes ran over Dog. 'But you are not flesh and blood. I cannot say how the magic will affect you.'

'I can taste now,' Dog said quietly, still marvelling at the fact.

Torrent's eyebrows shot up. 'So soon,' she murmured. Then, in response to Dog's quizzical look, 'Some of the effects are instantly felt; others take longer to come into being.' She frowned slightly. 'Prepare yourself for the fact that in the coming weeks there may be other changes in you.'

Dog didn't know what to say, so he just nodded. As he made to leave, a final thought occurred to him. 'It is unusual for me to see familiar faces between my awakenings,' he said over his shoulder to Torrent. 'Normally, those I knew are dead by the time I am called upon again. Seeing you has been . . . strange.'

Torrent smiled. 'It was a pleasure for me too.'

'Come on!' Sharpspark called from above, his impatience reaching incendiary levels.

Dog saw Torrent shoot a bemused look between him and the firesprite before he faced into the cold, snow-scented breeze from the north and began to run as fast as he could.

With each enormous bound, his heart lifted a little – he would see Phoenix again soon.

CHAPTER 32

Several days had passed since the wheever's invasion of Icegaard, but everyone was still on edge. The icemothers had scoured every inch of the lake and the Hunters the exterior of the palace, but none of them had discovered the creature's entry point. As a result, watches had been set inside, and the ice eagles were patrolling the skies.

Phoenix was exhausted. Her lessons with Nara had moved to one of the still-bright witcheries near the ingredients store. But otherwise progress had stalled. Phoenix still needed to be knocked out two or three times per session.

'This is useless,' she growled at the end of another fruitless class. Her head ached and her heart was pounding as though she'd been sprinting. She scuffed the heel of her boot on the floor. 'It's just the same thing every day. It doesn't *want* to be controlled.'

She tried not to think of the Shadowseam watching her, laughing at her. Sometimes, usually at night, the Croke and the Shadowseam merged in her mind into one terrifying darkness, leaving her gasping at the itching, creeping horror both entities instilled in her. Needless to say, between that and worrying about Dog, she hadn't been sleeping well.

'Your fire doesn't "want" anything, Phoenix,' Nara said gently. 'Magic doesn't have a will of its own.'

'Are you sure about that?'

'Quite sure,' said Nara. 'There will be a way for you to channel it more effectively. We just have to find it.'

The witch spoke calmly, but Phoenix knew that she was worried. Phoenix and her friends had been at the frost palace for a week now and she was no closer to controlling her fire than she had been on the first day. Meanwhile, the Shadowseam had drained five more witcheries, the sparring room and many of the unused bedrooms of their magic. Darkness was spreading through Icegaard at a frightening rate and water now flowed down the passage outside the ingredients store.

So much was riding on Phoenix, the pressure was unbearable. She saw the looks the witches gave her – painfully hopeful – and she wanted to hide from them, found herself avoiding them whenever she could.

On her shoulder, Widge pressed himself against her cheek, chittering his support.

'I'd better go,' she said tiredly to Nara. 'Yelara asked us to patrol the crypts. We're going to spend the night down there.'

'The whole night?' Nara asked, her eyebrows shooting up.

'We volunteered,' Phoenix said with a shrug. 'They're directly under the lake after all – it could be where the wheever got in.'

Since the wheever attack, Zenith and Five had moved past their altercation. Zenith still spouted Icegaard information at every opportunity, but Five now responded with facts about Ember instead of irritation. It was a situation that seemed to suit them both, to everyone's relief.

Nara sighed. 'I see. Do try to get some sleep down there, Phoenix. Our work here is so important and I'd like us to continue tomorrow if you're not too tired.'

Again, Phoenix felt the unbearable weight of the witches' hope pressing down on her. She nodded weakly. 'I'll do my best.'

Nara nodded, smiled. 'Good luck then. Not that you need it, of course.'

A short while later, Phoenix found Headwitch Yelara with Zenith at the bottom of the feasting tree. The two older witches, Fliss and Britt, were there too. Each of the three carried a bag of blankets and food. Phoenix checked her axes and hurried over, grinning when Zenith waved at her.

'Phoenix!' Yelara smiled as she arrived. 'Good. It's just Five and Six we're waiting for then.'

'They said they were going to search through the old

weapons for shields and a bow for Six,' Zenith said.

A minute later, the boys arrived, each triumphantly bearing an enormous wooden shield as thick as an arm. Six was also carrying a bow, freshly strung, the old wood gleaming with oil.

'I think it might actually be better than my other one,' he said, his face glowing with excitement. 'It shoots a bit further and doesn't drift to the left at all.'

'That straw dummy didn't stand a chance,' Five said drily.

'Nor will any dark creatures we meet,' Six beamed.

'Six is going to take care of everything while the rest of us hide behind these,' Five said jokingly, gesturing to the huge shields.

Phoenix laughed. 'Thanks, Six, that's generous of you! Are you both going to be able to carry those all night though?'

'Of course!' Six exclaimed.

Widge clambered out of Phoenix's bearskin to have a look and gave a doubtful chirp.

'Negativity is an unattractive trait in a squirrel, Widge,' Five said indignantly. 'I'll have you know I'm much stronger than I appear.'

'Same,' Six said cheerfully.

Widge's face seemed to say, 'We'll see'.

Britt smiled at the Hunters. 'So, which of you will be organising us?'

'Her.' Six and Five spoke in unison, both pointing at Phoenix.

A flicker of pride and fear sparked inside her, but she pushed it down. When she spoke, she was pleased her voice sounded authoritative.

'It's a massive space down there. We'll patrol to cover as much of it as possible, then split into two groups later to take turns to rest. Does that sound all right?'

Everyone nodded.

Yelara smiled at Phoenix. 'It sounds like you have a plan,' she said approvingly. Then she turned towards the lake to wave over the nearest icemothers.

In unison, the six closest statues stepped down from their plinths on to the water, which froze beneath them immediately. Together, they walked over to the assembled group, their footsteps crunching then melting behind them.

The statue in the lead was younger than the others, frost feathers braided in her icy hair. Phoenix tried not to shiver as the icemother bent down in front of Yelara, sending a gust of ferociously cold air over them, her frost-white eyes sweeping the group. 'The crypts?' she asked.

Yelara nodded. 'Yes, please, Linnet.'

The icemothers arrayed themselves in two rows of three on the lake. Then, as one, they reached up so their fingers brushed those of the statue opposite, creating an arched tunnel beneath them. Immediately, the water below began to seethe, pushing outwards so that a trench formed between two walls of gleaming, writhing liquid. Now the group could see what had been hidden: a dripping set of steps leading down to a door made of bone.

'Good luck!' Yelara called softly as the group descended.

'No need for it,' Five said cheerfully, patting his new shield.

Behind the door was a steeply descending path. Torches in sconces on the walls lit themselves as the group moved forward and the air grew noticeably cooler.

'Expect the unexpected,' Phoenix said to the others. 'Remember there could be anything down here.'

'Good thinking,' Five said seriously. 'Personally, I'm hoping for pepperroot biscuits.' He turned to Britt with a grin. 'How about you?'

The mousy-haired witch laughed. 'Some warm weather would be nice.'

'Honestly,' Phoenix muttered, trying to cover a sudden urge to smile.

Together, the group continued down until the path ended in a vanishing darkness. Five, Six and the witches gathered behind Phoenix, peering into the chill gloom. The darkness in the crypts wasn't caused by the Shadowseam, but it was still unnerving. In the distance, a torch flared, then another and another until pinpricks of light stretched away as far as Phoenix could see.

In every direction, shadowy rows of tombs appeared, sweeping away from the entrance. Here and there, the regularity of the lines was broken by the enormous roots of the feasting tree erupting from the ceiling to snake through the air before plunging into the ground again.

Phoenix suppressed a violent shiver of loathing: there was nothing about this place she liked. Beneath the roots and between the tombs, pools of blackness seemed to whisper to her to come closer, to see what hid within them. She shook the feeling away and stepped over to the nearest tomb.

On a shoulder-height block of ice lay a frighteningly lifelike effigy of a cloaked witch, her hands crossed peacefully over her chest. From each corner of her resting place rose sturdy posts, supporting an ice canopy carved with trailing leaves, flowers and fruits. The detail was startling, the cold, polished beauty of the tomb undeniable.

Each one was of the same design, but every frozen statue was unique: a perfect copy of the witch it commemorated.

Silence fell over the group as they gathered round Phoenix.

She shivered. 'Come on,' she said, leading them past rows of biers and under the feasting tree's enormous ice-gnarled roots.

She forced her gaze into every dark place, searching for anything that might give them an idea of how the wheever had broken into the frost palace.

Her neck prickled as though she was being watched and, without meaning to, she found herself thinking again of the Croke, of the Shadowseam and the strange darkness in the wheever's eyes. She glanced back at the witches as they walked, hoping to distract herself.

'If we're attacked, will you each be able to defend yourselves?'

Surprise flashed across their faces.

'Are we expecting to be attacked?' Zenith asked. 'I thought we were just seeing if creatures could get in down here.'

'Expect the unexpected,' Five and Six said together. They caught each other's eye and laughed, the sound bouncing off the tombs.

Phoenix tried to smile with them, but something about the crypts was sapping her humour. Her neck was still prickling and, beneath her furs, Widge was very still, his heart beating against hers.

'Yelara asked us to join you because of our battle-magic skills,' Fliss said steadily, her grey curls bobbing round her face, 'but they're untested in a real combat situation.'

It was an honest answer. 'None of us will be left alone and we're all responsible for each other's safety,'

Phoenix said steadily. She pointed back to the entrance. 'That is the only way in or out that we know of. If things get hairy, that's where we'll fall back to.' Everyone nodded, the witches suddenly looking a lot more nervous.

The torches in the crypts were widely spaced, pools of gloom lurking between them. Phoenix touched the moonstone in her pocket, wondering if she should take it out. Then Zenith murmured something, one of the slippery magical words that refused to be heard, and an orange orb of light appeared in front of her.

'Witchlight,' she said with a shrug, seeing the Hunters' surprise. She waved the ball of illumination ahead of them.

'Thanks,' Phoenix said, pleased. 'The more light the better.'

'Makes the place a bit less unnerving too,' Six added, shooting an uncomfortable glance at the nearest tomb.

'We've been in places much scarier than this!' Five exclaimed, immediately launching into a detailed description of the Frozen Forest for Zenith's benefit. The young witch listened intently, her expression rapt as he spoke.

'And what about the Great Woods? Have any of you been there?' Zenith asked when Five eventually stopped speaking. 'Did you know it was the witches who first discovered it was possible to communicate with the home-trees?'

'I didn't,' Six said, sounding interested.

'Do you know *why* the forest clan live in their home-trees?' Five countered.

'No!' Zenith said, sounding intrigued.

'Trapdoor deathspinners,' Phoenix said. 'There are loads of them in the Great Woods. They make living on the ground there pretty dangerous.'

Zenith's jaw dropped. 'A whole clan lives in trees because of a dark creature?'

'Well, lots of dark creatures, but yes,' Five said. 'That's what I meant about you not being able to understand the clans without understanding their monsters.'

Zenith absorbed this in thoughtful silence and the conversation ricocheted in another direction, with everyone listing all the places in Ember they'd like to see.

'Netherfoss,' Six said decisively. He gawped at Five's blank expression. 'Highest waterfall in Ember? You *must've* heard of it.'

'Nope.'

'You really should acquaint yourself with a book,' Phoenix said, rolling her eyes.

'Or a map,' Zenith smiled. 'I've never left the Frozen Wastes and even I know about Netherfoss.'

'All right, no need to rub it in,' Five said, a pained expression on his face. He glanced at Zenith, curious. 'What about you? You've never been anywhere. What do you want to see most?'

Zenith sighed. 'So many things! The home-trees and the floating market. The river clan's huge floating villages, the coloured grass of the desert clan—'

Five gave a great shout of laughter that raced away to echo wildly off the tombs. 'The coloured *what* of the desert clan?'

'Grass,' Zenith said with a small frown.

Five was laughing so hard he couldn't speak.

'Ignore him,' Six said, his mouth twitching. 'But . . . er . . . it's coloured *glass* the desert clan's known for, not grass.'

'Oh,' Zenith said, surprised. A moment later, she grinned. 'The desert probably looks quite different to how I imagined it then!'

'Probably,' Five gasped, clutching his side, and even Phoenix found herself laughing, the group's good humour infectious in spite of their strange surroundings.

Walking the periphery of the crypts took several hours. Eventually, they stopped by the tomb of a witch with a round, tranquil face and sat on the ground, nibbling the food they'd brought with them peaceably.

'How about Five, Fliss and I take the first watch?' Six said to Phoenix. 'We'll wake you when it's time to swap.'

Phoenix nodded, pulling her blanket close and settling herself down with her bag as a pillow. Widge crept out of her furs to curl up on her chest and Zenith's witchlight hovered nearby, its warmth a gentle touch on her cheek.

As an afterthought, she lifted her head and handed Five the moonstone from her pocket. 'Just in case,' she said in response to his questioning look, yawning. Her neck was still prickling with unease, but her eyes began to droop almost as soon as her head touched her bag.

'I'll set wards,' she heard Fliss murmur to Five and Six. 'They'll alert us if any dark creatures are close.'

'Really? You can do that?' Five asked, his voice squeaky with surprise. Then, in a much deeper tone: 'Excellent idea.'

Six managed to smother his laughter only with a superhuman effort as Phoenix felt herself drift towards sleep.

Darkness closed round her, watchful and malevolent.

'Hello?' she whispered.

Hello, hello, hello, came an echo.

Somewhere nearby, something moved. She tensed at the slither of sound, blinking desperately, willing her eyes to adjust.

'I know you're there,' she said, her voice trembling. 'Show yourself!'

Show yourself, show yourself, show yourself.

It took a moment for Phoenix to realise that this time it wasn't an echo that came back to her; the voice wasn't hers at all.

Panic crushed her as she turned on the spot.

Then, right by her ear, the Croke's toneless hiss: 'I see you.'

Phoenix sat bolt upright, heart hammering, just in time to see the torches in the crypts flicker out, one by one.

CHAPTER 33

'Phoenix!'

'I'm awake,' she gasped, jumping to her feet and sweeping the axes off her back. Behind her, Zenith and Britt struggled to their feet too. Five, Six and Fliss were positioned protectively round them, staring into the darkness.

'What's going on?' Zenith asked, her voice sleep-slurred.

'All the torches just went out,' Phoenix said, dropping her voice to a whisper.

'The witchlight too,' Britt gasped. She tried to cast another, but it faded the moment it appeared. 'What the . . .?'

'Shh!' Phoenix whispered.

The little group held their breath, clustering in the bubble of light cast by the moonstone in Five's hands. The darkness around them was absolute. Phoenix shot a glance over her shoulder, hoping to see the comforting golden glow of the entrance, but there was nothing, just infinite, disorientating black.

'Listen,' Five murmured.

Phoenix strained her ears past the rapid breathing of everyone around her out into the darkness. On her shoulder, Widge was stiff and still, his tail upright, the tension in him mirroring hers.

Suddenly, about thirty feet away, a red light began to pulse in mid-air. Phoenix almost cried out in shock.

Fliss gasped. 'The ward,' she said, her terror audible. 'Something's triggered it.'

'How close does a creature have to be to set it off?' Six whispered.

'I don't know exactly!' Fliss said, her voice shaking.

'*SHHHH!*' Phoenix hissed, straining her senses beyond the edge of the light.

The air had grown colder and round her ankles a thin grey mist was coiling. Every inch of her skin was prickling now, a sure sign that there was something unpleasant nearby.

'Cover me,' she breathed to Five and Six. She returned one of her axes to her back and took the moonstone from Five.

Beside her, Phoenix heard the gentle squeal of Six pulling his bowstring tight, of Five drawing his sword.

'Be careful,' they muttered together.

The bubble of moonstone-light inched forward as she did, illuminating tomb after tomb. As the others fell further behind, the mist grew thicker, reaching up to her knees now.

Scritch.

Phoenix froze, straining with every nerve to listen. It sounded as if it had come from directly in front of her, just beyond the reach of the moonstone-light. Her heart was thundering now, her grip slippery on her axe and the stone.

Scriiiiitch.

She took a steadying breath and forced herself further forward, painfully aware of her disadvantage. Whatever it was could see her clearly, but she couldn't see it at all.

In a quick, darting movement, she ducked and rolled forward, hoping to take it by surprise, or at least make herself a less obvious target.

She came upon it shockingly fast as she sprang back on her feet.

A shape almost too impossible to be alive, all sharp points and wild angles and jagged, sparkling edges. But alive it certainly was. It turned towards her as she landed, its movement slow and deadly.

Scriiiiitch.

The sound of ice scraping over ice. For a moment, Phoenix couldn't move, couldn't react. The creature was overwhelming in its size and strangeness, but it was its eyes she couldn't tear her gaze from: they were filled with shadows. Just like the wheever's had been.

'It's a skryll!' Five yelled from behind her. 'Phoenix, *run!*'

She froze, her mind reaching for the entry on them in *A Magical Bestiary*. To her horror, she found only fragments.

'*Skryll are highly dangerous . . . ability to divide themselves . . . slicing a victim to shreds so they can be easily absorbed.*

To permanently disable a skryll, you must wait until . . . Look for a slight blue-toned glow.'

Panic threatened to overwhelm her – most of the entry was a blank space in her mind and she couldn't recall a single one of the creature's rankings. Nor could she remember how to kill it.

An arrow flew past her to bounce uselessly off the skryll's icy body. Terrifyingly, it made no sound in response, seemed not to even notice. Then small cracks and fissures began appearing all over the creature. It was splitting and Phoenix remembered enough to know this was bad.

Finally, her instincts took over and she found herself sprinting back towards the others as fast as she could, arms pumping, legs driving as hard as they could.

'Come on!' Six yelled, waving her on as he and Five set their shields side by side, pulling the witches down behind them. 'Faster!'

Behind her, Phoenix heard the oddly musical tinkle of hundreds of icy fragments falling to the ground. Then an ominous rattle as they rose again.

CHAPTER 34

The air was suddenly full of whirling, whistling missiles. They surged after Phoenix, tearing through the air to shred her. With a last gargantuan burst of speed, she leaped over the two shields, hitting the ground hard and rolling straight into Fliss. The witch was thrown back, her head cracking against the base of the nearest tomb.

'Fliss!' Zenith screamed, her hands pressed over her mouth.

She lay perfectly still, knocked unconscious. Phoenix cursed, dropping the moonstone to drag her back into the protected space behind the shields just in time. Five and Six yelled with the effort of holding the shields steady while they were hammered by the skryll. Phoenix threw her weight behind theirs as some of the fragments flew over the top, skimming the crown of her head before circling back to attack them from behind.

'Look out!' she yelled, pulling her other axe off her back and just managing to deflect two flying shards that were as cruelly sharp and fast as throwing stars. Zenith flung herself out of the way just in time.

Phoenix gave a cry of dismay as she looked up to see at least a hundred other skryll fragments flying towards them. There was no way she could deflect them all. Suddenly her view was blocked by Britt, who'd leaped to her feet, arms outstretched. She must have said something, but all Phoenix could hear was a sudden gust of wind. In the moonstone-light, she saw a wall of bright, swirling air rush to meet the flying shards. The two forces collided hard, the sound making Phoenix's teeth ache. The skryll fragments were sent spinning away and the wall of light rebounded against Britt, flinging her through the air, straight into Five and Six.

'Britt!' Zenith gasped, running to where the witch lay, unmoving.

Five and Six were struggling to their feet, lunging for the shields, but the air around them was suddenly quiet, ominously still.

'I think it's . . . re-forming,' Six said, squinting into the gloom.

In a flash, Phoenix remembered more of the skryll's *Bestiary* entry. 'It can only be killed when it's whole,' she gasped. 'We have to strike it in its heart.'

'Yes,' Zenith agreed quickly. 'And its heart glows slightly blue. Can you see it?' Then, in response to their surprise: 'They're creatures of the Frozen Wastes, you know. I've learned a bit about them!'

Phoenix's heart lifted.

Five cursed. 'This is our chance then, but I can't see the heart at all!'

This *was* their chance, Phoenix realised, and it was slipping away. If they couldn't see it, they'd no chance of killing it. Sweat prickling her brow, she did the only thing she could. Praying the skryll hadn't shifted, she grabbed the moonstone from where it lay and tossed it underarm, watching it roll along the ground, illuminating the pitch-darkness.

'Come on, come on, come on,' Six muttered, his bowstring taut.

And then suddenly there it was. The moonstone came to a stop and just inside its bubble of light was the skryll, still complete.

'Shoot!' Five yelled, his voice shrill.

Six did, but, as his arrow winged through the breathless space, Phoenix saw they were too late: the creature was already breaking apart again.

'Shields!' she yelled, diving for Six's to cover him, Britt and Zenith.

Panic thrummed through her. Skryll were known to be stupid but not *that* stupid. Its fragments would circle the shields immediately this time, attacking from all angles at once.

'Witchlight, Zenith!' she shouted, realising they were almost outside the sphere of moonstone-light. She would need to see the flying fragments as early as possible to give her any chance of stopping them. 'And make it stick this time!'

A witchlight appeared above them, illuminating the space behind for an instant before it faded. Zenith cursed furiously and cast the spell again.

'Keep doing it,' Phoenix growled.

Then the air was full of the whine of missiles and there was no time to think. Six grabbed the shield from her and Phoenix stepped past Britt and Zenith to protect the group from behind. Already a cold fist of dread was in her stomach; she couldn't defend from every direction at once. She only had two axes. She was only human.

Zenith's witchlight pulsed on and off as she cast it again and again.

Five and Six clunked their shields together in front of the unconscious witches and knelt behind them, bracing for impact. Six glanced back at Phoenix, his face white and desperate. Then the skryll arrived. The force of the fragments driving into the shields pushed the two boys so hard they began to slide backwards.

A moment later, the shards circled to Phoenix and all thought stopped. There was only the whirl of her axes, the thunk of the fragments deflected off her blades and the high-pitched whine of them flying past her. Within moments, the first one broke through her defences. She swallowed a scream as it sliced through her furs and upper arm, flying past her, then whirling back to attack again. At almost the same moment, she felt a lightning bolt of pain in her thigh.

This is it. This is the end.

A sob of desperation was building in her, but she pushed it down: she couldn't let her concentration slip even for an instant. Bright drops of blood flew from her arm, splattering the peaceful tomb beside her as her axes became a frantic blur of motion.

As she twisted to one side, she caught sight of Zenith. The witch's face had changed, contorted in a great silent roar of quietspeech. A gust of powerful wind blasted outwards, so strong it almost lifted Phoenix off her feet. A wall of air rode on its tail, quickly solidifying before Phoenix into a shield of sparkling light. Skryll fragments bounced off it, and, as she pivoted back to Five and Six, she saw the same shield was holding all of them. Zenith was standing at the centre of it, her outstretched arms trembling with effort, eyes squeezed shut.

Five and Six gawped at her, both looking the worse for wear. Then, as suddenly as it began, the onslaught ceased, the skryll pieces racing away to re-form. This time, Phoenix saw, the skryll had moved further back, shifting into the safer darkness outside the pool of moonstone-light. Beside her, Zenith sucked in a breath, her eyes flickering open.

'Come on!' Six shouted, vaulting over the shields and racing to where the moonstone lay.

Five leaped after him, sword in hand, but Phoenix's leg almost gave out from beneath her as she made to follow. Swallowing a curse, she limped forward as fast as she could, her axe handles slick with blood. Up ahead, she saw Six smoothly scoop up the moonstone without even breaking stride, then skid to a halt as he almost ran into the fully formed skryll. Dropping the moonstone again, he fired arrow after arrow at the creature while Five plunged his sword into it, ducking a swing from either a tail or an arm.

It wasn't working, Phoenix realised, horror growing in her. Wherever its heart was, they weren't hitting it.

'Fall back!' she screamed, still limping towards them, her voice echoing all round her. It seemed as if everything was happening in slow motion. She saw cracks appear across the skryll as it began to fragment. She saw Five and Six exchange horrified glances and turn to flee, their arms pumping hard as they sprinted back towards her. She saw the first fragments peel free and give chase, impossibly fast. Too fast. They were gaining on the boys every second.

And suddenly Phoenix knew what to do.

The fire was just under the surface, as it always was, twisting, coiling, waiting to be used. She didn't think, just called it, raised her hand and unleashed it. The torrent of golden flame was blinding in the low light. It tore between Five and Six – who hurled themselves over the nearest tombs to shelter from the flames – and incinerated the flying fragments, ripping through the air to where the creature was still in the process of disintegrating. It gave an unearthly scream as the fire touched it, melting its impossible angles away, shards dripping off it.

'Phoenix, *stop*!' Six's head appeared over the top of the tomb. His bow was strung and he was aiming at the burning creature. 'I can see its heart!'

And, as fast as thought, the fire vanished.

Arrow after arrow flew from Six's bow, but the first was true and hit its mark. With another unearthly scream, the creature exploded, each piece dissolving into dust before it even touched the ground.

In the silence that followed, four rasping breaths could be heard.

From behind Phoenix, Zenith spoke, her voice shaking. 'That . . . was a *hunt*?' The witch's eyes were wide. 'The books were right. Hunters *are* mad!'

CHAPTER 35

Phoenix's whole body sagged with relief. The pain in her leg and arm ratcheted up instantly. She closed her eyes, stifling a groan. When she opened them, Five, Six and Zenith were standing in front of her. Five looked furious, but the other two were clearly awestruck.

'That. Was. Amazing.' Zenith's face was alight, her eyes fixed on Phoenix's face.

'Erm . . . thanks,' she said, managing a smile in spite of the pain. 'I mean, your shield thing was brilliant too. I think you saved my life.'

Six beamed. 'She definitely did!' He blinked at the look Phoenix shot him, and quickly corrected himself. 'But . . . I mean, you were doing really, *really* well by yourself.'

Five, meanwhile, crossed his arms over his chest and glared at Phoenix. 'You could've warned us you were going to do that. You almost cooked us! *Again!*'

'I'm sorry,' Phoenix winced. 'There wasn't time for a warning.'

'There's *always* time for a warning if you're about

to hurl that much magic at two of your friends,' he snapped.

Six's eyes widened. He looked Phoenix up and down as though seeing her for the first time. 'You're standing up!' he exclaimed.

'Yes?' Phoenix said, a questioning frown on her face.

'You used your magic and you're still standing up!'

He was right. The realisation caught her by surprise. She'd managed to stop the flow of fire. But how? Everything had happened so fast.

Behind them, Fliss stirred and groaned. To distract herself, Phoenix limped over to the other witches.

'Are you all right?' she asked, helping Fliss to sit up.

Her arm and leg throbbed horribly with each heartbeat. Everything felt fuzzy at the edges.

'Phoenix!' Five gasped, his anger vanishing as she wobbled, almost falling.

A moment later, everyone was clustered round her again. Unceremoniously, the sleeve of her tunic was hacked off and her trouser leg cut open to reveal the wounds.

'Too tight,' Phoenix groaned as Six tied a tourniquet round her leg. He silenced her with a look.

Phoenix took some slow, deep breaths through her nose and felt her head clear a little. 'I'm all right,' she said with a grimace, managing to push them back a half-step. 'How's Britt?' Phoenix's eyes were fixed on the small witch beside Fliss. She lay on the ground, frighteningly still. 'Is she . . . is she breathing?'

Fliss nodded, pressing her hand to her head where she'd hit it. 'She is, yes. Stunned though.'

Zenith nodded. 'Her shield spell rebounded on her.' Both of them winced.

'Hazard of battle magic,' Fliss muttered.

'How come yours didn't rebound?' Phoenix asked Zenith.

The young witch grimaced even as Fliss sat up straighter, her expression curious.

'You managed to hold it?' Fliss asked.

'It was brilliant,' Phoenix said, surprised by Zenith's reticence. 'The shield was all round us at once. She saved our lives.'

'A *perigon* shield?' Fliss gasped. 'Zenith, is that true?'

'Yes.' Zenith shrugged, standing up and brushing herself down.

Fliss laughed suddenly and clapped her hands together. 'But this is wonderful, Zenith! Wasn't that your last Proving spell? You're ready to Fledge!'

The sequence of emotions that passed over Zenith's face was too quick to identify. 'Perhaps,' was all she muttered before she offered Phoenix her hand and pulled her gently to her feet.

'Shh!' Five hissed suddenly, holding up his hand. Then: 'Shut up!' as Six turned to speak.

The air had grown colder, and Phoenix's skin was prickling again. 'Oh no,' she whispered.

Overhead, Zenith's witchlight finally stuck, but only weakly, its light dwindling. The moonstone still lay on the ground, several feet away. Five slipped forward and picked it up as Six restrung his bow to cover him.

'We should go,' Five muttered, backing towards them, his eyes everywhere at once.

Then, in heart-stopping unison, every statue in the crypts took a deep, rasping breath.

And the nearest one sat up.

CHAPTER 36

'We need to get out of here right now!' gasped Six. He stooped to heave the unconscious Britt over his shoulder. The others scrambled away from the sitting figure, but Phoenix felt frozen, heart hammering in her chest, legs uselessly numb.

The statue's spine was ramrod straight, the palm of its hands pressed down on to the top of its tomb. It was perfectly still beneath its canopy, as though it had been carved that way.

Phoenix forced herself to speak. 'It's not moving any more,' she whispered, hope flaring irrationally in her. 'I think—'

Her speech was cut off when the statue slowly turned its head to look at her. In the moonstone-light, its eyes were filled with shifting, oily shadows, just like the skryll's and the wheever's days before.

'Phoenix?' Six's voice shook.

'How is the Shadowseam *doing* this?' she murmured, her heart pulsing panic through her.

With steady, deadly purpose, the figure swung one

leg off the side of its tomb, then the other, dropping to the ground before straightening up slowly to regard them.

Widge gave a high, sharp alarm call, his tail lashing wildly.

'Go, go, go!' Phoenix screamed, pushing the others back towards the entrance tunnel.

If one statue could move like this, then what was to stop all of them doing it? She wasn't going to wait around to find out. Ahead of her ran Zenith, then Fliss and Six, staggering under the weight of Britt.

Where was Five? In a panic, Phoenix slowed, looking for him, and suddenly he was beside her, slinging her arm over his shoulder and yelling at her to limp faster. The moonstone was still clutched in his hand and, by its light, she saw the same shadows swimming in every statue's newly opened eyes. Up ahead, Zenith was trying to cast witchlights to guide everyone to the entrance, but they still refused to remain visible for more than a few seconds. In their flare-fade light, Phoenix could see other effigies beginning to move, their heads slowly turning.

The pain in her leg and arm was almost unbearable and her breath came in great heaving gasps.

An icy hand shot out from one of the tombs and Phoenix only just managed to hack at it before it grabbed her. It fractured with a crack, snapping off the statue and falling in fragments to the ground. The statue sat up, its dark, shifting gaze fixed on her. The loss of its hand seemed to have gone unnoticed.

'Keep going,' Five gasped as he felt her flinch, his arm tight round her waist. 'We're nearly there.'

They weren't. The others had pulled further ahead, but Phoenix could feel herself slowing down. Her leg felt as heavy as lead. It was starting to shake when she put weight on it.

'Why don't you go on,' she said to Five. 'I'll be right behind you.'

'Nice try.' Five's voice was harsh, his face stark in the moonstone-light. 'I'm not leaving you. *Move. Faster.*'

'I'm trying,' Phoenix hissed as another bolt of pain slammed through her.

A statue rolled to the ground in front of them with surprising speed. Phoenix raised her axe, but Five got there first, relieving the statue of its head in a swift, clean sweep. Phoenix staggered after him, using her axe as a crutch until she could sling her arm round his shoulder again. In front of them, more effigies were climbing from their resting places, turning to face them. Six, Zenith, Fliss and Britt were almost at the doorway, but Five and Phoenix were being cut off as the statues silently massed between them and the entrance.

'This way,' Five panted, pulling her between the tombs into another row. But it was no better: the statues were gathered there too.

With a half-gasp, half-sob, Five came to a stop. In front of them, the way was blocked and between each tomb more life-size figures of ice gathered.

Phoenix threw a desperate glance over her shoulder to see if they could switch back, find another way round, but they were cut off in every direction. In unison, the statues took a step closer, closing the gap between them.

'Phoenix,' Five whispered, his voice tiny, 'what do we do?'

Phoenix gritted her teeth, tried to force her brain into action, but her thoughts were skittering, panic making it impossible to think clearly.

It was Widge who showed them where to go. Wriggling free of Phoenix's furs, he scrambled on to her shoulder and leaped to the nearest tomb, now empty of its carving. He paused there, one paw raised, his eyes urgent as he looked back at her, then scampered up the post on to the canopy several feet above their heads.

'The tops of the tombs!' she gasped to Five. 'If they hold our weight, we might be able to defend ourselves from there. Climb up!'

For a moment, he stared at her blankly, then his face brightened as hope crept in. He threw himself up and then twisted back to haul Phoenix up too, grunting with the effort. The ice canopy creaked and groaned beneath their combined weight, but held.

The gap between each tomb was about five feet, just possible to leap across.

'Come on,' Five panted. '*Jump!*'

And then he was over, standing on the top of the next tomb along. Beneath them, hundreds of colourless faces tilted up, cold predators tracking their prey.

Phoenix grimaced. Her leg was a dead weight, barely able to hold her. She gritted her teeth and gave it her best shot, hobbling as fast as she could before throwing herself forward. Five's hand met hers in mid-air and, with a great heave, he pulled her across the gap. Immediately, frozen hands reached up, grabbing at their ankles.

'Five! Phoenix!' Six's voice was high and panicked, the echo bouncing wildly round the crypts.

Phoenix saw the rest of their group gathered by the entrance, staring back at them.

'We're surrounded!' she called, her voice cracking.

With steely resolve, Five dragged her forward and across the next gap. She cried out in pain as the impact jarred her injured leg and arm. Again and again, he pulled her on, until his breath was coming in great gasps and Phoenix felt her leg finally give out. Five swung viciously at an icy hand that grabbed for her, but his face was etched with despair.

Seeing him so desperate sparked something inside Phoenix and suddenly threads of heat were coursing

through her again. With a start, she realised she might be too injured to swing an axe, but not to wield her fire.

'Pull me up,' she gasped.

'You're going to try and incinerate me again, aren't you?' Five groaned, kicking back a statue that had almost managed to scramble on to their tomb.

The only magic out there now belongs to monsters. Suddenly his words were ringing in Phoenix's ears, deafening.

'Do you think I'm monstrous because I have magic?' she blurted.

'What?' Five turned to gape at her. 'What are you on about?'

On her shoulder, Widge looked as startled as Five, glancing back and forth between them, tail lashing with confusion.

'The day we arrived, you said to Zenith that magic—'

'You want to talk about this *now*?' Five interrupted. As if to confirm his point, an icy hand snaked to grab his ankle. He hacked at it viciously until it released him.

Phoenix swallowed a wave of pain. 'It's not the ideal moment,' she said, 'but it's . . . been on my mind.'

Five opened his mouth, then closed it again abruptly. 'All right,' he said. 'I see why it would've bothered you.'

'You're pretty scared of magic,' Phoenix said, retreating from another grasping hand. Her heart was racing unpleasantly and suddenly it didn't have anything to do with the situation they were in.

'I'm not *scared* of anything!' Five exclaimed, kicking away a statue that was trying to haul itself up to them. 'But . . . er . . . have you *seen* what's happening here? It's all magic's fault!' He spun back to her, talking quickly. 'If I didn't know you, I'd be terrified of you,' he said impatiently. 'But I do, so I'm not. Are you with me?'

Phoenix grinned.

'So can you please use your terrifying magic to save us now?' There was a sudden gleam in his eye that lifted her spirits more than he could have realised.

She beamed. 'I'll see what I can do.'

Fire coiled through her, warming her injured leg and arm, burning to get out. She was more determined to control it than she'd ever been. At her feet, another statue tried to heave itself up to her.

Small. Controlled.

Instead of a raging torrent, a single fireball exploded from her fingers. It hit the carved likeness in its chest, melting its right side and flinging it out of the moonstone-light back into the darkness. Phoenix caught her breath, a surge of delight rising in her.

'*Yes!*' Five whooped. 'That was amazing!' Then, worried, as more statues surged forward: 'Can you do it again?'

She could. It was just like Nara had suggested. Instead of flinging the door to her power wide, she could open it just an inch, just a crack. The results were no less powerful, but so much more controlled. Statue after statue was hurled away, smashed into pieces. Ice fragments glinted in the moonstone-light, but still they came.

'How long can you keep it up? Five asked anxiously as Phoenix blasted two more into oblivion.

Before she could reply, a hand grabbed her ankle and pulled. Suddenly she was falling, hitting the ground so hard the breath was knocked out of her.

'Phoenix!' Five yelled, springing down beside her. Distantly, she heard Six shouting too. Five swung wildly at the statues closing in. 'Get up!'

A statue grabbed her by the shoulders, pinning her down, its grip bruisingly strong. It thrust its expressionless face so close that she could see tiny bubbles of air trapped inside the ice there. Then it spoke.

'*I see you.*' Its voice was a rough, slithering horror, churning Phoenix's guts with terror.

She raised a hand to blast it away from her, then froze. The oily shadows in its eyes were running slowly down its cheeks like treacle, dripping off its chin, dissolving into smoke, then nothing. The statue grew still, its eyes returned to ice, its body no longer animated.

A cry of surprise rose from Five, and a moment later from Six, Zenith and Fliss as well. All the figures were still and silent, just statues once again.

Five stood frozen in shock, then looked down at Phoenix. 'Who knows how long this will last,' he said darkly, snapping the fingers off the ice statue holding her so she could wriggle free of its grip. 'Let's get out of here.'

Together, they limped towards Six, holding their breath when they squeezed between the tightly clustered statues.

Phoenix's heart hammered in her chest until they were back at the entrance. Six pulled them into a fierce, one-armed hug, Britt still unconscious over his shoulder.

'Out of here!' Fliss cried, herding them all back into the tunnel up to the lake. 'Quickly!'

Together, they raced up the sloping passage, through the door and up the steps to the lake's surface.

Immediately, Phoenix's vision filled with the concerned faces of icemothers, her ears with the sound of their chimed alarm. Then Seven was racing towards them, Yelara and the rest of the witches behind her.

'Are you all right?' the Headwitch cried. 'Seven just came to me. She said you were being attacked!'

Seven reached them first, her face deathly pale as she pulled Six into a hug, then Five and Phoenix too. 'You made it out,' she gasped. 'For a moment, I thought . . .' Phoenix could feel her trembling.

Six relinquished the unconscious Britt into the arms of several worried witches, who whisked her away immediately.

'We must seal the crypts,' Fliss said urgently to Yelara.

'It's beyond question that it's where the dark creatures are gaining access, although we still don't know how.'

'Agreed,' Yelara murmured. She turned to the witches behind her. 'We'll set as many wards and defences as we can down there.' She took a deep breath. 'And destroy the tunnel.'

Gasps of shock spread through the witches.

'We must,' Yelara said to them, 'and quickly. Until we know what's causing this and can put a stop to it.'

Most of the witches nodded, although Phoenix could see what it cost them. The remains of their loved ones were down here.

After the witches disappeared under the lake, Phoenix, Five, Six and Zenith collapsed on the island in stunned silence. Seven sank down too, wrapping her arms round her knees. She still looked pale.

'That,' Five said a minute later through gritted teeth, 'was worse than the Frozen Forest.' He shifted, shooting Phoenix a disapproving look. 'And, in future, can you *please* choose a less stressful moment for a heart-to-heart?'

Phoenix managed a weak laugh and a nod, waving away the others' questioning looks.

Zenith was slumped against the base of the feasting tree, exhaustion visible in every line of her body. Five raised his head to look at her. 'You were more useful than I thought you'd be,' he said grudgingly.

Zenith's shout of laughter took them all by surprise.

'All right,' Five admitted, a smile quirking, 'you were more than useful. I reckon you saved our necks down there with the skryll. I see why having a witch in a hunting team would be a good thing.'

Zenith was still laughing, but she nodded at Five. 'And I see why a witch might want to be part of one. That was –' she cast about for the right word – 'incredible!' Her grin was brighter than a witchlight. 'I never thought you'd all be so . . .' She trailed off, wincing.

'Brilliant?' Five said hopefully. 'Witty? Handsome?'

'Competent,' Zenith said drily, reminding Phoenix uncannily of Hoarfrost for a moment.

Six grinned. 'Yeah, we're all pretty good with our weapons. You know, for jumped-up little Hunters.'

Phoenix snorted. 'Stop making me laugh,' she said. 'It really hurts.'

Seven watched them all in silence, her cheeks still deathly pale.

Zenith hauled herself to her feet and offered Phoenix a hand. 'Come on,' she said. 'I'd better take you to the infirmary. You're bleeding everywhere.'

'I can do that,' Seven said quickly, leaping up and reaching for Phoenix too.

'It's all right,' Zenith said, waving her aside. 'I've got her.'

Phoenix didn't see Seven's face fall as she allowed herself to be pulled upright by the young witch.

'How did you do that?' Zenith asked as she helped Phoenix past Seven to the feasting tree, the others following. 'That thing with your axes when the skryll was attacking us. They moved so fast I could barely see them.'

'Oh.' Phoenix shrugged, then flinched at the bolt of pain that shot down her arm. 'That's just practice.' She paused. 'How did you do that thing with the shield being all round us at once?'

Zenith caught Phoenix's eye and grinned. 'Just practice.'

CHAPTER 37

'Well,' Yelara began, then stopped and shook her head, looking round at them.

Phoenix, Five, Six, Seven and Zenith were all in the infirmary. Of all the places in Icegaard, this was the one that most reminded Phoenix of the Hunting Lodge. Eight narrow beds were set in two neat rows facing each other. Furs were draped over wonderfully comfortable mattresses, and a fire crackled merrily in the grate. The pillows were stuffed with soft feathers and the very air seemed imbued with wellbeing.

Phoenix pinched herself to keep her eyes open, cursing the excessive comfort around her.

Five and Seven were perched at the bottom of her bed, Six and Zenith on the one next to her. Britt and Fliss were both asleep, their breathing soft and synchronous.

'Did you manage to seal the crypts?' Phoenix asked, shifting to a more comfortable position. Icegaard's healer, a tall, rangy witch called Retta, had smeared a pungent green goo on to her arm and leg. The wounds had knitted together astonishingly fast, but both limbs still throbbed.

'Yes,' Yelara said. 'I hope it will be a temporary measure, but—' She broke off, shaking her head. 'We took samples from the statues to try and find out what happened. I'm so very sorry though. I never, *never* would have sent you down there if—'

'We know,' Phoenix said quickly. 'And don't worry: it's part of a Hunter's job to expect the unexpected.'

Five made a choking sound and glared at her. 'That was *very* unexpected though.'

'Is there a-anything I can help with?' Seven asked, her eyes on the Headwitch.

'You've done quite enough already, Seven,' Yelara said warmly. 'If you hadn't come to get me when you did . . .'

'You didn't See what caused it, I suppose?' Five asked Seven. 'How the skryll got in? Why the statues . . . er . . . woke up?'

Seven shook her head, shoulders slumped. 'I'm sorry. I—' She stopped abruptly, shaking her head again.

'You don't have anything to be sorry for,' Six said fiercely.

'No,' Phoenix agreed. 'You're doing everything you can.'

Seven's smile was small and twisted. 'Y-yeah, it's so useful of me to be in the library while y-you're all fighting for your lives.'

Phoenix stared at her, troubled, unable to think of the right words to comfort her. Five and Six looked at a loss as well. Widge though leaped lightly from Phoenix's lap to Seven's shoulder, giving her earlobe a little lick and drawing a tremulous smile from her.

'It's the Shadowseam,' Phoenix said, turning her attention back to Yelara. 'It's got to be. The statues' eyes were all black, just like the wheever and the skryll. Its influence is spreading, changing.'

A horrible shiver ran through her and she pushed her hands into the fur covering her bed to hide their shaking. She knew what this meant: she would have to face the seam – soon. Perhaps very soon.

'I think you're probably right,' Yelara said, shaking her head. 'But we'll continue our tests to make sure. I'm overseeing them myself so I'd better get to the witcheries.' She sighed 'It's going to be a *long* day.' Then she smiled at each of them, genuine warmth in her gaze. 'You all did spectacularly tonight and should be very proud of yourselves.' She turned to go, then paused and looked back. 'Zenith,' she said, 'is it true that you cast a perigon shield?'

Zenith jumped, her surprise obvious, then nodded.

A small smile curved across the Headwitch's lips. 'Then something good has come out of all this. I've seen you cast an oculus and use the transforming spell successfully. Nara says you're proficient with the Veil and portals. The perigon shield was the final hurdle. Am I right in saying you've now cast all five Proving spells successfully?'

Zenith gulped and nodded again.

What was a Proving spell? Six caught Phoenix's eye and shrugged.

'Then you are ready to Fledge,' Yelara laughed, her face suddenly lighting up. 'And at only fifteen.' Her smile faded slightly and she added. 'Only if you want to though, Zenith. You don't have to do this now just because you can. You know that. Take your time – think about it.'

Zenith stood up, shaking her head. 'No,' she said, 'I'm ready. I want to do it.'

Yelara nodded. 'I thought you'd say that. In that case, one week from now. No magic until then.' She took Zenith's hand and squeezed it hard. A look passed between them, fierce and unreadable. Then Yelara was gone.

'What was all that about?' Five asked with a frown as the Headwitch's feathered cloak vanished round the door.

'A week to prepare before I Fledge,' Zenith said, suddenly looking nervous. More than nervous. 'Strengthening tonics every day and no magic.'

Five frowned. 'How come?

Zenith swallowed before speaking, choosing her words carefully. 'Magic uses your own energy to cause an effect.'

Phoenix started at this, sitting up straighter. Zenith could be talking about elemental magic rather than her own. She'd never considered that there could be such a similarity between them.

'The majority of spells just take a little energy,' Zenith went on, 'sometimes so little you wouldn't even feel it.' She stared into the fire, thoughtful. 'The Fledging spell is different though. You need to prepare for it.'

A sudden foreboding swept through Phoenix. She remembered how Zenith's arms had shaken when she'd cast the shield to protect them, as though it was a real physical weight she was holding.

'Is it dangerous?' Phoenix asked, fixing her eyes on Zenith's face.

The young witch pretended she hadn't heard, ducking her head, but not before Phoenix saw a spasm of fear cross her features.

'Zenith?' Phoenix prompted, her worry mirrored on the others' faces. Only Seven seemed unconcerned, suddenly very interested in the fireplace.

'Drink this, both of you,' interrupted the healer, Retta, bustling back in with two glasses of viciously blue liquid. Her tone brooked no argument as she handed one to Phoenix and the other to Zenith.

Phoenix took a sip and gagged. 'What *is* this?'

Even Widge, who considered most things potential food, recoiled from it.

'Looks like winter-wolf wee!' Five exclaimed, his lip curling in disgust.

Six leaned forward to get a closer look, then pulled back sharply. 'Eurgh! Smells like it too!'

'It is *not* winter-wolf wee!' Retta said, drawing herself up to her full, considerable height. 'Not least because that substance has no magical properties whatsoever.'

'That sounds just like what someone making you drink wee would say,' Five whispered.

'That's it – out!' Retta cried, incensed.

A furious, quivering finger pointed Five, Six and Seven to the door, and Widge returned to Phoenix's lap. Only when they'd vanished from view did Retta turn back to her patients, breathing hard.

'It's a strengthening potion,' she said shrilly. 'There's no urine whatsoever in—' She broke off and shook herself. Phoenix caught Zenith's eye and looked away quickly to stop herself bursting out laughing.

'It's one of our most potent brews,' Retta said with dignity. 'A very ancient recipe. You're to finish it all and you won't be leaving here until you do.' She glared at Phoenix and Zenith.

Phoenix was trained to recognise a battle she couldn't win. With a groan, she raised the foul-smelling cup to her lips once again.

Chapter 38

'How's the leg?' Nara asked the next day. She glanced up at Phoenix as she unloaded an array of mismatched boxes and bottles on to a long, low bench in the witchery they were now using for training.

Phoenix shrugged. 'It aches a bit but otherwise it's fine. Whatever that green goo was, it's even better than woundwort. My arm doesn't hurt at all!'

'Good!' said Nara. She straightened and looked Phoenix up and down, her gaze frank. 'You went through quite an ordeal last night.'

Phoenix pushed memories of the black-eyed effigies out of her head.

'So, what are we doing today?' she asked, changing the subject and eyeing the array of boxes and bottles the witch was fiddling with. For the first time, she felt properly excited about her lesson. The crypts had been a breakthrough with her powers and she was determined that it was just the beginning.

'A test of sorts, I suppose,' Nara explained. 'Something to build on the success you had controlling your fire last night.' She gestured to the items she'd laid out. 'I've brought a selection of magical substances ranging from the weakest to the most powerful. I thought by pitting your fire against them, working up the scale towards the more dangerous materials, we might get a better idea of what you're truly capable of.'

Phoenix hesitated. 'I'm not sure I understand.'

'You must try to destroy each one,' Nara said simply. 'To do it, you'll have to adjust the amount of fire you use each time, something we haven't attempted yet.'

'The next level of control.' Phoenix nodded slowly.

What Nara was suggesting did make sense. Sort of. She wanted to know if Phoenix's fire was powerful enough to destroy the Shadowseam. Phoenix pushed down a surge of fear.

Encouraged, Nara continued. 'We'll start with sandmadder skin. It's only weakly magical and its properties are purely defensive, so it won't retaliate in any way.'

'Fire-repellent?' Phoenix asked, remembering the cloak Nara had worn in her first lesson.

'Exactly,' Nara smiled.

Phoenix eyed the other items on the table warily. She didn't recognise most of them, but didn't doubt that some of them were dangerous.

'We'll come to those later,' Nara said. 'And we'll build up to them in small steps. We'll find your limit without putting you in danger.'

'All right then.' Phoenix nodded. 'Let's do it.' On her shoulder, Widge chirped his enthusiasm too.

'I'm going to create an oculus,' Nara said, swinging her cloak from her shoulders and suddenly looking very businesslike. 'Similar to what the Shadowseam is contained in, but much smaller.'

The room grew cold and a wind rushed past Phoenix, lifting her hair. A moment later, a vortex of air was swirling in front of Nara, its centre perfectly still and as clear as a mirror.

In front of her, Nara sagged slightly, suddenly breathless.

'That must have been a difficult spell,' Phoenix said, watching the witch step back to lean against the wall, head bowed.

'One of the toughest,' said Nara when she'd caught her breath. 'That's why it's so hard to keep renewing the spell round the Shadowseam.' She smiled weakly at Phoenix's questioning look. 'Have a closer look if you like: it's a more appealing prospect when it hasn't got a Shadowseam raging inside it. Don't touch it though. The main thing to understand is that it allows magic in, but not out again. So we'll throw my magical items and your fire in there, but nothing will be able to escape to harm us.'

While Nara unrolled the sandmadder skin, Phoenix stepped closer, her curiosity piqued. She found she could walk all the way round the vortex, but at no point could she see through it. The middle looked clear but also oddly . . . absent. The hairs on Phoenix's arms stood on end and Widge scrambled back down her collar.

By the time she'd finished her circumnavigation, Nara was ready, holding the sandmadder skin and wearing an excited smile.

'Here we go,' she said, tossing the skin lightly into the smooth centre of the spell. It hung in mid-air, eerily suspended. 'Ready?' Nara asked, beckoning Phoenix forward. Placing her hands on her shoulders, she guided Phoenix in front of the oculus until she was standing square to it. 'There,' she murmured, 'the perfect spot.'

Nodding, Phoenix drew in a careful breath and called the threads of fire, feeling them leap to attention. It was getting easier, she realised with a thrill of fear and delight. When her fingers were tingling, she raised her right hand and allowed a trickle of the flame out as a small fireball. It shot into the eye of the spell and raged across the sandmadder skin. Beside her, Phoenix heard Nara draw in a breath as the fire faded to nothing.

'Where is it?' Phoenix asked, peering into the vacant space. 'The skin? It's gone!'

Nara's lips curved into a satisfying smile and she nodded. 'As I suspected,' she said. 'Your fire is much more powerful than the magic in sandmadder skin.'

Phoenix winced. 'Good thing I didn't hit you with it on our first day then. That cloak of yours wouldn't have done much.'

Nara's smile faded. 'That's true,' she said sombrely. 'I'd never actually seen elemental fire at that point. Part of me thought the records I'd read couldn't possibly be true, that they must have been exaggerated somehow.' She turned to Phoenix. 'I was obviously wrong. How do you feel?'

Phoenix shrugged. 'Fine.'

'Then we'll move on,' Nara beamed, her excitement infectious.

Phoenix had worked her way through heartstone, darkwater and chimera breath before Nara handed her a pair of goggles.

'What are these for?' Phoenix asked, intrigued and a little troubled.

The darkwater particularly had taken a surprising amount of fire to destroy, perhaps because she'd been distracted by thoughts of Dog having to face its insidious power alone. He must have reached the Clasp days ago. She longed to hear news of him, to know he was all right. She wished she could see him, speak to him again.

'Our next substance is a fathomlight,' Nara said, nodding at the goggles in Phoenix's hand. 'Trust me when I say that you don't want to set eyes on one of them without those.' She paused and looked carefully at Phoenix. 'Do you need a break?'

Phoenix shook her head quickly. 'No,' she said. 'Let's do it.' She pulled the goggles on and adjusted them over her eyes, her mind flitting to what she could remember of *A Magical Bestiary*'s entry on the creatures that created fathomlights.

Fathomghasts are fearsome aquatic predators . . . be aware of a highly dangerous, land-based phenomenon connected to them.

If little prey is available in the water, the fathomghast will attach itself to the base of a cliff . . . release fathomlights . . . orbs of light that may float for many miles . . . impossibly fascinating . . . prey in thrall, it will lead them back to the cliff . . . into the waiting jaws of the fathomghast below.

. . . even snow bears and skryll . . . will follow them to their doom. These lights must be avoided at all costs. However, wearing desert-glass goggles does appear to dull their power.

Aggression: 9/10.
Danger posed: 9/10.
Difficulty to disable: 10/10.

Phoenix frowned. At least she could remember the rankings this time, but she really wished she'd had the time to sit down with *A Magical Bestiary* again; there were far too many gaps in her memory.

Widge chose this moment to scramble back out of her furs. She shook her head at him. 'Better stay out of the way for this, Widge,' she whispered. 'We don't have goggles in your size.' He gave a disgruntled chirp of agreement and promptly vanished again.

Nara put on her own pair of goggles, then flipped the catch on a box that looked like it was made of black stone, releasing the fathomlight into the oculus. It ricocheted around violently, blindingly white, jagged and furious.

Phoenix checked her goggles were secure and stepped a little closer. The fathomlight raged all the harder, exuding malice. She could feel its dark intentions even through the desert glass over her eyes.

Her battle with it was harder even than with the darkwater, mainly because the fathomlight was so quick and fierce. It dodged several of her fireballs and seemed to absorb two of them, becoming even brighter. That was a shock. With gritted teeth, Phoenix unleashed several generous torrents of fire over it, giving it no opportunity to wriggle away.

A few minutes later, she peeled off the goggles again, grinning and pleased with herself.

'How was that?' Nara asked, looking, Phoenix couldn't help but notice, hugely relieved.

'Fine,' Phoenix said, examining the empty oculus with some satisfaction. It was exhilarating winning against dangerous substances like this. 'What's next?'

'Actually, that's it,' said Nara. 'You've done brilliantly. I really thought the fathomlight would give you more trouble than that.'

'That's it?'

Phoenix felt her smile slip a little. Beneath her enjoyment of the test had been the hope that she'd prove to herself that she was capable of destroying the Shadowseam. But, as frightening as some of these substances were, none of them came close to the seam's strength.

Nara understood. 'There isn't really anything that compares directly with the seam,' she said, wincing. 'But I . . . I do think you're ready to face it.'

A terrible coldness spread through Phoenix, and Widge sensed it, returning to her shoulder to press himself against her cheek. She hadn't visited the seam since the wheever attack, but she knew it was growing all the time, steadily breaking through the defences the witches were using to hold it, draining the magic out of Icegaard, increasing the threat to Ember.

Nara was still talking. 'What you achieved in the crypts, and the level of mastery you showed me just now

– you've come on further than I imagined possible in such a short space of time. I—'

'You want me to face it *now*,' Phoenix whispered. A statement not a question.

'Not . . . now.' Nara grimaced, not quite meeting Phoenix's eye. 'But soon. The—' She broke off and passed a hand over her face. Then she straightened and looked at Phoenix. 'The passage to the Shadowseam is collapsing,' she said. 'The walls and floors there are more water than ice now, barely strong enough to hold our weight. Any magic we use to try to repair it is immediately drained away. If . . . if we can't get to the Shadowseam, we can't renew the oculus holding it, which means—'

'It could break free soon,' Phoenix finished for her, cold to the bone.

Nara nodded, her lips a thin line. 'Very soon.'

Phoenix's heart was racing now. She was more afraid of the Shadowseam than she'd ever been of anything. And she was sure that if she faced it she wouldn't win.

Could she tell Nara?

She looked into the witch's face, alive with hope and despair, and knew that she couldn't, not when there was so much riding on her.

'When?' Phoenix said quietly, dread making it hard to speak.

'The sooner the better,' Nara said, swallowing hard. 'Maybe—'

'Tomorrow then,' Phoenix said abruptly.

She turned and strode to the door so Nara couldn't see her face or the sudden sweat that had sprung up on her forehead. Widge dived into her bearskin, pressed himself against her in a tight, shivering ball as she said over her shoulder: 'I'll face the Shadowseam tomorrow morning. First thing.'

CHAPTER 39

In her room, Phoenix stared into the candle flame, willing herself to sleep with gritted teeth and clenched fists. She'd eaten her evening meal with her friends, but had somehow been unable to find the words to tell them what she would have to do the following day; that she was worried it would be her last.

Fear, more intense than she'd ever known it, galloped through her and her heart pounded as though she was being chased. Even Widge, pressed tightly against her neck, couldn't distract her from her terror.

How had she got herself into this situation? She didn't want to die; she wanted to live.

Maybe she could just get up and leave; put on her boots, walk out of Icegaard, cross the Frozen Wastes. She could escape. Survive.

But at what cost?

Slowly, unwillingly, Phoenix forced herself to consider the reality of what she was imagining. Would she abandon the witches who'd sought her help? Could she leave her friends in a place she knew to be dangerous?

Relinquish the Hunter name she'd fought so hard for? Allow Ember, and everyone in it, to be destroyed?

What would her little sister have thought of that? What would Dog say if he knew how she longed to flee?

Phoenix already understood that she wouldn't leave. *Couldn't* leave. The realisation didn't do anything to calm her ragged breaths, the sickened churning in her guts.

She made up her mind then and there that she would ask Nara to fly her friends and all the witches to Ledge before she faced the seam. The further they were from Icegaard when its magic failed, when it fulfilled its original deadly purpose, the better. At least Ledge was high up, might escape the worst of the wave's damage.

It seemed impossible, unthinkable, that she would sleep and yet suddenly she was back at the floating market.

'Good! That's it!' Reed called from the bank, encouraging Poppy enthusiastically. 'Kick harder.' Then, a moment later, 'Don't hold your breath!'

From her hiding place behind some crates stacked at the water's edge, Starling watched her sister's splashing movements carefully, tried to commit Reed's instructions to memory. The day was very warm, and sweat trickled down her back. The water looked wonderfully cool – she shook the thought away as soon as it occurred to her. She was there to make sure her sister was safe and for that reason alone.

That morning, Poppy had said again that Reed would be happy to teach her too, but something in Starling had railed against it. Partly it was because Poppy had suggested it – normally, it was Starling who planned their games – but another corner of her brain wondered if it was even allowed. If they'd been in Poa, a river-clan boy wouldn't be welcome, let alone allowed to give Poppy any kind of lesson. But the rules were different here, in this place that belonged to no one and everyone. Uncertainty itched beneath Starling's skin, sitting uncomfortably alongside Poppy's delight in the other clans' presence.

From the water, Poppy began to cough and Starling tensed, ready to run to her, but Reed was already there, hauling her out, banging her on the back.

'When I said "breathe", I meant when your head is above the water!' He was laughing but not unkindly.

'Thanks,' Poppy gasped when she'd caught her breath, plonking herself down and dangling her feet back into the water. 'It's harder than it looks.'

Reed sat next to her, shrugging. 'At first, maybe. I don't remember learning, but I suppose it's like anything: the more you do it, the more natural it feels.' He shot a sideways glance at Poppy. 'Starling didn't want to come then?'

Poppy shook her head, water-slicked hair flicking droplets over him. 'No.'

Starling tried not to feel guilty at how her little sister's shoulders slumped.

'She's quite different from you, isn't she?' Reed said. Not really a question.

'Maybe.' Poppy sounded uncertain. 'I've never really thought about it.'

'She's different,' Reed said with finality.

Starling's skin prickled unpleasantly. Suddenly she wished very much that she hadn't stayed once Poppy got out of the water. She could see her little sister was safe; now she was just eavesdropping. Something held her in place though, watching, listening. She had the strangest sensation that she was seeing Poppy through a stranger's eyes, that perhaps there were sides to her sister that she didn't know or hadn't noticed before. She was different with Reed, chattering away about the stories she'd heard, insisting they were true; more forceful than normal. Brighter.

'I've decided that, when I grow up, I'm going to be an adventurer,' she confided, pulling Reed to his feet.

'Can I be an adventurer with you?' he asked, eyes alight with excitement.

'Of course!' Poppy beamed. 'But I'm in charge.'

'Where shall we adventure first?' Reed asked. Then, distracted: 'Can we get lunch? I'm starving!'

Poppy's stomach rumbled audibly in response and, a moment later, they were both scampering away like rabbits, their laughter the last thing to vanish.

Starling sat for a long time, staring at the water. That Poppy was different here was beyond doubt; somehow their roles had been reversed. Usually, Starling was the one who was confident, in charge. Usually, the other clans were to be feared. Here, everything was upside down and inside out. Starling's head whirled with it all. She felt like she'd missed something important, been left behind.

The sunlight played over the lake's surface, the smell of the water fresh and green-tinged. Before she had time to think too hard about what she was doing, Starling stood and stripped down to her underthings. She stepped up to the water's edge and glared down into its glimmering depths. Beneath the surface, she could see green fronds waving gently, the flash of silver scales as fish darted by.

'Kick. Pull. Breathe,' Starling whispered to herself, remembering what Reed had shown Poppy.

She jumped in before she could change her mind, the cold a shock and a delight. Water shot painfully up her nose, and the peaceful scene beneath her was obscured by a thousand trails of bubbles streaming from her skin, her hair, her nose. She opened her eyes wide, heart beating wildly at the strangeness of everything. Above her was the bright sky, distorted and rippling, sunlight rolling across it. But, even as Starling watched, it drifted away from her, darkness gathering at its edges.

With a sudden flash of panic, Starling realised she wasn't swimming at all: she was sinking.

Kick. Pull. Breathe.

Frantically, she thrashed her arms and legs, wishing she'd picked up the piece of wood that Poppy had used as a float to start with. She'd expected this to be easy and it was anything but. By the time her head broke the surface, sucking in a huge, grateful breath, her arms were aching and her lungs were burning.

She hauled herself on to the bank and lay on the flattened reeds, coughing and cross. It was much harder than Reed made it look.

The sun climbed higher in the sky, its warmth melting away Starling's goosebumps as she sat up, frowned at the lake. Why was Poppy insisting on learning something so difficult and unnecessary? Starling was sure her little sister knew everyone in Poa would disapprove, but she wasn't letting that hold her back; she seemed determined to experience everything she could in her time here.

Was there something . . . brave in that?

Starling got to her feet, suddenly furious with herself for wasting two of her precious days here. Then she reached for Poppy's buoyant piece of wood and plunged herself back into the water.

CHAPTER 40

A soft sound woke Phoenix, and for a moment she lay still, stunned by the clarity of the dream. She could still taste the earthy silt of the lake on her tongue, sense the warmth of the sun on her cheeks. She could still feel what it was like to know her sister was alive and safe and nearby. Then, slowly, reality slipped back in.

Tomorrow she would face the Shadowseam.

Seven wasn't yet back, she saw. Her bedroll was still neatly made, half buried beneath scrolls, and in the midst of them all was Widge, happily chewing through a piece of paper.

'Widge!' Phoenix gasped. 'Stop that!'

She threw back her covers and grabbed him, snatching up the nibbled scroll to assess the damage. To her surprise, she quickly found herself immersed in it: 'Herbology in Auguring' by Banemage Sphagnum was fascinating. Phoenix would never have guessed there were so many plants to induce Sight, clarify it or prevent it altogether.

'Phoenix?'

She looked up to see Seven slip silently through the

door, looking distinctly nervous that Phoenix was touching one of her scrolls.

'Sorry,' Phoenix said quickly, putting it down again. 'Widge thought it was food, but I got it off him in time. It's interesting!'

Seven crouched over her bed to reroll the paper and nodded. 'I thought so too.'

She seemed subdued and Phoenix looked harder at her, eager to concentrate on something other than her own ever-growing terror of the next day. There were dark circles under Seven's eyes, a tremble in her hands.

'Are you all right?'

Seven opened her mouth, hesitated and shrugged.

Phoenix ploughed on. 'I know you're excited about all the information here, but there's still time for sleeping. You have to remember to look after yourself.' To her horror, tears welled in the other girl's eyes. 'Don't cry!' Phoenix exclaimed, panic rising in her. 'It was just a thought – nothing to get upset over!'

Seven snorted a laugh as she scrubbed the tears away. 'It's n-not that – I'm just tired,' she sniffed. 'And it's n-nice of you to worry about me.' She sat down, peeled off her boots.

'So, how is it going?' Phoenix ventured, returning to her own bed. 'In the library.'

'What do you m-mean?' Seven stiffened, looked up at her.

'Are you finding things that are helpful?' Phoenix asked, a little surprised. 'I've been so caught up in . . . stuff that I haven't talked to you about it properly.'

'Oh.' Seven relaxed. 'You've seen for yourself – there's l-loads. That's why I'm spending so l-long there.'

Phoenix stared at her, suddenly sure there was something more, something Seven was holding back.

For a moment, silence hung between them. Phoenix frowned. There was definitely a feeling in the room that she couldn't identify. Was Seven angry with her?

'Are you sure you're all right?' Phoenix asked again, uneasy. Seven really didn't seem herself.

'Fine,' Seven whispered, pushing the scrolls to one side and climbing into bed. 'Just t-tired, like I said.' She lay down, then turned to face Phoenix. 'Zenith is up on the eyrie. I think she c-could use a friend.'

Phoenix stared.

'A friend like you,' Seven pressed.

'All right,' Phoenix said, confused but grateful to have something to distract her. She pushed her feet into her boots before pausing to turn back to Seven with a frown. 'Why did you tell me that? You don't even like her, do you?'

She wasn't sure where the words had come from, but, as soon as Phoenix spoke them, she knew they were true. The others had warmed to Zenith since the wheever attack, but Seven had kept her distance.

'She h-helped you all down in the c-crypts,' Seven said. 'Without h-her shield, it would have been . . . bad.'

'You still don't like her though.'

'No,' Seven said eventually.

'Why not?'

'It doesn't matter.'

Phoenix hesitated, unsure how to proceed.

'She'll r-replace me,' Seven said suddenly, her outline stiff.

'What do you mean?' Phoenix asked, more confused than ever. 'No one can replace you, Seven.'

'As your friend,' Seven whispered. 'She'll replace me.'

She rolled over so her back was towards Phoenix, pulled the blanket up to her neck.

'Seven—' Phoenix broke off, utterly confused. 'That's just not true. I—'

'Ignore me,' Seven interrupted, her voice muffled. 'F-forget I said that. I'm just r-really tired.' She yanked the blanket over her head.

The conversation was over.

Phoenix stood, confusion raging in her. Was Seven . . . *jealous*? Should she say something else? Reassure her again? On her shoulder, Widge trilled softly, his tail brushing the back of her neck, his uncertainty matching her own.

In the end, Phoenix left the room silently, walking fast to outpace her bewilderment – and terror of the next day.

CHAPTER 41

The cold on the top of Icegaard was immediate and brutal; icy fingers plunged into Phoenix's mouth and up her nose, clawing inside her to scratch at her lungs. Widge gave her earlobe a sharp nip of displeasure before disappearing into her bearskin. But even the sudden slap of cold was not enough to distract Phoenix from the awe-inspiring beauty of the eyrie at night.

Inside Icegaard, it was easy to forget the structure's strange shape, but on top of it there was no denying the palace's watery origins. Flicks and splashes of ice twisted impossibly above her while spray whipped by an ancient wind hung in the air like diamonds. The moon glinted off a thousand gleaming surfaces, and tunnel-like pathways sparked silver before her. High up, within the cathedral of ice, Phoenix could just make out the sleeping ice eagles, heads tucked into their chests, their feathers seemingly made of moonlight. The voice of the Endless Ocean was soft, and the wind, for once, was still.

In the almost-silence, Phoenix's intake of breath was loud.

'Hello?' The voice was unmistakably Zenith's, and Phoenix made her way towards it, picking her way along rippling, watery paths of ice. She came into a central open area suddenly and there was Zenith, standing before a block of ice that towered over her.

'Phoenix,' Zenith said, her surprise obvious.

A spasm of shivering racked Phoenix, and her teeth clacked together until Zenith cast the warming spell over her.

'Thanks,' Phoenix sighed, feeling her muscles, and Widge, relax at the sudden kiss of heat. 'Wait, aren't you supposed to not be using magic?'

'That spell is so tiny it doesn't even count. It's using the bigger ones that could cause problems. How come you're up here in the middle of the night anyway?'

'Seven told me you could use some company,' Phoenix said.

'How did she know that?' Zenith frowned, immediately irritated.

Phoenix shrugged. 'How does she know anything? She just does.'

'Ugh,' Zenith said. 'It's like being spied on, isn't it, having someone know where you are and what you're thinking, even if you don't want them to?'

Phoenix hesitated. She wasn't about to admit that she'd had a couple of thoughts like that herself. 'I can go if you want,' she said, suddenly embarrassed.

'Not what I meant,' Zenith said, shaking her head. 'I just . . . doesn't it bother you? That she knows all this stuff about what's going to happen to us?'

'I don't think she does,' Phoenix said, springing to her friend's defence. 'She'd tell us if she saw something important.'

Zenith raised her eyebrows. 'If you say so.'

'I do,' Phoenix said firmly. 'Anyway, it's not her fault. She didn't ask for her power. I'm not sure she even likes it.'

Zenith shivered.'I wouldn't. Imagine knowing the future? Horrible.'

'Probably,' Phoenix said quietly. She shook herself. Thinking too much about Seven's gift always unnerved her. Her eyes ran over the block of ice instead. 'What's that?'

Zenith took a deep breath. 'My nemesis,' she said, a nervous laugh spilling out of her. She smiled at Phoenix's confusion. 'This is it,' she said quietly. 'The ice that I'll Fledge into my ice eagle.'

Phoenix stared. 'Can I . . .?' She nodded at the ice.

'Yes.' Zenith smiled. 'You can touch it.'

It felt like any other ice, smooth and stickily cold beneath Phoenix's fingers. In the tangle of frozen spray above their heads, an eagle ruffled its feathers. Phoenix stared at it and back at the ice, amazement growing in her at the impossibility of the magic.

'How do you do it?' she whispered.

'No one really understands how the spell itself works,' said Zenith. 'It's something we've known for as long as there have been witches at Icegaard. It's always been the hardest magic, the one that makes a witch.'

'Or breaks her,' Phoenix said quietly. Her eyes flicked to Zenith and away again. 'It could kill you, couldn't it?'

Zenith nodded slowly and Phoenix bit her lip to stop herself saying anything hasty.

'It takes more from you than other spells,' Zenith said. 'And, once you cast it, it can't be stopped. If you don't have enough strength to finish it . . .' She trailed off with a shrug, then added: 'The Blooding that made you a Hunter could have killed you, couldn't it? Perhaps they're not so different.'

Phoenix looked up, surprised, even as she realised it was true. 'My Blooding was sort of an accident,' she admitted. 'I didn't really know I was doing it at the time.'

Zenith laughed then, a deep, full-bellied sound that seemed to brighten the night around them. Phoenix found it impossible not to answer the witch's laughter with a smile of her own.

'You'll have to explain that to me sometime,' Zenith said. She turned back to the block of ice, staring at it thoughtfully. 'Do you know how much your arrival changed things for me?'

'It did?' Phoenix frowned.

'Why would I need an ice eagle if I can never go anywhere?' Zenith asked softly, her eyes unfocused. 'Before the seam-sickness, witches went out into the world; they *achieved* things. I've spent my whole life dreaming of doing the things they could do, never daring to believe it might actually happen. You coming here has been a huge shift. Things that seemed like wild dreams might be possible now, more than possible – likely!'

She shook her head. 'You wish for something your whole life, and then it's suddenly there in front of you, within reach.' She swallowed hard, giving Phoenix a shaky smile. 'I know it sounds stupid, but it's frightening.'

Phoenix nodded slowly. 'I think I understand.'

Zenith shook herself. 'Have you actually been up to the eyrie yet?'

'Isn't this it?' Phoenix asked, confused.

'No! Come on. You're going to love it!'

Grabbing Phoenix's hand, she pulled her along grooved, rippling passages through the ice. Every facet was alive with movement and light.

'How was Icegaard made?' Phoenix asked, the question occurring to her as she hurried after the witch.

'No one knows,' Zenith whispered. 'And keep your voice down by the way. We don't want to wake up the eagles. She hesitated, half looked back at Phoenix. 'There's a theory that an elemental made it.'

Phoenix gaped. 'What?'

'Well,' Zenith shrugged, 'you're a fire elemental. Water elementals wield the same power over water. But still –' she shook her head, staring around them – 'the power it would take to do something like this . . .'

A soft, warm feeling was unfurling in Phoenix's chest. Icegaard was beautiful, a place of wonder. She'd always thought of her power as something destructive and dangerous, but perhaps it didn't have to be, or perhaps there was more to it than she knew. Maybe she still didn't fully know what she was capable of, what the extent of her powers were. For a moment, a bubble of excitement swelled in her. Then she remembered the Shadowseam and it was like a door slamming shut in her face. In spite of Zenith's warmth spell, Phoenix felt chilled to the bone.

'Here,' Zenith said, coming to a sudden stop and nodding above her. '*That* is the eyrie.'

Phoenix gazed up, forcing her thoughts back into the moment. She stared, blinked and, to her surprise, laughed.

'That looks ridiculously dangerous.'

CHAPTER 42

High above their heads, perched at the wave's very highest point, sat a smooth, flat platform of ice. There were no railings, nothing to hold on to; it was a tiny raft tossed on the frozen wilderness.

'It *can* be dangerous,' said Zenith, grinning. 'But there's no wind tonight, so we'll be fine. Come on!'

She turned and began climbing the ladder propped against the platform and Phoenix followed, passing swirls of ice and wild brushstrokes of frozen spray.

Zenith's grip was surprisingly strong as she hauled her up on to the platform. 'How's that for a view?' she whispered, turning Phoenix in a circle to look all around.

For a painful moment, Phoenix couldn't speak. The beauty of it was shocking, a breath-thieving blow when you'd expected a smile. Behind Icegaard, stretching on as far as the eye could see, rolled the Endless Ocean. The moon cast a quicksilver path across it, beckoning Phoenix with its shimmer. In the other direction spread the glittering Frozen Wastes, its distances measured in days. Wind had scoured the ice into ridges that trapped moonlight in wavering liquid pools. Everything gleamed and winked and sparkled. The air was full of the tingle of magic, and the threads of fire running through Phoenix leaped with recognition.

Zenith's eyes were sharp on Phoenix's face.

'Good,' the witch sighed. 'I've always thought this was incredible. It's hard to know how it compares to the rest of the world when you've only seen drawings in books.'

'It's amazing,' Phoenix whispered, her voice hoarse.

She couldn't say anything more. Her heart ached. It always did when she saw something beautiful. If only her ma and da were here too. And Poppy of course; she especially would love this. For a moment, the image of her sister was so strong that she could see the little girl standing beside her, hair wild, expression blissful. She could feel Poppy's hand, small and warm, in Phoenix's own. She'd wanted to be an adventurer, and the knowledge coiled painfully in Phoenix's gut. She'd never know if that was something Poppy would have grown out of, but somehow she doubted it.

Zenith was still talking, Phoenix realised. With difficulty, she focused on what the other girl was saying. Tales of Icegaard rolled off Zenith's tongue. Of how she'd snuck up to the eyrie to watch a Fledging when she was tiny, and how much trouble she'd been in when she was caught. Of how, years before, five fathomghasts made the cliffs beneath Icegaard their home for a year, and no one could go outside until the spell to render their lights safe was rediscovered. She spoke of the rare creatures they sometimes saw out on the ice and in the ocean: the deliphins, stormflukes and, once, an ice giant.

'The ground moved,' Zenith whispered, her voice awestruck. 'Even though he was a day's walk away. We saw him through a spyglass.' She shivered and wrapped her arms round herself. 'I'll never forget it.'

In return, Phoenix spoke of her life at the Hunting Lodge, of the training they received, the legendary hunts they learned of. Zenith listened with such a fierce hunger on her face that Phoenix kept talking. And suddenly she found that she was telling Zenith about Silver and Dog; of how she'd hated Five and Six when they began their journey to the Frozen Forest to rescue Seven, of Sharpspark and Oakhammer, the horror of Victory's betrayal and the terror of the Croke. It all poured out of her in a hot liquid rush as she and Zenith sat side by side until the sky began to lighten in the east, and the icy pockets of moonlight dissolved.

When she finished speaking, Zenith's head was resting on her shoulder, her breath deep and even. Phoenix sat very still so as not to disturb her, her heart fuller than she could remember in a long time.

Her eyelids must have drooped for a moment as well.

Poppy sat with her back to her, dark hair lifting in a breeze that had risen.

'Poppy?' Phoenix murmured. The fading moon haloed her sister in silver and Phoenix raised a hand to shield her eyes.

'He's coming, Starling,' her little sister said, her voice as clear as a rung bell.

'Poppy!' Phoenix gasped, reaching for her. She wanted to see her face again, longed for it with every fibre of her being.

A cloud passed over the moon and her sister's outline shifted in the sudden dark.

'He's coming,' Poppy whispered again, but this time her voice was toneless, as empty and dead as an abyss: the Croke's voice.

The hairs rose on Phoenix's arms, but still she reached for her sister.

Poppy turned and Phoenix fell back with a cry of horror. Her sister's eyes were filled with swirling shadows. They spilled over her lashes, black, oily tears oozing slowly down her cheeks.

'I see you.'

Phoenix snapped awake with a stifled scream, lurching so hard that Zenith was thrown off.

'Ouch!' the witch gasped, and then, seeing Phoenix's face, 'Are you all right?'

Phoenix's heart was slamming against her ribs as she sucked in air, her eyes wild as she gazed around.

'What in Ember?' Zenith muttered, also looking around with a frown. The glistening ice had vanished, the ocean had vanished, even Icegaard beneath them was barely visible through a dense, roiling fog.

Phoenix stretched a hand out in front of her, shivering as it vanished eerily into curls of coiling mist. She'd never seen a fog so thick. Widge gave a low, fearful squeal.

Somewhere nearby, the ice eagles were agitated, their calls filling the air.

'Do you feel that?' Phoenix asked softly. The hairs on the back of her neck were prickling and her chest felt tight. Dark creatures were nearby.

Zenith nodded, her movements nervous as she stood. 'Quickly,' she whispered. 'We should get back inside.' With a yell, she pulled them both back down as an ice eagle exploded out of the fog, nearly sweeping them both off the platform in a flurry of feathers.

'Chiara!' Zenith called, raising a shaky arm in greeting. Phoenix recognised Nara's eagle as well. 'You gave me a shock. Do you see anything out there?'

Chiara landed next to them, but was visibly ruffled, her eyes everywhere at once.

'Not yet,' the eagle said, her soft voice still a surprise to Phoenix. 'But we all feel that we aren't alone. You should return inside.'

'Come on,' Phoenix whispered, tugging Zenith towards the ladder.

Together, the two girls stumbled through the fog, back down the steps into Icegaard.

The frost palace was full of the sound of the icemothers' chimes, beautiful and chilling.

Fear roared to life in Phoenix. What if something had happened with the Shadowseam? Had it broken free of its prison while she slept?

'Come on,' she said, speeding up. 'Let's find out what's going on.'

CHAPTER 43

On the stairs, they met Five and Six, freshly risen, both looking thoroughly confused.

'What's going on with the witchlights?' Six asked. I had one in my room and it just went out like a candle!' He pointed to one drifting aimlessly over their heads. It flickered oddly, then blinked out.

They all stared at the place the light had been, the afterglow of its image fading to darkness.

'Bit too much like the crypts for my liking,' Five said. His tone was light, but none of them were fooled; they exchanged an uneasy glance before starting down the stairs together.

Ahead of them, another witchlight winked out, throwing the steps into shadow. Phoenix plunged her hand into her pocket, gratefully pulling out the moonstone. It flared to life immediately, its reassuring silver-blue light spilling round them.

'What in Ember?' Six whispered. For a moment, Phoenix thought he was still talking about the lights, another of which had just blinked out. Then she saw he was staring intently at the wall. 'Phoenix, Five, Zenith, look at this!' he hissed, waving them closer.

Five made a sound of disgust. 'Ugh, another of those *things*. Why hasn't anything been done about them?'

Phoenix leaned forward, holding the moonstone closer to the wall before jerking away with a grimace. A glimmer's face stared at her, the moonstone-light cutting through the inches of ice to reveal its blunt reptilian face and serrated teeth. Its powerful body was covered in pearl-pale scales and studded with sharp spines, each of its four limbs terminating in wickedly long talons.

'Keep watching,' Six said, his voice urgent.

Five shot him a worried glance. 'Six,' he said carefully, 'it might be a dark creature, but it's been trapped in this wall for centuries, remember? It's *very* dead.'

'Why is it moving then?' Six asked steadily, not shifting his gaze an inch.

'You're seeing things,' Five insisted. To prove his point, he leaned towards the ice and rapped smartly on it. 'See?' He turned back to Six. 'It's fine.'

Beneath the ice, the creature's clawed hands curled ever so slowly into fists. Its eyes blinked open in time for them to see the vivid orange colour bleed into an oily shadow-blackness.

The four stood frozen, united in their disbelief.

'*Please* tell me we're hallucinating?' Five murmured.

The ice over the glimmer's face cracked with a whip-like sound.

'Get back!' Phoenix shouted, grabbing an axe off her back. The creature was struggling beneath the ice now, fighting to escape. Another crack snaked across the smooth surface.

Zenith's eyes were wide as she leaped away. 'Impossible,' she gasped. '*Impossible!*'

With a grinding groan, the wall exploded outwards, showering them with chunks of ice. And suddenly a full-grown glimmer was standing before them.

'Make as much noise as you can!' Phoenix called, swinging into gear. 'Try to confuse it!'

Six nodded, stumbling back and grabbing his bow.

The creature's head whipped towards him.

'Careful, Six!' Phoenix cried. She was desperately trying to remember the *Magical Bestiary* entry on glimmers.

Their shape may vary . . . but distinctive orange eyes . . . Their eyesight is extraordinarily good and they rely on this . . .
. . . the ability to . . . The best defence . . . back-to-back fighting stances . . . is strong, but . . .
killed in any of the usual ways.

Aggression: 8/10.

Danger posed: 8/10.

Difficulty to disable: ?/10.

Phoenix gritted her teeth: she'd forgotten more than she remembered. And there was something particularly important to know about glimmers, but what was it? She tried to force her mind to recall the missing facts – but couldn't.

The glimmer was slavering now, long strings of saliva hanging from its mouth.

'Yuck,' Five muttered. 'When was the last time it ate, do you think?'

Zenith shook her head, her shock visible. 'It's been in that wall my whole life!'

Five snorted as he and Six moved closer together. 'Great. Safe to say it's very hungry then.' He risked a glance at Phoenix. 'What do we need to know?'

The glimmer lunged at him as he spoke, scales luminous in the moonstone-light. Five's sword drove a wicked slice at it and it darted away.

'Er . . .' Phoenix hesitated, grasping her axe tighter as the creature circled, its hungry gaze fixed on them.

'The main thing is the invisibility,' Zenith said, somehow managing to sound matter-of-fact.

Phoenix groaned. *How* could she have forgotten that?

'This one's an adult,' Zenith went on, 'so, any moment now . . .'

As if on cue, the glimmer vanished.

'Invisibility?' Five muttered, his gaze roving the seemingly empty space around them. '*Wonderful.*'

Zenith cursed softly and whispered a word of quietspeech. A red light pulsed to life above her. 'Defensive spell,' she whispered. 'It will help when the glimmer creeps close to one of us.'

Phoenix pulled Zenith towards her until they were both pressed against the wall side by side. Very quietly, she slipped down into a crouch to place the moonstone on the ground and pull the other axe off her back.

Silently, she raised her fingers to her lips. Five, Six and Zenith nodded.

She held her breath to quell her pounding heart, and listened with everything she had. She heard the gentle tinkle of ice crystals, still falling from where the glimmer had burst out of the wall, Five and Six's breathing, and . . . Phoenix frowned and tried to home in on the sound, so quiet, so soft: the scratch of claws on ice, circling at the edge of the moonstone-light.

She gestured to the others just in time. The glimmer flew at Six, the moonstone revealing it as soon as it was within its sphere of light. Zenith's defensive spell sped down on to it, hitting the creature solidly in the chest and knocking it backwards. In quick succession, three of Six's arrows pierced it and, an instant later, Five was there, his sword carving a deadly arc to relieve it of its head. The oily darkness trickled out of its eyes and vanished.

For a moment, none of them spoke, each too shocked to move.

'Look!' Zenith breathed.

She was pointing at the wall where the glimmer had emerged. The ice seemed to be healing itself. Shards large and small jingled softly against each other as they slotted themselves back together, knitting the ragged wound until the wall was smooth and perfect again.

'Something smashed through the magic in Icegaard's walls to let the glimmer out,' Zenith whispered slowly. 'And now the magic is healing itself.'

'Could that have happened in the crypts too?' Phoenix whispered. 'If so, I think we've just seen how that skryll got in.'

Six nodded. 'And the wheever.'

'But . . . that glimmer was *dead*,' said Five. 'How did it come back to life?'

Zenith shook her head as silence fell between them.

'The glimmer's eyes were the same as the statues',' Six said eventually, almost making it a question.

Before anyone could say anything more, a scream sounded from lower down the feasting tree, echoing off the ice around them.

'I have an extremely bad feeling about this,' Five muttered, his eyes jumping between the dead glimmer and the direction of the yell.

'Come on,' Phoenix said darkly, shouldering her axes and sweeping the moonstone back into her hand.

Another yell tore through the air and the four set off at a hard run, racing towards the unknown.

CHAPTER 44

As the group pelted down the stairs, the witchlights vanished around them until the only illumination was the faint glow of the ice itself and the moon-stone in Phoenix's hand. The effect was eerie, light and shadow leaping to play tricks on them as they ran.

Six's hand on Phoenix's arm suddenly pulled her up short. 'Something's coming up,' he whispered, raising a finger to his lips, then silently stringing his bow. Beside him, Five drew his sword.

On Phoenix's shoulder, Widge's tail whipped back and forth, his agitation clear as she grabbed one of her axes. She could feel his fear in how his claws dug into her.

'Have I mentioned that I have a bad feeling about this?' Five muttered.

Round the twist in the stairs hurried four figures. Nara was leading the group and behind her were Seven, Thea and Libbet.

'By the frost, am I glad I've found you,' the witch gasped, her eyes raking over them.

Phoenix sagged with relief, loosening her grip on her axe.

At that moment, a boom rocked Icegaard, a hundred times stronger than the rhythmic pounding of the Endless Ocean.

Nara glanced behind them, her lips pressing into a narrow line.

'What was that? What's going on?' Zenith asked, pushing to the front.

'There are dark creatures massed in the fog outside,' Nara said quickly. 'They appear to be trying to break into Icegaard.' Her tone was light, but no one was fooled.

Widge squealed softly and vanished into Phoenix's bearskin.

Behind Nara, Libbet slipped her hand into Thea's.

The witch shook herself, focused on Zenith. 'I need you, Thea, Libbet and Seven to get somewhere safe and stay there until this is over.' She turned to Phoenix, Five and Six. 'Will you stay with them? Protect them?'

'Protect us?' Zenith gasped, affronted. 'I am quite capable—'

'Quiet, Zenith!' Nara losing her temper shocked them all into silence. When she spoke again, her voice trembled with the effort of sounding calm. 'There are more creatures out there than I've ever seen, and too few of us to defend the frost palace.' She raised a hand to cut off Zenith's objections. 'You cannot help us before you're Fledged. You just can't. What you *can* do is keep Thea and Libbet safe. Will you do that, Zenith? Promise me.'

Zenith's fingers had curled into fists, but she nodded once. A quick, angry gesture.

Phoenix couldn't peel her eyes from Nara, a deep dread growing in her. 'It's the Shadowseam,' she whispered, certainty hammering through her. 'It's drawn the creatures here.'

Nara winced as another boom rocked Icegaard. 'I have to return to the icemothers, help coordinate our defence.' Her eyes met Phoenix's. 'But I think you're right.'

Suddenly Phoenix remembered her idea from the night before. 'Why don't you reconnect the portal to Ledge?' she said, speaking fast. 'You could all fly through, then I can face the seam, and even if I fail—'

'You won't fail!' Nara spoke fiercely, looking angry that Phoenix had even entertained the possibility. 'And we witches will *never* leave Icegaard; it's our home, has been for a millennium. We won't abandon it in its hour of need and leave you to face the danger alone.'

'Yeah,' Five added crossly. 'And you can forget about us leaving you too. As if!'

Phoenix's stomach was suddenly writhing like a bag of worms, but she forced herself to nod, to straighten her spine. There wasn't time to argue now. 'I'll make sure the others are safe, then I'll head straight to the seam,' she said to Nara. 'I'll . . . I'll destroy it.' *Try to.*

'I'll meet you there,' Nara said, calm again, reaching out a hand to squeeze Phoenix's shoulder. 'You won't be by yourself.'

Phoenix nodded quickly, tried to force a smile on to her face and failed. Nara had already turned away, vanished round the curve in the stairs. Her footsteps faded rapidly as she raced down to the lake.

Another impact rocked the frost palace and a handful of ice dust rained down round them in a glittering, moonstone-lit shower.

'Is Icegaard going to fall down?' whispered Libbet.

'Of course not,' snapped Zenith. 'Don't be silly.' She grabbed the younger girl by the hand and pulled her up the stairs behind her. 'Come on – we'll head up to the eyrie.'

Libbet grinned, her cheer restored as she followed Zenith, but Thea glanced back down the steps, her brow furrowed into a worried frown.

'You're thinking the eyrie will be safe?' Phoenix asked, following Zenith too, an axe in one hand, the moonstone in the other.

'Yes,' Zenith said. 'We can put the girls on an ice eagle, fly them to safety.'

'What?' Thea spluttered. 'That's not what Nara said!

She didn't tell us to leave the frost palace and I don't want to! I'm not running away just because—'

'It's not running away,' Zenith snapped. 'It's a tactical retreat. With an ice eagle keeping you safe, I can help the witches defend Icegaard.'

Thea gasped. 'You're not even going to come with us?' Her steps slowed and Zenith grabbed her by the arm, hauling her forward.

'Don't be an idiot,' Zenith hissed. 'You know we're in trouble and you heard Nara: there aren't enough of us to defend the frost palace. Do you really want me to stay and babysit you instead of protecting our home?'

Phoenix winced at the hurt on the younger girl's face.

'No,' Thea said quietly.

Six slipped beside Phoenix. 'Are you all right with this?' he murmured.

Phoenix bit her lip. 'If the girls will really be safe on an ice eagle, then yes. I have to face the Shadowseam either way, but—'

'If they're safe, then Five and I could help Zenith and the witches,' Six interrupted eagerly. 'There are dark creatures down there and we're Hunters. We could be useful!'

'So could I!' Seven gasped from behind them, her breathing laboured with the exertion of running up so many steps.

'You're not a Hunter, Seven,' Six said, looking worried.

'I b-beat all of you in our last t-training session,' Seven said, her voice rising.

'One: that was ages ago,' Five said brutally. 'Two: you haven't trained since. Three: you didn't *actually* beat us. Hoarfrost would have our heads if we let you stay.'

Seven turned a hopeful gaze to her brother, but Six shook his head too. 'Can she fly with Thea and Libbet?' he asked Zenith, avoiding Seven's eye.

'Of course,' Zenith said grimly.

Phoenix caught Seven's hand, seeing despair and something like terror on the other girl's face. 'It'll be all right,' she murmured. 'It's better that you stay with Thea and Libbet. They've never left Icegaard, remember?' Seven didn't look convinced. 'You're not a Hunter yet,' Phoenix said, hoping that Seven didn't insist further. She didn't want to have to say it, but Seven wasn't a strong enough fighter to be of any use. To her relief, Seven nodded miserably.

The group surged up the stairs, past the dead glimmer and, further on, a cleft in the wall re-forming where another glimmer must have broken free.

'Look!' Libbet gasped, pointing.

Zenith pulled her on, her jaw set. Phoenix and Five sprinted to the front of the group, their weapons drawn. Nothing was going to take them by surprise.

'No stopping,' Zenith growled, 'and no more questions. We need to get you out of here.'

From behind them came another great boom that reverberated through the palace, quaking the steps beneath their feet. Zenith ran faster, a sheen of sweat visible on her forehead, her blue cloak billowing behind her.

A minute later, they were outside again, the eyrie a dull grey beneath the heavy, half-lit sky.

Phoenix dropped the moonstone back into her pocket. She saw with some relief that the fog had receded, was now coiled round the lower reaches of Icegaard. Weak winterlight smeared through the dense clouds above while the thick fog below remained dark.

'Can't see anything in that,' Six muttered, staring down at it. 'There could be a whole army there and you wouldn't know.'

Five hugged himself, shivering, and Zenith cast a warmth spell over the whole group.

'Thanks,' Phoenix said in unison with Five and Six. Seven was very pale, seemed barely to notice that the deathly cold had retreated.

'Quickly,' Zenith said, pushing Thea, Seven and Libbet away from the stairs towards the ladder leading to the platform of ice. She gazed around as they hurried, her brow furrowed. 'Where are all the ice eagles?'

Phoenix followed her gaze. The ice above them, so

full of feathers and movement during the night, was silent. Foreboding swept through her. Before she'd even opened her mouth, Six was waving her away.

'We'll stand guard here, shout if we hear anything coming up the stairs. You go with Zenith.' His eyes bored into hers and he lowered his voice. 'Make sure Seven is safe.'

Phoenix nodded once, his trust in her precious, and then she was off, haring along the sunken pathway, the ice curving up and round her as she raced to the ladder to reach Zenith and the others. Above her head, she heard the young witch give a short, sharp whistle, followed by a long note. There was something uncanny about it, haunting. Goosebumps broke out over Phoenix as she returned the axe to her back and began to climb. A moment later, she threw herself up on to the platform next to Seven, her eyes scanning the curlicues of ice beneath her, the low, snow-swollen sky above.

'Look!' gasped Libbet suddenly, her eyes turned skyward. She pointed into the cloud.

'What . . .' Zenith trailed off.

Widge poked his head out of Phoenix's bearskin, curiosity getting the better of him. He followed Libbet's gaze and gave a tiny mewl of fear.

Shapes moved above them: great pale wings beating rolls of cloud aside while smaller darker shadows harried them, ragged and strange.

'Glintwings!' Seven gasped.

As she spoke, one of the creatures burst free, streaming down towards them with terrifying speed. Phoenix stared, momentarily frozen. At first glance, the glintwing had the appearance of a large bird. But it wasn't. There was something wasted and rotten about it, the keel of its breastbone wrong, its chest sunken beneath the sheen of greasy black almost-feathers. Its beak was impossibly long and tooth-filled, its wings diaphanous, their shape shifting with the light.

A cry like a child's scream tore from it and brought Phoenix back to herself. Widge dived into her furs as she stepped in front of the others, pulling the axes off her back. The creature cut through the air like a vengeful spirit, its cry soul-wrenching, its appearance courage-breaking. As it dived, the diffuse light caught the front of its wings so they gleamed like blades. And Phoenix suddenly remembered from *A Magical Bestiary* that they *were* blades. The rest of the entry existed only in scraps.

These deadly creatures fly in flocks capable of scything through . . . devastatingly sharp wings. Do not be distracted by their toothed beaks . . . wings which cause the most damage . . .

Aggression: ?/10.
Danger posed: ?/10.
Difficulty to disable: ?/10.

Libbet's scream mingled with the creature's as Zenith raised her hands and Phoenix raised her axes, her vision filling with the hateful shape. She mightn't be able to remember the creature's ranking, but a glance was enough to tell her that one glintwing was incredibly dangerous, let alone a whole flock of them.

Then, like an arrow, an ice eagle emerged from the clouds in pursuit, its wings tucked tight to its sides as it dived.

'Chiara!' Thea screamed.

Nara's eagle caught the glintwing only a few feet above their heads, pulling it off course and slamming it into a twisting flume of ice. The glintwing scrabbled furiously, trying to dig its claws into Chiara's belly, stabbing at her with its serrated beak. But Chiara was too strong. A couple of slashes of her gleaming talons and the creature's black blood slipped down the ice, quickly followed by the glintwing itself.

A moment later, they all ducked as she swept just above their heads, banking tightly to land at the other end of the platform. She ruffled her feathers and eyed the group.

'Are you hurt?' she asked, her voice filled with urgency. Phoenix saw she had one eye on them and one on the sky above. A deep gash beneath her eye had stained her cheek feathers red.

'No,' Zenith gulped. 'What's happening up there?'

'The greatest flock of glintwings I have ever seen,' Chiara said, her talons rasping against the ice. She shook herself and stepped closer. 'What is happening in the frost palace? Nara is in danger – I feel it.'

'We're under attack from the ground too,' Zenith said quickly. 'Dark creatures are trying to break into Icegaard. Nara asked me to get Thea and Libbet to safety. Can you carry them?'

'And Seven,' Phoenix added.

In response, Chiara inclined her head slightly. 'Of course.' The great bird looked at the three girls, troubled. 'Though I fear it will not be an easy flight. Can you hold on tight and keep quiet, no matter what happens?'

Thea and Libbet nodded, their faces pale. Suddenly the danger was too real. Seven stepped closer, put a reassuring hand on Libbet's shoulder. 'It'll be all right,' she whispered.

'We will have to slip through the glintwings,' Chiara went on. 'The cloud covers them, but could hide us too if we are clever. Quickly, climb on.'

Zenith gave Thea a leg-up first, then helped Libbet too. Phoenix boosted Seven up last, noticing how she trembled. She sat stiff-backed behind Thea, her eyes wide and fixed on the back of the young witch's head. She looked terrified.

'It's just for a short while,' Zenith said, her smile wobbling as tears slid down Libbet's cheeks. 'Chiara will keep you all safe.'

'We should stay,' Thea whispered, her eyes huge on Zenith. 'We shouldn't be running away like this.'

Behind her, Seven was so rigid, Phoenix was worried she'd topple off Chiara. Widge scrambled on to her shoulder again to trill encouragement, but Seven didn't seem to hear him.

Then the great ice eagle spread her wings, powerful beats sending icy air curling down Phoenix's collar. Zenith moved to her side, their eyes fixed on the ice eagle as she rose higher, towards the cover and danger of the clouds.

'I should get to the Shadowseam,' Phoenix murmured, crushing her dread as she tracked Chiara's ascent.

Zenith nodded once, half turned to go, then gave a cry of alarm, her eyes still fixed on Nara's ice eagle.

Phoenix looked up just in time to see a change come over the beautiful bird. One moment she was flying, the next an awful stillness settled across her outstretched wings, the living lustre of her feathers shifting to the gleam of ice.

'No,' Zenith breathed. Then, as a sky-filling howl: '*NO!*'

Thea, Seven and Libbet only had time to scream once before Chiara disintegrated beneath them, her graceful lines dissolving into nothing more solid than shimmering ice dust.

The three girls plummeted towards the ground.

CHAPTER 45

'Thea! Libbet!' The screams tore from Zenith and she ran forward without thinking, would have run straight off the edge of the eyrie if Phoenix hadn't pulled her back, so roughly that the witch was flung to the ground.

Blood roared in Phoenix's ears as she watched Seven fall, cartwheeling limbs against a leaden sky. Widge's shrieks of horror were deafening in her ears and, beneath her, she could hear Six screaming. Her thoughts skipped, whipping back and forth like a flag in a storm. Bile rose in her throat and iron bands closed round her chest.

And then suddenly the girls stopped falling.

Her heart hammering, a sob trapped on her lips, it took Phoenix a moment to work out what had happened. The three girls hung in mid-air, still screaming but no longer tumbling, and Zenith was on her back, her arms raised towards them, lips whispering silent magic to life.

Phoenix held her breath until her lungs were burning, afraid to do anything that might break Zenith's concentration. But, slowly and steadily, she brought Thea, Libbet and Seven back to the platform.

Zenith leaped to her feet and the three witches clung to one another.

'You saved us,' Thea whispered, her arms tight round the older girl.

'Of course I did.' Zenith's voice cracked.

'Zenith will always save us,' Libbet gasped, her whole body trembling with shock.

Phoenix could feel Seven's terror radiating off her and wrapped her arms round the other girl. 'I'm sorry,' she whispered. Seven nodded dumbly, only reacting when Six's white face appeared at the top of the ladder.

'I'm all right,' she muttered as he pulled her into a hug. 'Honestly, I'm f-fine.' After a brief but obvious struggle, she turned to Zenith. 'Thanks to you,' she said stiffly.

Zenith laughed weakly and sat down rather suddenly. 'What are we going to do now?' she said to Phoenix. 'We can't put them on another ice eagle. You saw what just happened.'

A gentle rain of the shimmering ice dust was falling round them and Phoenix held out her hand to catch some of it, her throat tight. 'What happened?'

Zenith's voice shook. 'Ice eagles can die from injuries but more often they perish because their witch—' She broke off, smothering a sob.

'Nara?' Phoenix whispered.

'I think she's dead,' Zenith gasped, burying her face in shaking hands.

Widge gave a low croon of dismay as Phoenix swayed with shock.

No, that couldn't be true.

'Phoenix! Six!' Five's voice rose between the flares and twists of ice, cutting through their shock. 'I think you'd better get down here.'

'Listen . . .' he said when they were by his side a moment later.

Holding her breath, forcing her thoughts away from Nara, Phoenix listened. Below was the unmistakable sound of feet pounding up the stairs, approaching fast.

'It could be the other witches,' said Zenith, hope brightening her face.

Phoenix shook her head, dread building in her. 'Whatever's coming has claws,' she said.

She tried not to think about what that meant. Creatures – lots of them from the sound of it – had broken into the frost palace. How had they got past the witches? Why hadn't they been stopped?

Silently, she raged at herself. Now she was trapped at Icegaard's summit, unable to reach the Shadowseam. Nara had been counting on her. *Everyone* had been counting on her. What if she'd missed her chance to destroy it, and Icegaard – along with all of Ember – had to pay the price? Had she already broken her promise to Poppy? How could she have been so stupid?

Zenith's face fell and she pushed Thea and Libbet

back. 'Make yourselves small somewhere,' she instructed them.

'If you see or hear anything other than us, weave a V-Veil to hide,' Seven added.

Thea's eyes widened and Libbet gave a frightened squeak.

Zenith raised her eyebrows at Seven. 'You want Libbet to weave herself a Veil? She's only eight – that's some of the trickiest magic there is.'

The sound of clawed feet was very close now.

'Do what Zenith says,' Phoenix said to Thea and Libbet, forcing her thoughts away from the Shadowseam. 'Go and hide. Quickly.' Widge chirped his agreement, his worried eyes on the two girls. Phoenix took a deep breath. 'Seven, you too.'

Seven seemed to have expected this, visibly steeled herself. 'I have my dagger – I'm not useless. I can help.'

'If we need you, we'll shout,' Phoenix said ruthlessly.

Seven's face was very pale as the two girls regarded one another. For a moment, Phoenix thought she would argue, then Seven turned and walked away, her head held high.

'Thank you,' Six whispered, his relief obvious. 'So what exactly is our plan?'

Phoenix nodded quickly, her brain whirring. 'There's nowhere for us to fall back to,' she admitted. 'Holding this doorway is crucial.'

'Could we risk a different ice eagle?' Six asked.

'Only if we're comfortable with the thought of plummeting to our deaths,' Five snorted. 'Which, to be clear, I'm *definitely* not.'

'That would be a last resort,' Phoenix agreed, her stomach twisting.

Overhead, the glintwings were no longer silent; their childlike screams tore the air, setting Phoenix's nerves jangling. A soft, continuous rain of sparkling ice dust was falling over them. The witches' eagles were dying. Was it because the glintwings were killing them or were their witches dying inside the frost palace?

Zenith noticed it as well. Tears rolled silently down her cheeks, but she nodded when Phoenix looked at her. 'Don't let anything through. Got it?' she said, her voice harsh. Her eyes flicked to where Thea and Libbet had run to as she whispered defensive spells to life, sending many of them in their direction.

'We'll do everything we can,' Phoenix said to her. 'Strategically, this is a good position. The creatures can't come up the stairs more than two or three at a time. We can pick them off.' She glanced up. 'But we'll need to keep an eye out above us too.' She hesitated, then ploughed on. 'When there's a gap, I have to get to the Shadowseam. I have to destroy it. Will you stay here with Five and Six? It'll be safer that way.'

Before Zenith could reply, the first creature appeared

from round the curve in the stairs beneath them. A ripplewrack, damp and weedy, it scuttled up towards them with surprising speed, rivulets of water trailing behind it.

Six's bowstring twanged and the creature fell. Immediately, its place was taken by a winter wolf, a howl tearing from it when it scented them. One of Zenith's defensive spells dealt with that.

Soon there was no time to name the creatures. They appeared, leaped over the fallen bodies of those who'd gone before and were cut down by Six's arrows or Zenith's spells. Five and Phoenix stood, weapons in hand, ready to dispatch anything that slipped through.

Then suddenly Zenith turned, grabbed Phoenix by the wrist and pulled her forward to take her place.

'There's one ice eagle that *would* be safe for Thea and Libbet to ride,' she gasped. Her eyes were feverish and a faint sheen of sweat clung to her brow.

Instinctively, Phoenix knew what she was talking about. 'You want to try the Fledging spell now, don't you?' she said.

Zenith nodded. 'If I can do it, we'll know it's safe to fly on as long as I'm alive.'

'I thought you were supposed to rest, and not use magic, and take all those strengthening potions beforehand,' Phoenix said, sudden fear leaping through her.

Zenith nodded. 'But it's now or never. How else are we going to get out of here?'

Phoenix gestured at the growing pile of dark creatures beneath them. 'We can do this, Zenith,' she said quietly. 'It's what we're trained for. You don't have to put yourself at risk.'

The young witch shook her head, a smile playing across her lips. 'We don't know how many creatures are down there. We have to assume there are a lot more. What happens when Six runs out of arrows, when Five can't lift his sword any more?'

Phoenix opened her mouth, but Zenith cut her off.

'Don't. You'll fight for as long as you can, I know. I doubt there's anyone that would fight harder than you. And, when you can't use your axes any more, you'll unleash your fire. But when that's drained you? When I'm too exhausted to cast a spell? What then? I know you feel strong now, but what about in an hour? Two? In a day?'

She shook her head and Phoenix could see her mind was made up. 'If I'm going to do it with any chance of succeeding, then it has to be now, while I still have the strength, and you have the energy to defend me.'

Her eyes searched Phoenix's, full of fear and determination.

Phoenix could only nod, her voice gone. It was Five who spoke, his voice serious. 'It makes sense, Zenith. We'll protect you as long as we can.'

She nodded at him gratefully.

'Good luck,' he whispered to Zenith's back as she raced away, echoed by Six and, finally, Phoenix.

CHAPTER 46

'Phoenix! Concentrate!' Six shouted as a pair of winter wolves slunk into view side by side. The first had already flung itself at her, jaws angled towards her throat. Twisting to one side at the last possible second, she swung both axes crisply down on to the back of its neck. It was dead before it hit the ground, its momentum carrying it past Five, sliding gruesomely across the ice.

Phoenix drew a shaky breath. That had been too close.

'That can't happen again!' Six called.

She nodded, forcing her gaze into the gloom of the stairwell. 'It won't.' More than anything though she wanted to look behind her, see how Zenith was doing.

'Honestly,' Five growled, grabbing her and pulling her back so he could take her place, 'just watch if you have to.'

She didn't argue, but stepped away gratefully to position herself between the two groups, so she could keep half an eye on the doorway while still watching Zenith. Her heart was racing in her chest, her mouth very dry.

Thea and Libbet crept out of their hiding place, clearly knowing what was about to happen. Both stood well back, clutching one another. Zenith herself was in front of her block of ice. It towered over her, easily twice her height. In the dull morning light, it looked grey and solid and unyielding. An impossible challenge. How to transform a lump of ice into a living, breathing creature? Phoenix's mind couldn't comprehend it.

With a great roar, Five swung at an unseen creature just inside the stairwell.

Zenith didn't move, didn't even seem to hear him. All her energy was focused inwards, her hand stretched out. She must have spoken then and suddenly the air was full of wild, roaring magic. Gold-flecked radiance surged round her, fierce and frightening, binding her in place with thick ropes of light.

The spell whispered to the fire in Phoenix's blood, teasing it to the surface until her fingers began to tingle. She watched, heart in mouth, as Zenith's magic coiled itself round her chest and curled ribbon-like, along her outstretched arm. Phoenix could barely breathe. Part of her wanted to turn her gaze away, but she was riveted.

The spell wove past Zenith's wrist towards her fingers. She was beginning to shake, Phoenix saw, the tremors quickly becoming more obvious as the effort of controlling so much power took its toll.

Unconsciously, Phoenix moved closer, the strength of Zenith's magic magnetic, calling to her.

A trickle of blood slipped from one of the witch's nostrils as the spell moved beyond her fingers, tentatively bridging the space between her and the great block of ice. The strain was becoming more and more obvious: Zenith's legs were trembling, the knuckles of her right hand standing out in sharp definition. It looked as though she was fighting to stay standing, fighting even to stay conscious. Her eyes were burning coals of determination though. Phoenix felt that even if the world ended around them, Zenith wouldn't notice, so locked into the spell was she, so monumental was her will to succeed.

Phoenix held her breath: was it enough?

Zenith's knees gave way as blood began to drip from her chin, but still the magic flowed through her, over itself, towards the ice.

Thea was sobbing silently, one arm round Libbet, her tears dripping into the other girl's hair. Seven had crept closer to them, her eyes huge.

Phoenix couldn't move and Widge pressed himself against her cheek, offering all the comfort he could.

When Zenith's magic touched the ice, its flow increased to a howling torrent. Phoenix could barely see her through the ever-growing blaze of light. The little she could make out choked her with fear: Zenith, barely a shadow in the midst of the magic's fury, was slumped to one side, hardly enough energy left to keep her arm raised. But still her eyes focused the spell, tried to burn life into ice, even as she began to sway.

Slowly, impossibly, Phoenix saw the ice *was* beginning to change. The sharp edges softened, the shape blurred as the roar of magic grew and grew, pouring out of Zenith in a flood.

Phoenix could feel the spell forming; she realised it with a start, the connection making her blood sing. She could sense the magic weaving itself together: vast, complex, incomprehensible, becoming more intricate by the moment as the ice eagle began to take shape. Beneath its frozen surface, she could sense muscles knitting together, blood vessels multiplying through delicate organs, their functions hovering at the point of genesis.

Phoenix willed Zenith on with every fibre of her being. One final surge: that was all it would take to finish the spell, she was sure of it. But, instead of increasing, she felt the magic slow and, with horror, she saw Zenith topple to the ground, barely conscious, the magic a mere trickle.

'Zenith!' she heard herself cry.

'Zenith!' Libbet shrieked, racked with sobs. Thea held her back as the younger girl tried to run into the glow of magic and Seven jumped forward to help.

Impossibly, Zenith heard, responded. Phoenix sensed

it before she saw it, a final desperate handful of magic thrust towards the ice.

Details blossomed before Phoenix's eyes: the curve of a beak, the graceful sweep of a wing, powerful talons. The magic pulled at her and she felt a great gathering inside the statue until, like a wave's sudden surge, change swept over the ice. Delicately etched feathers took on a new, living lustre, claws curled and uncurled until finally the frozen eye brightened, blinked and swivelled towards its maker.

An ice eagle was born.

CHAPTER 47

For a moment, no one moved. The eagle watched Zenith and she watched it.

With a soft sound, it moved closer, ruffling its wings and dropping its head to peer closely at the girl on the ground.

'Xena,' Zenith whispered, her voice hoarse. She reached out a trembling hand and brushed the feathers beneath the bird's eye. The eagle allowed it, watching her all the time.

In a sudden rush, Thea and Libbet threw themselves on to Zenith.

'I thought it wasn't going to work,' sobbed Thea. 'I thought you were too tired.'

Libbet was too shocked to speak, just clung to the older girl with a ferocity that spoke louder than words.

Seven hadn't moved, something like longing on her face as she stared between Zenith and her newly fledged ice eagle.

Phoenix hung back, unable to peel her eyes away

from the huge bird in front of her. Xena was enormous, even larger than Chiara had been.

She couldn't find a way to put her wonder into words. Nothing sounded right and, to her horror, she felt tears stinging her eyes. It was too much to take in. Zenith had done it. She'd really done it.

'Xena,' Zenith said again softly.

'Zenith,' the eagle replied. Her voice was rougher than Chiara's, but the tenderness in it was unmistakable.

Before Phoenix could organise her thoughts, a panicked cry went up behind her.

'*Phoenix!*' It was Six.

She turned away from the witch and her eagle, racing back towards the stairs, axes in her hands.

The boys were planted in front of the door, chests heaving.

'Listen,' Six gasped.

Phoenix leaned into the stairwell, straining her ears, and immediately understood. Far beneath, something was climbing towards them fast, the ground vibrating with every step it took. Whatever was coming was huge.

'Zenith did it,' Phoenix gasped, stumbling back. 'Her ice eagle's called Xena. She's big enough to carry you all.'

'Why do you say that as if you're not coming with us?' Five asked.

Phoenix glanced at him, terror coursing through her.

For a moment, watching Zenith, she'd forgotten herself, forgotten what she had to do. Now it all came back in a sickening flood.

'I *have* to get to the Shadowseam. It might be the only way to end this. If I can destroy it, then maybe the dark creatures will . . .' She trailed off.

What did she think would happen? That the monsters would just go away? It was too late for that now, possibly even too late for the witches and Icegaard. But maybe she could still save Ember. She had to try.

'What?' Six sputtered. 'You've got to be joking – we're not leaving you here!'

'*Obviously*,' Five snorted, looking insulted at the thought. 'Don't worry, Six. She tried this before in the crypts. Coming over all heroic.' He glared at her. 'Idiot.'

Phoenix gulped, her eyes darting to the stairs. 'You don't understand,' she said. 'I'm just trying to—'

'Five's right,' Six said, cutting her off, nocking an arrow and aiming it down the steps. 'We face whatever it is together. And, if you're going to the Shadowseam, so are we.'

Phoenix fought down a scream of frustration. Why couldn't they just do as she said? *Why?*

In a line, they peered into the darkness of the stairwell, the ground trembling beneath their feet as their unknown enemy approached.

Six gulped and nocked another arrow so he could

fire two at a time. Phoenix tightened her grip on her axes, Widge a statue on her shoulder. Beside her, she could hear Five's breathing grow ragged.

Closer and closer the creature came, pounding towards them at terrifying speed.

Phoenix held her breath, tried not to give in to fear.

The darkness in the stairwell deepened as the creature turned the final corner, hurling itself up the last steps towards them.

Six let his arrows fly as soon as he saw the movement. Five and Phoenix leaped forward in synchrony, their weapons carving deadly arcs before them.

The creature, still only half lit, yelped and flinched when Six's arrows found their mark.

'PHOENIX!'

She only just managed to stop her axes in time, confusion raging through her.

'*Dog?*'

CHAPTER 48

Phoenix's joy and relief were so fierce she could have wept. She stumbled into the stairwell. 'DOG!' More of a scream than a shout. At any other time, she would have felt ashamed at the raw anguish in her voice, the desperate hope.

And suddenly the Guardian was there. Really there. He emerged from the darkness, eyes wide, ears pricked, bounding towards her in all his enormous glory.

She barely heard the others' shouts of delight, saw only Dog, his head dipping towards her as she flung her arms round his neck.

'I missed you,' she gasped. 'So much.'

'And I you,' he growled. 'I feared I was too late.' A shiver ran through him as Five, Seven and Six crowded round him.

To Phoenix's amazement, an instant later, a whirling bright spark appeared behind him, zooming down to meet them.

'Sharpspark!' she cried, her heart so full of unexpected joy that tears filled her eyes.

'I found them,' the sprite said to Dog, settling with satisfaction on Phoenix's shoulder. Widge immediately vanished into her furs with a disgruntled squeak. The heat rolling off him made the scar on her cheek tingle unpleasantly, but she'd never been so happy to feel it.

'What are you both doing here?'

'Rescuing you, of course,' Sharpspark said loftily.

'What's happening?' The voice was weak, and Phoenix turned to see Zenith limping towards them, supported on either side by Thea and Libbet. Her eyes widened as they swept over Dog. 'You're the Guardian of the Hunting Lodge,' she breathed. 'Phoenix told me about you.'

Behind her, Xena eyed Dog, her head tilted to one side.

'Dog, this is Zenith, Thea and Libbet.' Phoenix made the introductions quickly.

'And Xena,' Zenith added.

The eagle inclined her head gracefully at Dog. 'Greetings,' she murmured. Her eyes were curious, examining each aspect of him as though trying to understand how he worked.

'The other witches,' Libbet piped up, her eyes huge as she gazed at Dog, 'and the icemothers. Did you see them? Are they all right?'

A deep growl reverberated through him and Thea pulled the younger girl back, gulping. 'The icemothers are the statues?' he asked.

Libbet nodded.

'Broken,' Dog snarled, his hackles rising. 'Where I entered, they were in fragments.'

Libbet's bottom lip began to tremble.

'What of the witches?' Phoenix asked, suddenly dreading the answer.

'I saw none living,' Dog said.

Zenith gasped, and the younger girls whimpered as she slumped against them. Darkness whirled through Dog's words and Phoenix reeled, refused to believe him. Dog was wrong; he must be. Some of the witches would have found a place to hide. But under Phoenix's thoughts ran a dark current that whispered to her that this wasn't true.

'I saw many creatures though,' Dog went on, oblivious to Phoenix's agony. 'They are massed round Icegaard. Some hide in the fog. Some wander freely through the halls.' His eyes were intent on the Hunters. 'We must all leave. Now.' He nodded at Xena. 'The ice eagle will be safest. Take to the air and I will meet you back in Ledge.'

'So bossy,' Sharpspark muttered moodily from Phoenix's shoulder.

'Hush, Sharpspark,' Dog said firmly. 'You have seen what lurks down there. You know the sky is safer for them.'

'There are glintwings up there,' Phoenix said, forcing

herself to concentrate, nodding at the dark, shifting clouds. 'Lots of them.'

Her eyes darted to Dog's torn ear and away again. He'd told them once that it'd been glintwings that had caused the injury.

A snarl quivered on Dog's lips as he stared up too.

To Phoenix's surprise, Sharpspark glanced at Dog, pursed his lips, then said: 'I will lead them to Ledge, Dog. Protect them from the sky demons if need be.'

Dog nodded, his relief obvious. 'Thank you.'

'I can't go,' Phoenix said to Dog. 'Not yet. Not before I've destroyed the Shadowseam.'

Behind them, Zenith lifted Thea and Libbet on to Xena's back, then turned to Dog. 'I want to help.'

Phoenix's heart sank. 'You can't, Zenith, and you know it. You can barely stand. You've done everything possible and I'll feel better knowing you're away from here and safe.' She shook her head as Zenith opened her mouth to object. 'Then there's Thea and Libbet. If something happens to you, it's the end for them as well. You promised Nara you'd take care of them.'

The witch bowed her head, her fists clenched. When she looked up again, her face was tear-streaked, but she nodded.

Sharpspark yawned and rose off Phoenix's shoulder towards Xena. 'You will follow me,' he said imperiously. 'And fly *precisely* where I tell you.'

Xena narrowed her eyes, but inclined her head in agreement.

Phoenix turned to Seven, Five and Six, thoughts whirling. What could she say to make them leave with Zenith?

'D-don't,' Seven said sharply, anticipating what was coming. 'I don't c-care that I'm not a Hunter. I'm not flying on another of those birds. I'm not l-leaving you all. You can't make me and y-you'll need me anyway.'

'Oh great,' Five muttered, cutting off Phoenix's response. 'What is *that*?' He pointed towards the stairs. A green glow was bleeding up from the gloom below, growing steadily brighter. Something about it was horribly familiar.

Dog's lips quivered into a snarl as a kernel of suspicion grew in Phoenix.

'It's not . . . Morgren?' she whispered, her fear thundering in her ears so loudly she could barely hear her own voice.

Six had come to the same conclusion. 'Go!' he cried, whirling to see Thea pulling Zenith up on to Xena's back. He darted a glance at the green glow, his face alight with horror.

'Will you—' Zenith began.

'GO!' Phoenix shouted at Xena as a bright, crackling ball of green goblin magic shot out of the stairwell. Five and Phoenix managed to throw themselves out of the way just in time, and the spell slammed into a towering twist of ice behind them.

With an ear-splitting shriek of alarm, Xena spread her wings, taking to the air just in time to avoid a deluge of falling ice. It was her very first flight, but her wingbeats were powerful, confident. Together with Sharpspark, she whirled away, the young witches' faces on her back growing smaller by the moment.

Phoenix leaped to her feet, tearing her eyes from Zenith's with difficulty. Another bolt of magic flew out of the darkness and this time she managed to deflect it, in spite of the fact her arms felt suddenly shaky.

Morgren was here.

She hadn't destroyed the Shadowseam and now Morgren had arrived to release it.

She'd left it too late.

CHAPTER 49

There was a buzzing in Phoenix's head and her vision felt foggy. Then suddenly Seven was in front of her.

'When I tell you to run, do it,' she said. She spoke quickly and calmly, her composure startling. 'You have to get to the Shadowseam and you *have* to destroy it.' She glanced at Five, Six and Dog. 'You mustn't worry about leaving us. We'll be fine.'

Phoenix stared. She'd never seen the other girl so in command. It was like there was another Seven entirely standing in front of her. 'Seven, did you See—'

'Do as she says, Phoenix,' Six whispered, his eyes on the approaching green glow. 'We can look after ourselves.'

'Yeah,' Five agreed, although looking a little less certain. 'And try not to let the Shadowseam kill you.'

Another bolt of magic flew out from the stairwell and shot straight at Phoenix. She only just managed to deflect it in time, but right behind it was another. Before she knew what was happening, Dog had leaped to shield her, the impact of the magic hurling him to the ground.

Dog's yowl of pain tore at her and, as she rushed over to him, the scent of burning filled her nose.

'Phoenix, look out!' Six screamed, but it was too late. In her concern for Dog, another of Morgren's spells had gone unnoticed. It slammed into her chest, knocking the wind out of her and flinging her across the ice. For a moment, she lay stunned, drifting at the edge of consciousness, until her friends' cries of horror called her back to wakefulness.

Her first indication that something was wrong was a hot, angry, fizzing sensation that spread across her chest and round her back before beginning to tighten painfully. At the same moment, Widge gave a panicked squeal and shot out of her furs, clinging to her hair instead. With difficulty, she lifted her head and saw Morgren's green magic winding itself round her in a sort of rope. And it was squeezing the breath out of her. Hard.

'Phoenix!' Five yelled, his panic obvious as he raced to her side, Six and Seven right behind him.

Before they could reach her, the band of magic tightened itself again, crushing her until she felt her ribs creak, then she was wrenched up into the air above her friends, her arms pinned to her side, her legs kicking out frantically. Widge clung to her hair, squealing wildly, his claws digging into her scalp. Up and up she rose until she stopped fighting abruptly: to fall from this height would lead to serious injury at least, possibly death.

Despair clawed at her. Morgren had beaten her without even laying eyes on her.

The cruel laughter that reached her a moment later was a torment.

'Well, well, well,' drawled the mage, finally appearing at the top of the stairs, his violet eyes pinned on Phoenix dangling above him. 'The great and terrible elemental, trapped so easily. I'm almost disappointed.' His eyes swept across Dog, still trying to struggle to his feet, and his lips curved into a smile at the angry singe mark on the Guardian's side. 'And here's Dog brought low too. I really have excelled myself today.'

In an instant, Six strung an arrow and aimed it at the mage. 'Let Phoenix down!' he called. He sounded scared even though Phoenix knew how hard he was trying to hide it.

Morgren just smiled. 'Silly boy.' He nodded up at Phoenix, suspended high above them. 'It's not me you need to aim at.'

Even through her haze of pain, Phoenix wondered what he meant. It was Widge who warned her, clambering down to her chest and placing his paws on her chin, pushing her head back until she was staring into the clouds.

With a sound like silk tearing, glintwings plunged from above, gleaming ice-eagle feathers still caught in their beaks and claws, their dark wings rippling through the air. Phoenix's vision filled with them as they dived for her, their screams of bloodthirsty excitement suddenly all she could hear. She wriggled her arms as hard as she could, desperately trying to grab the dagger at her belt, but it was no good: Morgren's magical bonds held fast.

Below, her friends cried out their horror as the first creature reached her in a gust of rotting wings, jagged claws and carrion-stink. Phoenix swallowed a useless scream, still fighting to get her hands free, to protect Widge, as the wicked claws reached for them both.

Then, without warning, and at the very last minute, the glintwing veered sharply away from her, an arrow deeply embedded in its breast.

Below her, Six gave a roar of triumph as he fired another arrow and another, each one finding its mark, each driving another creature away from her.

Morgren's face twisted into a mask of rage, and Phoenix was just about to shout a warning to Six when Victory appeared on the stairs behind the mage, as unexpected as a squall, her sword in her hand, as tall and cold and proud as she'd ever been.

Until she saw what was happening.

'Morgren!' the weaponsmaster roared, her eyes wide. 'What in Ember are you doing?'

Another glintwing dived for Phoenix as the mage bared his sharpened teeth at Victory, and the hissing rope round her redoubled its attempt to crush her, forcing the air from her lungs.

'*Morgren!*' Victory shouted again.

Just as Phoenix's vision began to waver and she felt sure her ribs would snap, the vicious pressure subsided and she heaved in frantic breaths as she was lowered to the ground, away from the glintwings.

Fury and loathing rose in her as she gazed at her enemies, the people responsible for so much death and misery in her life and in so many others.

'It was just a bit of fun.' Morgren was scowling at Victory.

'Really?' Victory asked, quirking an eyebrow. 'It looked very much to me like you were trying to kill her.'

'Just maim actually,' said Morgren. 'When I kill her, it'll be with Skin.' He pulled his short flaying blade from his belt and waved it at the weaponsmaster, sickeningly cheerful at the thought.

A movement caught Phoenix's eye: Seven was beside Dog, whispering something in his ear. His head was bowed to hers and Phoenix couldn't help but notice that the scorch mark on his side was already much smaller. Together, they turned to look at Phoenix as she clambered shakily to her feet.

No, no, no, not yet.

But Seven couldn't read her mind and, before Phoenix could signal to her that she wasn't ready, the other girl opened her mouth and shouted, 'Now!' at the top of her lungs.

Instantly, Dog leaped for Morgren and Victory, knocking the mage to the ground, his jaws snapping closed barely an inch from Victory's sword arm. The weaponsmaster only just managed to dive out of the way, a cry of surprise tearing from her.

'Run, Phoenix!' Seven cried, her dagger clutched in both hands, the point of it trembling. '*Now!*'

There was no time to think. Her friends were risking themselves for her, to give her the chance to do what she'd come here for: to destroy the Shadowseam once and for all, to save Ember. Terror for them roared through her, but she couldn't squander the precious opportunity they'd given her. This might be Ember's last chance.

Every breath hurt her bruised ribs, but Phoenix sprinted forward as fast as she could nonetheless, making straight for the stairs, her arms pumping by her sides, urging her legs on. Widge squealed on her shoulder, his claws digging deeply into her bearskin to stop himself from falling. She ran as though the Croke was chasing her through every nightmare she'd ever had; as though she could outpace her horror at leaving her friends behind.

Her thoughts leaped like crickets, adrenaline fizzled through her veins, fire tingled in her fingertips, and a terrible hope grew in her.

It might not be too late.

CHAPTER 50

Phoenix tore down the stairs, through icy corridors that soon darkened. The Shadowseam's influence had spread further. Then, with no warning, the ground beneath her feet ceased to exist and suddenly she was falling. Icy water closed over her head, filling her mouth and nose. A silent, bubbling scream tore from her as her waterlogged furs pulled her down, down, down. Panic set in immediately, her lungs burning to take a breath, limbs thrashing helplessly.

She felt Widge struggle free of her bearskin and fight his way towards the surface, but she couldn't follow; it was as though the cold had frozen her ability to think, to move.

Poppy's voice. 'Shh, she'll hear you!'

Starling stopped her floundering and immediately began to sink. When she fought her way to the surface again, she was coughing and furious. Poppy and Reed were peeping out from the exact same hiding place she'd used to spy on them the day before.

'You're doing it, Starling!' Poppy beamed, seeing she'd

been spotted and coming to sit on the bank. She dangled her feet in the cool water. 'I knew you could if you tried.'

Reed plonked himself down beside her little sister, looking equally pleased. 'Kick, pull, breathe,' he called to her. 'You're doing great!'

To her annoyance, Starling realised the praise was actually working; she didn't even mind when Reed called out tips to her as she swam back and forth in front of them.

Kick. Pull. Breathe.

Breathe.

Phoenix's brain screamed the word at her. Under the water, her feet touched something semi-solid and she pushed off with all her might, forcing herself to fight against the dead weight of the clothes holding her down.

When she finally broke the surface, her lungs were aching and she sucked in a breath greedily, terror battering her. Widge scrambled up on to her head with a disgruntled squeal, his claws digging painfully into her scalp as she trod water.

For the briefest instant, Poppy felt very close.

'*I think it might be useful,*' her little sister had said of swimming three years before. Phoenix could have wept at how right she'd been. How had she never noticed Poppy's wisdom? Even Seven had commented on it and she'd never met Poppy.

Widge nipped her sharply, his squeals urging her to

concentrate on their predicament. Treading water, Phoenix forced herself to look around, realising what had happened with horror. The passage barely existed any more and the floor had fully reverted to water. She looked up at the walls and saw how they struggled to hold their shape, bulging and bowing inwards: an ocean-weight waiting to drown her.

Clenching her teeth, she looked ahead, paddling to stay afloat. The Shadowseam was still there, waiting for her. The way might be stranger and more perilous, but she couldn't turn back. And, if she couldn't walk, she would have to swim. She struck out towards the seam, her breath laboured, the splash of her strokes deafeningly loud. Reed and Poppy still felt present: she could almost hear them calling instructions and encouragement as her waterlogged furs tried to pull her under.

The air alternated hot and cold as she struggled past the flaming torches, somehow still clinging to the walls, and her heart raced with the exertion.

For an instant, Phoenix found herself hoping Nara would be waiting for her as she'd promised. Then she remembered that Nara was dead – and couldn't hold in her sob of horror. She hadn't realised how much she'd been counting on the witch's support.

But she couldn't stop, couldn't risk losing this chance, not when so much was at stake.

Part of her had expected to be chased, thought that

Morgren or Victory or, worst of all, the Croke would suddenly peel out of the darkness to stop her. But here she was, against the odds.

With a sinking heart, she swam through the archway, trying to keep her mind empty, not thinking about what would come next. Her feet touched something solid and, with gratitude, she realised she could stand, the water coming up to her waist, the constant ripples from the oculus breeze chilling her neck. Widge clambered on to her shoulder and shook himself vigorously.

When she lifted her face to the Shadowseam, Phoenix was calm: she would have her chance with it after all. That was all she could ask for now.

CHAPTER 51

Only a few steps ahead of her, the living darkness raged inside its oculus, a nightstorm trapped in a jar. Widge gave a low keen of fear and Phoenix raised a shivering hand to stroke him, hoping it would calm both of them. But her eyes never left the seam.

Yelara had said that it wasn't alive, but to Phoenix it appeared immediately aware of her presence. It contracted in front of her, becoming denser and thicker, its surface rippling like the pitch that kept torches burning in the Hunting Lodge. Its reflection, twisted and distorted, bunched in the water around her. She swore the temperature dropped lower and her teeth began to chatter.

Lightning quick, a coil formed and lashed towards her, shockingly fast. The whirling magic of the oculus held it in check, but Phoenix could see how the spell thinned and strained when the Shadowseam pushed against it.

Phoenix's mouth felt very dry and her heart skipped frantically in her chest. This was it: she was here, ready to face the Shadowseam.

Except she didn't feel ready at all.

She shook herself fiercely, quelled her shivering and clenched her fists, forcing her gaze up into the writhing, vicious darkness of the seam. She'd already hesitated and that might have cost the witches their lives, put all of Ember in jeopardy. Another bout of trembling racked her, but this time it had nothing to do with the cold.

She took a deep breath and tried to force order into her thoughts, to think like a Hunter. What were its strengths? What might be its weaknesses? What should her strategy be?

It will kill you.

It was the only thought she could formulate because it was true. The Shadowseam was stronger than her. Phoenix knew that with every fibre of her being. She could pour fire on to it until she was empty, until her heart had no energy to beat, but it would make no difference. This was a battle she wouldn't win.

The dangerous pull of the seam's magic prickled over her and the fire inside her throbbed in response, rose closer to the surface, its warmth welcome for once.

Her terror didn't want to be forgotten or pushed to the side though: it screamed the risks at her, battered her with the things she could lose until she felt sick with it.

She closed her eyes, blotted out the dark, and thought of her friends instead, of Seven, Six, Five, Widge and Dog;

the ones who had given her hope when she'd thought there was none, made her care again, both for them and herself. For years after she'd lost her family, existence had been a grey twilight, her connection to the world hanging by a thread, sustained only by Widge and her fierce hunger for revenge. But her friends had helped her see that life was possible, even after tragedy and a raging grief that left no facet of her unaltered. They were her anchors and there was nothing she wouldn't do for them. Right now, they were facing Morgren and Victory, buying her the time she needed to face the Shadowseam. She couldn't let them down.

She couldn't let *Ember* down, full of thousands of people she'd never met, but whose vivid lives were perilously connected to her own: if she succeeded, they lived; if she failed, they died.

Then there was Poppy. She'd been the one to open Phoenix's eyes to the wonders in the world, all those places beyond the clan they'd grown up in. She'd wanted to see them all. Now she was gone, and all Phoenix could do was try to preserve those places for her.

So many lives depending on her. She couldn't let any of them down.

Sucking in a breath, Phoenix faced the writhing darkness and pushed away the desperate wish that she didn't have to do this by herself, the thought that she'd never felt so small or so alone. As if hearing her, Widge began to chew her hair, tugging it gently as though to remind her he was there too.

Phoenix swallowed a sob that was part gratitude and part fear for him: she would push him off her if she thought he'd leave. But she already knew he wouldn't.

Her breath wrenched through her, terror making her sluggish. But she reached for her flames anyway, and they leaped to the surface, eager and hungry.

The Shadowseam massed before her inside the oculus, gathering itself. She gazed at it, steadied herself, then raised her dripping hand and threw open the door to her power.

Golden fire tore out of her, through the oculus and straight into the hungry darkness. When the two substances met, a shock wave reverberated through the magical cage. For a terrifying moment, Phoenix saw the oculus grow impossibly thin, tested to its limit, before it rallied again, still holding the seam, but only just. With gritted teeth, she pushed harder, forcing more and more fire into the darkness.

Widge's form was tense and his eyes narrowed as he watched what was unfolding, his warmth and presence something Phoenix was impossibly grateful for.

Then there was no room for thought of any kind, only battle. The seam caught her fire somehow, dragged on it with unimaginable strength. She fought to keep control, to pace herself, to keep the flow steady and manageable while quelling her own rising panic.

She didn't know how long they were locked in the struggle, but finally she felt her flames snag on something, some invisible part of the seam, catching there and beginning to cause some damage. But, in return, the entity only raged more furiously, pulling harder and harder. And something strange was happening: the Shadowseam was steadily leaching the colour out of her fire. Within the oculus, her flames were now a confusing whirl of ash-grey.

Phoenix redoubled her efforts, steadily increasing the torrent of fire until the whole cavern was gold-washed and gleaming.

Inside the oculus, the Shadowseam bucked and writhed, then condensed in on itself, becoming more compact and malevolent. Now she felt its true strength. With a power that was undeniable, it latched on to her fire again, ripping the flames out of her so hard Phoenix felt something wrench deep in her chest. Her heart began to flutter strangely and a new coldness swept over her.

Through a growing numbness, she could hear Widge squealing. With every breath, the Shadowseam took more and more command from her, wresting her fire away from her in reams and reams. Her heart began to slow and her legs began to shake. Suddenly it was all she could do to stay upright in the water.

Dark spots danced in front of her eyes, confusing what she was seeing. Was the seam really smaller, or was it a trick of the light? Perhaps it didn't matter either way. Phoenix didn't have enough left in her to finish it. It had won.

The dark spots spread and her vision narrowed. Her torrent of fire began to falter as her knees almost gave out, water lapping against her as fear swept all thought aside.

She saw herself from outside her body, struggling in front of the Shadowseam, bathed in darkness, barely able to hold up her arm.

Then the image flickered to Zenith's fledging, the witch bathed in light where Phoenix was mired in shadow. It almost made her laugh aloud, her mind suddenly loose and spinning and wild: she was a dark reversal of Zenith, a negative imprint; destruction instead of creation; failure against success.

The thought sobered her, grounded her.

How *had* Zenith found the strength for that last push, that last desperate surge of magic that had ensured her triumph?

And if Zenith could do it then couldn't she? Couldn't she do it for her friends who were relying on her, for the witches who'd asked for her help, for the people of Ember with all their unknown dreams? Couldn't she do it for Poppy?

The urgency of the feeling sparked and caught and Phoenix forced her chin up, searched desperately inside herself for something, *anything* that would help her.

Where was her anger? Where was her fortifying rage? Once it had felt bottomless, eternal; wasn't that why this burning gift had come to her in the first place?

What if she wasn't fighting the Shadowseam but Morgren? What if she could fight what he, Victory and the Croke had done to her family? What if she could fight the memory of her last night in Poa, of finding her kin murdered? Fight the idea that she'd never see them again, never hold them or hear them or kiss them? What if she could fight their very deaths?

If she could do that, if she had that chance, she knew without a doubt that she would win.

Phoenix lifted her gaze to the Shadowseam and raised her other hand.

CHAPTER 52

With fear swept aside, Phoenix's heart beat faster again, suddenly full and sure. She could do this. She *would* do this. She didn't notice the cold any more, or the water. There was only fire and certainty. Faster and faster the flames flooded out of her, from both hands now, her vision clearing enough to show that the seam really was shrinking. Still fighting furiously, still reaching for her, but shrinking nonetheless.

Then, with fierce delight, she felt it shift, retreat. Instead of pulling at her fire, now it was trying to flee from it. Only a fraction of the size it had been, it darted frantically round the oculus, unable to move out of reach of the flames, still reaching, but . . . Phoenix frowned, her senses peeled raw and sharper than normal. The Shadowseam wasn't reaching for *her*, but something beyond her.

She heard a battle cry tear from her lips at the same moment as a fierce squeal of encouragement burst from Widge. Success was within reach and nothing would stop her now. She redoubled her efforts, once again hurling everything she had at the curling edges of darkness until, with a terrible ripping sound, the Shadowseam tore into two, three, four . . . innumerable pieces and vanished.

Phoenix sagged, joy and disbelief mingling in her. She was barely able to hold up her head, but couldn't tear her eyes from the empty oculus. Had she really done it? Beneath her feet, she could feel the ice shifting, changing as the water retreated and refroze. She stared around in silent amazement as Icegaard's magic re-established itself.

Suddenly she was standing, dripping wet, on solid ground. And, before her, the ice began to glow again, softly at first, then brighter until her eyes hurt, unused to the light. Holding herself up felt like too much effort and she half sat, half fell, lowering her forehead to the newly formed ice as the torches sparked and danced around her, their light suddenly unnecessary.

Widge butted her cheek with his head, his chirps unmistakably ones of deepest relief.

She'd done it. After so much doubt, so much fear, she'd conquered the seam, saved Ember, thwarted Morgren and Victory. Phoenix knew she should get up, get back to the others to tell them, to make sure they were safe, but exhaustion, heavier than any she'd ever known, weighed her down.

Distantly, she heard footsteps approach.

Beside her, Widge began to growl before darting into her sodden bearskin to hide. Phoenix could barely lift her head to see who'd upset him.

Victory's sword was in her hand and her eyes were fixed on the empty oculus. Her expression was one of fierce delight.

Phoenix couldn't move, couldn't think straight, even when the weaponsmaster crouched by her side.

'I knew you wouldn't let me down, Phoenix,' she murmured, a rare smile playing across her lips.

Phoenix was fighting to stay conscious with every cell in her body, but darkness was creeping across her vision. What was happening? Why did Victory look so happy?

The last thing she heard was Victory's elated whisper as she lifted Phoenix gently from the ground. 'Our master will be so pleased with you, Phoenix. So very, very pleased.'

Then everything slipped into black.

CHAPTER 53

'. . . no need to bind her, she's spent.'

Sounds and images whirled hazily round Phoenix as she blinked open her eyes.

'And the Shadowseam?' The voice was unmistakably Morgren's – hungry, eager.

'Gone.' Victory lowered her voice. 'No thanks to you. What were you thinking, Morgren? Attacking her *before* she'd destroyed it? You'd better hope our master didn't—'

'Phoenix!' The yell was Six's, and, a moment later, Five, Seven and Dog joined in too until her ears rang with it.

Shadows were still dancing across her vision, but she forced her screaming muscles to push her up into a sitting position so she could squint around. Widge slipped out of her bearskin to press himself against her cheek, his shivers telling her how worried he'd been.

''S all right, Widge,' she whispered, not knowing if it was true.

Slowly, her vision cleared enough for her to see she

was back on the eyrie, Morgren and Victory standing nearby, both watching her with caution. A flat, diminishing grey spread as far from Icegaard as Phoenix could see, the clouds in the sky and the fog on the ground smudged together, hard to separate. The world had become a featureless void.

Where were her friends though? She could hear their voices, but couldn't see them anywhere.

'Up here!' Five called, his voice breathless.

Phoenix looked up and gave a cry of rage. Her friends were hanging above her, suspended with ropes of magic just as she'd been earlier. Even Dog was entangled, though she could see he was fighting with every ounce of his considerable strength. All around them, on every twist and curl of ice, sat glintwings, their black eyes following each twitch and wriggle her friends made with unmistakable greed.

'Let them down!' Phoenix cried, struggling to her feet and taking a shaky step towards Morgren. She reached for the dagger on her belt and found it gone.

Victory waved it at her, looking cheerful. 'I'm not an idiot, you know,' she grinned. Her smile grew even wider as she turned to the mage. 'Perhaps we should grant her request though, Morgren. After she's helped us so much, it's the least we can do.'

Phoenix's confusion and doubt threatened to overwhelm her.

'What are you talking about?' Five demanded, red-faced from fighting his bonds. 'Phoenix would never help *you*. Never.'

Phoenix couldn't help but feel lifted by the certainty in his voice. His eyes, when she caught his gaze, were full of conviction and outrage on her behalf.

Victory laughed. 'Oh, but she has.'

Phoenix had never seen the weaponsmaster smile so much and it was beginning to scare her. Her mind was racing to catch up, but she couldn't make sense of what was happening. She'd destroyed the Shadowseam, saved Ember from it, ruined all their plans. Hadn't she?

Unless . . .

'The Shadowseam wasn't what we thought it was, was it?' Six asked, his voice shaking. He wasn't fighting his bonds now, just hanging there, every angle of him etched with despair. Dog and the others grew still too, their horror palpable in the air between them.

Victory laughed, a full-bodied belly laugh that made Phoenix want to throw her axes at the weaponsmaster. If only she *had* her axes.

'It really wasn't,' gasped Victory, tears of mirth appearing in her eyes. 'Phoenix has . . . she's only gone and—' Victory couldn't finish her sentence and the corners of Morgren's lips twitched as he watched her.

'Your plans *are* always excellent, Victory,' the mage said grudgingly.

'What are you talking about?' shouted Five, covering fear with anger.

'The Shadowseam,' Morgren smirked. 'Let me guess: you thought it was a dark entity doing our bidding, that it wanted to devour Icegaard and perhaps even destroy Ember? You thought it was drawing dark creatures to the frost palace?' The mage laughed at everyone's uncertainty. 'Wrong on every count. That *thing* was only growing because our master is nearby.'

'I don't understand,' Six whispered, his voice small. Beside him, Dog whined.

'Of course you don't,' Morgren sneered. 'How could you comprehend the genius of the greatest piece of goblin magic ever created?'

'Careful, Morgren,' Victory warned, glancing around as though afraid he'd be overheard.

'The Shadowseam was a doorway to an empty world,' Morgren went on, ignoring Victory. 'The spell to open it was created by my ancestors to trap the Master in that dark place, away from Ember.'

'The seam was a portal?' Seven whispered.

'*Much* more than just a portal,' said Morgren, fierce pride shining in his face. 'It was both a doorway and a trap, sentient in its own way. It actively sought the Master, the thing it was created to ensnare. Had it reached him, it would've dragged him through itself and snapped shut. Lucky, really –' Morgren laughed nastily – 'that the witches so kindly trapped it in that oculus. For forty years it waited, hoping to imprison him again. This was its best chance. If you'd let it, the Shadowseam would have saved you all.'

Phoenix felt like she'd missed a step, like she was tumbling into an abyss she hadn't even noticed was there.

No. Impossible.

She'd stood before the Shadowseam, *felt* its malevolence. Hadn't she?

'But . . .' Five frowned. 'Why did the goblins want to trap the Master? *You're* helping him!'

For the first time, Morgren looked discomfited. 'The Master walked this world eons ago,' he said. 'Most of my ancestors worshipped him as a god, but a few . . . didn't. It was they who created the Shadowseam spell. To trap the Master, to banish him to a place he could never return from. Unless –' Morgren's smile sharpened – 'some idiot decided to use the spell again, to reopen the door and allow my master to escape.'

'Then . . . it wasn't an illness that killed the witches forty years ago, was it?' Six asked, his face deathly pale.

Morgren laughed. 'No, it was our master, finally escaped from his prison and feeding for the first time in many centuries.'

Phoenix couldn't breathe. Dizziness broke over her in waves.

'Feeding?' Dog growled, his voice laced with disgust.

'I assume the witch who opened the Shadowseam had no idea what it really was,' said Morgren with a shrug. 'Our master had to fight his way out. The seam fought to hold him of course, and he lost much of himself in order to escape, but once here –' Morgren bared his sharp teeth – 'that witch helpfully trapped the seam, held it separate from him. So he feasted and grew, feasted and grew.' The mage's smile was content. 'The witches were his first fodder. But many years have passed since then. He's strong now.'

'And with the Shadowseam gone . . .' Victory breathed.

Morgren nodded, matter of fact. 'Ember will be ours.'

'No. Ember will be his.' The voice from the darkness was flat and lifeless, seemed to whisper fear and pain into every ear that heard it. In its wake, a dense, thick silence fell, clogging throats and gagging mouths.

An unbearable itching, creeping feeling spread through Phoenix, making it impossible to follow what was being said. Her chest felt painfully tight, her palms grew sweaty and her skin prickled all over. Inside her furs, Widge was shivering. A sob gathered in her and she swallowed it down furiously, squeezing her fists to quell their trembling.

She couldn't tear her eyes from the stairs behind Morgren: the darkness there thickened and swirled as though alive, exuding menace. Even through Zenith's warmth spell, a terrible coldness seeped into Phoenix and breathing became even harder as pressure built around her. She'd felt this before, had dreamed of it for months, knew what it meant.

'The Croke is here,' Victory said, following her gaze over Morgren's shoulder. The humour vanished from the weaponsmaster's face and she drew back, watchful.

The Croke didn't emerge from the gloom so much as draw the darkness round itself. The black cloak, the faceless void beneath the hood, the sinister way of moving, Phoenix took it all in at a glance and felt her resolve slipping, panic overwhelming her. A muffled sob from Seven told her she wasn't the only one who felt that way.

The urge to flee was almost overwhelming, but Phoenix's legs were barely strong enough to hold her and she could never leave her friends, trussed and trapped above her. So she staggered away from the Croke, shivering with dread, until her back was pressed against a pillar of ice.

'I think she's afraid,' Morgren said to Victory, nodding at Phoenix with a smirk.

'Of course she is,' came the toneless voice again. 'I am her nightmare. I have made sure of it, placed myself in her dreams every night since long before she arrived here.'

Phoenix stiffened, tried to wrap her mind round what she'd just heard. The Croke had really been inside her dreams? Horror clawed at her and wouldn't let go.

Victory saw how her terror rocked her, and shook her head in disgust. 'You've gone soft, Phoenix,' she muttered.

'Leave her alone!' Five cried.

Victory turned her attention on to him. 'And you,' she sneered, 'pretending to grow a spine. You don't fool me. Your Hunter name should be Worm and you know it.'

'Shut up,' Six growled and Phoenix startled at the anger in his voice. 'Don't talk to him like that. No one has less of a right to discuss naming, *Victory*.'

She smirked. 'Oh, I don't know,' she said. She threw back her head and drew in a lungful of air beneath the swirling sky. 'Here I am, on the summit of Icegaard no less, the witches broken beneath me. Victorious.' Her lips curved into a real smile now. 'True to my name.'

'Our master grows impatient.'

The Croke's voice was despair woven into sound. It burned through hope and strength and happiness, leaving only darkness in its wake. Phoenix saw the others shrink back and tried to reach for her rage, anything other than the terrible numbness that was filling her. There had to be a way to resist. The thought was distant though, barely a whisper.

The Croke stepped away from the others, its hood turned towards the grey void of the Frozen Wastes. 'He comes.'

CHAPTER 54

Phoenix's eyes scoured the space around them. For months now, she'd wondered about who or what the 'Master' might be. She was loath to admit it, but there was a curiosity that burned brightly inside her. Who had managed to unite the dark creatures, return magic to the goblins, recruit Victory? What was it that had stealthily spread unrest through Ember for years without anyone realising it?

Victory's laughter was twisted through with cruelty. 'You're searching in the wrong place, Phoenix.' Her voice shook with fervour. 'Look further, think bigger. He's more powerful than you can imagine.'

Look further? Phoenix ignored the cold terror winding down her spine and scanned the sky instead, but there was nothing.

'The fog,' Seven whispered from above, her voice hitching. 'L-look at the fog.'

Phoenix stared, but didn't understand what she was seeing. It stretched as far as she could see, and every inch of it was suddenly seething, boiling, bubbling over itself as it surged towards the frost palace.

Dog gave a bark of alarm as a bank of mist crested Icegaard. It moved towards the Croke, slowly at first, then faster, gathering itself into coils that wound themselves up the hooded figure. Then suddenly one darted forward, snake-like, pushing itself into the void where the Croke's face should be.

Five gave a shout of alarm and Phoenix swallowed her rising bile.

The Croke, the figure of her nightmares, seemed suddenly helpless, held tightly by bands of fog while endless reams of grey shadow poured into it. On and on it went, all of the fog across the Frozen Wastes rushing to the frost palace, until suddenly, abruptly, it was done. The end of the darkness dived into the Croke and vanished.

In the space between breaths, Phoenix took in the scene before her. Something about the Croke's posture had changed, the alteration enough to convince Phoenix that this thing in front of her might now house an entirely different entity. Morgren and Victory stepped back, a new, careful watchfulness about them. Above her, her friends were fear-frozen, staring down in silent terror.

Phoenix had mentally flicked through every page of *A Magical Bestiary*, compared what she'd seen against every entry. Even with her imperfect memory, she knew there was nothing; the Master was an entirely unknown creature. Part of her had suspected this would be the case, but it didn't prepare her for the truth: she had no idea what he was, no idea of his strengths and weaknesses, no idea how to defeat him.

'Master,' Morgren said, bowing his head before the Croke's still figure. 'We have taken Icegaard. The elemental has destroyed the Shadowseam. Ember is yours for the taking.'

'You do not need to tell me this. I see all.'

Phoenix almost retched. Two voices now emanated from the Croke: the first was the toneless one Phoenix already associated with the cloaked figure, the second something else entirely. Its words slid like snakes, slippery and sickeningly smooth. They weaved through her head and warped her thoughts until she couldn't hold on to an idea. The creature's voice created a vacuum, sucking everything into it.

A terrible shivering fit came over Phoenix. She stared at her friends, trying to take strength from them, but saw only their terror and pain. When the creature spoke with both its voices, it brought tides of misery. Her worst memories surfaced: she lived again the discovery of her murdered family in Poa, facing Oakhammer, Silver's death, an Ygrex wearing her sister's face. Everything she was ashamed of rose in her, every regret clamoured for her attention. She felt a tear slide down her cheek and didn't raise a hand to wipe it away. Everything was hopeless.

Beneath her furs, she felt Widge shift and wriggle, agitated. He nipped her hard, teeth breaking the soft skin over her collarbone. Bright white pain cut through everything and, for an instant, Phoenix thought clearly.

The more violence, the more chaos and destruction, the stronger he grows.

Words Morgren had said about the Master months before.

This was the Master's power, she realised with a lurch. To strip away everything good and leave only what was rotten. Terror, shame, regret, hatred: he fed on them, grew stronger in their presence.

The Master turned to face Morgren, and Phoenix saw the mage become still beneath his gaze, his unease growing with each passing moment.

'I see all,' the Master repeated.

'Master,' Morgren began, his eyes flicking around as though seeking escape, 'I—'

'You would have killed the elemental. Your grudge against her was more important to you than me.'

Now Morgren was shaking his head, fear rolling off him in waves. Victory's face took on a strained, pinched look.

'No,' Morgren whispered. 'Master—'

'After all I have done for you. The gifts I have lavished on you.'

'I've been faithful always. I—'

'You were until today,' the Master allowed, 'so I will make your death painless.' A pause. 'Relatively painless.'

'Please! I've served you for years,' Morgren gasped, his eyes huge. He gazed around wildly, his eyes landing on Phoenix. 'I never would have *killed* her! I just wanted to frighten her. I only—'

'I see all.'

Morgren staggered back a step, looked like he was about to flee, but a strange rigidity suddenly came over him.

'Foolish. You know there is nowhere to run. Nowhere to hide. Not from me.'

It looked like Morgren was trying to speak, but couldn't. Only his eyes moved, flicking back and forth wildly, full of mad desperation. When the green flames first appeared in his hands, Phoenix thought he was trying to fight back. But then his sleeve caught fire.

Five gave a shout of horror from above her and Dog barked furiously. Six and Seven both appeared too shocked to make a sound. Phoenix's heart slammed against her ribs and she wrapped her arms round herself, feeling her knees begin to shake.

The goblin fire moved quickly, its heat building to something fierce. Within moments, Morgren was encased in a towering pillar of green flames.

Inside her bearskin, Widge gave a low keen of terror. When the fire died down – almost as fast as it had risen – Phoenix saw the mage again, blackened but still standing, eyes squeezed shut, his hands balled into fists. For a moment, she wondered if it had all been a trick to teach him a lesson. Then a breeze gusted across the eyrie and Morgren dissolved into feathers of ash, lifted by the wind and carried out to the Endless Ocean.

Victory turned away sharply, her fists tight by her sides, her shoulders shuddering as she heaved in noisy breaths. Her shock was palpable, as solid as Morgren had been moments before. Perhaps the weaponsmaster had only just realised how expendable she was. Phoenix almost felt sorry for her. *Almost.*

Abruptly, the magic binding Dog, Seven, Five and Six failed, and they dropped to the ground around her with yelps and cries of surprise. Dog landed so heavily the whole frost palace shuddered, but he stood and shook himself off immediately, seemingly unharmed. The first thing he did was plant himself between the Master and Phoenix, his hackles rising, his lips quivering into a snarl.

The void beneath the Croke's hood turned towards him and Phoenix saw a terrible shiver run through Dog as he fought to stand tall under the Master's gaze.

'Guardian.' The Master sounded pleased. 'I have heard much of you. And yet I find you are not at all as I expected.' He moved closer, the Croke's robes billowing round him.

'You will not harm these children,' Dog growled.

'Children? I thought they were Hunters?' The Master's tone was mocking.

'Not the Seer.' Victory regained her composure and turned back to them, the familiar disgust on her face as she regarded Seven. 'That one could never be a Hunter.'

Phoenix saw her friend shrivel beneath the weaponsmaster's gaze and felt some of her old fortifying rage return to her.

'What do you want from us?' Phoenix asked, hating how her voice came out sounding so small.

'You were right, Victory.' The Master spoke again, his voices coiling through each other. The faceless void turned to gaze at Phoenix. 'This one has spine, could have been formidable. You were wise to take note of her.'

As his attention focused on her, Phoenix fought with every cell to hold on to something worthy: Widge snuggled at her chest; Five refusing to leave her in the crypts; Dog crossing the Frozen Wastes for her. There were things in her that were shameful, but also parts that shone. Her friends proved it.

She gritted her teeth and raised her gaze to the emptiness beneath the Croke's hood.

'What do you want from us?'

'Everything, Phoenix. I am hungry. Always. I want everything.'

There was no answer to that, and Phoenix stared, helpless with fear. When she'd been small and afraid of the dark, she used to squeeze her eyes shut and bury her head under her blankets until her parents came. She longed for those times now with an urgency that shook her.

Dog sensed how she quailed, and compensated for it, standing even taller, his hackles rising higher. He stalked a step closer to the Master, his growl a threat, and Phoenix marvelled at how brave he was. It gave her hope, straightened her own spine, and she saw the same effect replicated in her friends.

'You will not harm these children,' Dog growled again, louder this time, bolder.

Victory's lips curved into a dark smile as her eyes flicked between Dog and the Master. For a moment, there was deathly silence, then, as one, the glintwings spread their wings and descended on the Guardian, their screams rattling Phoenix's brain in her skull. Dog vanished beneath a whirling maelstrom of stinking black feathers and teeth, his snarls and barks quickly descending into yelps and yowls.

'STOP!' Phoenix screamed, unable to bear his cries of pain.

For a moment, she thought she'd somehow commanded the creatures. As one, they lifted off Dog – crumpled and panting on the ice – to return to their perches around the eyrie. Then she felt the Master's attention on her.

'For you,' he said, 'I will. The Shadowseam would never have stopped, never given up. It would have dragged me back to that dead, empty place.' The pressure in the air around Phoenix grew unbearable. 'You have saved me from it. I reward those who help me.'

Phoenix shook her head, horror rolling through her. 'I would . . . I would *never* help you. My family is dead because of you. Victory killed them – slaughtered my whole village – on your orders.' She suppressed a sob of denial, of fear, of anguish. How had she got things so wrong?

'She did,' the Master laughed. 'I was so hungry. How I feasted on Victory's murderous work that night. The terror, the pain, the despair: glorious. I dream of it often.'

Phoenix shuddered, sickness roiling through her. She reached for anger, but found only paralysing grief and terror inside herself.

'Don't despair, Phoenix,' the Master said, his voice a parody of tenderness. 'You have won your friends' lives. That, surely, is worth something to you?'

'You're letting us go?' Five asked, his voice as doubt-filled as Phoenix had ever heard it.

'Of course,' the Master crooned. 'How else will I get my message to Ember?'

Phoenix forced herself to move, edging her way over to Dog. She saw with horror that his side had been raked and rent by the glintwings, the stone there deeply gouged.

'Can you stand up?' she whispered. For a moment,

he didn't answer and fear pulsed in her, then he struggled to his feet, swaying slightly. She could feel how tensely he held himself, how much pain he was in.

'Delightful.' The Master's laugh was sickening. Then: 'Come.'

Victory signalled the others to follow in single file. Seven walked ahead of Phoenix and she tried to catch the other girl's eye, but Seven seemed cut off, locked deep within a private misery.

The Master's soft footsteps forged ahead of them, the frost palace's ice lighting their way.

'Faster,' Victory said roughly, shoving Six from behind. 'Hurry up.' Her sword was in her hand. 'And don't try anything,' she said, her gaze lingering particularly on Dog. 'I may not have magic, but my sword will kill you as quickly as any spell.'

'There is no need for them to disobey,' the Master said, both voices speaking in unity. 'Not when they are about to be released.'

Staggering slightly, Phoenix followed the Master, unable to believe what was happening. This was some sort of trick, she was sure of it. Desperately, she tried to reach for the threads of fire again, the only weapon she had access to, but they were spent, echoing so faintly and so deeply that she knew it would be a while before she could call on them again. She raised a hand to stroke Widge instead, hoping to calm some of the fearful shivers racking him.

Dog butted her gently with his head. 'Are you all right?' he growled. 'Do you want to ride on my back?'

There was nothing Phoenix wanted more, but she shook her head nonetheless, seeing how he limped.

'Where are you taking us?' she muttered to Victory.

'To the entrance, of course,' the weaponsmaster grunted. 'Only way in and out of this place.'

'Where is everyone?' Six whispered as they walked. 'Where are the witches?'

'And the dark creatures,' Five muttered. 'It sounded like there were tons of them. Where are they all?'

Five's question was answered a moment later when they arrived at the base of the feasting tree.

A terrible groan tore from Seven, and Phoenix couldn't stop herself from shaking. Icegaard was broken: the great doors ripped from their hinges, gaping cracks in the walls letting in gusts of wind. The lake was frozen solid – how had that happened? – the multicoloured fish entombed beneath the surface. And atop the ice were the dark creatures. They filled the space entirely, standing shoulder to shoulder. Creatures with no business being this far north, creatures that never normally tolerated the presence of another living thing. In each one's eyes, oily shadows swarmed.

Phoenix had to know. 'Is it you?' she whispered. 'Is it you who puts the shadows in their eyes?'

The Master's laugh made her want to cringe, but she forced her chin up.

'Of course it is me. It's my greatest gift: to place my will in the bodies of dark creatures and dead things. They are mine.'

Phoenix thought of the glimmer – dead then not dead – and shuddered, forced herself to keep speaking. 'And the statues? In the crypts?'

'Each one is made using a drop of blood from the witch they commemorate. That is how the statues achieve their remarkable lifelikeness. And that is what allowed me into them: each contains a tiny part of that witch's death.'

His attention was heavy on Phoenix now, pressing down on her shoulders, squeezing her chest. Widge slipped back into her furs, unable to bear it.

'Did you enjoy them as much as I did? I hoped they'd . . . encourage you to control your fire faster than those ridiculous lessons. I was beginning to worry you'd never be able to destroy the Shadowseam for me.' His terrible laughter filled the whole cavern, the branches of the feasting tree shuddering with it. 'Lucky for both of us that I'm such a good teacher.'

Phoenix tried not to tremble, tried not to give in to despair. But it was very, very hard. The animated effigies, the glimmer, the skryll, the wheever: he'd been behind everything. It had never been the Shadowseam. Even worse, he'd been using them to manipulate her – and it had worked. Phoenix felt a sudden need to be sick, and took a slow, deep breath until it passed.

'Was it you draining the magic out of Icegaard too?' Six asked, his voice shaking

The Master's laughter redoubled. 'Yes. That's why the seam was growing: I was right in front of it for the first time in decades and it was desperate to recapture me. Icegaard's magic was too tempting for me to resist. Although,' he allowed, 'I had no desire to see Ember washed away by my . . . nibbling. I would have stopped before it came to that, put a little of the magic back, as I did for you when you destroyed the seam. When I pick Ember apart, it will be one household, one person at a time. I will savour every delicious morsel of it.'

Phoenix allowed her eyes to close. The Master had been toying with her, with all of them, since the very beginning. He'd been behind everything. The Shadowseam had done nothing more disagreeable than look frightening. It had been a door capable of catching him, capable of dragging him into a prison that would have held him. And she had destroyed it.

She'd got it all wrong; everything she'd done had been for nothing. Instead of saving Ember, she'd helped its most dangerous enemy. Thanks to her, the world had never been in more peril. She had let everyone down: the Hunters, the clans, the witches, her friends.

And Poppy. She'd failed her little sister. Again.

Despair was an abyss with sides too slippery to climb.

She felt Seven step closer, slip a comforting hand into hers. Inside her furs, Widge pressed himself against her heart.

'Where are the witches?' Five asked.

No one answered and, when Phoenix raised her gaze again, she saw with horror that some of the dark creatures were wearing witch cloaks. Once snow-white, pristine and gleaming, now the feathers were dull, trampled with filth. Phoenix gazed around with growing despair. Where *were* the witches? She could see none at all.

Phoenix swallowed a sob, thinking of Nara. The witch had helped her, trained her, and done it all with kindness and humour. She hadn't deserved this terrible end.

The Master nodded towards the doors, smashed open and hanging from their hinges. In unison, every dark creature shifted so that a clear, straight path opened before them to the outside word. Thousands of shadow-filled eyes rested on them, but not a single creature moved.

'Come,' Dog murmured, nudging her on to the path with his nose. 'We must go. Quickly.'

Phoenix stumbled blindly after him. Behind her, the others made to follow, when suddenly one of the Master's stick-thin arms shot out from beneath its cloak to grab Seven.

The girl screamed, trying to pull away, but as quickly as it had happened it was done.

'Your powers are not what I thought,' the Master said. Did Phoenix imagine a hint of annoyance in his voices? 'You are weak, growing weaker.'

'I . . .' Tears were spilling down Seven's cheeks and she couldn't speak, only shake her head. Everything in Phoenix leaned towards the girl in sympathy. To be touched by the Croke was an invasion of unparalleled horror; the Master must be a hundred times worse.

'Go then,' the Master said. 'Return to Ledge. Tell the Hunters of what you've seen here, that Ember is mine for the taking . . . unless they care to stop me.' He laughed his stomach-churning laugh. 'I cannot tell you how much I hope they try.'

Across the frozen lake, thousands of dark creatures shifted, the air throbbing with their hunger.

The Master turned back to the feasting tree, Victory moving with him.

Then, almost casually, he added: 'I do have need of one of them though. I thought the Seer would be the most useful, but she barely deserves the title. Take one of the boys instead.'

Victory's lips pressed together in a thin line, but she nodded once, spinning back to seize Six. Before anyone could react, she'd dragged him away from the others.

'What?' Six gasped, trying to twist free, but unable to wriggle out of Victory's iron grip.

Phoenix was too shocked to move, couldn't think, could barely breathe. The ranks of dark creatures shifted, moving across the space between the group and Victory, cutting them off from Six. Inside her furs, Widge gave a low keen of terror.

Sounds and shapes swooped dizzyingly round Phoenix and she felt herself sway dangerously. This couldn't be happening. She reached again desperately for her power, but it was too drained, a faded spark too deep inside her to be called upon. She was helpless.

'Six,' she whispered, watching Victory drag him away from them, back towards the feasting tree. *No.*

Seven was screaming now and Five was trying to force his way through the dark creatures, braving quills and claws and fangs to reach his friend. But it was no good; the monsters were like stone statues – immovable.

'Six!' Five cried, the panic in his voice heart-wrenching. 'SIX!'

'You have seconds to leave before I release my pets,' the Master said as he turned to follow Victory and Six. 'Go. Warn the Hunters. Tell them to prepare for me – if they can.'

'Or stay if you prefer,' Victory called back nastily. 'Find out just how hungry the Master's army is.'

A shiver seemed to travel through the creatures and

they moved infinitesimally closer to Phoenix and her friends.

Six was struggling with Victory now, fighting with everything he had to get back to his friends – until Victory struck him viciously in the face with the pommel of her sword. Six's head snapped back and he fell to the ground, unmoving. Victory scooped him up with ease.

'No!' Seven screamed, lunging forward to try to help Five shove past a glimmer. 'This isn't right!' she cried. 'This isn't h-how it was meant to be!'

Victory, Six and the Master began their ascent of the feasting tree and the attention of the dark creatures sharpened. Phoenix could almost feel their will returning.

A winter wolf growled, shaking itself before staring around, confused. Shadows dripped from its eyes like hot wax until their unnatural blueness shone through again. A string of saliva slipped from its mouth as its gaze locked on to Seven.

Other creatures were beginning to come back to themselves too. Deep within their ranks, a Grim shifted. Its hair began to writhe, its fingers twitching to life. Silently and ever so slowly, it reached for the spineghast next to it, leaching its life away, unnoticed.

'We must leave,' Dog barked, gazing round in horror. 'Now!'

'No!' Five yelled, springing forward to redouble his

efforts to reach Six. The glimmer before him twitched, a line of drool sliding from between its lips.

With a stone in her stomach, Phoenix caught his furs and dragged him back, fighting, towards Dog. There was no time. The huge space was suddenly filling with the growls and snarls of dark creatures waking up. Every inch of her itched with the terrible danger of them. From inside her furs, Widge was shrieking his alarm.

'What are you doing?' Five yelled, twisting, trying to fight her off. 'Are you mad? We can't leave him! Get off me!' Tears of grief and fury fell unchecked down his cheeks.

Dog grabbed Five from her and, with a reserve of strength she didn't know she had, Phoenix threw Seven – slack with shock – on to his back, climbing up behind her and dragging Five on too.

She turned to look at Six, the pain of it so great she felt that she might pass out. Victory had slung the unconscious boy over her shoulder, was ascending the stairs in front of the Master.

'Six!' Phoenix cried, her voice written through with despair. Six didn't move, didn't hear her. What was happening was surely impossible: an idea would come to her; Six would wake up; her fire would return so she could fight her way to him. *Something* would happen to reunite them.

Nothing happened.

Five and Seven were falling apart, only Phoenix's grip held them on Dog's back as he turned on the spot, a faint whine in his throat.

The light around them dimmed as the Master vanished from view. The air grew even colder and very, very still. The world held its breath. Then, with a cacophony of shrieks and snarls and howls, his dark creatures shook the shadows from their eyes and surged towards Phoenix.

Chapter 55

Dog sprang forward and an instant later he was barging through the press of monsters, the open path to the doors disappearing before their eyes.

Seven was shaking, oblivious as hands and claws and teeth tore at them. Five was frozen too, his face blank with shock.

'Hold on!' Dog barked as he sprang forward, faster and faster, surging towards the broken doors.

Phoenix yelled as an Ygrex lunged at Five, its teeth almost sinking into his leg before she managed to kick it away. She pushed the others' heads down as skryll fragments whistled over them, then suddenly they were outside, tearing away from the frost palace as fast as Dog could run.

Zenith's warmth spell had partly worn off and the cold hit them like a slap, the shock almost enough to knock Phoenix off Dog. Inside her still-damp furs, Widge tensed.

'Hold on to each other,' she gasped through chattering teeth. Gratefully, she felt Seven and Five's grip tighten. She was too tired to be able to support them any longer.

'Yes!' Dog howled. 'Hold on!' He sped up, the ground vanishing beneath his huge paws as he pounded across the ice.

Tears ran down Phoenix's face and in front of her Five shook with suppressed sobs. They'd left Six behind. The knowledge was a wound too painful to face, going against everything they'd ever been taught as Hunters.

When Phoenix glanced over her shoulder, she saw that none of the creatures had followed them. Instead, they were arrayed outside the empty frost palace, dark sentinels in the dying light. The Master really was letting them go.

The little group ploughed on in wretched silence, each wrapped in their own misery as the weak sun emerged from behind heavy clouds to dive into the ocean. For a moment, the ice around them turned a delicate pale gold, then the colour bled back into the ocean, leaving only grey behind.

'How will we get back?' Five asked a while later, the first of them to speak, his voice hoarse and dull. Overhead, the clouds were thinning, the odd star peeping through.

A shudder passed through Seven, and Phoenix knew exactly what she was thinking: they were weeks away from Ledge, they had no food, no weapons and they would have to travel through the Frozen Forest.

'I will carry you, of course,' Dog said steadily. 'And protect you.'

Phoenix suddenly wanted to cry. How had it come to this? Widge licked her cheek.

Dog slowed and looked back at them. For the first time, Phoenix felt how his sides moved beneath her, almost as if he was panting, except he didn't need to breathe.

'Are you all right?' she asked. 'Do you want to rest?'

'No,' Dog growled. 'I rarely require rest. But I will pace myself. Those glintwings injured me. This journey will be a test of even my stamina.' From then, he walked, sometimes breaking into a long, ground-covering lope. 'We will follow the coast until we are through the Frozen Forest,' he said, 'then cut through the Fangs towards the source of the Ilara. From there, our journey will be easier.'

Five laughed humourlessly. 'I'll say. Just the tiny challenges of the Frozen Forest and the Fangs to contend with first.'

'We cannot wish them away,' Dog said slowly. 'They must be faced. We will succeed because we have to. News of what has happened at Icegaard must be carried to Ledge. Hoarfrost has to know. The clans must be warned so they can prepare for what is coming.'

He was right, Phoenix realised. There was a chance that Zenith would find her way to Ledge, but what if she didn't? Or what if she wasn't believed? Witches hadn't been seen in Ember for decades, and they weren't loved.

'We'll make it,' Phoenix said darkly.

'We will,' Seven whispered, and Phoenix tried desperately not to read more into that than she should.

As night drew round them, Dog asked Phoenix to use the moonstone to light their way. Its glow was the first hope she'd felt since they'd left Icegaard. Five turned his face towards it and she knew that behind her Seven did the same.

'At least we still have the moonstone,' Five said eventually. Phoenix was relieved to hear his voice steadier, some of the old firmness back. 'That'll be useful in the Frozen Forest.'

Phoenix nodded, staring into its blazing depths. Even Widge seemed to take comfort in it, scampering down her arm to place his paws on it, the light turning his whiskers silver.

But no matter how she tried to turn her thoughts away from Six, she couldn't. She'd abandoned him, left him with their enemies. The hard knot of guilt inside her grew and grew until breathing felt difficult. Where was he? What was happening to him?

'We shouldn't have left him,' Five whispered. 'We should have stayed.'

'You would all be dead,' Dog murmured.

Five was quiet for a moment. '*We shouldn't have left him.*'

Dog looked back at them, his face kindly. 'Try to rest. The middle of the night is not the time for such—' He stopped talking suddenly, a new tension humming through him as his ears pricked.

Immediately, the others fell silent, each straining their ears too.

'Is it them? Are you sure?' A voice in the distance.

'How *dare* you question me!' This voice was tiny, yet distinctive.

Widge gave a high-pitched squeal of horrified recognition and dived into Phoenix's furs. She stood on Dog's back, her face turned to the sky, a flicker of hope leaping in her. 'Sharpspark! Zenith!' she cried. 'Over here!'

'We see you!' the witch cried. And suddenly the sky was full of sweeping wings, pale faces and a small, fiery, furious one staring down at them.

Moments later, Xena landed on the ice in front of them and the two groups fell into each other's arms, tears rolling down their cheeks as terror gave way to relief. Sharpspark flew straight to Dog, and Phoenix noticed with bemusement how pleased they looked to see each other.

A few hours had made all the difference for Zenith:

she was looking much stronger than on the eyrie. After a few moments of wild hugs and exclamations, she stood back, a small frown on her face as she scanned them.

'But . . . where's Six?' she asked.

CHAPTER 56

A while later, the group were sitting on the ice together. Zenith was still too weak to perform magic, but, under her instruction, Thea transfigured one of Xena's feathers into a huge log that Sharpspark was only too happy to set alight. Libbet managed to conjure a simple wind shield and, behind that, the group sat round the flames, feeling returning to their fingers and colour to their cheeks. The mood though was very sombre. Phoenix had relayed everything that had happened after Xena had flown, including the probable deaths of the witches.

'But you didn't *see* them?' Thea asked for the third time.

Phoenix shook her head unwillingly, knowing her answer was condemning the girl to hold on to a hope that someone had survived, escaped, maybe to reappear one day. Phoenix held no such hope. She'd seen the number of dark creatures in the great hall, the number of witches' cloaks taken by them as trophies. Grief for Nara threatened to strangle her. She pressed her lips together, unable to say anything more.

'And Six,' Libbet whispered, silver tear tracks visible on her cheeks in the firelight. 'What will happen to him?' She whispered it to herself and Phoenix felt a great sadness weigh down on her as she looked at the little girl. She already seemed so much older than when they'd met.

'We don't know,' Five said unsteadily. 'The . . . the Master said he needed one of us for something.' He looked up, his eyes wild. 'What could that be?'

Phoenix shook her head mutely.

Seven muffled a sob, ducked her head to hide it, then stood and slipped from the firelight into the darkness beyond the windshield. She had a way of making herself small and unnoticeable so that Phoenix almost missed it, but, as she saw the girl's bright hair disappear, a dark fear flooded her. Seven had just lost her family. There was no feeling Phoenix knew better than the bleak and lonely despair that lurked on the heels of such an event. What was Seven doing?

Phoenix leaped to her feet and hurried after her friend, panic flaring as she saw her at the cliff's edge, the ocean slamming into the wall of rock beneath her.

'Seven!' Phoenix called.

Seven half turned, shrugged when she saw Phoenix.

They stood side by side, staring out over the dark, surging water, Phoenix desperately searching for something to say that might ease Seven's pain. Everything seemed wrong and silence stretched between them.

'I didn't S-See that he'd be taken,' Seven whispered eventually, making Phoenix jump. Her fists were clenched by her sides and the moonlight on her face cast pools of fierce shadow round her eyes. 'How did I not S-See it?'

'You can't blame yourself,' Phoenix said quietly, reaching for her hand.

'Of c-course I c-can,' Seven hissed, her eyes fixed on the moon-silvered horizon. 'It must've been there in his Paths. I just didn't check them.'

Phoenix's heart ached for her friend. 'Your gift is amazing,' she said haltingly. 'But there's so much it hasn't shown you.' She swallowed, feeling out of her depth. 'I know I don't understand your power, but I do know you can't blame yourself for the things you don't See.'

'Can't I?'

Seven's face was in profile, made strange by the night. The wind had dropped and, in the sudden stillness, she was like a statue, the ocean reflected darkly in her eyes. In that moment, there was something uncanny about her, otherworldly.

Phoenix shivered, had to resist the urge to pull back. 'Seven?'

The other girl blinked, shook herself and was Phoenix's friend again, tears shining in her eyes. 'You're wrong, Phoenix,' she gasped. 'I could've Seen it. I should have. I just wasn't l-looking at his Paths – I was l-looking at yours.'

Seven stumbled back towards camp, arms wrapped round herself, leaving Phoenix stranded with the crash of waves and the thunder of her own heart.

This is all your fault.

Why had she let it happen? What had she done?

The night was very cold and very still. Phoenix stared down at the waves smashing relentlessly into the base of the cliff, vertigo making her light-headed. She'd tried to be a better person, tried to master her magic, hoped it would save Ember and the witches. Instead, she'd helped their enemies, closed the door to a prison that could have held the Master, and broken the lodge's most important rule: Hunters never left a member of their team behind. *Never.* But she had done it. She'd left Six. Self-loathing rose in her.

She thought of all that she and Six had been through together. He had saved her life, fought by her side, and it had been he who'd first extended the hand of friendship to her.

He'd changed her life.

And she'd abandoned him.

Phoenix's head ached and her limbs felt weak. She sat, her legs dangling over the cliff, replaying those last moments over and over. What should she have done differently? How could she have saved him? Questions and wild possibilities spun through her until she felt dizzy, sickened. Even Widge licking her cheek couldn't change the course of her thoughts.

She got up and turned back to the fire eventually, walking slowly over to the group.

Seven was sitting by the flames, hugging her knees. When she saw Phoenix looking at her, she turned away. Did Seven blame her? It would be no more than she deserved. Five was sitting apart from the others, his gaze far away. The young witches were huddled together, tear-streaked, talking softly.

Dog came to her and nudged her gently with his nose. She leaned gratefully against him. 'Zenith may have a solution to our problem,' he said.

'Six . . .?' Phoenix gasped, turning to the girl, hope suddenly flooding her.

Zenith winced. 'Sorry, no,' she said. 'We were talking about getting back to Ledge. Five said you travelled through a portal to reach Icegaard. That Nara said she left it open?'

'Oh.' Phoenix tried to take in what Zenith was saying, but Nara's name echoed again and again in her thoughts. Nara, who was dead. Dead like her family, dead like Silver.

Smothering grief rose in her and she held her breath to stop herself from sobbing aloud. Six, Nara, all the witches who had welcomed them, there was too much that pressed down on Phoenix, too much to bear. She wanted to curl up on the ground, pretend none of it was real.

'. . . problem will be connecting the portals,' Zenith was saying. 'It's worth a try. If I can do it, it will save us a lot of time.'

There was something brittle about her in the firelight, as though a breath of wind might blow her away. Phoenix suspected she was only holding herself together for the sake of Thea and Libbet, and only through an extraordinary force of will.

'It would save us from danger too,' Xena added, the ice eagle speaking for the first time since they'd set off.

'Can you try now?' Phoenix asked, rousing herself to look at the young witch.

Zenith hesitated but Xena didn't. 'She cannot,' the ice eagle said simply. 'She is dangerously drained. Maybe tomorrow. Perhaps the day after.' Zenith sagged, her relief obvious.

Dog growled. 'We are still too close to Icegaard for my liking. We must keep moving.'

'Why?' Phoenix heard herself say, her voice dull. 'The Master wants us to spread the word of what happened at Icegaard for him. Why would he harm his own messengers?'

Saying the words out loud made her feel ill. Dog moved closer to her, nudged her gently again with his nose.

'Let them rest,' Xena said gently, turning her head from Phoenix to take in the whole group. 'I can patrol the sky. There is no cover for miles, no way anything can creep up on us.'

The witches looked as relieved as Phoenix felt when Dog acquiesced. The ground was not comfortable, but at least with the windshield and the warmth spells they weren't cold. One by one, the others fell into an uneasy sleep; even Sharpspark was curled up and quiet in the flames.

Only Phoenix stayed awake, thoughts tormenting her.

What if she never saw Six again?

Widge pressed himself to her cheek, but even he couldn't comfort her.

She rolled on to her back and stared up at the sharp, watchful stars, but there were no answers there for her.

CHAPTER 57

Dog lay by the fire, watching Phoenix toss and turn. He could feel her distress, her regret, knew she was thinking of Six. He wanted to comfort her: several times he almost said something, then stopped himself at the last minute, unable to find the right words.

Guilt weighed heavily on him. What sort of a Guardian was he to let a brand-new Hunter be taken from right under his nose? Why hadn't he fought his way to Six, dragged him from Victory with his own teeth?

You were afraid.

Dog examined the thought carefully. It was true: his size and strength had never granted him immunity from fear. And he *had* been afraid, but never before had that stopped him from achieving his purpose. There'd been something more at play.

He shifted slightly, trying to get comfortable on the ice, his belly still unpleasantly cold despite the witch's warmth spells. His senses were growing sharper every day and he wasn't entirely sure it was a good thing: two weeks ago he could've lain on this ice without feeling anything at all. That was before the lutra though. Torrent had said its touch bestowed health, cured all ills. So far, it seemed to have done the opposite: he was in more discomfort than he'd ever known in his long, long life.

Still, he could taste now. And, when Phoenix and the others had sat on his back, he'd felt their warmth. He'd never experienced that before, only ever perceived their weight.

He rested his head on his paws, wincing slightly. One of them still hurt from where he'd fallen on it when Morgren died. He licked it tentatively and found that soothed the throbbing a little. Numerous other aches and pains clamoured for attention too.

He thought he'd hidden it well earlier though, had still managed to carry Five, Seven and Phoenix to safety. In their shock, they hadn't noticed how often he'd slowed down, how every step felt laboured. There'd been a few moments where he'd doubted he could go on.

And there it was.

Doubt.

Dog understood with horror the reason he hadn't tried to get Six back. He'd told himself in the heat of the moment that he couldn't leave Phoenix, Five and Seven surrounded by so many dark creatures while he fought his way to the other boy. But the truth was much worse: he hadn't *believed* he could do it. Reaching Six, let alone getting him back, had seemed an impossible task. The realisation tolled through him like a bell. Never before had he questioned his own strength.

Something had shifted in him on that frozen lake. The fear had been terrible and the pain had been very great, and somehow, together, they had drained him of his confidence. He had felt small and weak. But, even worse, he had allowed those feelings to convince him he *was* small and weak. And that was much, much more dangerous.

What was happening to him?

Dog couldn't stop the whimper.

Phoenix rolled to face him at once. 'Dog,' she whispered. 'Are you all right?'

He only hesitated for an instant.

'Of course,' he lied. 'Try to get some sleep.'

She turned on to her back with a sigh, squeezed her eyes tight shut.

Dog watched her for a moment, his heart brimming with a tenderness that solidified into a rock-hard determination. He'd let her down terribly, but it would never happen again. Ember was about to be dragged into a conflict likely to be as vicious as the Dark War. His strength would be needed, perhaps more than ever. The Hunting Lodge would count on him, as it always had. And Phoenix would rely on him because they were – he almost stumbled over the word – friends.

He was the Glorious Guardian of the Hunting Lodge, and nothing – not fear, not pain, nor the lutra's touch with its strange effects – would make him ever forget that again.

He would be the formidable weapon everyone needed him to be.

Dog went back to licking his sore paw, and, although it still hurt, his heart felt much lighter.

CHAPTER 58

'I can do it,' Zenith said the next day, resting a hand against Xena's soft, snowy feathers. The ice eagle's gaze was sharp on her, searching. 'I'll open two portals here, one on the ground and one in the sky. Xena and I will fly through to the window Nara left outside Ledge, then land and connect the one on the ground there so you can all walk through to join me.'

Phoenix forced herself to nod, to smile encouragingly, even though her exhaustion was a dead weight round her. She stared across the fire at Seven, who looked as bad as she felt: hunched and small, so insubstantial she was almost grey round the edges. Her forehead rested on her knees and she showed no interest in what the witches were saying.

'That all sounds good.' Thea frowned. 'Except that you only Fledged yesterday, Zenith. You need to rest.'

'I would if I could,' Zenith said patiently. 'But we have to get out of here as fast as possible, for our own safety and to warn Ember of what is coming.' She turned to Xena, and there was something almost pleading in her look.

'I agree,' Xena said eventually, dipping her feathered head to the younger girls. 'We must try at least. I will be with Zenith all the time. If the magic is too much of a strain, I will bring her safely back down.'

Phoenix stared at Xena. In fact, it was hard for her to peel her eyes away. Yesterday this creature hadn't existed. Today she stood before them, fully formed, intelligent and aware. The scale of the Fledging spell took her breath away. Xena was the only spark of joy among them – Phoenix saw how the young witches gazed at her, touched her as they would a talisman, a symbol of hope in a time of darkest despair.

'I'm scared,' Libbet whispered. 'What will it be like, this Ledge place?'

Zenith swallowed hard. 'I always thought it looked beautiful in the drawings,' she said. 'Imagine hundreds of homes sticking out of an enormous cliff face. It isn't magic but it looks like it. And . . . and the witches gifted Ledge ice-eagle feathers for their first-ever pair of wings. We helped them build the wing shed above the village too. I hope we'll be welcome there if . . . if they remember those things.' She looked more uncertain than Phoenix had ever seen her.

Five, who hadn't spoken a word all morning, raised his head, saw the fear on the girl's face. 'They'll remember,' he said quietly. 'Even if I have to remind them myself, they will.'

Zenith nodded. Phoenix's heart lifted a little at the sight of Five talking again.

When she turned back to Zenith, she saw a whisper of quietspeech slipping from the witch's lips. The air in front of her rippled, then stilled, seemingly no different than before.

Phoenix gazed at it, uncertain. Had the spell worked?

'It won't open until I connect the other side of it at Ledge,' Zenith said, seeing her look as she swung herself up on to Xena's back. 'Wish me luck,' she added as the ice eagle spread her wings.

'Do you need it?' Phoenix asked, a sudden fear leaping in her. Then quickly: 'Good luck!'

'Don't worry,' Zenith called as they rose into the sky. 'I'll see you in Ledge.'

In silence, the group watched the two climb high into the sky before turning and—

'They're gone,' Thea gasped.

'It worked!' Libbet squealed, bouncing on the balls of her feet.

Dog and Phoenix exchanged a look and she turned away quickly, pacing by the remains of the fire, Widge pressed against her cheek.

The minutes trickled by and tension grew in the waiting group. Phoenix stared out to the Endless Ocean, trying not to notice how sweat prickled on her palms, how her heart raced in her chest.

'How long would it take her to find somewhere to land?' Thea whispered eventually. 'Might it be a while?'

The fear in all of them was palpable now.

'We must give her a chance,' Dog said calmly, although Phoenix could see the worry vibrating through him. 'She may need some time to recuperate before she attempts the spell again.'

Thea nodded quickly. 'That's true.'

Phoenix resumed her pacing, keeping her focus firmly on her feet, anything to stop her imagining the things that could have gone wrong.

It was Five who saw the disturbance first. 'Look!' he cried, leaping to his feet and pointing.

There was a movement in the air where Zenith had stood before, a distortion that rippled, swirling like a stirred cup of tea. As they watched, light began to bleed out of it, and, an instant later, they were staring into a perfectly round window of daylight, the ground through it scattered with snow-dusted rocks, scrubby trees visible further on.

And Zenith. She appeared in the window, staggering slightly, but almost glowing with delight.

Phoenix breathed again, her relief dizzying. In spite of everything they'd been through, she felt her lips curve into a smile.

A few moments later, they were all standing on the thyme-scented mountainside below Ledge, sagging with relief as Zenith closed both portals behind them. The group stood in silence, the witches marvelling at the daylight and the fact the land here had a shape, unlike the impossibly flat Wastes.

'If you like this, you'll love the view from up in Ledge,' Five said, Libbet's amazement impossible to ignore.

'Come,' Dog said, leading them away. 'We must get to Hoarfrost as quickly as possible. We may not have long to prepare the clans and it will not be an easy job.'

The urgency in his voice drove them all on.

'Hoarfrost will be pleased about one thing at least,' Five said, his hands clenched into fists. 'I've chosen my Hunter name.'

Phoenix started, turned to stare at him. 'You have?'

'Thorn,' he said shortly.

'I don't understand—'

'I'll be a thorn in their side,' he said, his expression dark. 'I'll make them wish they'd never set eyes on us. Never taken Six . . .'

Phoenix pressed her lips together miserably to stop herself from saying anything more. A few months ago, she would have said it was the perfect name for Five, but now she knew him better. There *was* a sharp, difficult side to him, but he was so much more than that. It was a name chosen in the agony of loss: one that didn't do him justice.

'We will get him back,' Five – Thorn – said. His voice was flinty, his hands clenched into fists. He nodded to himself. 'We have the magic of Icegaard in Zenith, elemental magic in you. We'll gather the clan chiefs, *force* them to work together for once, for the good of everyone.' He looked up. 'And Dog, of course. He's unbeatable.'

Phoenix thought she saw the Guardian flinch, but a moment later was sure she'd imagined it; he was as huge and strong and powerful as he'd ever been. The memory of his whimper, of him licking his paw, bothered her though: she'd never seen him do anything like that before. But another, more careful, glance at him reassured her all was well.

Dog growled softly. 'You are right to have hope, Five.' He shook himself. 'I mean Thorn. The Master has a power that is undeniable. But, if we can unite the clans, anything is possible.'

His words slipped through Phoenix like a balm and, for the first time since she'd destroyed the Shadowseam, she felt a stirring of hope.

Dog's eyes were gentle on her. 'It wasn't your fault,' he said firmly as though he could hear her tangled thoughts. 'You did not know what the Shadowseam was. No one did.'

Phoenix gulped, unable to meet his eye. If only she could make herself believe he was right. But still the kernel of hope grew inside her, hardened. This wasn't the end; if anything, it was only the beginning. The Master had revealed himself, but he hadn't won yet. Far from it. There was still a chance for Phoenix to right her many wrongs.

'Uniting the clans,' she said softly, puffing slightly as the ground began to rise towards Ledge. 'We'll just have to overcome millennia of prejudice and hatred.'

Thorn nodded. 'And we might only have weeks to do it. A smile slipped across his features for the first time since they'd left Six. 'We do like a challenge.'

'We do,' she smiled back, her heart lifting further to see he felt the same hope as her. She took his hand and squeezed it. 'And we *will* get Six back,' she whispered.

A muscle flickered in his jaw as he squeezed her hand too. 'We will.'

Over their heads, Sharpspark darted back and forth, watched by Dog. The air was very still and the first sounds from Ledge drifted down to them: cries of awe as Xena took to the skies again. In front of Phoenix walked Zenith, Thea and Libbet, their arms interlinked, grief, fear and excitement spun tight between them.

Only Widge seemed downcast. He sat backwards on Phoenix's shoulder, gazing at where they'd come from, tail drooping.

'What's up, Widge?' she asked, glancing behind them, confused.

She frowned. Stopped.
A flare of wild panic.
'Where's Seven?'

CHAPTER 59

The portal closed.

Seven allowed the Veil to fall from her, the magic trickling away into the wind of the Wastes. She'd taught herself that spell and a few others in the library at Icegaard, but hadn't realised how much more draining it would be using it for real. A wave of dizziness broke over her and she closed her eyes, swallowed hard. Phoenix had almost seen her, almost remembered her, and she'd had to pour everything into the invisibility spell to stay hidden, stay forgotten.

And now she was alone. An icy breeze coiled round her wrists and ankles, lifted her hair, then dropped it again. The silence was crushing.

What had she done?

What you always knew you'd have to do!

Seven forced her eyes open, forced herself to run through recent events.

The dark army had come exactly when she'd expected. Phoenix had closed the Shadowseam just as she'd foreseen. And then the Master had tried to keep her with him, as she'd known he would. She'd prepared for that moment for days, eaten copious amounts of erebus leaf from the ingredients store to dull her Sight. When he'd touched her, she'd looked weak, her power barely there, certainly not enough to help him conquer Ember.

But then he'd taken her brother instead. After all her careful planning, how had she not Seen that?

Panic rose in her. How had she missed something so huge?

The answer was obvious. The Paths were fiendishly complex, impossible to navigate fully. She'd focused on the one that had seemed the most important: Phoenix's. In the last couple of weeks, she hadn't checked her brother's once.

Lazy. Careless.

She was afraid to look at the Paths now, sure they'd be changed beyond recognition. They were there at the edge of her vision, as they always were. It was just the slightest adjustment to reach them, a refocusing of her eyes, a shift in her attention, a step sideways. And suddenly she wasn't in the Frozen Wastes, but the complicated, ever-shifting landscape of fate.

Paths stretched away from her in multitudes, crisscrossing each other, circling back, splintering, kaleidoscoping into an ocean of possibilities.

Seven turned on the spot – and frowned. Everything looked the same.

She blinked, shook her head, then pushed down her confusion and searched for her own Path. It appeared unchanged, still a perilous, narrow track scratched across an impossibly steep mountainside. She gathered her courage and followed the trail onwards, shivering and stumbling as it grew ever steeper, ever narrower. Images of the future flashed like lightning behind her eyes.

A waterfall at full moon.

A black shingle beach, deep underground.

Ranks of silent warriors, terrified gazes probing the watchful dark.

Seven swallowed hard. Her Path petrified her as it always had. But it was the same one she'd Seen before, unaltered by her brother being taken. How could that be? How could he be gone and her Path remain the same?

She looked again, followed her Path further to be sure: so many points of danger, so many places to fall.

The things she would have to do.

But the same things she'd always known she'd have to do.

Her fingernails carved crescents into her palms as she stepped away from the Paths, back into the Wastes.

For a long time, she stood motionless, trying to comprehend what she'd seen. Her Path was as clear as it had always been. Her fate was the same.

But, if she'd missed her own brother being taken,

what else might have slipped by unnoticed? Suddenly everything felt impossible, her vast, fragile plan teetering on the sharpest knife edge, pulled this way and that by forces she could only half see.

Your Path is clear. You know what you must do next, where you must go.

But what of her brother, the last of her family, the one who'd always stood by her, protected her?

Seven listened to the swish-boom of the waves against the cliffs, the soul-freezing whisper of the wind. Could she still do this? Even now? Even with Six taken and her faith in herself shaken to the very core?

There was no choice: she *had* to – it was the only Path there was.

Then make a new Path!

The anguished thought rose up in her like a scream and Seven closed her eyes, trying to find her courage again.

She would stick to her fragile, impossible plan. She would do what had to be done. The alternative . . .

Seven shivered, wrapped her arms round herself and began to walk.

Acknowledgements

There's a rumour that second books are hard to write and this one certainly seems to prove it true. Extra special thanks to my husband, Ben, and my fantastic agent, Claire, who talked me through a disastrous first draft and convinced me that I could still write. I don't know where I'd be without you both!

The Fireborn series is blessed to have such dedicated teams on both sides of the Atlantic. Thanks so much to my fantastic editors: Nick, Kristen and Megan whose insights have improved the story immeasurably. To everyone in Marketing, PR, Design and Rights – a huge thanks for everything you do in helping the series find its readers. Special thanks to Tina Mories for just being brilliant every day.

Thank you to Sophie Medvedeva for her wondrous cover art and internal illustrations.

Huge, huge thanks to all the booksellers, librarians, teachers and book bloggers who have championed this series and continue to do so. You are all stars.

To all the friends and family who've supported me

through the ups and downs of writing in a pandemic, I'm eternally grateful and appreciate each and every one of you. Special thanks to Jo, Claire, Miguel, Laura, Dashe and Annabel who read early drafts of this story and gave invaluable feedback.

I edited this book in Sydney and was incredibly fortunate to meet a wonderful group of writers out there. Thank you to Roger, Triona, Beth, Tom, Erik, Jesse and the extended Marrickville crew for welcoming me so warmly.

Last but not least, thanks to you, dear reader. It's been quite a journey, but we still have a way to go . . . I hope you'll join Phoenix and me for the third book.

THE ADVENTURE
CONTINUES IN...

THE FINAL BATTLE IGNITES

AISLING
FOWLER

FIREBORN
STARLING AND THE CAVERN OF LIGHT